STRANGE TALES

STRANGE TALES

Rudyard Kipling

with an Introduction by
DAVID STUART DAVIES

WORDSWORTH EDITIONS

In loving memory of
MICHAEL TRAYLER
the founder of Wordsworth Editions

ɪ

Readers who are interested in other titles from
Wordsworth Editions are invited to visit our website at
www.wordsworth-editions.com

For our latest list and a full mail-order service contact
Bibliophile Books, 5 Thomas Road, London E14 7BN
Tel: +44 0207 515 9222 Fax: +44 0207 538 4115
e-mail: orders@bibliophilebooks.com

This edition published 2006 by
Wordsworth Editions Limited
8B East Street, Ware, Hertfordshire SG12 9HJ

ISBN 1 84022 532 7

Typeset in Great Britain by Antony Gray
Printed by Clays Ltd, St Ives plc

CONTENTS

INTRODUCTION

When one is considering writers involved in the creation of ghost stories, supernatural and horror tales, or those concocted especially to unnerve the reader, one does not immediately think of Rudyard Kipling, the author of *The Jungle Book* and the *Just So Stories*. And yet, like many successful storytellers of the Victorian era, he was drawn from time to time to this particular genre. In some ways it is less surprising that he turned his hand to Gothic entertainments than other English scribes who were lodged in the safe and mundane environs of leafy suburbia, for Kipling spent a great deal of his early life in India at a time when mysticism was almost a way of life there. Indeed, a significant number of the stories in this collection have an Indian background, which sympathetically enhances the strangeness of the narrative. The richness and alien qualities of this locale allied to the unusual occurrences in Kipling's plots give the stories an extra unsettling *frisson* which increases their power to disturb and intrigue the reader.

In this collection we have distilled the best of Kipling's chilling narratives, presenting you with tales of hauntings, magic, violence, horror and the unforgiving power of the supernatural. Where India is the setting, the surroundings and strangeness of the country insinuate their way into the lives of colonial men and women stationed on the subcontinent in a bygone era. The term 'imperial gothic' has been coined especially to describe these supernatural tales. Equally effective are the other stories, whether set in the time of war at sea or in the leafy shires, thanks to Kipling's word wizardry.

* * *

Rudyard Kipling was born in Bombay (now Mumbai) in India, in 1865, at a time when the country was ruled by the British. His father, John Lockwood Kipling, was an arts and crafts teacher at the Jeejeebhoy School of Art and his mother, Alice, was a sister-in-law of the pre-Raphaelite painter Edward Burne-Jones. While Ruddy, as he was affectionately known, grew up in the atmosphere of a white middle-class artistic family, he was also influenced by the Indian culture on his doorstep. Indeed, he was brought up by an ayah, his Indian nurse, who taught him Hindustani as his first language.

His early years were blissfully happy in this exotic world of vivid colours, strange animals and wonderful sights, smells and sounds, but at the age of five he was shipped off to cold, alien England by his parents and left for five years in a foster home at Southsea. Here he was treated harshly and beaten for the mildest misdemeanour. The contrast between the happiness of his Indian experience and the cold brutality of his British one would colour much of his later writing.

When he was twelve he entered the United Services College at Westward Ho! near Bideford. It was an expensive establishment that specialised in training boys for a military life. However Kipling's poor eyesight and his mediocre academic achievements ruled out any hopes of a successful career in the forces. Nevertheless, one good thing did come out of his time at the college: the headmaster, Cormell Price, a friend of his father and uncles, fostered his literary abilities.

In 1882, aged sixteen, with great joy he returned to India, to Lahore, where his parents now lived, to work on the *Civil and Military Gazette* (1882–7), and later on its sister paper, the *Pioneer*, in Allahabad (1887–9). In his limited spare time he wrote many poems and stories, which were published alongside his reporting, and his literary career began to flourish. It was during this period that he wrote most of his tales of the supernatural, influenced to some extent by the unhappy memories he carried with him of his adolescence in England.

As Kipling's output increased, so did his fame and the respect of critics and readers. When he returned to Britain in 1889, he was hailed as a literary heir to Charles Dickens. He remained in London, continuing with his writing, until 1892, when he married Caroline Starr Balestier, the sister of an American publisher whom he had known. After a world trip, he returned with Carrie to her family home in Brattleboro, Vermont, USA, with the intention of settling down there. It was at Brattleboro, deep in New England, that he wrote *Captains Courageous* and *The Jungle Books*, and that the couple's first two children, Josephine and Elsie, were born.

Kipling was dissatisfied with his life in Vermont and a quarrel with his brother-in-law drove the family back to England in 1896. They settled at Rottingdean, near Brighton, where their son John was born the following year. Life was contented and fulfilling until, tragically, Josephine died while the family were on a visit to the United States in early 1899; things were never the same again after Josephine's death. Living so close to Brighton, Kipling had become a tourist attraction, so in 1902 he sought the seclusion of a lovely seventeenth-century house called Bateman's, south of Burwash, nearby in Sussex, where he spent his remaining years. Widely regarded as the unofficial poet laureate, Kipling refused the actual post and many other honours, among them the Order of Merit. However, in 1907 he was the first author to be awarded the Nobel Prize for Literature. His years were darkened by the death of his son John in the the First World War. Kipling died in 1936 and is buried in Poet's Corner at Westminster Abbey.

* * *

Rudyard Kipling's literary output was immense, ranging from the fairytale-like excursions of the *Just So Stories* and children's fiction such as *Stalky & Co* and the adventure tales *Kim* and *Captains Courageous* to the vast array of poems which he penned, the most famous perhaps being 'If'. Therefore it is easy to see how his strange and supernatural tales have been overlooked. But we have dug deep into the wonderful literary pudding left behind by Kipling and for this edition we have extracted a fine collection of spine-chilling plums for your edification and delight.

The collection kicks off with one of the more graphically horrific of the author's tales, 'The Mark of the Beast', a story of lycanthropy. It is one of Kipling's early pieces, written in India before his return to England. By the kind offices of Sir Ian Hamilton, an army officer who was keen to promote Kipling's work, the story found its way on to the desks of two important editors, Andrew Lang and William Sharp, who both recoiled in horror when they read the story. Lang commented, ' . . . this [is] poisonous stuff which has left an extremely disagreeable impression on my mind.' Sharp was equally perturbed, writing to Hamilton stating, 'I strongly recommend you instantly burn this detestable piece of work. I would like to hazard a guess that the writer of the article in question is very young, that he will die mad before he has reached thirty.' Nevertheless the story was published in the *Pioneer*, the Allahabad newspaper, in 1890 and later Kipling wrote a sequel, 'The Return of Imray', the plot of which, like the original, hinges on an insult to an Indian which results in tragic consequences.

'The Phantom Rickshaw' also leans towards the horror end of the ghost-story spectrum. The central character is haunted by visions of a spectral rickshaw inhabited by his dead mistress that drive him towards madness. There is more than a touch of the styling and subject matter of Edgar Allan Poe about this tale and yet it is perhaps less predictable, far removed from the stifling atmosphere of the dark gothic environs of Poe's landscape and situated in Kipling's Simla.

Another story in the Edgar Allan Poe manner is 'The Strange Ride of Morrowbie Jukes', with its vivid description of 'the horrible little burrows of the nightmare village of the living dead'. However, it has been noted by several critics that for all its obvious dreadfulness, fundamentally this story exhibits a perceptive assessment of the Anglo-Indian position at the time. Though Jukes's superiority as a sahib appears to be threatened by the equality of life in the valley, it is reaffirmed when Jukes is rescued by his Indian servant. No such rescue awaits the two other characters, Peachy and Dravott. They, too, assert their superiority, and by acting as gods, they carry their roles as sahibs to its logical conclusion. But when they are revealed to be mere mortals on an equal footing with others, the natives destroy them. In this scenario Kipling cleverly illustrates the paradox of British rule in India. Having conquered, the British had to govern; in order to govern they had to act as gods; to act as gods was ultimately impossible and so the crack in the armour was inevitably revealed and the weakness exposed.

Perhaps 'They' is Kipling's greatest ghost story. Certainly it is his most sensitive and most tender, engendering a sense of unease and melancholy rather than shock and horror. We are very much into the twentieth century here – the story was written in 1904 – with the motor car featuring strongly in the plot. The narrator driving around the Sussex countryside in the spring finds himself lost and discovers an old country house belonging to a blind woman who looks after several 'elusive' children. It is only on further visits that he learns the poignant secret of the house and of the children. Kipling's habit of exorcising his own pain and doubt in his poetry and prose provides no finer example than in this story. It was written by the author to help him move on from the grief he felt at his young daughter's death some five years earlier. The final parting in the story represents on the page Kipling's acceptance of the loss of his own child and is all the more moving because of this personal involvement with the narrative.

One of the incidental pleasures of 'They' is Kipling's rare celebration of the English landscape, which the narrator describes with elegiac freshness:

I let the country flow under my wheels. The orchid-studded flats of the East gave way to the thyme, ilex, and grey grass of the Downs; these again to the rich cornland and fig-trees of the lower coast, where you can carry the beat of the tide on your left hand for fifteen level miles . . .

'In The Same Boat' is an odd little story concerning a young man and woman who suffer from a strange affliction. They are troubled by unsettling dreams which make them weak and gloomy for days afterwards and as a result the pair have become addicts of Najdolene, a calming drug. Kipling maintains a subdued satirical tone throughout, faintly mocking this couple, implying that they are somewhat self-indulgent. The cause of their dilemma is solved not by a doctor but by the common-sense companion of the young lady.

We have what Kipling regarded as a 'supernatural country-house canine love story' in 'The Dog Hervey' (almost something for everyone then). Kipling had a great love of dogs. It was the unconditional affection that the creatures give to their owners which appealed to him. The hound Malachi, owned by the narrator of this story, was named after one of Kipling's own dogs. The name is taken from Thomas More's line, 'When Malachi wore a collar of gold.'

Kipling was an acquaintance and indeed a fan of Arthur Conan Doyle, the creator of the detective Sherlock Holmes, and he gave a nod and wink to his friend when he created the psychic detective story, 'The House Surgeon', which is about a house which he called Holmescroft.

It can be seen in certain stories that Kipling's desire for accuracy in presenting characters with their anomalies of speech and accents can actually hinder the flow of the narrative. This is certainly the case with 'The Wish House' in which the plot unravels through the conversation of Mrs Ashcroft and Mrs Fettley, which is carried on in Sussex dialect. However, the premise of the story – the lengths someone will go to to keep a person 'where I want 'im' – is chilling and highly original.

The monster sea serpent at the centre of the wise little story 'A Matter of Fact' allows Kipling to play about with the notion of truth and lies; what it is appropriate to reveal and when it is right to play on people's gullibility. As the seasoned old journalist who narrates the

story observes, ' . . . Truth is a naked lady, and if by accident she is
drawn up from the bottom of the sea, it behoves a gentleman either
to give her a print petticoat or turn his face to the wall and vow that
he did not see.'

The incidental horrors of war are suggested in the eerie visitation
of five children in 'Swept and Garnished' which was first published
in January 1915, shortly after the outbreak of World War I. The
war affected Kipling profoundly; another tale written in 1915 is the
bitter and angry 'Mary Postgate', which Stanley Baldwin's son called
'the wickedest story ever written'. This attack was inspired by the
shocking nature of the apparent pleasure experienced by Mary as she
watches a German soldier die, and of the implied sexual satisfaction
she gains from the act. It has been claimed that Kipling wrote this
story as a superstitious attempt to avert the evil eye: if he wrote a
story in which he imagined his deepest fears, the gods may spare his
son John who was fighting in the war. If this is true, this desperate
ploy did not work for John was killed in the trenches in 1917. His
death devastated his father.

'A Madonna of the Trenches' was written while the author was
working on a history of his son's regiment, his book, *The Irish Guards
in the Great War* (1923). Kipling's sense of loss pervades the text
which includes some horrifyingly graphic descriptions of conditions
in the trenches of the Western Front. The story is one of his most
complex and, because of the apparent acceptance of adulterous love,
one of his most controversial.

We are back in India for the final selection of tales. 'At the End of
the Passage' is a ghost story which takes place in a run-down outpost
in a remote area of the country. Here four men, adrift in their
isolation, fight the heat, themselves and the fear that there is a
strange presence in the room at the end of the passage. This tale also
reflects the strain and claustrophobia felt by the English when they
are so far removed from what they regard as normality, trapped as it
were in a hot, sticky bubble miles away from 'civilisation'.

While 'The Bisara of Pooree' is a warning parable ('You will say
that all this story is made up'), 'The Lost Legion' reads like an old
soldier's tale told around the campfire late at night, one which has
grown more fantastic with the repeated tellings. This may well have
been its origin, for, like most great writers, Kipling borrowed from
life and embroidered the 'truth' with his own imagination.

'The Dream of Duncan Parrenness' is a kind of Anglo-Indian
version of John Bunyan's *Pilgrim's Progress* and is peppered with

archaic prose to underline the comparison. Kipling was a great ad-
mirer of Bunyan and his work and advised would-be writers to: 'Go
home and read him. Read the *Pilgrim's Progress* half-a-dozen times
before you try to write prose.'

'The Tomb of His Ancestors' introduces the rare beast, the
Clouded Tiger and once again reveals the unique and delicate
balance inherent in the relationship between the British invaders and
the native Indians.

'By Word of Mouth' is one of the most famous of Kipling's supernatural tales. It is chilling because of its simplicity and the bitter-
sweet outcome.

The final story, 'My Own True Ghost Story', is a convincing
personal anecdote with a suitable twist in the tale. It ends this
collection with an authorly flourish.

*   *   *

Rudyard Kipling spent his formative years in India, a country where
there was wide belief in ghosts and the supernatural; at the same
period of history, Europe was buzzing with speculation concerning
matters involving psychic and spiritualist beliefs. Therefore it is no
wonder that such an imaginative and informed writer should include
other-worldly elements in his fiction. And similarly, it is no wonder
that a writer of Kipling's brilliance should make these tales thrilling
and engrossing.

Kipling is an entertaining writer, but like all great wordsmiths he
also provides some enriching and elevating insight or illumination
about human nature and the world in which we live. These are
strange tales indeed, but insightful and rewarding into the bargain.

DAVID STUART DAVIES

STRANGE TALES

The Mark of the Beast

Your Gods and my Gods – do you or I know
which are the stronger?

Native Proverb

East of Suez, some hold, the direct control of Providence ceases;
Man being there handed over to the power of the Gods and Devils of
Asia, and the Church of England Providence only exercising an
occasional and modified supervision in the case of Englishmen.

This theory accounts for some of the more unnecessary horrors of
life in India: it may be stretched to explain my story.

My friend Strickland of the Police, who knows as much of natives
of India as is good for any man, can bear witness to the facts of the
case. Dumoise, our doctor, also saw what Strickland and I saw. The
inference which he drew from the evidence was entirely incorrect.
He is dead now; he died, in a rather curious manner, which has been
elsewhere described.

When Fleete came to India he owned a little money and some land
in the Himalayas, near a place called Dharmsala. Both properties had
been left him by an uncle, and he came out to finance them. He was
a big, heavy, genial, and inoffensive man. His knowledge of natives
was, of course, limited, and he complained of the difficulties of the
language.

He rode in from his place in the hills to spend New Year in the
station, and he stayed with Strickland. On New Year's Eve there was a
big dinner at the club, and the night was excusably wet. When men
foregather from the uttermost ends of the Empire, they have a right to
be riotous. The Frontier had sent down a contingent o' Catch-'em-
Alive-O's who had not seen twenty white faces for a year, and were
used to ride fifteen miles to dinner at the next Fort at the risk of a
Khyberee bullet where their drinks should lie. They profited by their
new security, for they tried to play pool with a curled-up hedgehog
found in the garden, and one of them carried the marker round the

room in his teeth. Half a dozen planters had come in from the south and were talking 'horse' to the Biggest Liar in Asia, who was trying to cap all their stories at once. Everybody was there, and there was a general closing up of ranks and taking stock of our losses in dead or disabled that had fallen during the past year. It was a very wet night, and I remember that we sang 'Auld Lang Syne' with our feet in the Polo Championship Cup, and our heads among the stars, and swore that we were all dear friends. Then some of us went away and annexed Burma, and some tried to open up the Soudan and were opened up by Fuzzies in that cruel scrub outside Suakim, and some found stars and medals, and some were married, which was bad, and some did other things which were worse, and the others of us stayed in our chains and strove to make money on insufficient experiences.

Fleete began the night with sherry and bitters, drank champagne steadily up to dessert, then raw, rasping Capri with all the strength of whisky, took Benedictine with his coffee, four or five whiskies and sodas to improve his pool strokes, beer and bones at half-past two, winding up with old brandy. Consequently, when he came out, at half-past three in the morning, into fourteen degrees of frost, he was very angry with his horse for coughing, and tried to leapfrog into the saddle. The horse broke away and went to his stables; so Strickland and I formed a Guard of Dishonour to take Fleete home.

Our road lay through the bazaar, close to a little temple of Hanuman, the Monkey-god, who is a leading divinity worthy of respect. All gods have good points, just as have all priests. Personally, I attach much importance to Hanuman, and am kind to his people – the great grey apes of the hills. One never knows when one may want a friend.

There was a light in the temple, and as we passed, we could hear voices of men chanting hymns. In a native temple, the priests rise at all hours of the night to do honour to their god. Before we could stop him, Fleete dashed up the steps, patted two priests on the back, and was gravely grinding the ashes of his cigar-butt into the forehead of the red stone image of Hanuman. Strickland tried to drag him out, but he sat down and said solemnly: 'Shee that? Mark of the B-beasht! *I* made it. Ishn't it fine?'

In half a minute the temple was alive and noisy, and Strickland, who knew what came of polluting gods, said that things might occur. He, by virtue of his official position, long residence in the country, and weakness for going among the natives, was known to the priests and he felt unhappy. Fleete sat on the ground and refused to move. He said that 'good old Hanuman' made a very soft pillow.

Then, without any warning, a Silver Man came out of a recess behind the image of the god. He was perfectly naked in that bitter, bitter cold, and his body shone like frosted silver, for he was what the Bible calls 'a leper as white as snow'. Also he had no face, because he was a leper of some years' standing and his disease was heavy upon him. We two stooped to haul Fleete up, and the temple was filling and filling with folk who seemed to spring from the earth, when the Silver Man ran in under our arms, making a noise exactly like the mewing of an otter, caught Fleete round the body and dropped his head on Fleete's breast before we could wrench him away. Then he retired to a corner and sat mewing while the crowd blocked all the doors.

The priests were very angry until the Silver Man touched Fleete. That nuzzling seemed to sober them.

At the end of a few minutes' silence one of the priests came to Strickland and said, in perfect English, 'Take your friend away. He has done with Hanuman, but Hanuman has not done with him.' The crowd gave room and we carried Fleete into the road.

Strickland was very angry. He said that we might all three have been knifed, and that Fleete should thank his stars that he had escaped without injury.

Fleete thanked no-one. He said that he wanted to go to bed. He was gorgeously drunk.

We moved on, Strickland silent and wrathful, until Fleete was taken with violent shivering fits and sweating. He said that the smells of the bazaar were overpowering, and he wondered why slaughter-houses were permitted so near English residences. 'Can't you smell the blood?' said Fleete.

We put him to bed at last, just as the dawn was breaking, and Strickland invited me to have another whisky and soda. While we were drinking he talked of the trouble in the temple, and admitted that it baffled him completely. Strickland hates being mystified by natives, because his business in life is to overmatch them with their own weapons. He has not yet succeeded in doing this, but in fifteen or twenty years he will have made some small progress.

'They should have mauled us,' he said, 'instead of mewing at us. I wonder what they meant. I don't like it one little bit.'

I said that the Managing Committee of the temple would in all probability bring a criminal action against us for insulting their religion. There was a section of the Indian Penal Code which exactly met Fleete's offence. Strickland said he only hoped and prayed that they would do this. Before I left I looked into Fleete's room, and saw him lying on his right side, scratching his left breast. Then. I went to bed cold, depressed, and unhappy, at seven o'clock in the morning.

At one o'clock I rode over to Strickland's house to enquire after Fleete's head. I imagined that it would be a sore one. Fleete was breakfasting and seemed unwell. His temper was gone, for he was abusing the cook for not supplying him with an underdone chop. A man who can eat raw meat after a wet night is a curiosity. I told Fleete this and he laughed.

'You breed queer mosquitoes in these parts,' he said. 'I've been bitten to pieces, but only in one place.'

'Let's have a look at the bite,' said Strickland. 'It may have gone down since this morning.'

While the chops were being cooked, Fleete opened his shirt and showed us, just over his left breast, a mark, the perfect double of the black rosettes – the five or six irregular blotches arranged in a circle – on a leopard's hide. Strickland looked and said, 'It was only pink this morning. It's grown black now.'

Fleete ran to a glass.

'By Jove!' he said, 'this is nasty. What is it?'

We could not answer. Here the chops came in, all red and juicy, and Fleete bolted three in a most offensive manner. He ate on his right grinders only, and threw his head over his right shoulder as he snapped the meat. When he had finished, it struck him that he had been behaving strangely, for he said apologetically, 'I don't think I ever felt so hungry in my life. I've bolted like an ostrich.'

After breakfast Strickland said to me, 'Don't go. Stay here, and stay for the night.'

Seeing that my house was not three miles from Strickland's, this request was absurd. But Strickland insisted, and was going to say something when Fleete interrupted by declaring in a shamefaced way that he felt hungry again. Strickland sent a man to my house to fetch over my bedding and a horse, and we three went down to Strickland's stables to pass the hours until it was time to go out for a ride. The man who has a weakness for horses never wearies of inspecting them; and when two men are killing time in this way they gather knowledge and lies the one from the other.

There were five horses in the stables, and I shall never forget the scene as we tried to look them over. They seemed to have gone mad. They reared and screamed and nearly tore up their pickets; they sweated and shivered and lathered and were distraught with fear.

Strickland's horses used to know him as well as his dogs; which made the matter more curious. We left the stable for fear of the brutes throwing themselves in their panic. Then Strickland turned back and called me. The horses were still frightened, but they let us 'gentle' and make much of them, and put their heads in our bosoms.

'They aren't afraid of *us*,' said Strickland. 'D'you know, I'd give three months' pay if Outrage here could talk.'

But Outrage was dumb, and could only cuddle up to his master and blow out his nostrils, as is the custom of horses when they wish to explain things but can't. Fleete came up when we were in the stalls, and as soon as the horses saw him, their fright broke out afresh. It was all that we could do to escape from the place unkicked. Strickland said, 'They don't seem to love you, Fleete.'

'Nonsense,' said Fleete; 'my mare will follow me like a dog.' He went to her; she was in a loose-box; but as he slipped the bars she plunged, knocked him down, and broke away into the garden. I laughed, but Strickland was not amused. He took his moustache in both fists and pulled at it till it nearly came out. Fleete, instead of going off to chase his property, yawned, saying that he felt sleepy. He went to the house to lie down, which was a foolish way of spending New Year's Day.

Strickland sat with me in the stables and asked if I had noticed anything peculiar in Fleete's manner. I said that he ate his food like a beast; but that this might have been the result of living alone in the hills out of the reach of society as refined and elevating as ours for instance. Strickland was not amused. I do not think that he listened to me, for his next sentence referred to the mark on Fleete's breast, and I said that it might have been caused by blister-flies, or that it was possibly a birth-mark newly born and now visible for the first time. We both agreed that it was unpleasant to look at, and Strickland found occasion to say that I was a fool.

'I can't tell you what I think now,' said he, 'because you would call me a madman; but you must stay with me for the next few days, if you can. I want you to watch Fleete, but don't tell me what you think till I have made up my mind.'

'But I am dining out tonight,' I said. 'So am I,' said Strickland, 'and so is Fleete. At least if he doesn't change his mind.'

We walked about the garden smoking, but saying nothing – because we were friends, and talking spoils good tobacco – till our pipes were out. Then we went to wake up Fleete. He was wide awake and fidgeting about his room.

'I say, I want some more chops,' he said. 'Can I get them?'

We laughed and said, 'Go and change. The ponies will be round in a minute.'

'All right,' said Fleete. I'll go when I get the chops – underdone ones, mind.'

He seemed to be quite in earnest. It was four o'clock, and we had had breakfast at one; still, for a long time, he demanded those underdone chops. Then he changed into riding clothes and went out into the verandah. His pony – the mare had not been caught – would not let him come near. All three horses were unmanageable – mad with fear – and finally Fleete said that he would stay at home and get something to eat. Strickland and I rode out wondering. As we passed the temple of Hanuman, the Silver Man came out and mewed at us.

'He is not one of the regular priests of the temple,' said Strickland. 'I think I should particularly like to lay my hands on him.'

There was no spring in our gallop on the racecourse that evening. The horses were stale, and moved as though they had been ridden out.

'The fright after breakfast has been too much for them,' said Strickland.

That was the only remark he made through the remainder of the ride. Once or twice I think he swore to himself; but that did not count.

We came back in the dark at seven o'clock, and saw that there were no lights in the bungalow. 'Careless ruffians my servants are!' said Strickland.

My horse reared at something on the carriage drive, and Fleete stood up under its nose.

'What are you doing, grovelling about the garden?' said Strickland.

But both horses bolted and nearly threw us. We dismounted by the stables and returned to Fleete, who was on his hands and knees under the orange bushes.

'What the devil's wrong with you?' said Strickland.

'Nothing, nothing in the world,' said Fleete, speaking very quickly and thickly. 'I've been gardening – botanising you know. The smell of the earth is delightful. I think I'm going for a walk – a long walk – all night.'

Then I saw that there was something excessively out of order somewhere, and I said to Strickland, 'I am not dining out.'

'Bless you!' said Strickland. 'Here, Fleete, get up. You'll catch fever there. Come in to dinner and let's have the lamps lit. We'll all dine at home.'

Fleete stood up unwillingly, and said, 'No lamps – no lamps. It's much nicer here. Let's dine outside and have some more chops – lots of 'em and underdone – bloody ones with gristle.'

Now a December evening in Northern India is bitterly cold, and Fleete's suggestion was that of a maniac.

'Come in,' said Strickland sternly. 'Come in at once.'

Fleete came, and when the lamps were brought, we saw that he was literally plastered with dirt from head to foot. He must have been rolling in the garden. He shrank from the light and went to his room. His eyes were horrible to look at. There was a green light behind them, not in them, if you understand, and the man's lower lip hung down.

Strickland said, 'There is going to be trouble – big trouble – tonight. Don't you change your riding-things.'

We waited and waited for Fleete's reappearance, and ordered dinner in the meantime. We could hear him moving about his own room, but there was no light there. Presently from the room came the long-drawn howl of a wolf.

People write and talk lightly of blood running cold and hair standing up and things of that kind. Both sensations are too horrible to be trifled with. My heart stopped as though a knife had been driven through it, and Strickland turned as white as the tablecloth.

The howl was repeated, and was answered by another howl far across the fields.

That set the gilded roof on the horror. Strickland dashed into Fleete's room. I followed, and we saw Fleete getting out of the window. He made beast-noises in the back of his throat. He could not answer us when we shouted at him. He spat.

I don't quite remember what followed, but I think that Strickland must have stunned him with the long boot-jack or else I should never have been able to sit on his chest. Fleete could not speak, he could only snarl, and his snarls were those of a wolf, not of a man. The human spirit must have been giving way all day and have died out with the twilight. We were dealing with a beast that had once been Fleete.

The affair was beyond any human and rational experience. I tried to say 'Hydrophobia', but the word wouldn't come, because I knew that I was lying.

We bound this beast with leather thongs of the punkah-rope, and tied its thumbs and big toes together, and gagged it with a shoe-horn, which makes a very efficient gag if you know how to arrange it. Then we carried it into the dining-room, and sent a man to

Dumoise, the doctor, telling him to come over at once. After we had despatched the messenger and were drawing breath, Strickland said, 'It's no good. This isn't any doctor's work.' I, also, knew that he spoke the truth.

The beast's head was free, and it threw it about from side to side. Anyone entering the room would have believed that we were curing a wolf's pelt. That was the most loathsome accessory of all.

Strickland sat with his chin in the heel of his fist, watching the beast as it wriggled on the ground, but saying nothing. The shirt had been torn open in the scuffle and showed the black rosette mark on the left breast. It stood out like a blister.

In the silence of the watching we heard something without mewing like a she-otter. We both rose to our feet, and, I answer for myself, not Strickland, felt sick – actually and physically sick. We told each other, as did the men in Pinafore, that it was the cat.

Dumoise arrived, and I never saw a little man so unprofessionally shocked. He said that it was a heart-rending case of hydrophobia, and that nothing could be done. At least any palliative measures would only prolong the agony. The beast was foaming at the mouth. Fleete, as we told Dumoise, had been bitten by dogs once or twice. Any man who keeps half a dozen terriers must expect a nip now and again. Dumoise could offer no help. He could only certify that Fleete was dying of hydrophobia. The beast was then howling, for it had managed to spit out the shoe-horn. Dumoise said that he would be ready to certify to the cause of death, and that the end was certain. He was a good little man, and he offered to remain with us; but Strickland refused the kindness. He did not wish to poison Dumoise's New Year. He would only ask him not to give the real cause of Fleete's death to the public.

So Dumoise left, deeply agitated; and as soon as the noise of the cart-wheels had died away, Strickland told me, in a whisper, his suspicions. They were so wildly improbable that he dared not say them out aloud; and I, who entertained all Strickland's beliefs, was so ashamed of owning to them that I pretended to disbelieve.

'Even if the Silver Man had bewitched Fleete for polluting the image of Hanuman, the punishment could not have fallen so quickly.'

As I was whispering this the cry outside the house rose again, and the beast fell into a fresh paroxysm of struggling till we were afraid that the thongs that held it would give way.

'Watch!' said Strickland. 'If this happens six times I shall take the law into my own hands. I order you to help me.'

He went into his room and came out in a few minutes with the barrels of an old shotgun, a piece of fishing-line, some thick cord, and his heavy wooden bedstead. I reported that the convulsions had followed the cry by two seconds in each case, and the beast seemed perceptibly weaker.

Strickland muttered, 'But he can't take away the life! He can't take away the life!'

I said, though I knew that I was arguing against myself, 'It may be a cat. It must be a cat. If the Silver Man is responsible, why does he dare to come here?'

Strickland arranged the wood on the hearth, put the gun-barrels into the glow of the fire, spread the twine on the table and broke a walking stick in two. There was one yard of fishing line, gut, lapped with wire, such as is used for mahseer-fishing, and he tied the two ends together in a loop.

Then he said, 'How can we catch him? He must be taken alive and unhurt.'

I said that we must trust in Providence, and go out softly with polo-sticks into the shrubbery at the front of the house. The man or animal that made the cry was evidently moving round the house as regularly as a night-watchman. We could wait in the bushes till he came by and knock him over.

Strickland accepted this suggestion, and we slipped out from a bathroom window into the front verandah and then across the carriage drive into the bushes.

In the moonlight we could see the leper coming round the corner of the house. He was perfectly naked, and from time to time he mewed and stopped to dance with his shadow. It was an unattractive sight, and thinking of poor Fleete, brought to such degradation by so foul a creature, I put away all my doubts and resolved to help Strickland from the heated gun-barrels to the loop of twine – from the loins to the head and back again – with all tortures that might be needful.

The leper halted in the front porch for a moment and we jumped out on him with the sticks. He was wonderfully strong, and we were afraid that he might escape or be fatally injured before we caught him. We had an idea that lepers were frail creatures, but this proved to be incorrect. Strickland knocked his legs from under him and I put my foot on his neck. He mewed hideously, and even through my riding-boots I could feel that his flesh was not the flesh of a clean man.

He struck at us with his hand and feet-stumps. We looped the lash of a dog-whip round him, under the armpits, and dragged him backwards into the hall and so into the dining-room where the beast lay. There we tied him with trunk-straps. He made no attempt to escape, but mewed.

When we confronted him with the beast the scene was beyond description. The beast doubled backwards into a bow as though he had been poisoned with strychnine, and moaned in the most pitiable fashion. Several other things happened also, but they cannot be put down here.

'I think I was right,' said Strickland. 'Now we will ask him to cure this case.'

But the leper only mewed. Strickland wrapped a towel round his hand and took the gun-barrels out of the fire. I put the half of the broken walking stick through the loop of fishing-line and buckled the leper comfortably to Strickland's bedstead. I understood then how men and women and little children can endure to see a witch burnt alive; for the beast was moaning on the floor, and though the Silver Man had no face, you could see horrible feelings passing through the slab that took its place, exactly as waves of heat play across red-hot iron – gun-barrels for instance.

Strickland shaded his eyes with his hands for a moment and we got to work. This part is not to be printed.

The dawn was beginning to break when the leper spoke. His mewings had not been satisfactory up to that point. The beast had fainted from exhaustion and the house was very still. We un-strapped the leper and told him to take away the evil spirit. He crawled to the beast and laid his hand upon the left breast. That was all. Then he fell face down and whined, drawing in his breath as he did so.

We watched the face of the beast, and saw the soul of Fleete coming back into the eyes. Then a sweat broke out on the forehead and the eyes – they were human eyes – closed. We waited for an hour but Fleete still slept. We carried him to his room and bade the leper go, giving him the bedstead, and the sheet on the bedstead to cover his nakedness, the gloves and the towels with which we had touched him, and the whip that had been hooked round his body. He put the sheet about him and went out into the early morning without speaking or mewing.

Strickland wiped his face and sat down. A night-gong, far away in the city, made seven o'clock.

'Exactly four-and-twenty hours!' said Strickland. 'And I've done enough to ensure my dismissal from the service, besides permanent quarters in a lunatic asylum. Do you believe that we are awake?'

The red-hot gun-barrel had fallen on the floor and was singeing the carpet. The smell was entirely real.

That morning at eleven we two together went to wake up Fleete. We looked and saw that the black leopard-rosette on his chest had disappeared. He was very drowsy and tired, but as soon as he saw us, he said, 'Oh! Confound you fellows. Happy New Year to you. Never mix your liquors. I'm nearly dead.'

'Thanks for your kindness, but you're over time,' said Strickland. 'Today is the morning of the second. You've slept the clock round with a vengeance.'

The door opened, and little Dumoise put his head in. He had come on foot, and fancied that we were laying out Fleete.

'I've brought a nurse,' said Dumoise. 'I suppose that she can come in for . . . what is necessary.'

'By all means,' said Fleete cheerily, sitting up in bed. 'Bring on your nurses.'

Dumoise was dumb. Strickland led him out and explained that there must have been a mistake in the diagnosis. Dumoise remained dumb and left the house hastily. He considered that his professional reputation had been injured, and was inclined to make a personal matter of the recovery. Strickland went out too. When he came back, he said that he had been to call on the Temple of Hanuman to offer redress for the pollution of the god, and had been solemnly assured that no white man had ever touched the idol and that he was an incarnation of all the virtues labouring under a delusion.

'What do you think?' said Strickland.

I said, ' "There are more things . . . " '

But Strickland hates that quotation. He says that I have worn it threadbare.

One other curious thing happened which frightened me as much as anything in all the night's work. When Fleete was dressed he came into the dining-room and sniffed. He had a quaint trick of moving his nose when he sniffed. 'Horrid doggy smell, here,' said he. 'You should really keep those terriers of yours in better order. Try sulphur, Strick.'

But Strickland did not answer. He caught hold of the back of a chair, and, without warning, went into an amazing fit of hysterics. It is terrible to see a strong man overtaken with hysteria. Then it struck me that we had fought for Fleete's soul with the Silver Man in that room, and had disgraced ourselves as Englishmen for ever, and I laughed and gasped and gurgled just as shamefully as Strickland, while Fleete thought that we had both gone mad. We never told him what we had done.

Some years later, when Strickland had married and was a church-going member of society for his wife's sake, we reviewed the incident dispassionately, and Strickland suggested that I should put it before the public.

I cannot myself see that this step is likely to clear up the mystery; because, in the first place, no-one will believe a rather unpleasant story, and, in the second, it is well known to every right-minded man that the gods of the heathen are stone and brass, and any attempt to deal with them otherwise is justly condemned.

The Return of Imray

The doors were wide, the story saith,
Out of the night came the patient wraith,
He might not speak, and he could not stir
A hair of the Baron's minniver –

Speechless and strengthless, a shadow thin,
He roved the castle to seek his kin.
And oh, 'twas a piteous thing to see
The dumb ghost follow his enemy!

The Baron

Imray achieved the impossible. Without warning, for no conceivable motive, in his youth, at the threshold of his career he chose to disappear from the world – which is to say, the little Indian station where he lived.

Upon a day he was alive, well, happy, and in great evidence among the billiard-tables at his Club. Upon a morning, he was not, and no manner of search could make sure where he might be. He had stepped out of his place; he had not appeared at his office at the proper time, and his dogcart was not upon the public roads. For these reasons, and because he was hampering, in a microscopical degree, the administration of the Indian Empire, that Empire paused for one microscopical moment to make inquiry into the fate of Imray. Ponds were dragged, wells were plumbed, telegrams were despatched down the lines of railways and to the nearest seaport town – twelve hundred miles away; but Imray was not at the end of the drag-ropes nor the telegraph wires. He was gone, and his place knew him no more.

Then the work of the great Indian Empire swept forward, because it could not be delayed, and Imray from being a man became a mystery – such a thing as men talk over at their tables in the Club for a month, and then forget utterly. His guns, horses, and carts were sold to the highest bidder. His superior officer wrote an altogether absurd letter to his mother, saying that Imray had unaccountably disappeared, and his bungalow stood empty.

After three or four months of the scorching hot weather had gone by, my friend Strickland, of the Police, saw fit to rent the bungalow from the native landlord. This was before he was engaged to Miss Youghal – an affair which has been described in another place – and while he was pursuing his investigations into native life. His own life was sufficiently peculiar, and men complained of his manners and customs. There was always food in his house, but there were no regular times for meals. He ate, standing up and walking about, whatever he might find at the sideboard, and this is not good for human beings. His domestic equipment was limited to six rifles, three shotguns, five saddles, and a collection of stiff-jointed mah-seer-rods, bigger and stronger than the largest salmon-rods. These occupied one half of his bungalow, and the other half was given up to Strickland and his dog Tietjens – an enormous Rampur slut who devoured daily the rations of two men. She spoke to Strickland in a language of her own; and whenever, walking abroad, she saw things calculated to destroy the peace of Her Majesty the Queen-Empress, she returned to her master and laid information. Strickland would take steps at once, and the end of his labours was trouble and fine and imprisonment for other people. The natives believed that Tietjens was a familiar spirit, and treated her with the great reverence that is born of hate and fear. One room in the bungalow was set apart for her special use. She owned a bedstead, a blanket, and a drinking-trough, and if anyone came into Strickland's room at night her custom was to knock down the invader and give tongue till someone came with a light. Strickland owed his life to her, when he was on the Frontier, in search of a local murderer, who came in the grey dawn to send Strickland much farther than the Andaman Islands. Tietjens caught the man as he was crawling into Strickland's tent with a dagger between his teeth; and after his record of iniquity was established in the eyes of the law he was hanged. From that date Tietjens wore a collar of rough silver, and employed a monogram on her night-blanket; and the blanket was of double woven Kashmir cloth, for she was a delicate dog.

Under no circumstances would she be separated from Strickland; and once, when he was ill with fever, made great trouble for the doctors, because she did not know how to help her master and would not allow another creature to attempt aid. Macarnaght, of the Indian Medical Service, beat her over her head with a gun-butt before she could understand that she must give room for those who could give quinine.

A short time after Strickland had taken Imray's bungalow, my business took me through that Station, and naturally, the Club quarters being full, I quartered myself upon Strickland. It was a desirable bungalow, eight-roomed and heavily thatched against any chance of leakage from rain. Under the pitch of the roof ran a ceiling-cloth which looked just as neat as a whitewashed ceiling. The landlord had repainted it when Strickland took the bungalow. Unless you knew how Indian bungalows were built you would never have suspected that above the cloth lay the dark three-cornered cavern of the roof, where the beams and the underside of the thatch harboured all manner of rats, bats, ants, and foul things.

Tietjens met me in the verandah with a bay like the boom of the bell of St. Paul's, putting her paws on my shoulder to show she was glad to see me. Strickland had contrived to claw together a sort of meal which he called lunch, and immediately after it was finished went out about his business. I was left alone with Tietjens and my own affairs. The heat of the summer had broken up and turned to the warm damp of the rains. There was no motion in the heated air, but the rain fell like ramrods on the earth, and flung up a blue mist when it splashed back. The bamboos, and the custard-apples, the poinsettias, and the mango trees in the garden stood still while the warm water lashed through them, and the frogs began to sing among the aloe hedges. A little before the light failed, and when the rain was at its worst, I sat in the back verandah and heard the water roar from the eaves, and scratched myself because I was covered with the thing called prickly-heat. Tietjens came out with me and put her head in my lap and was very sorrowful; so I gave her biscuits when tea was ready, and I took tea in the back verandah on account of the little coolness found there. The rooms of the house were dark behind me. I could smell Strickland's saddlery and the oil on his guns, and I had no desire to sit among these things. My own servant came to me in the twilight, the muslin of his clothes clinging tightly to his drenched body, and told me that a gentleman had called and wished to see someone. Very much against my will, but only because of the darkness of the rooms, I went into the naked drawing-room, telling my man to bring the lights. There might or might not have been a caller waiting – it seemed to me that I saw a figure by one of the windows – but when the lights came there was nothing save the spikes of the rain without, and the smell of the drinking earth in my nostrils. I explained to my servant that he was no wiser than he ought to be, and went back to the verandah to talk to Tietjens. She had gone out into the wet, and I could hardly coax her back to me, even with biscuits with sugar tops. Strickland came home, dripping wet, just before dinner, and the first thing he said was: 'Has anyone called?'

I explained, with apologies, that my servant had summoned me into the drawing-room on a false alarm; or that some loafer had tried to call on Strickland, and thinking better of it had fled after giving his name. Strickland ordered dinner, without comment, and since it was a real dinner with a white tablecloth attached, we sat down.

At nine o'clock Strickland wanted to go to bed, and I was tired too. Tietjens, who had been lying underneath the table, rose up, and swung into the least exposed verandah as soon as her master moved to his own room, which was next to the stately chamber set apart for Tietjens. If a mere wife had wished to sleep out of doors in that pelting rain it would not have mattered; but Tietjens was a dog, and therefore the better animal. I looked at Strickland, expecting to see him flay her with a whip. He smiled queerly, as a man would smile after telling some unpleasant domestic tragedy. 'She has done this ever since I moved in here,' said he. 'Let her go.'

The dog was Strickland's dog, so I said nothing, but I felt all that Strickland felt in being thus made light of. Tietjens encamped outside my bedroom window, and storm after storm came up, thundered on the thatch, and died away. The lightning spattered the sky as a thrown egg spatters a barn door, but the light was pale blue, not yellow; and, looking through my split bamboo blinds, I could see the great dog standing, not sleeping, in the verandah, the hackles alift on her back and her feet anchored as tensely as the drawn wire-rope of a suspension bridge. In the very short pauses of the thunder I tried to sleep, but it seemed that someone wanted me very urgently. He, whoever he was, was trying to call me by name, but his voice was no more than a husky whisper. The thunder ceased, and Tietjens went into the garden and howled at the low moon. Somebody tried to open my door, walked about and about through the house and stood breathing heavily in the verandahs, and just when I was falling asleep I fancied that I heard a wild hammering and clamouring above my head or on the door.

I ran into Strickland's room and asked him whether he was ill, and had been calling for me. He was lying on his bed half-dressed, a pipe in his mouth. 'I thought you'd come,' he said. 'Have I been walking round the house recently?'

I explained that he had been tramping in the dining-room and the smoking-room and two or three other places, and he laughed and told me to go back to bed. I went back to bed and slept till the morning, but through all my mixed dreams I was sure I was doing someone an injustice in not attending to his wants. What those wants were I could not tell; but a fluttering, whispering, bolt-fumbling, lurking, loitering Someone was reproaching me for my slackness, and, half-awake, I heard the howling of Tietjens in the garden and the threshing of the rain.

I lived in that house for two days. Strickland went to his office daily, leaving me alone for eight or ten hours with Tietjens for my only companion. As long as the full light lasted I was comfortable, and so was Tietjens; but in the twilight she and I moved into the back verandah and cuddled each other for company. We were alone in the house, but none the less it was much too fully occupied by a tenant with whom I did not wish to interfere. I never saw him, but I could see the curtains between the rooms quivering where he had just passed through; I could hear the chairs creaking as the bamboos sprung under a weight that had just quitted them; and I could feel when I went to get a book from the dining-room that somebody was waiting in the shadows of the front verandah till I should have gone away. Tietjens made the twilight more interesting by glaring into the darkened rooms with every hair erect, and following the motions of something that I could not see. She never entered the rooms, but her eyes moved interestedly: that was quite sufficient. Only when my servant came to trim the lamps and make all light and habitable she would come in with me and spend her time sitting on her haunches, watching an invisible extra man as he moved about behind my shoulder. Dogs are cheerful companions.

I explained to Strickland, gently as might be, that I would go over to the Club and find for myself quarters there. I admired his hospitality, was pleased with his guns and rods, but I did not much care for his house and its atmosphere. He heard me out to the end, and then smiled very wearily, but without contempt, for he is a man who understands things. 'Stay on,' he said, 'and see what this thing means. All you have talked about I have known since I took the bungalow. Stay on and wait. Tietjens has left me. Are you going too?'

I had seen him through one little affair, connected with a heathen idol, that had brought me to the doors of a lunatic asylum, and I had no desire to help him through further experiences. He was a man to whom unpleasantnesses arrived as do dinners to ordinary people.

Therefore I explained more clearly than ever that I liked him immensely, and would be happy to see him in the daytime; but that I did not care to sleep under his roof. This was after dinner, when Tietjens had gone out to lie in the verandah.

' 'Pon my soul, I don't wonder,' said Strickland, with his eyes on the ceiling-cloth. 'Look at that!'

The tails of two brown snakes were hanging between the cloth and the cornice of the wall. They threw long shadows in the lamplight.

'If you are afraid of snakes of course – ' said Strickland.

I hate and fear snakes, because if you look into the eyes of any snake you will see that it knows all and more of the mystery of man's fall, and that it feels all the contempt that the Devil felt when Adam was evicted from Eden. Besides which its bite is generally fatal, and it twists up trouser legs.

'You ought to get your thatch overhauled,' I said. 'Give me a mahseer-rod, and we'll poke 'em down.'

'They'll hide among the roof-beams,' said Strickland. 'I can't stand snakes overhead. I'm going up into the roof. If I shake 'em down, stand by with a cleaning-rod and break their backs.'

I was not anxious to assist Strickland in his work, but I took the cleaning-rod and waited in the dining-room, while Strickland brought a gardener's ladder from the verandah, and set it against the side of the room.

The snake-tails drew themselves up and disappeared. We could hear the dry rushing scuttle of long bodies running over the baggy ceiling-cloth. Strickland took a lamp with him, while I tried to make clear to him the danger of hunting roof-snakes between a ceiling-cloth and a thatch, apart from the deterioration of property caused by ripping out ceiling-cloths.

'Nonsense!' said Strickland. 'They're sure to hide near the walls by the cloth. The bricks are too cold for 'em, and the heat of the room is just what they like.' He put his hand to the corner of the stuff and ripped it from the cornice. It gave with a great sound of tearing, and Strickland put his head through the opening into the dark of the angle of the roof-beams. I set my teeth and lifted the rod, for I had not the least knowledge of what might descend.

'H'm!' said Strickland, and his voice rolled and rumbled in the roof. 'There's room for another set of rooms up here, and, by Jove, someone is occupying 'em!'

'Snakes?' I said from below.

'No. It's a buffalo. Hand me up the two last joints of a mahseer-rod, and I'll prod it. It's lying on the main roof-beam.'

I handed up the rod.

'What a nest for owls and serpents! No wonder the snakes live here,' said Strickland, climbing farther into the roof. I could see his elbow thrusting with the rod. 'Come out of that, whoever you are! Heads below there! It's falling.'

I saw the ceiling-cloth nearly in the centre of the room bag with a shape that was pressing it downwards and downwards towards the lighted lamp on the table. I snatched the lamp out of danger and stood back. Then the cloth ripped out from the walls, tore, split, swayed, and shot down upon the table something that I dared not look at, till Strickland had slid down the ladder and was standing by my side.

He did not say much, being a man of few words; but he picked up the loose end of the tablecloth and threw it over the remnants on the table.

'It strikes me,' said he, putting down the lamp, 'our friend Imray has come back. Oh! you would, would you?'

There was a movement under the cloth, and a little snake wriggled out, to be back-broken by the butt of the mahseer-rod. I was sufficiently sick to make no remarks worth recording.

Strickland meditated, and helped himself to drinks. The arrangement under the cloth made no more signs of life.

'Is it Imray?' I said.

Strickland turned back the cloth for a moment, and looked.

'It is Imray,' he said; 'and his throat is cut from ear to ear.'

Then we spoke, both together and to ourselves: 'That's why he whispered about the house.'

Tietjens, in the garden, began to bay furiously. A little later her great nose heaved open the dining-room door.

She sniffed and was still. The tattered ceiling-cloth hung down almost to the level of the table, and there was hardly room to move away from the discovery.

Tietjens came in and sat down; her teeth bared under her lip and her forepaws planted. She looked at Strickland.

'It's a bad business, old lady,' said he. 'Men don't climb up into the roofs of their bungalows to die, and they don't fasten up the ceiling cloth behind 'em. Let's think it out.'

'Let's think it out somewhere else,' I said.

'Excellent idea! Turn the lamps out. We'll get into my room.'

I did not turn the lamps out. I went into Strickland's room first, and allowed him to make the darkness. Then he followed me, and we lit tobacco and thought. Strickland thought. I smoked furiously, because I was afraid.

'Imray is back,' said Strickland. 'The question is – who killed Imray? Don't talk, I've a notion of my own. When I took this bungalow I took over most of Imray's servants. Imray was guileless and inoffensive, wasn't he?'

I agreed; though the heap under the cloth had looked neither one thing nor the other.

'If I call in all the servants they will stand fast in a crowd and lie like Aryans. What do you suggest?'

'Call 'em in one by one,' I said.

'They'll run away and give the news to all their fellows,' said Strickland. 'We must segregate 'em. Do you suppose your servant knows anything about it?'

'He may, for aught I know; but I don't think it's likely. He has only been here two or three days,' I answered. 'What's your notion?'

'I can't quite tell. How the dickens did the man get the wrong side of the ceiling-cloth?'

There was a heavy coughing outside Strickland's bedroom door. This showed that Bahadur Khan, his body-servant, had waked from sleep and wished to put Strickland to bed.

'Come in,' said Strickland. 'It's a very warm night, isn't it?'

Bahadur Khan, a great, green-turbaned, six-foot Mahomedan, said that it was a very warm night; but that there was more rain pending, which, by his Honour's favour, would bring relief to the country.

'It will be so, if God pleases,' said Strickland, tugging off his boots. 'It is in my mind, Bahadur Khan, that I have worked thee remorselessly for many days – ever since that time when thou first camest into my service. What time was that?'

'Has the Heaven-born forgotten? It was when Imray Sahib went secretly to Europe without warning given; and I – even I – came into the honoured service of the protector of the poor.'

'And Imray Sahib went to Europe?'

'It is so said among those who were his servants.'

'And thou wilt take service with him when he returns?'

'Assuredly, Sahib. He was a good master, and cherished his dependants.'

'That is true. I am very tired, but I go buck-shooting tomorrow. Give me the little sharp rifle that I use for black-buck; it is in the case yonder.'

The man stooped over the case; handed barrels, stock, and fore-end to Strickland, who fitted all together, yawning dolefully. Then he reached down to the gun-case, took a solid-drawn cartridge, and slipped it into the breech of the '360 Express.

'And Imray Sahib has gone to Europe secretly! That is very strange, Bahadur Khan, is it not?'

'What do I know of the ways of the white man. Heaven-born?'

'Very little, truly. But thou shalt know more anon. It has reached me that Imray Sahib has returned from his so long journeyings, and that even now he lies in the next room, waiting his servant.'

'Sahib!'

The lamplight slid along the barrels of the rifle as they levelled themselves at Bahadur Khan's broad breast.

'Go and look!' said Strickland. 'Take a lamp. Thy master is tired, and he waits thee. Go!'

The man picked up a lamp, and went into the dining-room, Strickland following, and almost pushing him with the muzzle of the rifle. He looked for a moment at the black depths behind the ceiling-cloth; at the writhing snake under foot; and last, a grey glaze settling on his face, at the thing under the tablecloth.

'Hast thou seen?' said Strickland after a pause.

'I have seen. I am clay in the white man's hands. What does the Presence do?'

'Hang thee within the month. What else?'

'For killing him? Nay, Sahib, consider. Walking among us, his servants, he cast his eyes upon my child, who was four years old. Him he bewitched, and in ten days he died of the fever – my child!'

'What said Imray Sahib?'

'He said he was a handsome child, and patted him on the head; wherefore my child died. Wherefore I killed Imray Sahib in the twilight, when he had come back from office, and was sleeping. Wherefore I dragged him up into the roof-beams and made all fast behind him. The Heaven-born knows all things. I am the servant of the Heaven-born.'

Strickland looked at me above the rifle, and said, in the vernacular, 'Thou art witness to this saying? He has killed.'

Bahadur Khan stood ashen grey in the light of the one lamp. The need for justification came upon him very swiftly. 'I am trapped,' he said, 'but the offence was that man's. He cast an evil eye upon my child, and I killed and hid him. Only such as are served by devils,' he glared at Tietjens, couched stolidly before him, 'only such could know what I did.'

'It was clever. But thou shouldst have lashed him to the beam with a rope. Now, thou thyself wilt hang by a rope. Orderly!'

A drowsy policeman answered Strickland's call. He was followed by another, and Tietjens sat wondrous still.

'Take him to the police-station,' said Strickland. 'There is a case toward.'

'Do I hang, then?' said Bahadur Khan, making no attempt to escape, and keeping his eyes on the ground.

'If the sun shines or the water runs – yes!' said Strickland.

Bahadur Khan stepped back one long pace, quivered, and stood still. The two policemen waited further orders.

'Go!' said Strickland.

'Nay; but I go very swiftly,' said Bahadur Khan. 'Look! I am even now a dead man.'

He lifted his foot, and to the little toe there clung the head of the half-killed snake, firm fixed in the agony of death.

'I come of land-holding stock,' said Bahadur Khan, rocking where he stood. 'It were a disgrace to me to go to the public scaffold: therefore I take this way. Be it remembered that the Sahib's shirts are correctly enumerated, and that there is an extra piece of soap in his washbasin. My child was bewitched, and I slew the wizard. Why should you seek to slay me with the rope? My honour is saved, and – and – I die.'

At the end of an hour he died, as they die who are bitten by the little brown karait, and the policemen bore him and the thing under the tablecloth to their appointed places. All were needed to make clear the disappearance of Imray.

'This,' said Strickland, very calmly, as he climbed into bed, 'is called the nineteenth century. Did you hear what that man said?'

'I heard,' I answered. 'Imray made a mistake.'

'Simply and solely through not knowing the nature of the Oriental, and the coincidence of a little seasonal fever. Bahadur Khan had been with him for four years.'

I shuddered. My own servant had been with me for exactly that length of time. When I went over to my own room I found my man waiting, impassive as the copper head on a penny, to pull off my boots.

'What has befallen Bahadur Khan?' said I.

'He was bitten by a snake and died. The rest the Sahib knows,' was the answer.

'And how much of this matter hast thou known?'

'As much as might be gathered from One coming in in the twilight to seek satisfaction. Gently, Sahib. Let me pull off those boots.'

I had just settled to the sleep of exhaustion when I heard Strickland shouting from his side of the house – 'Tietjens has come back to her place!'

And so she had. The great deerhound was couched statelily on her own bedstead on her own blanket, while, in the next room, the idle, empty, ceiling-cloth waggled as it trailed on the table.

The Phantom Rickshaw

May no ill dreams disturb my rest,
Nor Powers of Darkness me molest.

Evening Hymn

One of the few advantages that India has over England is a great Knowability. After five years' service a man is directly or indirectly acquainted with the two or three hundred Civilians in his Province, all the Messes of ten or twelve Regiments and Batteries, and some fifteen hundred other people of the non-official caste. In ten years his knowledge should be doubled, and at the end of twenty he knows, or knows something about, every Englishman in the Empire, and may travel anywhere and everywhere without paying hotel-bills.

Globe-trotters who expect entertainment as a right, have, even within my memory, blunted this open-heartedness, but none the less today, if you belong to the Inner Circle and are neither a Bear nor a Black Sheep, all houses are open to you, and our small world is very, very kind and helpful.

Rickett of Kamartha stayed with Polder of Kumaon some fifteen years ago. He meant to stay two nights, but was knocked down by rheumatic fever, and for six weeks disorganised Polder's establishment, stopped Polder's work, and nearly died in Polder's bedroom. Polder behaves as though he had been placed under eternal obligation by Rickett, and yearly sends the little Ricketts a box of presents and toys. It is the same everywhere. The men who do not take the trouble to conceal from you their opinion that you are an incompetent ass, and the women who blacken your character and misunderstand your wife's amusements, will work themselves to the bone in your behalf if you fall sick or into serious trouble.

Heatherlegh, the Doctor, kept, in addition to his regular practice, a hospital on his private account – an arrangement of loose boxes for Incurables, his friend called it – but it was really a sort of fitting-up shed for craft that had been damaged by stress of weather. The weather in India is often sultry, and since the tale of bricks is always a fixed quantity, and the only liberty allowed is permission to work overtime and get no thanks, men occasionally break down and become as mixed as the metaphors in this sentence.

Heatherlegh is the dearest doctor that ever was, and his invariable prescription to all his patients is, 'lie low, go slow, and keep cool.' He says that more men are killed by overwork than the importance of this world justifies. He maintains that overwork slew Pansay, who died under his hands about three years ago. He has, of course, the right to speak authoritatively, and he laughs at my theory that there was a crack in Pansay's head and a little bit of the Dark World came through and pressed him to death. 'Pansay went off the handle,' says Heatherlegh, 'after the stimulus of long leave at Home. He may or he may not have behaved like a blackguard to Mrs Keith-Wessington. My notion is that the work of the Katabundi Settlement ran him off his legs, and that he took to brooding and making much of an ordinary P. & O. flirtation. He certainly was engaged to Miss Mannering, and she certainly broke off the engagement. Then he took a feverish chill and all that nonsense about ghosts developed. Overwork started his illness, kept it alight, and killed him, poor devil. Write him off to the System – one man to take the work of two and a half men.'

I do not believe this. I used to sit up with Pansay sometimes when Heatherlegh was called out to patients, and I happened to be within claim. The man would make me most unhappy by describing in a low, even voice, the procession that was always passing at the bottom of his bed. He had a sick man's command of language.

When he recovered I suggested that he should write out the whole affair from beginning to end, knowing that ink might assist him to ease his mind. When little boys have learned a new bad word they are never happy till they have chalked it up on a door. And this also is Literature.

He was in a high fever while he was writing, and the blood-and-thunder Magazine diction he adopted did not calm him. Two months afterward he was reported fit for duty, but, in spite of the fact that he was urgently needed to help an undermanned Commission stagger through a deficit, he preferred to die; vowing at the last that he was hag-ridden. I got his manuscript before he died, and this is his version of the affair, dated 1885.

* * *

My doctor tells me that I need rest and change of air. It is not improbable that I shall get both ere long – rest that neither the red-coated messenger nor the midday gun can break, and change of air far beyond that which any homeward-bound steamer can give me. In the meantime I am resolved to stay where I am; and, in flat defiance of my doctor's orders, to take all the world into my confidence. You shall learn for yourselves the precise nature of my malady; and shall, too, judge for yourselves whether any man born of woman on this weary earth was ever so tormented as I.

Speaking now as a condemned criminal might speak ere the drop-bolts are drawn, my story, wild and hideously improbable as it may appear, demands at least attention. That it will ever receive credence I utterly disbelieve. Two months ago I should have scouted as mad or drunk the man who had dared tell me the like. Two months ago I was the happiest man in India. Today, from Peshawar to the sea, there is no-one more wretched. My doctor and I are the only two who know this. His explanation is, that my brain, digestion, and eyesight are all slightly affected, giving rise to my frequent and persistent 'delusions'. Delusions, indeed! I call him a fool; but he attends me still with the same unwearied smile, the same bland professional manner, the same neatly trimmed red whiskers, till I begin to suspect that I am an ungrateful, evil-tempered invalid. But you shall judge for yourselves.

Three years ago it was my fortune – my great misfortune – to sail from Gravesend to Bombay, on return from long leave, with one Agnes Keith-Wessington, wife of an officer on the Bombay side. It does not in the least concern you to know what manner of woman she was. Be content with the knowledge that, ere the voyage had ended, both she and I were desperately and unreasoningly in love with one another. Heaven knows that I can make the admission now without one particle of vanity. In matters of this sort there is always one who gives and another who accepts. From the first day of our ill-omened attachment, I was conscious that Agnes's passion was a stronger, a more dominant, and – if I may use the expression – a purer sentiment than mine. Whether she recognised the fact then, I do not know. Afterward it was bitterly plain to both of us.

Arrived at Bombay in the spring of the year, we went our respective ways, to meet no more for the next three or four months, when my leave and her love took us both to Simla. There we spent the season together; and there my fire of straw burned itself out to a pitiful end with the closing year. I attempt no excuse. I make no apology. Mrs Wessington had given up much for my sake, and was prepared to give

up all. From my own lips, in August, 1882, she learned that I was sick
of her presence, tired of her company, and weary of the sound of her
voice. Ninety-nine women out of a hundred would have wearied of
me as I wearied of them; seventy-five of that number would have
promptly avenged themselves by active and obtrusive flirtation with
other men. Mrs Wessington was the hundredth. On her neither my
openly expressed aversion nor the cutting brutalities with which I
garnished our interviews had the least effect.

'Jack, darling!' was her one eternal cuckoo cry: 'I'm sure it's all a
mistake – a hideous mistake; and we'll be good friends again some
day. *Please* forgive me, Jack, dear.'

I was the offender, and I knew it. That knowledge transformed my
pity into passive endurance, and, eventually, into blind hate – the
same instinct, I suppose, which prompts a man to savagely stamp on
the spider he has but half killed. And with this hate in my bosom the
season of 1882 came to an end.

Next year we met again at Simla – she with her monotonous face
and timid attempts at reconciliation, and I with loathing of her in
every fibre of my frame. Several times I could not avoid meeting her
alone; and on each occasion her words were identically the same.
Still the unreasoning wail that it was all a 'mistake'; and still the hope
of eventually 'making friends'. I might have seen, had I cared to look,
that that hope only was keeping her alive. She grew more wan and
thin month by month. You will agree with me, at least, that such
conduct would have driven anyone to despair. It was uncalled for;
childish; unwomanly. I maintain that she was much to blame. And
again, sometimes, in the black, fever-stricken night-watches, I have
begun to think that I might have been a little kinder to her. But that
really is a 'delusion'. I could not have continued pretending to love
her when I didn't, could I? It would have been unfair to us both.

Last year we met again – on the same terms as before. The same
weary appeal, and the same curt answers from my lips. At least I would
make her see how wholly wrong and hopeless were her attempts at
resuming the old relationship. As the season wore on, we fell apart –
that is to say, she found it difficult to meet me, for I had other and
more absorbing interests to attend to. When I think it over quietly
in my sick-room, the season of 1884 seems a confused nightmare
wherein light and shade were fantastically intermingled – my court-
ship of little Kitty Mannering; my hopes, doubts, and fears; our long
rides together; my trembling avowal of attachment; her reply; and
now and again a vision of a white face flitting by in the rickshaw with

the black and white liveries I once watched for so earnestly; the wave of Mrs Wessington's gloved hand; and, when she met me alone, which was but seldom, the irksome monotony of her appeal. I loved Kitty Mannering; honestly, heartily loved her, and with my love for her grew my hatred for Agnes. In August Kitty and I were engaged. The next day I met those accursed 'magpie' *jhampanies* at the back of Jakko, and, moved by some passing sentiment of pity, stopped to tell Mrs Wessington everything. She knew it already.

'So I hear you're engaged, Jack dear.' Then, without a moment's pause: 'I'm sure it's all a mistake – a hideous mistake. We shall be as good friends some day, Jack, as we ever were.'

My answer might have made even a man wince. It cut the dying woman before me like the blow of a whip. 'Please forgive me, Jack; I didn't mean to make you angry; but it's true, it's true!'

And Mrs Wessington broke down completely. I turned away and left her to finish her journey in peace, feeling, but only for a moment or two, that I had been an unutterably mean hound. I looked back, and saw that she had turned her rickshaw with the idea, I suppose, of overtaking me.

The scene and its surroundings were photographed on my memory. The rain-swept sky (we were at the end of the wet weather), the sodden, dingy pines, the muddy road, and the black powder-riven cliffs formed a gloomy background against which the black and white liveries of the *jhampanies*, the yellow-panelled rickshaw and Mrs Wessington's down-bowed golden head stood out clearly. She was holding her handkerchief in her left hand and was leaning back exhausted against the rickshaw cushions. I turned my horse up a bypath near the Sanjowlie Reservoir and literally ran away. Once I fancied I heard a faint call of 'Jack!' This may have been imagination. I never stopped to verify it. Ten minutes later I came across Kitty on horseback; and, in the delight of a long ride with her, forgot all about the interview.

A week later Mrs Wessington died, and the inexpressible burden of her existence was removed from my life. I went plainsward perfectly happy. Before three months were over I had forgotten all about her, except that at times the discovery of some of her old letters reminded me unpleasantly of our bygone relationship. By January I had disinterred what was left of our correspondence from among my scattered belongings and had burned it. At the beginning of April of this year, 1885, I was at Simla – semi-deserted Simla – once more, and was deep in lover's talks and walks with Kitty. It was decided that we should be married at the end of June. You will understand, therefore, that, loving Kitty as I did, I am not saying too much when I pronounce myself to have been, at that time, the happiest man in India.

Fourteen delightful days passed almost before I noticed their flight. Then, aroused to the sense of what was proper among mortals circumstanced as we were, I pointed out to Kitty that an engagement ring was the outward and visible sign of her dignity as an engaged girl; and that she must forthwith come to Hamilton's to be measured for one. Up to that moment, I give you my word, we had completely forgotten so trivial a matter. To Hamilton's we accordingly went on the 15th of April, 1885. Remember that – whatever my doctor may say to the contrary – I was then in perfect health, enjoying a well-balanced mind and an *absolutely* tranquil spirit. Kitty and I entered Hamilton's shop together, and there, regardless of the order of affairs, I measured Kitty for the ring in the presence of the amused assistant. The ring was a sapphire with two diamonds. We then rode out down the slope that leads to the Combermere Bridge and Peliti's shop.

While my Waler was cautiously feeling his way over the loose shale, and Kitty was laughing and chattering at my side – while all Simla, that is to say as much of it as had then come from the Plains, was grouped round the Reading Room and Peliti's veranda – I was aware that someone, apparently at a vast distance, was calling me by my Christian name. It struck me that I had heard the voice before, but when and where I could not at once determine. In the short space it took to cover the road between the path from Hamilton's shop and the first plank of the Combermere Bridge I had thought over half a dozen people who might have committed such a solecism, and had eventually decided that it must have been singing in my ears. Immediately opposite Peliti's shop my eye was arrested by the sight of four *jhampanies* in 'magpie' livery, pulling a yellow-panelled, cheap, bazaar rickshaw. In a moment my mind flew back to the previous season and Mrs Wessington with a sense of irritation and disgust. Was it not enough that the woman was dead and done with, without her black and white servitors reappearing to spoil the day's happiness? Whoever employed them now I thought I would call upon, and ask as a personal favour to change her *jhampanies'* livery. I would hire the men myself, and, if necessary, buy their coats from off their backs. It is impossible to say here what a flood of undesirable memories their presence evoked.

'Kitty,' I cried, 'there are poor Mrs Wessington's *jhampanies* turned up again! I wonder who has them now?'

Kitty had known Mrs Wessington slightly last season, and had always been interested in the sickly woman.

'What? Where?' she asked. 'I can't see them anywhere.'

Even as she spoke her horse, swerving from a laden mule, threw himself directly in front of the advancing rickshaw. I had scarcely time to utter a word of warning when, to my unutterable horror, horse and rider passed *through* men and carriage as if they had been thin air.

'What's the matter?' cried Kitty; 'what made you call out so foolishly, Jack? If I *am* engaged I don't want all creation to know about it. There was lots of space between the mule and the veranda; and, if you think I can't ride – There!'

Whereupon wilful Kitty set off, her dainty little head in the air, at a hand-gallop in the direction of the Bandstand; fully expecting, as she herself afterward told me, that I should follow her. What was the matter? Nothing indeed. Either that I was mad or drunk, or that Simla was haunted with devils. I reined in my impatient cob, and turned round. The rickshaw had turned too, and now stood immediately facing me, near the left railing of the Combermere Bridge.

'Jack! Jack, darling!' (There was no mistake about the words this time: they rang through my brain as if they had been shouted in my ear.) 'It's some hideous mistake, I'm sure. *Please* forgive me, Jack, and let's be friends again.'

The rickshaw-hood had fallen back, and inside, as I hope and pray daily for the death I dread by night, sat Mrs Keith-Wessington, handkerchief in hand, and golden head bowed on her breast.

How long I stared motionless I do not know. Finally, I was aroused by my *sais* taking the Waler's bridle and asking whether I was ill. From the horrible to the commonplace is but a step. I tumbled off my horse and dashed, half fainting, into Peliti's for a glass of cherry brandy. There two or three couples were gathered round the coffee-tables discussing the gossip of the day. Their trivialities were more comforting to me just then than the consolations of religion could have been. I plunged into the midst of the conversation at once; chatted, laughed, and jested with a face (when I caught a glimpse of it in a mirror) as white and drawn as that of a corpse. Three or four men noticed my condition; and, evidently setting it down to the results of over-many pegs, charitably endeavoured to draw me apart from the rest of the loungers. But I refused to be led away. I wanted the company of my kind – as a child rushes into the midst of the dinner-party after a fright in the dark. I must have talked for about ten minutes or so, though it seemed an eternity to me, when I heard Kitty's clear voice outside enquiring for me. In another minute she had entered the shop, prepared to roundly upbraid me for failing so signally in my duties. Something in my face stopped her.

'Why, Jack,' she cried, 'what *have* you been doing? What has happened? Are you ill?' Thus driven into a direct lie, I said that the sun had been a little too much for me. It was close upon five o'clock of a cloudy April afternoon, and the sun had been hidden all day. I saw my mistake as soon as the words were out of my mouth: attempted to recover it; blundered hopelessly and followed Kitty in a regal rage, out of doors, amid the smiles of my acquaintances. I made some excuse (I have forgotten what) on the score of my feeling faint; and cantered away to my hotel, leaving Kitty to finish the ride by herself.

In my room I sat down and tried calmly to reason out the matter. Here was I, Theobald Jack Pansay, a well-educated Bengal Civilian in the year of grace, 1885, presumably sane, certainly healthy, driven in terror from my sweetheart's side by the apparition of a woman who had been dead and buried eight months ago. These were facts that I could not blink. Nothing was further from my thought than any memory of Mrs Wessington when Kitty and I left Hamilton's shop. Nothing was more utterly commonplace than the stretch of wall opposite Peliti's. It was broad daylight. The road was full of people; and yet here, look you, in defiance of every law of probability, in direct outrage of Nature's ordinance, there had appeared to me a face from the grave.

Kitty's Arab had gone *through* the rickshaw: so that my first hope that some woman marvellously like Mrs Wessington had hired the carriage and the coolies with their old livery was lost. Again and again I went round this treadmill of thought; and again and again gave up baffled and in despair. The voice was as inexplicable as the apparition. I had originally some wild notion of confiding it all to Kitty; of begging her to marry me at once; and in her arms defying the ghostly occupant of the rickshaw. 'After all,' I argued, 'the presence of the rickshaw is in itself enough to prove the existence of a spectral illusion. One may see ghosts of men and women, but surely never of coolies and carriages. The whole thing is absurd. Fancy the ghost of a hillman!'

Next morning I sent a penitent note to Kitty, imploring her to overlook my strange conduct of the previous afternoon. My Divinity was still very wroth, and a personal apology was necessary. I explained, with a fluency born of night-long pondering over a falsehood, that I had been attacked with sudden palpitation of the heart – the result of indigestion. This eminently practical solution had its effect; and Kitty and I rode out that afternoon with the shadow of my first lie dividing us.

Nothing would please her save a canter round Jakko. With my nerves still unstrung from the previous night I feebly protested against the notion, suggesting Observatory Hill, Jutogh, the Boileaugunge road – anything rather than the Jakko round. Kitty was angry and a little hurt: so I yielded from fear of provoking further misunderstanding, and we set out together toward Chota Simla. We walked a greater part of the way, and, according to our custom, cantered from a mile or so below the Convent to the stretch of level road by the Sanjowlie Reservoir. The wretched horses appeared to fly, and my heart beat quicker and quicker as we neared the crest of the ascent. My mind had been full of Mrs Wessington all the afternoon; and every inch of the Jakko road bore witness to our old-time walks and talks. The bowlders were full of it; the pines sang it aloud overhead; the rain-fed torrents giggled and chuckled unseen over the shameful story; and the wind in my ears chanted the iniquity aloud.

As a fitting climax, in the middle of the level men call the Ladies' Mile the Horror was awaiting me. No other rickshaw was in sight – only the four black and white *jhampanies*, the yellow-panelled carriage, and the golden head of the woman within – all apparently just as I had left them eight months and one fortnight ago! For an instant I fancied that Kitty *must* see what I saw – we were so marvellously sympathetic in all things. Her next words undeceived me – 'Not a soul in sight! Come along, Jack, and I'll race you to the Reservoir buildings!' Her wiry little Arab was off like a bird, my Waler following close behind, and in this order we dashed under the cliffs. Half a minute brought us within fifty yards of the rickshaw. I pulled my Waler and fell back a little. The rickshaw was directly in the middle of the road; and once more the Arab passed through it, my horse following. 'Jack! Jack dear! *Please* forgive me,' rang with a wail in my ears, and, after an interval – 'It's a mistake, a hideous mistake!'

I spurred my horse like a man possessed. When I turned my head at the Reservoir works, the black and white liveries were still waiting – patiently waiting – under the grey hillside, and the wind brought me a mocking echo of the words I had just heard. Kitty bantered me a good deal on my silence throughout the remainder of the ride. I had been talking up till then wildly and at random. To save my life I could not speak afterward naturally, and from Sanjowlie to the Church wisely held my tongue.

I was to dine with the Mannerings that night, and had barely time to canter home to dress. On the road to Elysium Hill I overheard two men talking together in the dusk. – 'It's a curious thing,' said one, 'how completely all trace of it disappeared. You know my wife was insanely fond of the woman (never could see anything in her myself), and wanted me to pick up her old rickshaw and coolies if they were to be got for love or money. Morbid sort of fancy I call it; but I've got to do what the *Memsahib* tells me. Would you believe that the man she hired it from tells me that all four of the men – they were brothers – died of cholera on the way to Hardwar, poor devils, and the rickshaw has been broken up by the man himself. Told me he never used a dead *Memsahib's* rickshaw. Spoiled his luck. Queer notion, wasn't it? Fancy poor little Mrs Wessington spoiling anyone's luck except her own!' I laughed aloud at this point; and my laugh jarred on me as I uttered it. So there *were* ghosts of rickshaws after all, and ghostly employments in the other world! How much did Mrs Wessington give her men? What were their hours? Where did they go?

And for visible answer to my last question I saw the infernal Thing blocking my path in the twilight. The dead travel fast, and by short cuts unknown to ordinary coolies. I laughed aloud a second time and checked my laughter suddenly, for I was afraid I was going mad. Mad to a certain extent I must have been, for I recollect that I reined in my horse at the head of the rickshaw, and politely wished Mrs Wessington 'Good-evening'. Her answer was one I knew only too well. I listened to the end; and replied that I had heard it all before, but should be delighted if she had anything further to say. Some malignant devil stronger than I must have entered into me that evening, for I have a dim recollection of talking the commonplaces of the day for five minutes to the Thing in front of me.

'Mad as a hatter, poor devil – or drunk. Max, try and get him to come home.'

Surely *that* was not Mrs Wessington's voice! The two men had overheard me speaking to the empty air, and had returned to look after me. They were very kind and considerate, and from their words evidently gathered that I was extremely drunk. I thanked them confusedly and cantered away to my hotel, there changed, and arrived at the Mannerings' ten minutes late. I pleaded the darkness of the night as an excuse; was rebuked by Kitty for my unlover-like tardiness; and sat down.

The conversation had already become general; and under cover of it, I was addressing some tender small talk to my sweetheart when I was aware that at the further end of the table a short red-whiskered man was describing, with much broidery, his encounter with a mad unknown that evening.

A few sentences convinced me that he was repeating the incident of half an hour ago. In the middle of the story he looked round for applause, as professional storytellers do, caught my eye, and straightway collapsed. There was a moment's awkward silence, and the red-whiskered man muttered something to the effect that he had 'forgotten the rest', thereby sacrificing a reputation as a good storyteller which he had built up for six seasons past. I blessed him from the bottom of my heart, and – went on with my fish.

In the fullness of time that dinner came to an end; and with genuine regret I tore myself away from Kitty – as certain as I was of my own existence that It would be waiting for me outside the door. The red-whiskered man, who had been introduced to me as Doctor Heatherlegh, of Simla, volunteered to bear me company as far as our roads lay together. I accepted his offer with gratitude.

My instinct had not deceived me. It lay in readiness in the Mall, and, in what seemed devilish mockery of our ways, with a lighted headlamp. The red-whiskered man went to the point at once, in a manner that showed he had been thinking over it all dinner-time.

'I say, Pansay, what the deuce was the matter with you this evening on the Elysium road?' The suddenness of the question wrenched an answer from me before I was aware.

'That!' said I, pointing to It.

'*That* may be either D.T. or Eyes for aught I know. Now you don't liquor. I saw as much at dinner, so it can't be D. T. There's nothing whatever where you're pointing, though you're sweating and trembling with fright like a scared pony. Therefore, I conclude that it's Eyes. And I ought to understand all about them. Come along home with me. I'm on the Blessington lower road.'

To my intense delight the rickshaw instead of waiting for us kept about twenty yards ahead – and this, too whether we walked, trotted, or cantered. In the course of that long night ride I had told my companion almost as much as I have told you here.

'Well, you've spoiled one of the best tales I've ever laid tongue to,' said he, 'but I'll forgive you for the sake of what you've gone through. Now come home and do what I tell you; and when I've cured you, young man, let this be a lesson to you to steer clear of women and indigestible food till the day of your death.'

The rickshaw kept steady in front; and my red-whiskered friend seemed to derive great pleasure from my account of its exact where-abouts.

'Eyes, Pansay – all Eyes, Brain, and Stomach. And the greatest of these three is Stomach. You've too much conceited Brain, too little Stomach, and thoroughly unhealthy Eyes. Get your Stomach straight and the rest follows. And all that's French for a liver pill. I'll take sole medical charge of you from this hour, for you're too interesting a phenomenon to be passed over!'

By this time we were deep in the shadow of the Blessington lower road and the rickshaw came to a dead stop under a pine-clad, over-hanging shale cliff. Instinctively I halted too, giving my reason. Heatherlegh rapped out an oath.

'Now, if you think I'm going to spend a cold night on the hillside for the sake of a stomach-*cum*-Brain-*cum*-Eye illusion . . . Lord, ha' mercy! What's that?'

There was a muffled report, a blinding smother of dust just in front of us, a crack, the noise of rent boughs, and about ten yards of the cliff-side – pines, undergrowth, and all – slid down into the road below, completely blocking it up. The uprooted trees swayed and tottered for a moment like drunken giants in the gloom, and then fell prone among their fellows with a thunderous crash. Our two horses stood motionless and sweating with fear. As soon as the rattle of falling earth and stone had subsided, my companion muttered: 'Man, if we'd gone forward we should have been ten feet deep in our graves by now. "There are more things in heaven and earth" . . . Come home, Pansay, and thank God. I want a peg badly.'

We retraced our way over the Church Ridge, and I arrived at Dr Heatherlegh's house shortly after midnight.

His attempts toward my cure commenced almost immediately, and for a week I never left his sight. Many a time in the course of that week did I bless the good fortune which had thrown me in contact with Simla's best and kindest doctor. Day by day my spirits grew lighter and more equable. Day by day, too, I became more and more inclined to fall in with Heatherlegh's 'spectral illusion' theory, implicating eyes, brain, and stomach. I wrote to Kitty, telling her that a slight sprain caused by a fall from my horse kept me indoors for a few days; and that I should be recovered before she had time to regret my absence.

Heatherlegh's treatment was simple to a degree. It consisted of liver pills, cold-water baths, and strong exercise, taken in the dusk or at early dawn – for, as he sagely observed: 'A man with a sprained ankle doesn't walk a dozen miles a day, and your young woman might be wondering if she saw you.'

At the end of the week, after much examination of pupil and pulse, and strict injunctions as to diet and pedestrianism, Heatherlegh dismissed me as brusquely as he had taken charge of me. Here is his parting benediction: 'Man, I can certify to your mental cure, and that's as much as to say I've cured most of your bodily ailments. Now, get your traps out of this as soon as you can; and be off to make love to Miss Kitty.'

I was endeavouring to express my thanks for his kindness. He cut me short.

'Don't think I did this because I like you. I gather that you've behaved like a blackguard all through. But, all the same, you're a phenomenon, and as queer a phenomenon as you are a blackguard. No!' – checking me a second time – 'not a rupee, please. Go out and see if you can find the eyes-brain-and-stomach business again. I'll give you a lakh for each time you see it.'

Half an hour later I was in the Mannerings' drawing-room with Kitty – drunk with the intoxication of present happiness and the foreknowledge that I should never more be troubled with Its hideous presence. Strong in the sense of my new-found security, I proposed a ride at once; and, by preference, a canter round Jakko.

Never had I felt so well, so overladen with vitality and mere animal spirits, as I did on the afternoon of the 30th of April. Kitty was delighted at the change in my appearance, and complimented me on it in her delightfully frank and outspoken manner. We left the Mannerings' house together, laughing and talking, and cantered along the Chota Simla road as of old.

I was in haste to reach the Sanjowlie Reservoir and there make my assurance doubly sure. The horses did their best, but seemed all too slow to my impatient mind. Kitty was astonished at my boisterousness. 'Why, Jack!' she cried at last, 'you are behaving like a child. What are you doing?'

We were just below the Convent, and from sheer wantonness I was making my Waler plunge and curvet across the road as I tickled it with the loop of my riding-whip.

'Doing?' I answered; 'nothing, dear. That's just it. If you'd been doing nothing for a week except lie up, you'd be as riotous as I.

> Singing and murmuring in your feastful mirth,
>   Joying to feel yourself alive;
> Lord over Nature, Lord of the visible Earth,
>   Lord of the senses five.'

My quotation was hardly out of my lips before we had rounded the corner above the Convent; and a few yards further on could see across to Sanjowlie. In the centre of the level road stood the black and white liveries, the yellow-panelled rickshaw, and Mrs Keith-Wessington. I pulled up, looked, rubbed my eyes, and, I believe must have said something. The next thing I knew was that I was lying face downward on the road with Kitty kneeling above me in tears.

'Has it gone, child!' I gasped. Kitty only wept more bitterly.

'Has *what* gone, Jack dear? What does it all mean? There must be a mistake somewhere, Jack. A hideous mistake.' Her last words brought me to my feet – mad – raving for the time being.

'Yes, there is a mistake somewhere,' I repeated, 'a hideous mistake. Come and look at It.'

I have an indistinct idea that I dragged Kitty by the wrist along the road up to where It stood, and implored her for pity's sake to speak to It; to tell It that we were betrothed; that neither Death nor Hell could break the tie between us; and Kitty only knows how much more to the same effect. Now and again I appealed passionately to the Terror in the rickshaw to bear witness to all I had said, and to release me from a torture that was killing me. As I talked I suppose I must have told Kitty of my old relations with Mrs Wessington, for I saw her listen intently with white face and blazing eyes.

'Thank you, Mr Pansay,' she said, 'that's *quite* enough. *Sais, ghora láo.*'

The *saises*, impassive as Orientals always are, had come up with the recaptured horses; and as Kitty sprang into her saddle I caught hold of the bridle, entreating her to hear me out and forgive. My answer was the cut of her riding-whip across my face from mouth to eye, and a word or two of farewell that even now I cannot write down. So I judged, and judged rightly, that Kitty knew all; and I staggered back to the side of the rickshaw. My face was cut and bleeding, and the blow of the riding-whip had raised a livid blue weal on it. I had no self-respect. Just then, Heatherlegh, who must have been following Kitty and me at a distance, cantered up.

'Doctor,' I said, pointing to my face, 'here's Miss Mannering's signature to my order of dismissal and . . . I'll thank you for that lakh as soon as convenient.'

Heatherlegh's face, even in my abject misery, moved me to laughter.

'I'll stake my professional reputation' – he began.

'Don't be a fool,' I whispered. 'I've lost my life's happiness and you'd better take me home.'

As I spoke the rickshaw was gone. Then I lost all knowledge of what was passing. The crest of Jakko seemed to heave and roll like the crest of a cloud and fall in upon me.

Seven days later (on the 7th of May, that is to say) I was aware that I was lying in Heatherlegh's room as weak as a little child. Heatherlegh was watching me intently from behind the papers on his writing-table. His first words were not encouraging; but I was too far spent to be much moved by them.

'Here's Miss Kitty has sent back your letters. You corresponded a good deal, you young people. Here's a packet that looks like a ring, and a cheerful sort of a note from Mannering Papa, which I've taken the liberty of reading and burning. The old gentleman's not pleased with you.'

'And Kitty?' I asked, dully.

'Rather more drawn than her father from what she says. By the same token you must have been letting out any number of queer reminiscences just before I met you. Says that a man who would have behaved to a woman as you did to Mrs Wessington ought to kill himself out of sheer pity for his kind. She's a hot-headed little virago, your mash. Will have it too that you were suffering from D. T. when that row on the Jakko road turned up. Says she'll die before she ever speaks to you again.'

I groaned and turned over to the other side.

'Now you've got your choice, my friend. This engagement has to be broken off; and the Mannerings don't want to be too hard on you. Was it broken through D. T. or epileptic fits? Sorry I can't offer you a better exchange unless you'd prefer hereditary insanity. Say the word and I'll tell 'em it's fits. All Simla knows about that scene on the Ladies' Mile. Come! I'll give you five minutes to think over it.'

During those five minutes I believe that I explored thoroughly the lowest circles of the Inferno which it is permitted man to tread on earth. And at the same time I myself was watching myself faltering through the dark labyrinths of doubt, misery, and utter despair. I wondered, as Heatherlegh in his chair might have wondered, which dreadful alternative I should adopt. Presently I heard myself answering in a voice that I hardly recognised – 'They're confoundedly particular about morality in these parts. Give 'em fits, Heatherlegh, and my love. Now let me sleep a bit longer.'

Then my two selves joined, and it was only I (half-crazed, devil-driven I) that tossed in my bed, tracing step by step the history of the past month.

'But I am in Simla,' I kept repeating to myself. 'I, Jack Pansay, am in Simla and there are no ghosts here. It's unreasonable of that woman to pretend there are. Why couldn't Agnes have left me alone? I never did her any harm. It might just as well have been me as Agnes. Only I'd never have come hack on purpose to kill *her*. Why can't I be left alone – left alone and happy?'

It was high noon when I first awoke: and the sun was low in the sky before I slept – slept as the tortured criminal sleeps on his rack, too worn to feel further pain.

Next day I could not leave my bed. Heatherlegh told me in the morning that he had received an answer from Mr Mannering, and that, thanks to his (Heatherlegh's) friendly offices, the story of my affliction had travelled through the length and breadth of Simla, where I was on all sides much pitied.

'And that's rather more than you deserve,' he concluded, pleasantly, 'though the Lord knows you've been going through a pretty severe mill. Never mind; we'll cure you yet, you perverse phenomenon.'

I declined firmly to be cured. 'You've been much too good to me already, old man,' said I; 'but I don't think I need trouble you further.'

In my heart I knew that nothing Heatherlegh could do would lighten the burden that had been laid upon me.

With that knowledge came also a sense of hopeless, impotent rebellion against the unreasonableness of it all. There were scores of men no better than I whose punishments had at least been reserved for another world; and I felt that it was bitterly, cruelly unfair that I alone should have been singled out for so hideous a fate. This mood would in time give place to another where it seemed that the rickshaw and I were the only realities in a world of shadows; that Kitty was a ghost; that Mannering, Heatherlegh, and all the other men and women I knew were all ghosts; and the great, grey hills themselves but vain shadows devised to torture me. From mood to mood I tossed backward and forward for seven weary days, my body growing daily stronger and stronger, until the bedroom looking-glass told me that I had returned to everyday life, and was as other men once more. Curiously enough my face showed no signs of the struggle I had gone through. It was pale indeed, but as expressionless and commonplace as ever. I had expected some permanent alteration – visible evidence of the disease that was eating me away. I found nothing.

On the 15th of May, I left Heatherlegh's house at eleven o'clock in the morning; and the instinct of the bachelor drove me to the Club. There I found that every man knew my story as told by Heatherlegh, and was, in clumsy fashion, abnormally kind and attentive. Nevertheless I recognised that for the rest of my natural life I should be among but not of my fellows; and I envied very bitterly indeed the laughing coolies on the Mall below. I lunched at the Club, and at four o'clock wandered aimlessly down the Mall in the vague hope of meeting Kitty. Close to the Bandstand the black and white liveries joined me; and I heard Mrs Wessington's old appeal at my side. I had been expecting this ever since I came out; and was only surprised at her delay. The phantom rickshaw and I went side by side along the Chota Simla road in silence. Close to the bazar, Kitty and a man on horseback overtook and passed us. For any sign she gave I might have been a dog in the road. She did not even pay me the compliment of quickening her pace, though the rainy afternoon had served for an excuse.

So Kitty and her companion, and I and my ghostly Light-o'-Love, crept round Jakko in couples. The road was streaming with water; the pines dripped like roof-pipes on the rocks below, and the air was full of fine, driving rain. Two or three times I found myself saying to myself almost aloud: 'I'm Jack Pansay on leave at Simla – *at Simla!* Everyday, ordinary Simla. I mustn't forget that – I mustn't forget that.' Then I would try to recollect some of the gossip I had heard at the Club: the prices of So-and-So's horses – anything, in fact, that related to the workaday Anglo-Indian world I knew so well. I even repeated the multiplication-table rapidly to myself, to make quite sure that I was not taking leave of my senses. It gave me much comfort; and must have prevented my hearing Mrs Wessington for a time.

Once more I wearily climbed the Convent slope and entered the level road. Here Kitty and the man started off at a canter, and I was left alone with Mrs Wessington. 'Agnes,' said I, 'will you put back your hood and tell me what it all means?' The hood dropped noiselessly, and I was face to face with my dead and buried mistress. She was wearing the dress in which I had last seen her alive; carried the same tiny handkerchief in her right hand; and the same card-case in her left. (A woman eight months dead with a card-case!) I had to pin myself down to the multiplication-table, and to set both hands on the stone parapet of the road, to assure myself that that at least was real.

'Agnes,' I repeated, 'for pity's sake tell me what it all means.' Mrs Wessington leaned forward, with that odd, quick turn of the head I used to know so well, and spoke.

If my story had not already so madly overleaped the bounds of all human belief I should apologise to you now. As I know that no-one – no, not even Kitty, for whom it is written as some sort of justification of my conduct – will believe me, I will go on. Mrs Wessington spoke and I walked with her from the Sanjowlie road to the turning below the Commander-in-Chief's house as I might walk by the side of any living woman's rickshaw, deep in conversation. The second and most tormenting of my moods of sickness had suddenly laid hold upon me, and like the Prince in Tennyson's poem, 'I seemed to move amid a world of ghosts.' There had been a garden-party at the Commander-in-Chief's, and we two joined the crowd of homeward-bound folk. As I saw them then it seemed that *they* were the shadows – impalpable, fantastic shadows – that divided for Mrs Wessington's rickshaw to pass through. What we said during the course of that weird interview I cannot – indeed, I dare not – tell. Heatherlegh's comment would have been a short laugh and a remark that I had been 'mashing a brain-eye-and-stomach chimera'. It was a ghastly and yet in some indefinable way a marvellously dear experience. Could it be possible, I wondered, that I was in this life to woo a second time the woman I had killed by my own neglect and cruelty?

I met Kitty on the homeward road – a shadow among shadows.

If I were to describe all the incidents of the next fortnight in their order, my story would never come to an end; and your patience would be exhausted. Morning after morning and evening after evening the ghostly rickshaw and I used to wander through Simla together. Wherever I went there the four black and white liveries followed me and bore me company to and from my hotel. At the Theatre I found them amid the crowd or yelling *jhampanies*; outside the Club veranda, after a long evening of whist; at the Birthday Ball, waiting patiently for my reappearance; and in broad daylight when I went calling. Save that it cast no shadow, the rickshaw was in every respect as real to look upon as one of wood and iron. More than once, indeed, I have had to check myself from warning some hard-riding friend against cantering over it. More than once I have walked down the Mall deep in conversation with Mrs Wessington to the unspeakable amazement of the passers-by.

Before I had been out and about a week I learned that the 'fit' theory had been discarded in favour of insanity. However, I made no change in my mode of life. I called, rode, and dined out as freely as ever. I had a passion for the society of my kind which I had never felt before; I hungered to be among the realities of life; and at the same time I felt vaguely unhappy when I had been separated too long from my ghostly companion. It would be almost impossible to describe my varying moods from the 15th of May up to today.

The presence of the rickshaw filled me by turns with horror, blind fear, a dim sort of pleasure, and utter despair. I dared not leave Simla; and I knew that my stay there was killing me. I knew, moreover, that it was my destiny to die slowly and a little every day. My only anxiety was to get the penance over as quietly as might be. Alternately I hungered for a sight of Kitty and watched her outrageous flirtations with my successor – to speak more accurately, my successors – with amused interest. She was as much out of my life as I was out of hers. By day I wandered with Mrs Wessington almost content. By night I implored Heaven to let me return to the world as I used to know it. Above all these varying moods lay the sensation of dull, numbing wonder that the Seen and the Unseen should mingle so strangely on this earth to hound one poor soul to its grave.

* * *

August 27 – Heatherlegh has been indefatigable in his attendance on me; and only yesterday told me that I ought to send in an application for sick leave. An application to escape the company of a phantom! A request that the Government would graciously permit me to get rid of five ghosts and an airy rickshaw by going to England. Heatherlegh's proposition moved me to almost hysterical laughter. I told him that I should await the end quietly at Simla; and I am sure that the end is not far off. Believe me that I dread its advent more than any word can say; and I torture myself nightly with a thousand speculations as to the manner of my death.

Shall I die in my bed decently and as an English gentleman should die; or, in one last walk on the Mall, will my soul be wrenched from me to take its place forever and ever by the side of that ghastly phantasm? Shall I return to my old lost allegiance in the next world, or shall I meet Agnes loathing her and bound to her side through all eternity? Shall we two hover over the scene of our lives till the end of Time? As the day of my death draws nearer, the intense horror that all living flesh feels toward escaped spirits from beyond the grave grows more and more powerful. It is an awful thing to go down quick among the dead with scarcely one-half of your life completed. It is a thousand times more awful to wait as I do in your midst, for I know not what unimaginable terror. Pity me, at least on the score of my 'delusion', for I know you will never believe what I have written here. Yet as surely as ever a man was done to death by the Powers of Darkness I am that man.

In justice, too, pity her. For as surely as ever woman was killed by man, I killed Mrs Wessington. And the last portion of my punishment is ever now upon me.

The Strange Ride of Morrowbie Jukes

Alive or dead – there is no other way.

Native Proverb

There is, as the conjurers say, no deception about this tale. Jukes by accident stumbled upon a village that is well known to exist, though he is the only Englishman who has been there. A somewhat similar institution used to flourish on the outskirts of Calcutta, and there is a story that if you go into the heart of Bikanir, which is in the heart of the Great Indian Desert, you shall come across not a village but a town where the Dead who did not die but may not live have established their headquarters. And, since it is perfectly true that in the same Desert is a wonderful city where all the rich moneylenders retreat after they have made their fortunes (fortunes so vast that the owners cannot trust even the strong hand of the Government to protect them, but take refuge in the waterless sands), and drive sumptuous C-spring barouches, and buy beautiful girls and decorate their palaces with gold and ivory and Minton tiles and mother-o'-pearl, I do not see why Jukes's tale should not be true. He is a Civil Engineer, with a head for plans and distances and things of that kind, and he certainly would not take the trouble to invent imaginary traps. He could earn more by doing his legitimate work. He never varies the tale in the telling, and grows very hot and indignant when he thinks of the disrespectful treatment he received. He wrote this quite straightforwardly at first, but he has since touched it up in places and introduced Moral Reflections, thus –

In the beginning it all arose from a slight attack of fever. My work necessitated my being in camp for some months between Pakpattan and Muharakpur – a desolate sandy stretch of country, as everyone who has had the misfortune to go there may know. My coolies were neither more nor less exasperating than other gangs, and my work demanded sufficient attention to keep me from moping, had I been inclined to so unmanly a weakness.

On the 23d December, 1884, I felt a little feverish. There was a full moon at the time, and, in consequence, every dog near my tent was baying it. The brutes assembled in twos and threes and drove me frantic. A few days previously I had shot one loud-mouthed singer and suspended his carcase *in terrorem* about fifty yards from my tent-door. But his friends fell upon, fought for, and ultimately devoured the body; and, as it seemed to me, sang their hymns of thanksgiving afterward with renewed energy.

The lightheartedness which accompanies fever acts differently on different men. My irritation gave way, after a short time, to a fixed determination to slaughter one huge black and white beast who had been foremost in song and first in flight throughout the evening. Thanks to a shaking hand and a giddy head I had already missed him twice with both barrels of my shotgun, when it struck me that my best plan would be to ride him down in the open and finish him off with a hog-spear. This, of course, was merely the semi-delirious notion of a fever patient; but I remember that it struck me at the time as being eminently practical and feasible.

I therefore ordered my groom to saddle Pornic and bring him round quietly to the rear of my tent. When the pony was ready, I stood at his head prepared to mount and dash out as soon as the dog should again lift up his voice. Pornic, by the way, had not been out of his pickets for a couple of days; the night air was crisp and chilly; and I was armed with a specially long and sharp pair of persuaders with which I had been rousing a sluggish cob that afternoon. You will easily believe, then, that when he was let go he went quickly. In one moment, for the brute bolted as straight as a die, the tent was left far behind, and we were flying over the smooth sandy soil at racing speed.

In another we had passed the wretched dog, and I had almost forgotten why it was that I had taken the horse and hog-spear.

The delirium of fever and the excitement of rapid motion through the air must have taken away the remnant of my senses. I have a faint recollection of standing upright in my stirrups, and of brandishing my hog-spear at the great white Moon that looked down so calmly on my mad gallop; and of shouting challenges to the camel-thorn bushes as they whizzed past. Once or twice I believe, I swayed forward on Pornic's neck, and literally hung on by my spurs – as the marks next morning showed.

The wretched beast went forward like a thing possessed, over what seemed to be a limitless expanse of moonlit sand. Next, I remember, the ground rose suddenly in front of us, and as we topped the ascent I saw the waters of the Sutlej shining like a silver bar below. Then Pornic blundered heavily on his nose, and we rolled together down some unseen slope.

I must have lost consciousness, for when I recovered I was lying on my stomach in a heap of soft white sand, and the dawn was beginning to break dimly over the edge of the slope down which I had fallen. As the light grew stronger I saw that I was at the bottom of a horseshoe-shaped crater of sand, opening on one side directly on to the shoals of the Sutlej. My fever had altogether left me, and, with the exception of a slight dizziness in the head, I felt no bad effects from the fall over night.

Pornic, who was standing a few yards away, was naturally a good deal exhausted, but had not hurt himself in the least. His saddle, a favourite polo one, was much knocked about, and had been twisted under his belly. It took me some time to put him to rights, and in the meantime I had ample opportunities of observing the spot into which I had so foolishly dropped.

At the risk of being considered tedious, I must describe it at length: inasmuch as an accurate mental picture of its peculiarities will be of material assistance in enabling the reader to understand what follows.

Imagine then, as I have said before, a horseshoe-shaped crater of sand with steeply graded sand walls about thirty-five feet high. (The slope, I fancy, must have been about 65 degrees.) This crater enclosed a level piece of ground about fifty yards long by thirty at its broadest part, with a crude well in the centre. Round the bottom of the crater, about three feet from the level of the ground proper, ran a series of eighty-three semi-circular ovoid, square, and multilateral holes, all about three feet at the mouth. Each hole on inspection showed that it was carefully shored internally with driftwood and bamboos, and over the mouth a wooden drip-board projected, like the peak of a jockey's cap, for two feet. No sign of life was visible in these tunnels, but a most sickening stench pervaded the entire amphitheatre – a stench fouler than any which my wanderings in Indian villages have introduced me to.

Having remounted Pornic, who was as anxious as I to get back to camp, I rode round the base of the horseshoe to find some place whence an exit would be practicable. The inhabitants, whoever they might be, had not thought fit to put in an appearance, so I was left to my own devices. My first attempt to 'rush' Pornic up the steep sandbanks showed me that I had fallen into a trap exactly on the same model as that which the ant-lion sets for its prey. At each step the shifting sand poured down from above in tons, and rattled on the drip-boards of the holes like small shot. A couple of ineffectual charges sent us both rolling down to the bottom, half choked with the torrents of sand; and I was constrained to turn my attention to the river-bank.

Here everything seemed easy enough. The sand hills ran down to the river edge, it is true, but there were plenty of shoals and shallows across which I could gallop Pornic, and find my way back to *terra firma* by turning sharply to the right or left. As I led Pornic over the sands I was startled by the faint pop of a rifle across the river; and at the same moment a bullet dropped with a sharp '*whit*' close to Pornic's head.

There was no mistaking the nature of the missile – a regulation Martini-Henry 'picket'. About five hundred yards away a country-boat was anchored in midstream; and a jet of smoke drifting away from its bows in the still morning air showed me whence the delicate attention had come. Was ever a respectable gentleman in such an *impasse*? The treacherous sand slope allowed no escape from a spot which I had visited most involuntarily, and a promenade on the river frontage was the signal for a bombardment from some insane native in a boat. I'm afraid that I lost my temper very much indeed.

Another bullet reminded me that I had better save my breath to cool my porridge; and I retreated hastily up the sands and back to the horseshoe, where I saw that the noise of the rifle had drawn sixty-five human beings from the badger-holes which I had up till that point supposed to be untenanted. I found myself in the midst of a crowd of spectators – about forty men, twenty women, and one child who could not have been more than five years old. They were all scantily clothed in that salmon-coloured cloth which one associates with Hindu mendicants, and, at first sight, gave me the impression of a band of loathsome *fakirs*. The filth and repulsiveness of the assembly were beyond all description, and I shuddered to think what their life in the badger-holes must be.

Even in these days, when local self-government has destroyed the greater part of a native's respect for a Sahib, I have been accustomed to a certain amount of civility from my inferiors, and on approaching the crowd naturally expected that there would be some recognition of my presence. As a matter of fact there was; but it was by no means what I had looked for.

The ragged crew actually laughed at me – such laughter I hope I may never hear again. They cackled, yelled, whistled, and howled as I walked into their midst; some of them literally throwing themselves down on the ground in convulsions of unholy mirth. In a moment I had let go Pornic's head, and, irritated beyond expression at the morning's adventure, commenced cuffing those nearest to me with all the force I could. The wretches dropped under my blows like ninepins, and the laughter gave place to wails for mercy; while those yet untouched clasped me round the knees, imploring me in all sorts of uncouth tongues to spare them.

In the tumult, and just when I was feeling very much ashamed of myself for having thus easily given way to my temper, a thin, high voice murmured in English from behind my shoulder: 'Sahib! Sahib! Do you not know me? Sahib, it is Gunga Dass, the telegraph-master.'

I spun round quickly and faced the speaker.

Gunga Dass (I have, of course, no hesitation in mentioning the man's real name) I had known four years before as a Deccanee Brahmin loaned by the Punjab Government to one of the Khalsia States. He was in charge of a branch telegraph-office there, and when I had last met him was a jovial, full-stomached, portly Government servant with a marvellous capacity for making bad puns in English – a peculiarity which made me remember him long after I had forgotten his services to me in his official capacity. It is seldom that a Hindu makes English puns.

Now, however, the man was changed beyond all recognition. Caste-mark, stomach, slate-coloured continuations, and unctuous speech were all gone. I looked at a withered skeleton, turban-less and almost naked, with long matted hair and deepset codfish-eyes. But for a crescent-shaped scar on the left cheek – the result of an accident for which I was responsible – I should never have known him. But it was indubitably Gunga Dass, and – for this I was thankful – an English-speaking native who might at least tell me the meaning of all that I had gone through that day.

The crowd retreated to some distance as I turned toward the miserable figure, and ordered him to show me some method of escaping from the crater. He held a freshly plucked crow in his hand, and in reply to my question climbed slowly on a platform of sand which ran in front of the holes, and commenced lighting a fire there in silence. Dried bents, sand-poppies, and driftwood burn quickly;

and I derived much consolation from the fact that he lit them with an ordinary sulphur-match. When they were in a bright glow, and the crow was nearly spitted in front thereof, Gunga Dass began without a word of preamble: 'There are only two kinds of men, Sar. The alive and the dead. When you are dead you are dead, but when you are alive you live.' (Here the crow demanded his attention for an instant as it twirled before the fire in danger of being burned to a cinder.) 'If you die at home and do not die when you come to the *ghât* to be burned you come here.'

The nature of the reeking village was made plain now, and all that I had known or read of the grotesque and the horrible paled before the fact just communicated by the ex-Brahmin. Sixteen years ago, when I first landed in Bombay, I had been told by a wandering Armenian of the existence, somewhere in India, of a place to which such Hindus as had the misfortune to recover from trance or cata-lepsy were conveyed and kept, and I recollect laughing heartily at what I was then pleased to consider a traveller's tale.

Sitting at the bottom of the sand-trap, the memory of Watson's Hotel, with its swinging punkahs, white-robed attendants, and the sallow-faced Armenian, rose up in my mind as vividly as a photograph, and I burst into a loud fit of laughter. The contrast was too absurd!

Gunga Dass, as he bent over the unclean bird, watched me curi-ously. Hindus seldom laugh, and his surroundings were not such as to move Gunga Dass to any undue excess of hilarity. He removed the crow solemnly from the wooden spit and as solemnly devoured it. Then he continued his story, which I give in his own words.

'In epidemics of the cholera you are carried to be burned almost before you are dead. When you come to the riverside the cold air, perhaps, makes you alive, and then, if you are only little alive, mud is put on your nose and mouth and you die conclusively. If you are rather more alive, more mud is put; but if you are too lively they let you go and take you away. I was too lively, and made protestation with anger against the indignities that they endeavoured to press upon me. In those days I was Brahmin and proud man. Now I am dead man and eat' – here he eyed the well-gnawed breast bone with the first sign of emotion that I had seen in him since we met – 'crows, and other things. They took me from my sheets when they saw that I was too lively and gave me medicines for one week, and I survived successfully. Then they sent me by rail from my place to Okara Station, with a man to take care of me; and at Okara Station we met two other men, and they conducted we three on camels, in the night, from Okara Station to this place, and they propelled me from the top to the bottom, and the other two succeeded, and I have been here ever since two and a half years. Once I was Brahmin and proud man, and now I eat crows.'

'There is no way of getting out?'

'None of what kind at all. When I first came I made experiments frequently and all the others also, but we have always succumbed to the sand which is precipitated upon our heads.'

'But surely,' I broke in at this point, 'the river-front is open, and it is worth while dodging the bullets; while at night' – I had already matured a rough plan of escape which a natural instinct of selfishness forbade me sharing with Gunga Dass. He, however, divined my unspoken thought almost as soon as it was formed; and, to my intense astonishment, gave vent to a long low chuckle of derision – the laughter, be it understood, of a superior or at least of an equal.

'You will not' – he had dropped the Sir completely after his opening sentence – 'make any escape that way. But you can try. I have tried. Once only.'

The sensation of nameless terror and abject fear which I had in vain attempted to strive against overmastered me completely. My long fast – it was now close upon ten o'clock, and I had eaten nothing since tiffin on the previous day – combined with the violent and unnatural agitation of the ride had exhausted me, and I verily believe that, for a few minutes, I acted as one mad. I hurled myself against the pitiless sand-slope. I ran round the base of the crater, blaspheming and praying by turns. I crawled out among the sedges of the river-front, only to be driven back each time in an agony of nervous dread by the rifle-bullets which cut up the sand round me – for I dared not face the death of a mad dog among that hideous crowd – and finally fell, spent and raving, at the curb of the well. No-one had taken the slightest notion of an exhibition which makes me blush hotly even when I think of it now.

Two or three men trod on my panting body as they drew water, but they were evidently used to this sort of thing, and had no time to waste upon me. The situation was humiliating. Gunga Dass, indeed, when he had banked the embers of his fire with sand, was at some pains to throw half a cupful of fetid water over my head, an attention for which I could have fallen on my knees and thanked him, but he was laughing all the while in the same mirthless, wheezy key that greeted me on my first attempt to force the shoals. And so, in a semi-comatose condition, I lay till noon.

Then, being only a man after all, I felt hungry, and intimated as much to Gunga Dass, whom I had begun to regard as my natural protector. Following the impulse of the outer world when dealing with natives, I put my hand into my pocket and drew out four annas. The absurdity of the gift struck me at once, and I was about to replace the money.

Gunga Dass, however, was of a different opinion. 'Give me the money,' said he; 'all you have, or I will get help, and we will kill you!' All this as if it were the most natural thing in the world!

A Briton's first impulse, I believe, is to guard the contents of his pockets; but a moment's reflection convinced me of the futility of differing with the one man who had it in his power to make me comfortable; and with whose help it was possible that I might eventually escape from the crater. I gave him all the money in my possession, Rs. 9-8-5 – nine rupees eight annas and five pie – for I always keep small change as *bakshish* when I am in camp. Gunga Dass clutched the coins, and hid them at once in his ragged loin cloth, his expression changing to something diabolical as he looked round to assure himself that no-one had observed us.

'*Now* I will give you something to eat,' said he.

What pleasure the possession of my money could have afforded him I am unable to say; but inasmuch as it did give him evident delight I was not sorry that I had parted with it so readily, for I had no doubt that he would have had me killed if I had refused. One does not protest against the vagaries of a den of wild beasts; and my companions were lower than any beasts. While I devoured what Gunga Dass had provided, a coarse *chapatti* and a cupful of the foul well-water, the people showed not the faintest sign of curiosity – that curiosity which is so rampant, as a rule, in an Indian village.

I could even fancy that they despised me. At all events they treated me with the most chilling indifference, and Gunga Dass was nearly as bad. I plied him with questions about the terrible village, and received extremely unsatisfactory answers. So far as I could gather, it had been in existence from time immemorial – whence I concluded that it was at least a century old – and during that time no-one had ever been known to escape from it. [I had to control myself here with both hands, lest the blind terror should lay hold of me a second time and drive me raving round the crater.] Gunga Dass took a malicious pleasure in emphasising this point and in watching me wince. Nothing that I could do would induce him to tell me who the mysterious 'They' were.

'It is so ordered,' he would reply, 'and I do not yet know anyone who has disobeyed the orders.'

'Only wait till my servants find that I am missing,' I retorted, 'and I promise you that this place shall be cleared off the face of the earth, and I'll give you a lesson in civility, too, my friend.'

'Your servants would be torn in pieces before they came near this place; and, besides, you are dead, my dear friend. It is not your fault, of course, but none the less you are dead and buried.'

At irregular intervals supplies of food, I was told, were dropped down from the land side into the amphitheatre, and the inhabitants fought for them like wild beasts. When a man felt his death coming on he retreated to his lair and died there. The body was sometimes dragged out of the hole and thrown on to the sand, or allowed to rot where it lay.

The phrase 'thrown on to the sand' caught my attention, and I asked Gunga Dass whether this sort of thing was not likely to breed a pestilence.

'That,' said he with another of his wheezy chuckles, 'you may see for yourself subsequently. You will have much time to make observations.'

Whereat, to his great delight, I winced once more and hastily continued the conversation: 'And how do you live here from day to day? What do you do?' The question elicited exactly the same answer as before – coupled with the information that 'this place is like your European heaven; there is neither marrying nor giving in marriage.'

Gunga Dass had been educated at a Mission School, and, as he himself admitted, had he only changed his religion 'like a wise man', might have avoided the living grave which was now his portion. But as long as I was with him I fancy he was happy.

Here was a Sahib, a representative of the dominant race, helpless as a child and completely at the mercy of his native neighbours. In a deliberate lazy way he set himself to torture me as a schoolboy would devote a rapturous half-hour to watching the agonies of an impaled beetle, or as a ferret in a blind burrow might glue himself comfortably to the neck of a rabbit. The burden of his conversation was that there was no escape 'of no kind whatever', and that I should stay here till I died and was 'thrown on to the sand'. If it were possible to forejudge the conversation of the Damned on the advent of a new soul in their abode, I should say that they would speak as Gunga Dass did to me throughout that long afternoon. I was powerless to protest or answer, all my energies being devoted to a struggle against the inexplicable terror that threatened to overwhelm me again and again. I can compare the feeling to nothing except the struggles of a man against the overpowering nausea of the Channel passage – only my agony was of the spirit and infinitely more terrible.

As the day wore on, the inhabitants began to appear in full strength to catch the rays of the afternoon sun, which were now sloping in at the mouth of the crater. They assembled in little knots, and talked among themselves without even throwing a glance in my direction. About four o'clock, as far as I could judge, Gunga Dass rose and dived into his lair for a moment, emerging with a live crow in his hands. The wretched bird was in a most draggled and deplorable condition, but seemed to be in no way afraid of its master. Advancing cautiously to the river front, Gunga Dass stepped from tussock to tussock until he had reached a smooth patch of sand directly in the line of the boat's fire. The occupants of the boat took no notice. Here he stopped, and, with a couple of dexterous turns of the wrist, pegged the bird on its back with outstretched wings. As was only natural, the crow began to shriek at once and beat the air with its claws. In a few seconds the clamour had attracted the attention of a bevy of wild crows on a shoal a few hundred yards away, where they were discussing something that looked like a corpse. Half a dozen crows flew over at once to see what was going on, and also, as it proved, to attack the pinioned bird. Gunga Dass, who had lain down on a tussock, motioned to me to be quiet, though I fancy this was a needless precaution. In a moment, and before I could see how it happened, a wild crow, who had grappled with the shrieking and helpless bird, was entangled in the latter's claws, swiftly disengaged by Gunga Dass, and pegged down beside its companion in adversity. Curiosity, it seemed, overpowered the rest of the flock, and almost before Gunga Dass and I had time to withdraw to the tussock, two more captives were struggling in the upturned claws of the decoys. So the chase – if I can give it so dignified a name – continued until Gunga Dass had captured seven crows. Five of them he throttled at once, reserving two for further operations another day. I was a good deal impressed by this, to me, novel method of securing food, and complimented Gunga Dass on his skill.

'It is nothing to do,' said he. 'Tomorrow you must do it for me. You are stronger than I am.'

This calm assumption of superiority upset me not a little, and I answered peremptorily: 'Indeed, you old ruffian! What do you think I have given you money for?'

'Very well,' was the unmoved reply. 'Perhaps not tomorrow, nor the day after, nor subsequently; but in the end, and for many years, you will catch crows and eat crows, and you will thank your European God that you have crows to catch and eat.'

I could have cheerfully strangled him for this; but judged it best under the circumstances to smother my resentment. An hour later I was eating one of the crows; and, as Gunga Dass had said, thanking my God that I had a crow to eat. Never as long as I live shall I forget that evening meal. The whole population were squatting on the hard sand platform opposite their dens, huddled over tiny fires of refuse and dried rushes. Death, having once laid his hand upon these men and forborne to strike, seemed to stand aloof from them now; for most of our company were old men, bent and worn and twisted with years, and women aged to all appearance as the Fates themselves. They sat together in knots and talked – God only knows what they found to discuss – in low equable tones, curiously in contrast to the strident babble with which natives are accustomed to make day hideous. Now and then an access of that sudden fury which had possessed me in the morning would lay hold on a man or woman; and with yells and imprecations the sufferer would attack the steep slope until, baffled and bleeding, he fell back on the platform incapable of moving a limb. The others would never even raise their eyes when this happened, as men too well aware of the futility of their fellows' attempts and wearied with their useless repetition. I saw four such outbursts in the course of the evening.

Gunga Dass took an eminently businesslike view of my situation, and while we were dining – I can afford to laugh at the recollection now, but it was painful enough at the time – propounded the terms on which he would consent to 'do' for me. My nine rupees eight annas, he argued, at the rate of three annas a day, would provide me with food for fifty-one days, or about seven weeks; that is to say, he would be willing to cater for me for that length of time. At the end of it I was to look after myself. For a further consideration – *videlicet* my boots – he would be willing to allow me to occupy the den next to his own, and would supply me with as much dried grass for bedding as he could spare.

'Very well, Gunga Dass,' I replied; 'to the first terms I cheerfully agree, but, as there is nothing on earth to prevent my killing you as you sit here and taking everything that you have' (I thought of the two invaluable crows at the time), 'I flatly refuse to give you my boots and shall take whichever den I please.'

The stroke was a bold one, and I was glad when I saw that it had succeeded. Gunga Dass changed his tone immediately, and disavowed all intention of asking for my boots. At the time it did not strike me as at all strange that I, a Civil Engineer, a man of thirteen years' standing in the Service, and, I trust, an average Englishman, should thus calmly threaten murder and violence against the man who had, for a consideration it is true, taken me under his wing. I had left the world, it seemed, for centuries. I was as certain then as I am now of my own existence, that in the accursed settlement there was no law save that of the strongest; that the living dead men had thrown behind them every canon of the world which had cast them out; and that I had to depend for my own life on my strength and vigilance alone. The crew of the ill-fated *Mignonette* are the only men who would understand my frame of mind. 'At present,' I argued to myself, 'I am strong and a match for six of these wretches. It is imperatively necessary that I should, for my own sake, keep both health and strength until the hour of my release comes – if it ever does.'

Fortified with these resolutions, I ate and drank as much as I could, and made Gunga Dass understand that I intended to be his master, and that the least sign of insubordination on his part would be visited with the only punishment I had it in my power to inflict – sudden and violent death. Shortly after this I went to bed. That is to say, Gunga Dass gave me a double armful of dried bents which I thrust down the mouth of the lair to the right of his, and followed myself, feet foremost; the hole running about nine feet into the sand with a slight downward inclination, and being neatly shored with timbers. From my den, which faced the river-front, I was able to watch the waters of the Sutlej flowing past under the light of a young moon and compose myself to sleep as best I might.

The horrors of that night I shall never forget. My den was nearly as narrow as a coffin, and the sides had been worn smooth and greasy by the contact of innumerable naked bodies, added to which it smelled abominably. Sleep was altogether out of question to one in my excited frame of mind. As the night wore on, it seemed that the entire amphitheatre was filled with legions of unclean devils that, trooping up from the shoals below, mocked the unfortunates in their lairs.

Personally I am not of an imaginative temperament – very few Engineers are – but on that occasion I was as completely prostrated with nervous terror as any woman. After half an hour or so, however,

I was able once more to calmly review my chances of escape. Any exit by the steep sand walls was, of course, impracticable. I had been thoroughly convinced of this some time before. It was possible, just possible, that I might, in the uncertain moonlight, safely run the gauntlet of the rifle shots. The place was so full of terror for me that I was prepared to undergo any risk in leaving it. Imagine my delight, then, when after creeping stealthily to the river-front I found that the infernal boat was not there. My freedom lay before me in the next few steps!

By walking out to the first shallow pool that lay at the foot of the projecting left horn of the horseshoe, I could wade across, turn the flank of the crater, and make my way inland. Without a moment's hesitation I marched briskly past the tussocks where Gunga Dass had snared the crows, and out in the direction of the smooth white sand beyond. My first step from the tufts of dried grass showed me how utterly futile was any hope of escape; for, as I put my foot down, I felt an indescribable drawing, sucking motion of the sand below. Another moment and my leg was swallowed up nearly to the knee. In the moonlight the whole surface of the sand seemed to be shaken with devilish delight at my disappointment. I struggled clear, sweating with terror and exertion, back to the tussocks behind me and fell on my face.

My only means of escape from the semicircle was protected with a quicksand!

How long I lay I have not the faintest idea; but I was roused at last by the malevolent chuckle of Gunga Dass at my ear: 'I would advise you, Protector of the Poor,' (the ruffian was speaking English) 'to return to your house. It is unhealthy to lie down here. Moreover, when the boat returns, you will most certainly be rifled at.' He stood over me in the dim light of the dawn, chuckling and laughing to himself. Suppressing my first impulse to catch the man by the neck and throw him on to the quicksand, I rose sullenly and followed him to the platform below the burrows.

Suddenly, and futilely as I thought while I spoke, I asked: 'Gunga Dass, what is the good of the boat if I can't get out *anyhow*?' I recollect that even in my deepest trouble I had been speculating vaguely on the waste of ammunition in guarding an already well protected foreshore.

Gunga Dass laughed again and made answer: 'They have the boat only in daytime. It is for the reason that *there is a way*. I hope we shall have the pleasure of your company for much longer time. It is a pleasant spot when you have been here some years and eaten roast crow long enough.'

I staggered, numbed and helpless, toward the fetid burrow allotted to me, and fell asleep. An hour or so later I was awakened by a piercing scream – the shrill, high-pitched scream of a horse in pain. Those who have once heard that will never forget the sound. I found some little difficulty in scrambling out of the burrow. When I was in the open, I saw Pornic, my poor old Pornic, lying dead on the sandy soil. How they had killed him I cannot guess. Gunga Dass explained that horse was better than crow, and 'greatest good of greatest number is political maxim. We are now Republic, Mister Jukes, and you are entitled to a fair share of the beast. If you like, we will pass a vote of thanks. Shall I propose?'

Yes, we were a Republic indeed! A Republic of wild beasts penned at the bottom of a pit, to eat and fight and sleep till we died. I attempted no protest of any kind, but sat down and stared at the hideous sight in front of me. In less time almost than it takes me to write this, Pornic's body was divided, in some unclear way or other; the men and women had dragged the fragments on to the platform and were preparing their normal meal. Gunga Dass cooked mine. The almost irresistible impulse to fly at the sand walls until I was wearied laid hold of me afresh, and I had to struggle against it with all my might. Gunga Dass was offensively jocular till I told him that if he addressed another remark of any kind whatever to me I should strangle him where he sat. This silenced him till silence became insupportable, and I bade him say something.

'You will live here till you die like the other Feringhi,' he said, coolly, watching me over the fragment of gristle that he was gnawing.

'What other Sahib, you swine? Speak at once, and don't stop to tell me a lie.'

'He is over there,' answered Gunga Dass, pointing to a burrow-mouth about four doors to the left of my own. 'You can see for yourself. He died in the burrow as you will die, and I will die, and as all these men and women and the one child will also die.'

'For pity's sake tell me all you know about him. Who was he? When did he come, and when did he die?'

This appeal was a weak step on my part. Gunga Dass only leered and replied: 'I will not – unless you give me something first.'

Then I recollected where I was, and struck the man between the eyes, partially stunning him. He stepped down from the platform at once, and, cringing and fawning and weeping and attempting to embrace my feet, led me round to the burrow which he had indicated.

'I know nothing whatever about the gentleman. Your God be my witness that I do not. He was as anxious to escape as you were, and he was shot from the boat, though we all did all things to prevent him from attempting. He was shot here.' Gunga Dass laid his hand on his lean stomach and bowed to the earth.

'Well, and what then? Go on!'

'And then – and then, Your Honour, we carried him in to his house and gave him water, and put wet cloths on the wound, and he laid down in his house and gave up the ghost.'

'In how long? In how long?'

'About half an hour, after he received his wound. I call Vishnu to witness,' yelled the wretched man, 'that I did everything for him. Everything which was possible, that I did!'

He threw himself down on the ground and clasped my ankles. But I had my doubts about Gunga Dass's benevolence, and kicked him off as he lay protesting.

'I believe you robbed him of everything he had. But I can find out in a minute or two. How long was the Sahib here?'

'Nearly a year and a half. I think he must have gone mad. But hear me swear, Protector of the Poor! Won't Your Honour hear me swear that I never touched an article that belonged to him? What is Your Worship going to do?'

I had taken Gunga Dass by the waist and had hauled him on to the platform opposite the deserted burrow. As I did so I thought of my wretched fellow-prisoner's unspeakable misery among all these horrors for eighteen months, and the final agony of dying like a rat in a hole, with a bullet-wound in the stomach. Gunga Dass fancied I was going to kill him and howled pitifully. The rest of the population, in the plethora that follows a full flesh meal, watched us without stirring.

'Go inside, Gunga Dass,' said I, 'and fetch it out.'

I was feeling sick and faint with horror now. Gunga Dass nearly rolled off the platform and howled aloud.

'But I am Brahmin, Sahib – a high-caste Brahmin. By your soul, by your father's soul, do not make me do this thing!'

'Brahmin or no Brahmin, by my soul and my father's soul, in you go!' I said, and, seizing him by the shoulders, I crammed his head into the mouth of the burrow, kicked the rest of him in, and, sitting down, covered my face with my hands.

At the end of a few minutes I heard a rustle and a creak; then Gunga Dass in a sobbing, choking whisper speaking to himself; then a soft thud – and I uncovered my eyes.

The dry sand had turned the corpse entrusted to its keeping into a yellow-brown mummy. I told Gunga Dass to stand off while I examined it. The body – clad in an olive-green hunting-suit much stained and worn, with leather pads on the shoulders – was that of a man between thirty and forty, above middle height, with light, sandy hair, long mustache, and a rough unkempt beard. The left canine of the upper jaw was missing, and a portion of the lobe of the right ear was gone. On the second finger of the left hand was a ring – a shield-shaped bloodstone set in gold, with a monogram that might have been either 'B.K.' or 'B.L.' On the third finger of the right hand was a silver ring in the shape of a coiled cobra, much worn and tarnished. Gunga Dass deposited a handful of trifles he had picked out of the burrow at my feet, and, covering the face of the body with my handkerchief, I turned to examine these. I give the full list in the hope that it may lead to the identification of the unfortunate man:

1 Bowl of a briarwood pipe, serrated at the edge; much worn and blackened; bound with string at the crew.
2 Two patent-lever keys; wards of both broken.
3 Tortoiseshell-handled penknife, silver or nickel, name-plate, marked with monogram 'B.K.'
4 Envelope, postmark undecipherable, bearing a Victorian stamp, addressed to 'Miss Mon – ' (rest illegible) – 'ham' – 'nt.'
5 Imitation crocodile-skin notebook with pencil. First forty-five pages blank; four and a half illegible; fifteen others filled with private memoranda relating chiefly to three persons – a Mrs L. Singleton, abbreviated several times to 'Lot Single', 'Mrs S. May', and 'Garmison', referred to in places as 'Jerry' or 'Jack'.
6 Handle of small-sized hunting-knife. Blade snapped short. Buck's horn, diamond cut, with swivel and ring on the butt; fragment of cotton cord attached.

It must not be supposed that I inventoried all these things on the spot as fully as I have here written them down. The notebook first attracted my attention, and I put it in my pocket with a view of studying it later on.

The rest of the articles I conveyed to my burrow for safety's sake, and there being a methodical man, I inventoried them. I then returned to the corpse and ordered Gunga Dass to help me to carry it out to the river-front. While we were engaged in this, the exploded shell of an old brown cartridge dropped out of one of the pockets and rolled at my feet. Gunga Dass had not seen it; and I fell to thinking that a man does not carry exploded cartridge-cases, especially 'browns', which will not bear loading twice, about with him when shooting. In other words, that cartridge-case had been fired inside the crater. Consequently there must be a gun somewhere. I was on the verge of asking Gunga Dass, but checked myself, knowing that he would lie. We laid the body down on the edge of the quicksand by the tussocks. It was my intention to push it out and let it be swallowed up – the only possible mode of burial that I could think of. I ordered Gunga Dass to go away.

Then I gingerly put the corpse out on the quicksand. In doing so, it was lying face downward, I tore the frail and rotten khaki shooting-coat open, disclosing a hideous cavity in the back. I have already told you that the dry sand had, as it were, mummified the body. A moment's glance showed that the gaping hole had been caused by a gunshot wound; the gun must have been fired with the muzzle almost touching the back. The shooting-coat, being intact, had been drawn over the body after death, which must have been instantaneous. The secret of the poor wretch's death was plain to me in a flash. Someone of the crater, presumably Gunga Dass, must have shot him with his own gun – the gun that fitted the brown cartridges. He had never attempted to escape in the face of the rifle-fire from the boat.

I pushed the corpse out hastily, and saw it sink from sight literally in a few seconds. I shuddered as I watched. In a dazed, half-conscious way I turned to peruse the notebook. A stained and discoloured slip of paper had been inserted between the binding and the back, and dropped out as I opened the pages. This is what it contained: '*Four out from crow-clump: three left; nine out; two right; three back; two left; fourteen out; two left; seven out; one left; nine back; two right; six back; four right; seven back*.' The paper had been burned and charred at the edges. What it meant I could not understand. I sat down on the dried bents turning it over and over between my fingers, until I was aware of Gunga Dass standing immediately behind me with glowing eyes and outstretched hands.

'Have you got it?' he panted. 'Will you not let me look at it also? I swear that I will return it.'

'Got what? Return what?' I asked.

'That which you have in your hands. It will help us both.' He stretched out his long, bird-like talons, trembling with eagerness.

'I could never find it,' he continued. 'He had secreted it about his person. Therefore I shot him, but nevertheless I was unable to obtain it.'

Gunga Dass had quite forgotten his little fiction about the rifle-bullet. I received the information perfectly calmly. Morality is blunted by consorting with the Dead who are alive.

'What on earth are you raving about? What is it you want me to give you?'

'The piece of paper in the notebook. It will help us both. Oh, you fool! You fool! Can you not see what it will do for us? We shall escape!'

His voice rose almost to a scream, and he danced with excitement before me. I own I was moved at the chance of my getting away.

'Don't skip! Explain yourself. Do you mean to say that this slip of paper will help us? What does it mean?'

'Read it aloud! Read it aloud! I beg and I pray you to read it aloud.'

I did so. Gunga Dass listened delightedly, and drew an irregular line in the sand with his fingers.

'See now! It was the length of his gun-barrels without the stock. I have those barrels. Four gun-barrels out from the place where I caught crows. Straight out; do you follow me? Then three left. Ah! how well I remember when that man worked it out night after night. Then nine out, and so on. Out is always straight before you across the quicksand. He told me so before I killed him.'

'But if you knew all this why didn't you get out before?'

'I did *not* know it. He told me that he was working it out a year and a half ago, and how he was working it out night after night when the boat had gone away, and he could get out near the quicksand safely. Then he said that we would get away together. But I was afraid that he would leave me behind one night when he had worked it all out, and so I shot him. Besides, it is not advisable that the men who once get in here should escape. Only I, and *I* am a Brahmin.'

The prospect of escape had brought Gunga Dass's caste back to him. He stood up, walked about and gesticulated violently. Eventually I managed to make him talk soberly, and he told me how this Englishman had spent six months night after night in exploring, inch by inch, the passage across the quicksand; how he had declared it to be simplicity itself up to within about twenty yards of the river bank after turning the flank of the left horn of the horseshoe. This much he had evidently not completed when Gunga Dass shot him with his own gun.

In my frenzy of delight at the possibilities of escape I recollect shaking hands effusively with Gunga Dass, after we had decided that we were to make an attempt to get away that very night. It was weary work waiting throughout the afternoon.

About ten o'clock, as far as I could judge, when the Moon had just risen above the lip of the crater, Gunga Dass made a move for his burrow to bring out the gun-barrels whereby to measure our path. All the other wretched inhabitants had retired to their lairs long ago. The guardian boat drifted downstream some hours before, and we were utterly alone by the crow-clump. Gunga Dass, while carrying the gun-barrels, let slip the piece of paper which was to be our guide. I stooped down hastily to recover it, and, as I did so, I was aware that the diabolical Brahmin was aiming a violent blow at the back of my head with the gun-barrels. It was too late to turn round. I must have received the blow somewhere on the nape of my neck. A hundred thousand fiery stars danced before my eyes, and I fell forwards senseless at the edge of the quicksand.

When I recovered consciousness, the Moon was going down, and I was sensible of intolerable pain in the back of my head. Gunga Dass had disappeared and my mouth was full of blood. I lay down again and prayed that I might die without more ado. Then the unreasoning fury which I had before mentioned, laid hold upon me, and I staggered inland toward the walls of the crater. It seemed that someone was calling to me in a whisper – 'Sahib! Sahib! Sahib!' exactly as my bearer used to call me in the morning. I fancied that I was delirious until a handful of sand fell at my feet. Then I looked up and saw a head peering down into the amphitheatre – the head of Dunnoo, my dog-boy, who attended to my collies. As soon as he had attracted my attention, he held up his hand and showed a rope. I motioned, staggering to and fro for the while, that he should throw it down. It was a couple of leather punkah-ropes knotted together, with a loop at one end. I slipped the loop over my head and under my arms; heard Dunnoo urge something forward; was conscious that I was being dragged, face downward, up the steep sand slope, and the next instant found myself choked and half fainting on the sand hills overlooking the crater. Dunnoo, with his face ashy grey in the moonlight, implored me not to stay but to get back to my tent at once.

It seems that he had tracked Pornic's footprints fourteen miles across the sands to the crater; had returned and told my servants, who flatly refused to meddle with anyone, white or black, once fallen into the hideous Village of the Dead; whereupon Dunnoo had taken one of my ponies and a couple of punkah-ropes, returned to the crater, and hauled me out as I have described.

To cut a long story short, Dunnoo is now my personal servant on a gold mohur a month – a sum which I still think far too little for the services he has rendered. Nothing on earth will induce me to go near that devilish spot again, or to reveal its whereabouts more clearly than I have done. Of Gunga Dass I have never found a trace, nor do I wish to do so. My sole motive in giving this to be published is the hope that someone may possibly identify, from the details and the inventory which I have given above, the corpse of the man in the olive-green hunting-suit.

'They'

One view called me to another; one hill top to its fellow, half across the county, and since I could answer at no more trouble than the snapping forward of a lever, I let the country flow under my wheels. The orchid-studded flats of the East gave way to the thyme, ilex, and grey grass of the Downs; these again to the rich cornland and fig trees of the lower coast, where you carry the beat of the tide on your left hand for fifteen level miles; and when at last I turned inland through a huddle of rounded hills and woods I had run myself clean out of my known marks. Beyond that precise hamlet which stands godmother to the capital of the United States, I found hidden villages where bees, the only things awake, boomed in eighty-foot lindens that overhung grey Norman churches; miraculous brooks diving under stone bridges built for heavier traffic than would ever vex them again; tithe barns larger than their churches, and an old smithy that cried out aloud how it had once been a hall of the Knights of the Temple. Gypsies I found on a common where the gorse, bracken, and heath fought it out together up a mile of Roman road; and a little farther on I disturbed a red fox rolling dog-fashion in the naked sunlight.

As the wooded hills closed about me I stood up in the car to take the bearings of that great Down whose ringed head is a landmark for fifty miles across the low countries. I judged that the lie of the country would bring me across some westward running road that went to his feet, but I did not allow for the confusing veils of the woods. A quick turn plunged me first into a green cutting brimful of liquid sunshine, next into a gloomy tunnel where last year's dead leaves whispered and scuffled about my tyres. The strong hazel stuff meeting overhead had not been cut for a couple of generations at least, nor had any axe helped the moss-cankered oak and beech to spring above them. Here the road changed frankly into a carpeted ride on whose brown velvet spent primrose-clumps showed like jade, and a few sickly, white-stalked bluebells nodded together. As the slope favoured I shut off the power and slid over the whirled leaves, expecting every moment to meet a keeper; but I only heard a jay, far off, arguing against the silence under the twilight of the trees.

Still the track descended. I was on the point of reversing and working my way back on the second speed ere I ended in some swamp, when I saw sunshine through the tangle ahead and lifted the brake.

It was down again at once. As the light beat across my face my fore-wheels took the turf of a great still lawn from which sprang horsemen ten feet high with levelled lances, monstrous peacocks, and sleek round-headed maids of honour – blue, black, and glistening – all of clipped yew. Across the lawn – the marshalled woods besieged it on three sides – stood an ancient house of lichened and weather-worn stone, with mullioned windows and roofs of rose-red tile. It was flanked by semi-circular walls, also rose-red, that closed the lawn on the fourth side, and at their feet a box hedge grew man-high. There were doves on the roof about the slim brick chimneys, and I caught a glimpse of an octagonal dove-house behind the screening wall.

Here, then, I stayed, a horseman's green spear laid at my breast, held by the exceeding beauty of that jewel in that setting.

'If I am not packed off for a trespasser, or if this knight does not ride a wallop at me,' thought I, 'Shakespeare and Queen Elizabeth at least must come out of that half-open garden door and ask me to tea.'

A child appeared at an upper window, and I thought the little thing waved a friendly hand. But it was to call a companion, for presently another bright head showed. Then I heard a laugh among the yew-peacocks, and turning to make sure (till then I had been watching the house only) I saw the silver of a fountain behind a hedge thrown up against the sun. The doves on the roof cooed to the cooing water; but between the two notes I caught the utterly happy chuckle of a child absorbed in some light mischief.

The garden door – heavy oak sunk deep in the thickness of the wall – opened further: a woman in a big garden hat set her foot slowly on the time-hollowed stone step and as slowly walked across the turf. I was forming some apology when she lifted up her head and I saw that she was blind.

'I heard you,' she said. 'Isn't that a motor car?'

'I'm afraid I've made a mistake in my road. I should have turned off up above – I never dreamed – ' I began.

'But I'm very glad. Fancy a motor car coming into the garden! It will be such a treat – ' She turned and made as though looking about her. 'You – you haven't seen anyone have you – perhaps?'

'No-one to speak to, but the children seemed interested at a distance.'

'Which?'

'I saw a couple up at the window just now, and I think I heard a little chap in the grounds.'

'Oh, lucky you!' she cried, and her face brightened. 'I hear them, of course, but that's all. You've seen them and heard them?'

'Yes,' I answered. 'And if I know anything of children one of them's having a beautiful time by the fountain yonder. Escaped, I should imagine.'

'You're fond of children?'

I gave her one or two reasons why I did not altogether hate them.

'Of course, of course,' she said. 'Then you understand. Then you won't think it foolish if I ask you to take your car through the gardens, once or twice – quite slowly. I'm sure they'd like to see it. They see so little, poor things. One tries to make their life pleasant, but – ' she threw out her hands towards the woods. 'We're so out of the world here.'

'That will be splendid,' I said. 'But I can't cut up your grass.'

She faced to the right. 'Wait a minute,' she said. 'We're at the South gate, aren't we? Behind those peacocks there's a flagged path. We call it the Peacock's Walk. You can't see it from here, they tell me, but if you squeeze along by the edge of the wood you can turn at the first peacock and get on to the flags.'

It was sacrilege to wake that dreaming house-front with the clatter of machinery, but I swung the car to clear the turf, brushed along the edge of the wood and turned in on the broad stone path where the fountain-basin lay like one star-sapphire.

'May I come too?' she cried. 'No, please don't help me. They'll like it better if they see me.'

She felt her way lightly to the front of the car, and with one foot on the step she called: 'Children, oh, children! Look and see what's going to happen!'

The voice would have drawn lost souls from the Pit, for the yearning that underlay its sweetness, and I was not surprised to hear an answering shout behind the yews. It must have been the child by the fountain, but he fled at our approach, leaving a little toy boat in the water. I saw the glint of his blue blouse among the still horsemen.

Very disposedly we paraded the length of the walk and at her request backed again. This time the child had got the better of his panic, but stood far off and doubting.

'The little fellow's watching us,' I said. 'I wonder if he'd like a ride.'

'They're very shy still. Very shy. But, oh, lucky you to be able to see them! Let's listen.'

I stopped the machine at once, and the humid stillness, heavy with the scent of box, cloaked us deep. Shears I could hear where some gardener was clipping; a mumble of bees and broken voices that might have been the doves.

'Oh, unkind!' she said weariedly.

'Perhaps they're only shy of the motor. The little maid at the window looks tremendously interested.'

'Yes?' She raised her head. 'It was wrong of me to say that. They are really fond of me. It's the only thing that makes life worth living – when they're fond of you, isn't it? I daren't think what the place would be without them. By the way, is it beautiful?'

'I think it is the most beautiful place I have ever seen.'

'So they all tell me. I can feel it, of course, but that isn't quite the same thing.'

'Then have you never – ?' I began, but stopped abashed.

'Not since I can remember. It happened when I was only a few months old, they tell me. And yet I must remember something, else how could I dream about colours. I see light in my dreams, and colours, but I never see *them*. I only hear them just as I do when I'm awake.'

'It's difficult to see faces in dreams. Some people can, but most of us haven't the gift,' I went on, looking up at the window where the child stood all but hidden.

'I've heard that too,' she said. 'And they tell me that one never sees a dead person's face in a dream. Is that true?'

'I believe it is – now I come to think of it.'

'But how is it with yourself – yourself?' The blind eyes turned towards me.

'I have never seen the faces of my dead in any dream,' I answered.

'Then it must be as bad as being blind.'

The sun had dipped behind the woods and the long shades were possessing the insolent horsemen one by one. I saw the light die from off the top of a glossy-leaved lance and all the brave hard green turn to soft black. The house, accepting another day at end, as it had accepted an hundred thousand gone, seemed to settle deeper into its rest among the shadows.

'Have you ever wanted to?' she said after the silence.

'Very much sometimes,' I replied. The child had left the window as the shadows closed upon it.

'Ah! So've I, but I don't suppose it's allowed . . . Where d'you live?'

'Quite the other side of the county – sixty miles and more, and I must be going back. I've come without my big lamp.'

'But it's not dark yet. I can feel it.'

'I'm afraid it will be by the time I get home. Could you lend me someone to set me on my road at first? I've utterly lost myself.'

'I'll send Madden with you to the crossroads. We are so out of the world, I don't wonder you were lost! I'll guide you round to the front of the house; but you will go slowly, won't you, till you're out of the grounds? It isn't foolish, do you think?'

'I promise you I'll go like this,' I said, and let the car start herself down the flagged path.

We skirted the left wing of the house, whose elaborately cast lead guttering alone was worth a day's journey; passed under a great rose-grown gate in the red wall, and so round to the high front of the house which in beauty and stateliness as much excelled the back as that all others I had seen.

'Is it so very beautiful?' she said wistfully when she heard my raptures. 'And you like the lead figures too? There's the old azalea garden behind. They say that this place must have been made for children. Will you help me out, please? I should like to come with you as far as the crossroads, but I mustn't leave them. Is that you, Madden? I want you to show this gentleman the way to the crossroads. He has lost his way but – he has seen them.'

A butler appeared noiselessly at the miracle of old oak that must be called the front door, and slipped aside to put on his hat. She stood looking at me with open blue eyes in which no sight lay, and I saw for the first time that she was beautiful.

'Remember,' she said quietly, 'if you are fond of them you will come again,' and disappeared within the house.

The butler in the car said nothing till we were nearly at the lodge gates, where catching a glimpse of a blue blouse in a shrubbery I swerved amply lest the devil that leads little boys to play should drag me into child-murder.

'Excuse me,' he asked of a sudden, 'but why did you do that, Sir?'

'The child yonder.'

'Our young gentleman in blue?'

'Of course.'

'He runs about a good deal. Did you see him by the fountain, Sir?'

'Oh, yes, several times. Do we turn here?'

'Yes, Sir. And did you 'appen to see them upstairs too?'

'At the upper window? Yes.'

'Was that before the mistress come out to speak to you, Sir?'

'A little before that. Why d'you want to know?'

He paused a little. 'Only to make sure that – that they had seen the car, Sir, because with children running about, though I'm sure you're driving particularly careful, there might be an accident. That was all, Sir. Here are the crossroads. You can't miss your way from now on. Thank you, Sir, but that isn't *our* custom, not with – '

'I beg your pardon,' I said, and thrust away the British silver.

'Oh, it's quite right with the rest of 'em as a rule. Goodbye, Sir.'

He retired into the armour-plated conning tower of his caste and walked away. Evidently a butler solicitous for the honour of his house, and interested, probably through a maid, in the nursery.

Once beyond the signposts at the crossroads I looked back, but the crumpled hills interlaced so jealously that I could not see where the house had lain. When I asked its name at a cottage along the road, the fat woman who sold sweetmeats there gave me to understand that people with motor cars had small right to live – much less to 'go about talking like carriage folk'. They were not a pleasant-mannered community.

When I retraced my route on the map that evening I was little wiser. Hawkin's Old Farm appeared to be the survey title of the place, and the old County Gazetteer, generally so ample, did not allude to it. The big house of those parts was Hodnington Hall, Georgian with early Victorian embellishments, as an atrocious steel engraving attested. I carried my difficulty to a neighbour – a deep-rooted tree of that soil – and he gave me a name of a family which conveyed no meaning.

A month or so later – I went again, or it may have been that my car took the road of her own volition. She overran the fruitless Downs, threaded every turn of the maze of lanes below the hills, drew through the high-walled woods, impenetrable in their full leaf, came out at the crossroads where the butler had left me, and a little further on developed an internal trouble which forced me to turn her in on a grass way-waste that cut into a summer-silent hazel wood. So far as I could make sure by the sun and a six-inch Ordnance map, this should be the road flank of that wood which I had first explored from the heights above. I made a mighty serious business of my repairs and a glittering shop of my repair kit,

spanners, pump, and the like, which I spread out orderly upon a
rug. It was a trap to catch all childhood, for on such a day, I argued,
the children would not be far off. When I paused in my work I
listened, but the wood was so full of the noises of summer (though
the birds had mated) that I could not at first distinguish these from
the tread of small cautious feet stealing across the dead leaves. I
rang my bell in an alluring manner, but the feet fled, and I re-
pented, for to a child a sudden noise is very real terror. I must have
been at work half an hour when I heard in the wood the voice of the
blind woman crying: 'Children, oh children, where are you?' and
the stillness made slow to close on the perfection of that cry. She
came towards me, half feeling her way between the tree boles, and
though a child it seemed clung to her skirt, it swerved into the
leafage like a rabbit as she drew nearer.

'Is that you?' she said, 'from the other side of the county?'

'Yes, it's me from the other side of the county.'

'Then why didn't you come through the upper woods? They were
there just now.'

'They were here a few minutes ago. I expect they knew my car had
broken down, and came to see the fun.'

'Nothing serious, I hope? How do cars break down?'

'In fifty different ways. Only mine has chosen the fifty-first.'

She laughed merrily at the tiny joke, cooed with delicious laughter,
and pushed her hat back.

'Let me hear,' she said.

'Wait a moment,' I cried, 'and I'll get you a cushion.'

She set her foot on the rug all covered with spare parts, and stooped
above it eagerly. 'What delightful things!' The hands through which
she saw glanced in the chequered sunlight. 'A box here – another box!
Why you've arranged them like playing shop!'

'I confess now that I put it out to attract them. I don't need half
those things really.'

'How nice of you! I heard your bell in the upper wood. You say
they were here before that?'

'I'm sure of it. Why are they so shy? That little fellow in blue who
was with you just now ought to have got over his fright. He's been
watching me like a Red Indian.'

'It must have been your bell,' she said. 'I heard one of them go past
me in trouble when I was coming down. They're shy – so shy even
with me.' She turned her face over her shoulder and cried again:
'Children! Oh, children! Look and see!'

'They must have gone off together on their own affairs,' I suggested, for there was a murmur behind us of lowered voices broken by the sudden squeaking giggles of childhood. I returned to my tinkerings and she leaned forward, her chin on her hand, listening interestedly.

'How many are they?' I said at last. The work was finished, but I saw no reason to go.

Her forehead puckered a little in thought. 'I don't quite know,' she said simply. 'Sometimes more – sometimes less. They come and stay with me because I love them, you see.'

'That must be very jolly,' I said, replacing a drawer, and as I spoke I heard the inanity of my answer.

'You – you aren't laughing at me,' she cried. 'I – I haven't any of my own. I never married. People laugh at me sometimes about them because – because – '

'Because they're savages,' I returned. 'It's nothing to fret for. That sort laugh at everything that isn't in their own fat lives.'

'I don't know. How should I? I only don't like being laughed at about *them*. It hurts; and when one can't see . . . I don't want to seem silly,' her chin quivered like a child's as she spoke, 'but we blindies have only one skin, I think. Everything outside hits straight at our souls. It's different with you. You've such good defences in your eyes – looking out – before anyone can really pain you in your soul. People forget that with us.'

I was silent reviewing that inexhaustible matter – the more than inherited (since it is also carefully taught) brutality of the Christian peoples, beside which the mere heathendom of the West Coast nigger is clean and restrained. It led me a long distance into myself.

'Don't do that!' she said of a sudden, putting her hands before her eyes.

'What?'

She made a gesture with her hand.

'That! It's – it's all purple and black. Don't! That colour hurts.'

'But, how in the world do you know about colours?' I exclaimed, for here was a revelation indeed.

'Colours as colours?' she asked.

'No. *Those* Colours which you saw just now.'

'You know as well as I do,' she laughed, 'else you wouldn't have asked that question. They aren't in the world at all. They're in *you* – when you went so angry.'

'D'you mean a dull purplish patch, like port wine mixed with ink?' I said.

'I've never seen ink or port wine, but the colours aren't mixed. They are separate – all separate.'

'Do you mean black streaks and jags across the purple?'

She nodded. 'Yes – if they are like this,' and zigzagged her finger again, 'but it's more red than purple – that bad colour.'

'And what are the colours at the top of the – whatever you see?'

Slowly she leaned forward and traced on the rug the figure of the Egg itself.

'I see them so,' she said, pointing with a grass stem, 'white, green, yellow, red, purple, and when people are angry or bad, black across the red – as you were just now.'

'Who told you anything about it – in the beginning?' I demanded.

'About the colours? No-one. I used to ask what colours were when I was little – in table-covers and curtains and carpets, you see – because some colours hurt me and some made me happy. People told me; and when I got older that was how I saw people.' Again she traced the outline of the Egg which it is given to very few of us to see.

'All by yourself?' I repeated.

'All by myself. There wasn't anyone else. I only found out afterwards that other people did not see the Colours.'

She leaned against the tree-hole plaiting and unplaiting chance-plucked grass stems. The children in the wood had drawn nearer. I could see them with the tail of my eye frolicking like squirrels.

'Now I am sure you will never laugh at me,' she went on after a long silence. 'Nor at *them*.'

'Goodness, no!' I cried, jolted out of my train of thought. 'A man who laughs at a child – unless the child is laughing too – is a heathen!'

'I didn't mean that of course. You'd never laugh *at* children, but I thought – I used to think – that perhaps you might laugh *about* them. So now I beg your pardon . . . What are you going to laugh at?'

I had made no sound, but she knew.

'At the notion of your begging my pardon. If you had done your duty as a pillar of the state and a landed proprietress you ought to have summoned me for trespass when I barged through your woods the other day. It was disgraceful of me – inexcusable.'

She looked at me, her head against the tree trunk – long and steadfastly – this woman who could see the naked soul.

'How curious,' she half whispered. 'How very curious.'

'Why, what have I done?'

'You don't understand . . . and yet you understood about the Colours. Don't you understand?'

She spoke with a passion that nothing had justified, and I faced her bewilderedly as she rose. The children had gathered themselves in a roundel behind a bramble bush. One sleek head bent over something smaller, and the set of the little shoulders told me that fingers were on lips. They, too, had some child's tremendous secret. I alone was hopelessly astray there in the broad sunlight.

'No,' I said, and shook my head as though the dead eyes could note. 'Whatever it is, I don't understand yet. Perhaps I shall later – if you'll let me come again.'

'You will come again,' she answered. 'You will surely come again and walk in the wood.'

'Perhaps the children will know me well enough by that time to let me play with them – as a favour. You know what children are like.'

'It isn't a matter of favour but of right,' she replied, and while I wondered what she meant, a dishevelled woman plunged round the bend of the road, loose-haired, purple, almost lowing with agony as she ran. It was my rude, fat friend of the sweetmeat shop. The blind woman heard and stepped forward. 'What is it, Mrs Madehurst?' she asked.

The woman flung her apron over her head and literally grovelled in the dust, crying that her grandchild was sick to death, that the local doctor was away fishing, that Jenny the mother was at her wits end, and so forth, with repetitions and bellowings.

'Where's the next nearest doctor?' I asked between paroxysms.

'Madden will tell you. Go round to the house and take him with you. I'll attend to this. Be quick!' She half-supported the fat woman into the shade. In two minutes I was blowing all the horns of Jericho under the front of the House Beautiful, and Madden, in the pantry, rose to the crisis like a butler and a man.

A quarter of an hour at illegal speeds caught us a doctor five miles away. Within the half-hour we had decanted him, much interested in motors, at the door of the sweetmeat shop, and drew up the road to await the verdict.

'Useful things cars,' said Madden, all man and no butler. 'If I'd had one when mine took sick she wouldn't have died.'

'How was it?' I asked.

'Croup. Mrs Madden was away. No-one knew what to do. I drove eight miles in a tax cart for the doctor. She was choked when we came back. This car'd ha' saved her. She'd have been close on ten now.'

'I'm sorry,' I said. 'I thought you were rather fond of children from what you told me going to the crossroads the other day.'

'Have you seen 'em again, Sir – this mornin'?'

'Yes, but they're well broke to cars. I couldn't get any of them within twenty yards of it.'

He looked at me carefully as a scout considers a stranger – not as a menial should lift his eyes to his divinely appointed superior.

'I wonder why,' he said just above the breath that he drew.

We waited on. A light wind from the sea wandered up and down the long lines of the woods, and the wayside grasses, whitened already with summer dust, rose and bowed in sallow waves.

A woman, wiping the suds off her arms, came out of the cottage next the sweetmeat shop.

'I've be'n listenin' in de back-yard,' she said cheerily. 'He says Arthur's unaccountable bad. Did ye hear him shruck just now? Unaccountable bad. I reckon t'will come Jenny's turn to walk in de wood nex' week along, Mr Madden.'

'Excuse me, Sir, but your lap-robe is slipping,' said Madden deferentially. The woman started, dropped a curtsey, and hurried away.

'What does she mean by "walking in the wood"?' I asked.

'It must be some saying they use hereabouts. I'm from Norfolk myself,' said Madden. 'They're an independent lot in this county. She took you for a chauffeur, Sir.'

I saw the Doctor come out of the cottage followed by a draggle-tailed wench who clung to his arm as though he could make treaty for her with Death. 'Dat sort,' she wailed – 'dey're just as much to us dat has 'em as if dey was lawful born. Just as much – just as much! An' God he'd be just as pleased if you saved 'un, Doctor. Don't take it from me. Miss Florence will tell ye de very same. Don't leave 'im, Doctor!'

'I know. I know,' said the man, 'but he'll be quiet for a while now. We'll get the nurse and the medicine as fast as we can.' He signalled me to come forward with the car, and I strove not to be privy to what followed; but I saw the girl's face, blotched and frozen with grief, and I felt the hand without a ring clutching at my knees when we moved away.

The Doctor was a man of some humour, for I remember he claimed my car under the Oath of Aesculapius, and used it and me without mercy. First we convoyed Mrs Madehurst and the blind woman to wait by the sickbed till the nurse should come. Next we invaded a neat county town for prescriptions (the Doctor said the trouble was cerebro-spinal meningitis), and when the County Institute, banked and flanked with scared market cattle, reported itself out of nurses for the moment we literally flung ourselves loose upon the county. We conferred with the owners of great houses – magnates at the ends of overarching avenues whose big-boned womenfolk strode away from their tea-tables to listen to the imperious Doctor. At last a white-haired lady sitting under a cedar of Lebanon and surrounded by a court of magnificent Borzois – all hostile to motors – gave the Doctor, who received them as from a princess, written orders which we bore many miles at top speed, through a park, to a French nunnery, where we took over in exchange a pallid-faced and trembling Sister. She knelt at the bottom of the *tonneau* telling her beads without pause till, by short cuts of the Doctor's invention, we had her to the sweetmeat shop once more. It was a long afternoon crowded with mad episodes that rose and dissolved like the dust of our wheels; cross-sections of remote and incomprehensible lives through which we raced at right angles; and I went home in the dusk, wearied out, to dream of the clashing horns of cattle; round-eyed nuns walking in a garden of graves; pleasant tea-parties beneath shaded trees; the carbolic-scented, grey-painted corridors of the County Institute; the steps of shy children in the wood, and the hands that clung to my knees as the motor began to move.

* * *

I had intended to return in a day or two, but it pleased Fate to hold me from that side of the county, on many pretexts, till the elder and the wild rose had fruited. There came at last a brilliant day, swept clear from the south-west, that brought the hills within hand's reach – a day of unstable airs and high filmy clouds. Through no merit of my own I was free, and set the car for the third time on that known road. As I reached the crest of the Downs I felt the soft air change, saw it glaze under the sun; and, looking down at the sea, in that instant beheld the blue of the Channel turn through polished silver and dulled steel to dingy pewter. A laden collier hugging the coast steered outward for deeper water and, across copper-coloured haze, I saw sails rise one by one on the anchored fishing-fleet. In a deep dene behind me an eddy of sudden wind drummed through sheltered oaks, and spun aloft the first-day sample of autumn leaves. When I reached the beach road the sea-fog fumed over the brickfields, and the tide was telling all the groynes of the gale beyond Ushant. In less than an hour summer England vanished in chill grey. We were again the shut island of the North, all the ships of the world bellowing at our perilous gates; and between their outcries ran the piping of bewildered gulls. My cap dripped moisture, the folds of the rug held it in pools or sluiced it away in runnels, and the salt-rime stuck to my lips.

Inland the smell of autumn loaded the thickened fog among the trees, and the drip became a continuous shower. Yet the late flowers – mallow of the wayside, scabious of the field, and dahlia of the garden – showed gay in the mist, and beyond the sea's breath there was little sign of decay in the leaf. Yet in the villages the house doors were all open, and bare-legged, bare-headed children sat at ease on the damp doorsteps to shout 'pip-pip' at the stranger.

I made bold to call at the sweetmeat shop, where Mrs Madehurst met me with a fat woman's hospitable tears. Jenny's child, she said, had died two days after the nun had come. It was, she felt, best out of the way, even though insurance offices, for reasons which she did not pretend to follow, would not willingly insure such stray lives. 'Not but what Jenny didn't tend to Arthur as though he'd come all proper at de end of de first year – like Jenny herself.' Thanks to Miss Florence, the child had been buried with a pomp which, in Mrs Madehurst's opinion, more than covered the small irregularity of its birth. She described the coffin, within and without, the glass hearse, and the evergreen lining of the grave.

'But how's the mother?' I asked.

'Jenny? Oh, she'll get over it. I've felt dat way with one or two o' my own. She'll get over. She's walkin' in de wood now.'

'In this weather?'

Mrs Madehurst looked at me with narrowed eyes across the counter.

'I dunno but it opens de 'eart like. Yes, it opens de 'eart. Dat's where losin' and bearin' comes so alike in de long run, we do say.'

Now the wisdom of the old wives is greater than that of all the Fathers, and this last oracle sent me thinking so extendedly as I went up the road, that I nearly ran over a woman and a child at the wooded corner by the lodge gates of the House Beautiful.

'Awful weather!' I cried, as I slowed dead for the turn.

'Not so bad,' she answered placidly out of the fog. 'Mine's used to 'un. You'll find yours indoors, I reckon.'

Indoors, Madden received me with professional courtesy, and kind enquiries for the health of the motor, which he would put under cover.

I waited in a still, nut-brown hall, pleasant with late flowers and warmed with a delicious wood fire – a place of good influence and great peace. (Men and women may sometimes, after great effort, achieve a creditable lie; but the house, which is their temple, cannot say anything save the truth of those who have lived in it.) A child's cart and a doll lay on the black-and-white floor, where a rug had been kicked back. I felt that the children had only just hurried away – to hide themselves, most like – in the many turns of the great adzed staircase that climbed statelily out of the hall, or to crouch at gaze behind the lions and roses of the carven gallery above. Then I heard her voice above me, singing as the blind sing – from the soul –

> 'In the pleasant orchard-closes,'

and all my early summer came back at the call.

> 'In the pleasant orchard-closes,
>   God bless all our gains say we –
> But may God bless all our losses,
>   Better suits with our degree,'

she dropped the marring fifth line, and repeated –

> 'Better suits with our degree!'

I saw her lean over the gallery, her linked hands white as pearl against the oak.

'Is that you – from the other side of the county?' she called.

'Yes, me – from the other side of the county,' I answered laughing.

'What a long time before you had to come here again.' She ran down the stairs, one hand lightly touching the broad rail. 'It's two months and four days. Summer's gone!'

'I meant to come before, but Fate prevented.'

'I knew it. Please do something to that fire. They won't let me play with it, but I can feel it's behaving badly. Hit it!'

I looked on either side of the deep fireplace, and found but a half-charred hedge-stake with which I punched a black log into flame.

'It never goes out, day or night,' she said, as though explaining. 'In case anyone comes in with cold toes, you see.'

'It's even lovelier inside than it was out,' I murmured. The red light poured itself along the age-polished dusky panels till the Tudor roses and lions of the gallery took colour and motion. An old eagle-topped convex mirror gathered the picture into its mysterious heart, distorting afresh the distorted shadows, and curving the gallery lines into the curves of a ship. The day was shutting down in half a gale as the fog turned to stringy scud. Through the uncurtained mullions of

the broad window I could see valiant horsemen of the lawn rear and
recover against the wind that taunted them with legions of dead
leaves. 'Yes, it must be beautiful,' she said. 'Would you like to go
over it? There's still light enough upstairs.'

I followed her up the unflinching, wagon-wide staircase to the
gallery whence opened the thin fluted Elizabethan doors.

'Feel how they put the latch low down for the sake of the children.'
She swung a light door inward.

'By the way, where are they?' I asked. 'I haven't even heard them
today.'

She did not answer at once. Then, 'I can only hear them,' she
replied softly. 'This is one of their rooms – everything ready, you see.'

She pointed into a heavily-timbered room. There were little low
gate tables and children's chairs. A doll's house, its hooked front half
open, faced a great dappled rocking-horse, from whose padded saddle
it was but a child's scramble to the broad window-seat overlooking the
lawn. A toy gun lay in a corner beside a gilt wooden cannon.

'Surely they've only just gone,' I whispered. In the failing light a
door creaked cautiously. I heard the rustle of a frock and the patter of
feet – quick feet through a room beyond.

'I heard that,' she cried triumphantly. 'Did you? Children, O
children, where are you?'

The voice filled the walls that held it lovingly to the last perfect
note, but there came no answering shout such as I had heard in the
garden. We hurried on from room to oak-floored room; up a step
here, down three steps there; among a maze of passages; always
mocked by our quarry. One might as well have tried to work an
unstopped warren with a single ferret. There were boltholes innumerable – recesses in walls, embrasures of deep slitten windows now
darkened, whence they could start up behind us; and abandoned
fireplaces, six feet deep in the masonry, as well as the tangle of
communicating doors. Above all, they had the twilight for their
helper in our game. I had caught one or two joyous chuckles of
evasion, and once or twice had seen the silhouette of a child's frock
against some darkening window at the end of a passage; but we
returned empty-handed to the gallery, just as a middle-aged woman
was setting a lamp in its niche.

'No, I haven't seen her either this evening, Miss Florence,' I heard
her say, 'but that Turpin he says he wants to see you about his shed.'

'Oh, Mr Turpin must want to see me very badly. Tell him to come
to the hall, Mrs Madden.'

I looked down into the hall whose only light was the dulled fire, and deep in the shadow I saw them at last. They must have slipped down while we were in the passages, and now thought themselves perfectly hidden behind an old gilt leather screen. By child's law, my fruitless chase was as good as an introduction, but since I had taken so much trouble I resolved to force them to come forward later by the simple trick, which children detest, of pretending not to notice them. They lay close, in a little huddle, no more than shadows except when a quick flame betrayed an outline.

'And now we'll have some tea,' she said. 'I believe I ought to have offered it you at first, but one doesn't arrive at manners somehow when one lives alone and is considered – h'm – peculiar.' Then with very pretty scorn, 'would you like a lamp to see to eat by?'

'The firelight's much pleasanter, I think.' We descended into that delicious gloom and Madden brought tea.

I took my chair in the direction of the screen ready to surprise or be surprised as the game should go, and at her permission, since a hearth is always sacred, bent forward to play with the fire.

'Where do you get these beautiful short faggots from?' I asked idly. 'Why, they are tallies!'

'Of course,' she said. 'As I can't read or write I'm driven back on the early English tally for my accounts. Give me one and I'll tell you what it meant.'

I passed her an unburned hazel-tally, about a foot long, and she ran her thumb down the nicks.

'This is the milk-record for the home farm for the month of April last year, in gallons,' said she. 'I don't know what I should have done without tallies. An old forester of mine taught me the system. It's out of date now for everyone else; but my tenants respect it. One of them's coming now to see me. Oh, it doesn't matter. He has no business here out of office hours. He's a greedy, ignorant man – very greedy or – he wouldn't come here after dark.'

'Have you much land then?'

'Only a couple of hundred acres in hand, thank goodness. The other six hundred are nearly all let to folk who knew my folk before me, but this Turpin is quite a new man – and a highway robber.'

'But are you sure I shan't be – ?'

'Certainly not. You have the right. He hasn't any children.'

'Ah, the children!' I said, and slid my low chair back till it nearly touched the screen that hid them. 'I wonder whether they'll come out for me.'

There was a murmur of voices – Madden's and a deeper note – at the low, dark side door, and a ginger-headed, canvas-gaitered giant of the unmistakable tenant farmer type stumbled or was pushed in.

'Come to the fire, Mr Turpin,' she said.

'If – if you please, Miss, I'll – I'll be quite as well by the door.' He clung to the latch as he spoke like a frightened child. Of a sudden I realised that he was in the grip of some almost overpowering fear.

'Well?'

'About that new shed for the young stock – that was all. These first autumn storms settin' in . . . but I'll come again, Miss.' His teeth did not chatter much more than the door latch.

'I think not,' she answered levelly. 'The new shed – m'm. What did my agent write you on the 15th?'

'I – fancied p'raps that if I came to see you – ma – man to man like, Miss. But – '

His eyes rolled into every corner of the room wide with horror. He half opened the door through which he had entered, but I noticed it shut again – from without and firmly.

'He wrote what I told him,' she went on. 'You are overstocked already. Dunnett's Farm never carried more than fifty bullocks – even in Mr Wright's time. And *he* used cake. You've sixty-seven and you don't cake. You've broken the lease in that respect. You're dragging the heart out of the farm.'

'I'm – I'm getting some minerals – superphosphates – next week. I've as good as ordered a truckload already. I'll go down to the station tomorrow about 'em. Then I can come and see you man to man like, Miss, in the daylight . . . That gentleman's not going away, is he?' He almost shrieked.

I had only slid the chair a little further back, reaching behind me to tap on the leather of the screen, but he jumped like a rat.

'No. Please attend to me, Mr Turpin.' She turned in her chair and faced him with his back to the door. It was an old and sordid little piece of scheming that she forced from him – his plea for the new cowshed at his landlady's expense, that he might with the covered manure pay his next year's rent out of the valuation after, as she made clear, he had bled the enriched pastures to the bone. I could not but admire the intensity of his greed, when I saw him outfacing for its sake whatever terror it was that ran wet on his forehead.

I ceased to tap the leather – was, indeed, calculating the cost of the shed – when I felt my relaxed hand taken and turned softly between the soft hands of a child. So at last I had triumphed. In a moment I would turn and acquaint myself with those quick-footed wanderers . . .

The little brushing kiss fell in the centre of my palm – as a gift on which the fingers were, once, expected to close: as the all-faithful half-reproachful signal of a waiting child not used to neglect even when grown-ups were busiest – a fragment of the mute code devised very long ago.

Then I knew. And it was as though I had known from the first day when I looked across the lawn at the high window.

I heard the door shut. The woman turned to me in silence, and I felt that she knew.

What time passed after this I cannot say. I was roused by the fall of a log, and mechanically rose to put it back. Then I returned to my place in the chair very close to the screen.

'Now you understand,' she whispered, across the packed shadows.

'Yes, I understand – now. Thank you.'

'I – I only hear them.' She bowed her head in her hands. 'I have no right, you know – no other right. I have neither borne nor lost – neither borne nor lost!'

'Be very glad then,' said I, for my soul was torn open within me.

'Forgive me!'

She was still, and I went back to my sorrow and my joy.

'It was because I loved them so,' she said at last, brokenly. '*That* was why it was, even from the first – even before I knew that they – they were all I should ever have. And I loved them so!'

She stretched out her arms to the shadows and the shadows within the shadow.

'They came because I loved them – because I needed them. I – I must have made them come. Was that wrong, think you?'

'No – no.'

'I – I grant you that the toys and – and all that sort of thing were nonsense, but – but I used to so hate empty rooms myself when I was little.' She pointed to the gallery. 'And the passages all empty. . . . And how could I ever bear the garden door shut? Suppose – '

'Don't! For pity's sake, don't!' I cried. The twilight had brought a cold rain with gusty squalls that plucked at the leaded windows.

'And the same thing with keeping the fire in all night. *I* don't think it so foolish – do you?'

I looked at the broad brick hearth, saw, through tears I believe, that there was no unpassable iron on or near it, and bowed my head.

'I did all that and lots of other things – just to make believe. Then they came. I heard them, but I didn't know that they were not mine by right till Mrs Madden told me – '

'The butler's wife? What?'

'One of them – I heard – she saw. And knew. Hers! *Not* for me. I didn't know at first. Perhaps I was jealous. Afterwards, I began to understand that it was only because I loved them, not because . . . Oh, you *must* bear or lose,' she said piteously. 'There is no other way – and yet they love me. They must! Don't they?'

There was no sound in the room except the lapping voices of the fire, but we two listened intently, and she at least took comfort from what she heard. She recovered herself and half rose. I sat still in my chair by the screen.

'Don't think me a wretch to whine about myself like this, but – but I'm all in the dark, you know, and *you* can see.'

In truth I could see, and my vision confirmed me in my resolve, though that was like the very parting of spirit and flesh. Yet a little longer I would stay since it was the last time.

'You think it is wrong, then?' she cried sharply, though I had said nothing.

'Not for you. A thousand times no. For you it is right . . . I am grateful to you beyond words. For me it would be wrong. For me only . . . '

'Why?' she said, but passed her hand before her face as she had done at our second meeting in the wood. 'Oh, I see,' she went on simply as a child. 'For you it would be wrong.' Then with a little indrawn laugh, 'and, d'you remember, I called you lucky – once – at first. You who must never come here again!'

She left me to sit a little longer by the screen, and I heard the sound of her feet die out along the gallery above.

In the Same Boat

'A throbbing vein,' said Dr Gilbert soothingly, 'is the mother of delusion.'

'Then how do you account for my knowing when the thing is due?' Conroy's voice rose almost to a break.

'Of course, but you should have consulted a doctor before using – palliatives.'

'It was driving me mad. And now I can't give them up.'

'Not so bad as that! One doesn't form fatal habits at twenty-five. Think again. Were you ever frightened as a child?'

'I don't remember. It began when I was a boy.'

'With or without the spasm? By the way, do you mind describing the spasm again?'

'Well,' said Conroy, twisting in the chair, 'I'm no musician, but suppose you were a violin-string – vibrating – and someone put his finger on you? As if a finger were put on the naked soul! Awful!'

'So's indigestion – so's nightmare – while it lasts.'

'But the horror afterwards knocks me out for days. And the waiting for it . . . and then this drug habit! It can't go on!' He shook as he spoke, and the chair creaked.

'My dear fellow,' said the doctor, 'when you're older you'll know what burdens the best of us carry. A fox to every Spartan.'

'That doesn't help *me*. I can't! I can't!' cried Conroy, and burst into tears.

'Don't apologise,' said Gilbert, when the paroxysm ended. 'I'm used to people coming a little – unstuck in this room.'

'It's those tabloids!' Conroy stamped his foot feebly as he blew his nose. 'They've knocked me out. I used to be fit once. Oh, I've tried exercise and everything. But – if one sits down for a minute when it's due – even at four in the morning – it runs up behind one.'

'Ye-es. Many things come in the quiet of the morning. You always know when the visitation is due?'

'What would I give not to be sure!' he sobbed.

'We'll put that aside for the moment. I'm thinking of a case where what we'll call anaemia of the brain was masked (I don't say cured) by vibration. He couldn't sleep, or thought he couldn't, but a steamer voyage and the thump of the screw – '

'A steamer? After what I've told you!' Conroy almost shrieked. 'I'd sooner . . . '

'Of course *not* a steamer in your case, but a long railway journey the next time you think it will trouble you. It sounds absurd, but – '

'I'd try anything. I nearly have,' Conroy sighed.

'Nonsense! I've given you a tonic that will clear *that* notion from your head. Give the train a chance, and don't begin the journey by bucking yourself up with tabloids. Take them along, but hold them in reserve – in reserve.'

'D'you think I've self-control enough, after what you've heard?' said Conroy.

Dr Gilbert smiled. 'Yes. After what I've seen,' he glanced round the room, 'I have no hesitation in saying you have quite as much self-control as many other people. I'll write you later about your journey. Meantime, the tonic,' and he gave some general directions before Conroy left.

An hour later Dr Gilbert hurried to the links, where the others of his regular weekend game awaited him. It was a rigid round, played as usual at the trot, for the tension of the week lay as heavy on the two King's Counsels and Sir John Chartres as on Gilbert. The lawyers were old enemies of the Admiralty Court, and Sir John of the frosty eyebrows and Abernethy manner was bracketed with, but before, Rutherford Gilbert among nerve-specialists.

At the Clubhouse afterwards the lawyers renewed their squabble over a tangled collision case, and the doctors as naturally compared professional matters.

'Lies – all lies,' said Sir John, when Gilbert had told him Conroy's trouble. '*Post hoc, propter hoc*. The man or woman who drugs is *ipso facto* a liar. You've no imagination.'

'Pity you haven't a little – occasionally.'

'I have believed a certain type of patient in my time. It's always the same. For reasons not given in the consulting room they take to the drug. Certain symptoms follow. They will swear to you, and believe it, that they took the drug to mask the symptoms. What does your man use? Najdolene? I thought so. I had practically the duplicate of your case last Thursday. Same old Najdolene – same old lie.'

'Tell me the symptoms, and I'll draw my own inferences, Johnnie.'

'Symptoms! The girl was rank poisoned with Najdolene. Ramping, stamping possession. Gad, I thought she'd have the chandelier down.'

'Mine came unstuck too, and he has the physique of a bull,' said Gilbert. 'What delusions had yours?'

'Faces – faces with mildew on them. In any other walk of life we'd call it the Horrors. She told me, of course, she took the drugs to mask the faces. *Post hoc, propter hoc* again. All liars!'

'What's that?' said the senior K.C. quickly. 'Sounds professional.'

'Go away! Not for you, Sandy.' Sir John turned a shoulder against him and walked with Gilbert in the chill evening.

To Conroy in his chambers came, one week later, this letter:

DEAR MR CONROY – If your plan of a night's trip on the 17th still holds good, and you have no particular destination in view, you could do me a kindness. A Miss Henschil, in whom I am interested, goes down to the West by the 10.8 from Waterloo (Number 3 platform) on that night. She is not exactly an invalid, but, like so many of us, a little shaken in her nerves. Her maid, of course, accompanies her, but if I knew you were in the same train it would be an additional source of strength. Will you please write and let me know whether the 10.8 from Waterloo, Number 3 platform, on the 17th, suits you, and I will meet you there? Don't forget my caution, and keep up the tonic.

                    Yours sincerely,
                              L. RUTHERFORD GILBERT

'He knows I'm scarcely fit to look after myself,' was Conroy's thought. 'And he wants me to look after a woman!'

Yet, at the end of half an hour's irresolution, he accepted.

Now Conroy's trouble, which had lasted for years, was this.

On a certain night, while he lay between sleep and wake, he would be overtaken by a long shuddering sigh, which he learned to know was the sign that his brain had once more conceived its horror, and in time – in due time – would bring it forth.

Drugs could so well veil that horror that it shuffled along no worse than as a freezing dream in a procession of disorderly dreams; but over the return of the event drugs had no control. Once that sigh had passed his lips the thing was inevitable, and through the days granted before its rebirth he walked in torment. For the first two years he had striven to fend it off by distractions, but neither exercise nor drink availed. Then he had come to the tabloids of

the excellent M. Najdol. These guarantee, on the label, 'Refreshing
and absolutely natural sleep to the soul-weary.' They are carried in
a case with a spring which presses one scented tabloid to the end of
the tube, whence it can be lipped off in stroking the moustache or
adjusting the veil.

Three years of M. Najdol's preparations do not fit a man for
many careers. His friends, who knew he did not drink, assumed that
Conroy had strained his heart through valiant outdoor exercises,
and Conroy had with some care invented an imaginary doctor,
symptoms, and regimen, which he discussed with them and with his
mother in Hereford. She maintained that he would grow out of it,
and recommended *nux vomica*.

When at last Conroy faced a real doctor, it was, he hoped, to be
saved from suicide by a strait-waistcoat. Yet Dr Gilbert had but
given him more drugs – a tonic, for instance, that would couple
railway carriages – and had advised a night in the train. Not alone
the horrors of a railway journey (for which a man who dare keep no
servant must e'en pack, label, and address his own bag), but the
necessity for holding himself in hand before a stranger 'a little
shaken in her nerves'.

He spent a long forenoon packing, because when he assembled and
counted things his mind slid off to the hours that remained of the day
before his night, and he found himself counting minutes aloud. At
such times the injustice of his fate would drive him to revolts which
no servant should witness, but on this evening Dr Gilbert's tonic
held him fairly calm while he put up his patent razors.

Waterloo Station shook him into real life. The change for his
ticket needed concentration, if only to prevent shillings and pence
turning into minutes at the booking-office; and he spoke quickly to a
porter about the disposition of his bag. The old 10.8 from Waterloo
to the West was an all-night caravan that halted, in the interests of
the milk traffic, at almost every station.

Dr Gilbert stood by the door of the one composite corridor-coach;
an older and stouter man behind him. 'So glad you're here!' he cried.
'Let me get your ticket.'

'Certainly not,' Conroy answered. 'I got it myself – long ago. My
bag's in too,' he added proudly.

'I beg your pardon. Miss Henschil's here. I'll introduce you.'

'But – but,' he stammered – 'think of the state I'm in. If anything
happens I shall collapse.'

'Not you. You'd rise to the occasion like a bird. And as for the self-control you were talking of the other day' – Gilbert swung him round – 'look!'

A young man in an ulster over a silk-faced frock-coat stood by the carriage window, weeping shamelessly.

'Oh, but that's only drink,' Conroy said. 'I haven't had one of my – my things since lunch.'

'Excellent!' said Gilbert. 'I knew I could depend on you. Come along. Wait for a minute, Chartres.'

A tall woman, veiled, sat by the far window. She bowed her head as the doctor murmured Conroy knew not what. Then he disappeared and the inspector came for tickets.

'My maid – next compartment,' she said slowly.

Conroy showed his ticket, but in returning it to the sleeve-pocket of his ulster the little silver Najdolene case slipped from his glove and fell to the floor. He snatched it up as the moving train flung him into his seat.

'How nice!' said the woman. She leisurely lifted her veil, un-buttoned the first button of her left glove, and pressed out from its palm a Najdolene-case.

'Don't!' said Conroy, not realising he had spoken.

'I beg your pardon.' The deep voice was measured, even, and low. Conroy knew what made it so.

'I said "don't"! He wouldn't like you to do it!'

'No, he would not.' She held the tube with its ever-presented tabloid between finger and thumb. 'But aren't you one of the – ah – "soul-weary" too?'

'That's why. Oh, please don't! Not at first. I – I haven't had one since morning. You – you'll set me off!'

'You? Are you so far gone as that?'

He nodded, pressing his palms together. The train jolted through Vauxhall points, and was welcomed with the clang of empty milk-cans for the West.

After long silence she lifted her great eyes, and, with an innocence that would have deceived any sound man, asked Conroy to call her maid to bring her a forgotten book.

Conroy shook his head. 'No. Our sort can't read. Don't!'

'Were you sent to watch me?' The voice never changed.

'Me? I need a keeper myself much more – *this* night of all!'

'This night? Have you a night, then? They disbelieved *me* when I told them of mine.' She leaned back and laughed, always slowly. 'Aren't doctors stu-upid? They don't know.'

She leaned her elbow on her knee, lifted her veil that had fallen, and, chin in hand, stared at him. He looked at her – till his eyes were blurred with tears.

'Have *I* been there, think you?' she said.

'Surely – surely,' Conroy answered, for he had well seen the fear and the horror that lived behind the heavy-lidded eyes, the fine tracing on the broad forehead, and the guard set about the desirable mouth.

'Then – suppose we have one – just one apiece? I've gone without since this afternoon.'

He put up his hand, and would have shouted, but his voice broke.

'Don't! Can't you see that it helps me to help you to keep it off? Don't let's both go down together.'

'But I want one. It's a poor heart that never rejoices. Just one. It's my night.'

'It's mine – too. My sixty-fourth, fifth, sixth, seventh.' He shut his lips firmly against the tide of visualised numbers that threatened to carry him along.

'Ah, it's only my thirty-ninth.' She paused as he had done. 'I wonder if I shall last into the sixties . . . Talk to me or I shall go crazy. You're a man. You're the stronger vessel. Tell me when you went to pieces.'

'One, two, three, four, five, six, seven – eight – I beg your pardon.'

'Not in the least. I always pretend I've dropped a stitch of my knitting. I count the days till the last day, then the hours, then the minutes. Do you?'

'I don't think I've done very much else for the last – ' said Conroy, shivering, for the night was cold, with a chill he recognised.

'Oh, how comforting to find someone who can talk sense! It's not always the same date, is it?'

'What difference would that make?' He unbuttoned his ulster with a jerk. 'You're a sane woman. Can't you see the wicked – wicked – wicked' (dust flew from the padded arm-rest as he struck it) 'unfairness of it? What have *I* done?'

She laid her large hand on his shoulder very firmly.

'If you begin to think over that,' she said, 'you'll go to pieces and be ashamed. Tell me yours, and I'll tell you mine. Only be quiet – be quiet, lad, or you'll set me off!' She made shift to soothe him, though her chin trembled.

'Well,' said he at last, picking at the arm-rest between them, 'mine's nothing much, of course.'

'Don't be a fool! That's for doctors – and mothers.'

'It's Hell,' Conroy muttered. 'It begins on a steamer – on a stifling hot night. I come out of my cabin. I pass through the saloon where the stewards have rolled up the carpets, and the boards are bare and hot and soapy.'

'I've travelled too,' she said.

'Ah! I come on deck. I walk down a covered alleyway. Butcher's meat, bananas, oil, that sort of smell.'

Again she nodded.

'It's a lead-coloured steamer, and the sea's lead-coloured. Perfectly smooth sea – perfectly still ship, except for the engines running, and her waves going off in lines and lines and lines – dull grey. All this time I know something's going to happen.'

'*I* know. Something's going to happen,' she whispered.

'Then I hear a thud in the engine-room. Then the noise of machinery falling down – like fire-irons – and then two most awful yells. They're more like hoots, and I know – I know while I listen – that it means that two men have died as they hooted. It was their last breath hooting out of them – in most awful pain. Do you understand?'

'I ought to. Go on.'

'That's the first part. Then I hear bare feet running along the alleyway. One of the scalded men comes up behind me and says quite distinctly, "My friend! All is lost!" Then he taps me on the shoulder and I hear him drop down dead.' He panted and wiped his forehead.

'So that is your night?' she said.

'That is my night. It comes every few weeks – so many days after I get what I call sentence. Then I begin to count.'

'Get sentence? D'you mean *this*?' She half closed her eyes, drew a deep breath, and shuddered. ' "Notice" I call it. Sir John thought it was all lies.'

She had unpinned her hat and thrown it on the seat opposite, showing the immense mass of her black hair, rolled low in the nape of the columnar neck and looped over the left ear. But Conroy had no eyes except for her grave eyes.

'Listen now!' said she. 'I walk down a road, a white sandy road near the sea. There are broken fences on either side, and Men come and look at me over them.'

'Just men? Do they speak?'

'They try to. Their faces are all mildewy – eaten away,' and she hid her face for an instant with her left hand. 'It's the Faces – the Faces!'

'Yes. Like my two hoots. I know.'

'Ah! But the place itself – the bareness – and the glitter and the salt smells, and the wind blowing the sand! The Men run after me and I run . . . I know what's coming too. One of them touches me.'

'Yes! What comes then? We've both shirked that.'

'One awful shock – not palpitation, but shock, shock, shock!'

'As though your soul were being stopped – as you'd stop a finger-bowl humming?' he said.

'Just that,' she answered. 'One's very soul – the soul that one lives by – stopped. So!'

She drove her thumb deep into the arm-rest. 'And now,' she whined to him, 'now that we've stirred each other up this way, mightn't we have just one?'

'No,' said Conroy, shaking. 'Let's hold on. We're past' – he peered out of the black windows – 'Woking. There's the Necropolis. How long till dawn?'

'Oh, cruel long yet. If one dozes for a minute, it catches one.'

'And how d'you find that this' – he tapped the palm of his glove – 'helps you?'

'It covers up the thing from being too real – if one takes enough – you know. Only – only – one loses everything else. I've been no more than a bogie-girl for two years. What would you give to be real again? This lying's such a nuisance.'

'One must protect oneself – and there's one's mother to think of,' he answered.

'True. I hope allowances are made for us somewhere. Our burden – can you hear? – our burden is heavy enough.'

She rose, towering into the roof of the carriage. Conroy's ungentle grip pulled her back.

'Now *you* are foolish. Sit down,' said he.

'But the cruelty of it! Can't you see it? Don't you feel it? Let's take one now – before I –'

'Sit down!' cried Conroy, and the sweat stood again on his forehead. He had fought through a few nights, and had been defeated on more, and he knew the rebellion that flares beyond control to exhaustion.

She smoothed her hair and dropped back, but for a while her head and throat moved with the sickening motion of a captured wryneck.

'Once,' she said, spreading out her hands, 'I ripped my counter-pane from end to end. That takes strength. I had it then. I've little now. "All dorn", as my little niece says. And you, lad?'

' "All dorn"! Let me keep your case for you till the morning.'

'But the cold feeling is beginning.'

'Lend it me, then.'

'And the drag down my right side. I shan't be able to move in a minute.'

'I can scarcely lift my arm myself,' said Conroy. 'We're in for it.'

'Then why are you so foolish? You know it'll be easier if we have only one – only one apiece.'

She was lifting the case to her mouth. With tremendous effort Conroy caught it. The two moved like jointed dolls, and when their hands met it was as wood on wood.

'You must – not!' said Conroy. His jaws stiffened, and the cold climbed from his feet up.

'Why – must – I – not?' She repeated the words idiotically.

Conroy could only shake his head, while he bore down on the hand and the case in it.

Her speech went from her altogether. The wonderful lips rested half over the even teeth, the breath was in the nostrils only, the eyes dulled, the face set grey, and through the glove the hand struck like ice.

Presently her soul came back and stood behind her eyes – only thing that had life in all that place – stood and looked for Conroy's soul. He too was fettered in every limb, but somewhere at an immense distance he heard his heart going about its work as the engine-room carries on through and beneath the all but over-whelming wave. His one hope, he knew, was not to lose the eyes that clung to his, because there was an Evil abroad which would possess him if he looked aside by a hair-breadth.

The rest was darkness through which some distant planet spun while cymbals clashed. (Beyond Farnborough the 10.8 rolls out many empty milk-cans at every halt.) Then a body came to life with intolerable pricklings. Limb by limb, after agonies of terror, that body returned to him, steeped in most perfect physical weariness such as follows a long day's rowing. He saw the heavy lids droop over her eyes – the watcher behind them departed – and, his soul sinking into assured peace, Conroy slept.

Light on his eyes and a salt breath roused him without shock. Her hand still held his. She slept, forehead down upon it, but the movement of his waking waked her too, and she sneezed like a child.

'I – I think it's morning,' said Conroy.

'And nothing has happened! Did you see your Men? I didn't see my Faces. Does it mean we've escaped? Did – did you take any after I went to sleep? I'll swear *I* didn't,' she stammered.

'No, there wasn't any need. We've slept through it.'

'No need! Thank God! There was no need! Oh, look!'

The train was running under red cliffs along a sea-wall washed by waves that were colourless in the early light. Southward the sun rose mistily upon the Channel.

She leaned out of the window and breathed to the bottom of her lungs, while the wind wrenched down her dishevelled hair and blew it below her waist.

'Well!' she said with splendid eyes. 'Aren't you still waiting for something to happen?'

'No. Not till next time. We've been let off,' Conroy answered, breathing as deeply as she.

'Then we ought to say our prayers.'

'What nonsense! Someone will see us.'

'We needn't kneel. Stand up and say "Our Father". We *must*!'

It was the first time since childhood that Conroy had prayed. They laughed hysterically when a curve threw them against an arm-rest.

'Now for breakfast!' she cried. 'My maid – Nurse Blaber – has the basket and things. It'll be ready in twenty minutes. Oh! Look at my hair!' and she went out laughing.

Conroy's first discovery, made without fumbling or counting letters on taps, was that the London and South Western's allowance of washing-water is inadequate. He used every drop, rioting in the cold tingle on neck and arms. To shave in a moving train balked him, but the next halt gave him a chance, which, to his own surprise, he took. As he stared at himself in the mirror he smiled and nodded. There were points about this person with the clear, if sunken, eye and the almost uncompressed mouth. But when he bore his bag back to his compartment, the weight of it on a limp arm humbled that new pride.

'My friend,' he said, half aloud, 'you go into training. You're putty.'

She met him in the spare compartment, where her maid had laid breakfast.

'By Jove!' he said, halting at the doorway, 'I hadn't realised how beautiful you were!'

'The same to you, lad. Sit down. I could eat a horse.'

'I shouldn't,' said the maid quietly. 'The less you eat the better.' She was a small, freckled woman, with light fluffy hair and pale-blue eyes that looked through all veils.

'This is Miss Blaber,' said Miss Henschil. 'He's one of the soul-weary too, Nursey.'

'I know it. But when one has just given it up a full meal doesn't agree. That's why I've only brought you bread and butter.'

She went out quietly, and Conroy reddened.

'We're still children, you see,' said Miss Henschil. 'But I'm well enough to feel some shame of it. D'you take sugar?'

They starved together heroically, and Nurse Blaber was good enough to signify approval when she came to clear away.

'Nursey?' Miss Henschil insinuated, and flushed.

'Do you smoke?' said the nurse coolly to Conroy.

'I haven't in years. Now you mention it, I think I'd like a cigarette – or something.'

'I used to. D'you think it would keep me quiet?' Miss Henschil said.

'Perhaps. Try these.' The nurse handed them her cigarette-case.

'Don't take anything else,' she commanded, and went away with the tea-basket.

'Good!' grunted Conroy, between mouthfuls of tobacco.

'Better than nothing,' said Miss Henschil; but for a while they felt ashamed, yet with the comfort of children punished together.

'Now,' she whispered, 'who were you when you were a man?'

Conroy told her, and in return she gave him her history. It delighted them both to deal once more in worldly concerns – families, names, places, and dates – with a person of understanding.

She came, she said, of Lancashire folk – wealthy cotton-spinners, who still kept the broadened *a* and slurred aspirate of the old stock. She lived with an old masterful mother in an opulent world north of Lancaster Gate, where people in Society gave parties at a Mecca called the Langham Hotel.

She herself had been launched into Society there, and the flowers at the ball had cost eighty-seven pounds; but, being reckoned peculiar, she had made few friends among her own sex. She had attracted many men, for she was a beauty – *the* beauty, in fact, of Society, she said.

She spoke utterly without shame or reticence, as a life-prisoner tells his past to a fellow-prisoner; and Conroy nodded across the smoke-rings.

'Do you remember when you got into the carriage?' she asked. '(Oh, I wish I had some knitting!) Did you notice aught, lad?'

Conroy thought back. It was ages since. 'Wasn't there someone outside the door – crying?' he asked.

'He's – he's the little man I was engaged to,' she said. 'But I made him break it off. I told him 'twas no good. But he won't, yo' see.'

'*That* fellow? Why, he doesn't come up to your shoulder.'

'That's naught to do with it. I think all the world of him. I'm a foolish wench' – her speech wandered as she settled herself cosily, one elbow on the arm-rest. 'We'd been engaged – I couldn't help that – and he worships the ground I tread on. But it's no use. I'm not responsible, you see. His two sisters are against it, though I've the money. They're right, but they think it's the dri-ink,' she drawled. 'They're Methody – the Skinners. You see, their grandfather that started the Patton Mills, he died o' the dri-ink.'

'I see,' said Conroy. The grave face before him under the lifted veil was troubled.

'George Skinner.' She breathed it softly. 'I'd make him a good wife, by God's gra-ace – if I could. But it's no use. I'm not responsible. But he'll not take "No" for an answer. I used to call him "Toots". He's of no consequence, yo' see.'

'That's in Dickens,' said Conroy, quite quickly. 'I haven't thought of Toots for years. He was at Doctor Blimber's.'

'And so – that's my trouble,' she concluded, ever so slightly wringing her hands. 'But I – don't you think – there's hope now?'

'Eh?' said Conroy. 'Oh yes! This is the first time I've turned my corner without help. With your help, I should say.'

'It'll come back, though.'

'Then shall we meet it in the same way? Here's my card. Write me your train, and we'll go together.'

'Yes. We must do that. But between times – when we want – ' She looked at her palm, the four fingers working on it. 'It's hard to give 'em up.'

'But think what we have gained already, and let me have the case to keep.'

She shook her head, and threw her cigarette out of the window. 'Not yet.'

'Then let's lend our cases to Nurse, and we'll get through today on cigarettes. I'll call her while we feel strong.'

She hesitated, but yielded at last, and Nurse accepted the offerings with a smile.

'*You'll* be all right,' she said to Miss Henschil. 'But if I were you' – to Conroy – 'I'd take strong exercise.'

When they reached their destination Conroy set himself to obey Nurse Blaber. He had no remembrance of that day, except one streak of blue sea to his left, gorse bushes to his right, and, before him, a coastguard's track marked with whitewashed stones that he

counted up to the far thousands. As he returned to the little town he
saw Miss Henschil on the beach below the cliffs. She kneeled at
Nurse Blaber's feet, weeping and pleading.

*   *   *

Twenty-five days later a telegram came to Conroy's rooms: NOTICE
GIVEN. WATERLOO AGAIN. TWENTY-FOURTH. That same evening he
was wakened by the shudder and the sigh that told him his sentence
had gone forth. Yet he reflected on his pillow that he had, in spite
of lapses, snatched something like three weeks of life, which included several rides on a horse before breakfast – the hour one
most craves Najdolene; five consecutive evenings on the river at
Hammersmith in a tub where he had well stretched the white arms
that passing crews mocked at; a game of rackets at his club; three
dinners, one small dance, and one human flirtation with a human
woman. More notable still, he had settled his month's accounts,
only once confusing petty cash with the days of grace allowed him.
Next morning he rode his hired beast in the park victoriously. He
saw Miss Henschil on horseback near Lancaster Gate, talking to a
young man at the railings.

She wheeled and cantered toward him.

'By Jove! How well you look!' he cried, without salutation. 'I didn't
know you rode.'

'I used to once,' she replied. 'I'm all soft now.'

They swept off together down the ride.

'Your beast pulls,' he said.

'Wa-ant him to. Gi-gives me something to think of. How've you
been?' she panted. 'I wish chemists' shops hadn't red lights.'

'Have you slipped out and bought some, then?'

'You don't know Nursey. Eh, but it's good to be on a horse again!
This chap cost me two hundred.'

'Then you've been swindled,' said Conroy.

'I know it, but it's no odds. I must go back to Toots and send him
away. He's neglecting his work for me.'

She swung her heavy-topped animal on his none too sound hocks.
'Sentence come, lad?'

'Yes. But I'm not minding it so much this time.'

'Waterloo, then – and God help us!' She thundered back to the
little frock-coated figure that waited faithfully near the gate.

Conroy felt the spring sun on his shoulders and trotted home.
That evening he went out with a man in a pair oar, and was rowed to

a standstill. But the other man owned he could not have kept the pace five minutes longer.

*　　*　　*

He carried his bag all down Number 3 platform at Waterloo, and hove it with one hand into the rack.

'Well done!' said Nurse Blaber, in the corridor. 'We've improved too.'

Dr Gilbert and an older man came out of the next compartment.

'Hallo!' said Gilbert. 'Why haven't you been to see me, Mr Conroy? Come under the lamp. Take off your hat. No – no. Sit, you young giant. Ve-ry good. Look here a minute, Johnnie.'

A little, round-bellied, hawk-faced person glared at him.

'Gilbert was right about the beauty of the beast,' he muttered. 'D'you keep it in your glove now?' he went on, and punched Conroy in the short ribs.

'No,' said Conroy meekly, but without coughing. 'Nowhere – on my honour! I've chucked it for good.'

'Wait till you are a sound man before you say *that*, Mr Conroy.' Sir John Chartres stumped out, saying to Gilbert in the corridor, 'It's all very fine, but the question is shall I or we "Sir Pandarus of Troy become", eh? We're bound to think of the children.'

'Have you been vetted?' said Miss Henschil, a few minutes after the train started. 'May I sit with you? I – I don't trust myself yet. I can't give up as easily as you can, seemingly.'

'Can't you? I never saw anyone so improved in a month.'

'Look here!' She reached across to the rack, single-handed lifted Conroy's bag, and held it at arm's length. 'I counted ten slowly. And I didn't think of hours or minutes,' she boasted.

'Don't remind me,' he cried.

'Ah! Now I've reminded myself. I wish I hadn't. Do you think it'll be easier for us tonight?'

'Oh, don't.' The smell of the carriage had brought back all his last trip to him, and Conroy moved uneasily.

'I'm sorry. I've brought some games,' she went on. 'Draughts and cards – but they all mean counting. I wish I'd brought chess, but I can't play chess. What can we do? Talk about something.'

'Well, how's Toots, to begin with?' said Conroy.

'Why? Did you see him on the platform?'

'No. Was he there? I didn't notice.'

'Oh yes. He doesn't understand. He's desperately jealous. I told him it doesn't matter. Will you please let me hold your hand? I believe I'm beginning to get the chill.'

'Toots ought to envy me,' said Conroy.

'He does. He paid you a high compliment the other night. He's taken to calling again – in spite of all they say.'

Conroy inclined his head. He felt cold, and knew surely he would be colder.

'He said,' she yawned. '(Beg your pardon.) He said he couldn't see how I could help falling in love with a man like you; and he called himself a damned little rat, and he beat his head on the piano last night.'

'The piano? You play, then?'

'Only to him. He thinks the world of my accomplishments. Then I told him I wouldn't have you if you were the last man on earth instead of only the best-looking – not with a million in each stocking.'

'No, not with a million in each stocking,' said Conroy vehemently. 'Isn't that odd?'

'I suppose so – to anyone who doesn't know. Well, where was I? Oh, George as good as told me I was deceiving him, and he wanted to go away without saying good-night. He hates standing a-tiptoe, but he must if I won't sit down.'

Conroy would have smiled, but the chill that foreran the coming of the Lier-in-Wait was upon him, and his hand closed warningly on hers.

'And – and so –' she was trying to say, when her hour also overtook her, leaving alive only the fear-dilated eyes that turned to Conroy. Hand froze on hand and the body with it as they waited for the horror in the blackness that heralded it. Yet through the worst Conroy saw, at an uncountable distance, one minute glint of light in his night. Thither would he go and escape his fear; and behold, that light was the light in the watch-tower of her eyes, where her locked soul signalled to his soul: 'Look at me!'

In time, from him and from her, the Thing sheered aside, that each soul might step down and resume its own concerns. He thought confusedly of people on the skirts of a thunderstorm, withdrawing from windows where the torn night is, to their known and furnished beds. Then he dozed, till in some drowsy turn his hand fell from her warmed hand.

'That's all. The Faces haven't come,' he heard her say. 'All – thank God! I don't feel even I need what Nursey promised me. Do you?'

'No.' He rubbed his eyes. 'But don't make too sure.'

'Certainly not. We shall have to try again next month. I'm afraid it will be an awful nuisance for you.'

'Not to me, I assure you,' said Conroy, and they leaned back and laughed at the flatness of the words, after the hells through which they had just risen.

'And now,' she said, strict eyes on Conroy, '*why* wouldn't you take me – not with a million in each stocking?'

'I don't know. That's what I've been puzzling over.'

'So have I. We're as handsome a couple as I've ever seen. Are you well off, lad?'

'They call me so,' said Conroy, smiling.

'That's North country.' She laughed again. Setting aside my good looks and yours, I've four thousand a year of my own, and the rents should make it six. That's a match some old cats would lap tea all night to fettle up.'

'It is. Lucky Toots!' said Conroy.

'Ay,' she answered, 'he'll be the luckiest lad in London if I win through. Who's yours?'

'No – no-one, dear. I've been in Hell for years. I only want to get out and be alive and – so on. Isn't that reason enough?'

'Maybe, for a man. But I never minded things much till George came. I was all stu-upid like.'

'So was I, but now I think I can live. It ought to be less next month, oughtn't it?' he said.

'I hope so. Ye-es. There's nothing much for a maid except to be married, and *7* ask no more. Whoever yours is, when you've found her, she shall have a wedding present from Mrs George Skinner that – '

'But she wouldn't understand it any more than Toots.'

'He doesn't matter – except to me. I can't keep my eyes open, thank God! Good-night, lad.'

Conroy followed her with his eyes. Beauty there was, grace there was, strength, and enough of the rest to drive better men than George Skinner to beat their heads on piano-tops – but for the new-found life of him Conroy could not feel one flutter of instinct or emotion that turned to herward. He put up his feet and fell asleep, dreaming of a joyous, normal world recovered – with interest on arrears. There were many things in it, but no one face of any one woman.

* * *

Thrice afterward they took the same train, and each time their trouble shrank and weakened. Miss Henschil talked of Toots, his multiplied calls, the things he had said to his sisters, the much worse things his sisters had replied; of the late (he seemed very dead to them) M. Najdol's gifts for the soul-weary; of shopping, of house rents, and the cost of really artistic furniture and linen.

Conroy explained the exercises in which he delighted – mighty labours of play undertaken against other mighty men, till he sweated and, having bathed, slept. He had visited his mother, too, in Hereford, and he talked something of her and of the home-life, which his body, cut out of all clean life for five years, innocently and deeply enjoyed. Nurse Blaber was a little interested in Conroy's mother, but, as a rule, she smoked her cigarette and read her paper-backed novels in her own compartment.

On their last trip she volunteered to sit with them, and buried herself in *The Cloister and the Hearth* while they whispered together. On that occasion (it was near Salisbury) at two in the morning, when the Lier-in-Wait brushed them with his wing, it meant no more than that they should cease talk for the instant, and for the instant hold hands, as even utter strangers on the deep may do when their ship rolls underfoot.

'But still,' said Nurse Blaber, not looking up, 'I think your Mr Skinner might feel jealous of all this.'

'It would be difficult to explain,' said Conroy.

'Then you'd better not be at my wedding,' Miss Henschil laughed.

'After all we've gone through, too. But I suppose you ought to leave me out. Is the day fixed?' he cried.

'Twenty-second of September – in spite of both his sisters. I can risk it now.' Her face was glorious as she flushed.

'My dear chap!' He shook hands unreservedly, and she gave back his grip without flinching. 'I can't tell you how pleased I am!'

'Gracious Heavens!' said Nurse Blaber, in a new voice. 'Oh, I beg your pardon. I forgot I wasn't paid to be surprised.'

'What at? Oh, I see!' Miss Henschil explained to Conroy. 'She expected you were going to kiss me, or I was going to kiss you, or something.'

'After all you've gone through, as Mr Conroy said,'

'But I couldn't, could you?' said Miss Henschil, with a disgust as frank as that on Conroy's face. 'It would be horrible – horrible. And yet, of course, you're wonderfully handsome. How d'you account for it, Nursey?'

Nurse Blaber shook her head. 'I was hired to cure you of a habit, dear. When you're cured I shall go on to the next case – that senile-decay one at Bournemouth I told you about.'

'And I shall be left alone with George! But suppose it isn't cured,' said Miss Henschil of a sudden. Suppose it comes back again. What can I do? I can't send for *him* in this way when I'm a married woman!' She pointed like an infant.

'I'd come, of course,' Conroy answered. 'But, seriously, that is a consideration.'

They looked at each other, alarmed and anxious, and then toward Nurse Blaber, who closed her book, marked the place, and turned to face them.

'Have you ever talked to your mother as you have to me?' she said.

'No. I might have spoken to dad – but mother's different. What d'you mean?'

'And you've never talked to your mother either, Mr Conroy?'

'Not till I took Najdolene. Then I told her it was my heart. There's no need to say anything, now that I'm practically over it, is there?'

'Not if it doesn't come back, but – ' She beckoned with a stumpy, triumphant finger that drew their heads close together. 'You know I always go in and read a chapter to mother at tea, child.'

'I know you do. You're an angel,' Miss Henschil patted the blue shoulder next her. 'Mother's Church of England now,' she explained. 'But she'll have her Bible with her pikelets at tea every night like the Skinners.'

'It was Naaman and Gehazi last Tuesday that gave me a clue. I said I'd never seen a case of leprosy, and your mother said she'd seen too many.'

'Where? She never told me,' Miss Henschil began.

'A few months before you were born – on her trip to Australia – at Mola or Molo something or other. It took me three evenings to get it all out.'

'Ay – mother's suspicious of questions,' said Miss Henschil to Conroy. 'She'll lock the door of every room she's in, if it's but for five minutes. She was a Tackberry from Jarrow way, yo' see.'

'She described your men to the life – men with faces all eaten away, staring at her over the fence of a lepers' hospital in this Molo Island. They begged from her, and she ran, she told me, all down the street, back to the pier. One touched her and she nearly fainted. She's ashamed of that still.'

'My men? The sand and the fences?' Miss Henschil muttered.

'Yes. You know how tidy she is and how she hates wind. She remembered that the fences were broken – she remembered the wind blowing. Sand – sun – salt wind – fences – faces – I got it all out of her, bit by bit. You don't know what I know! And it all happened three or four months before you were born. There!' Nurse Blaber slapped her knee with her little hand triumphantly.

'Would that account for it?' Miss Henschil shook from head to foot.

'Absolutely. I don't care who you ask! You never imagined the thing. It was *laid* on you. It happened on earth to *you*! Quick, Mr Conroy, she's too heavy for me! I'll get the flask.'

Miss Henschil leaned forward and collapsed, as Conroy told her afterwards, like a factory chimney. She came out of her swoon with teeth that chattered on the cup.

'No – no,' she said, gulping. 'It's not hysterics. Yo' see I've no call to hev 'em any more. No call – no reason whatever. God be praised! Can't yo' *feel* I'm a right woman now?'

'Stop hugging me!' said Nurse Blaber. 'You don't know your strength. Finish the brandy and water. It's perfectly reasonable, and I'll lay long odds Mr Conroy's case is something of the same. I've been thinking – '

'I wonder – ' said Conroy, and pushed the girl back as she swayed again.

Nurse Blaber smoothed her pale hair. 'Yes. Your trouble, or something like it, happened somewhere on earth or sea to the mother who bore you. Ask her, child. Ask her and be done with it once for all.'

'I will,' said Conroy . . . 'There ought to be – ' He opened his bag and hunted breathlessly.

'Bless you! Oh, God bless you, Nursey!' Miss Henschil was sobbing. 'You don't know what this means to me. It takes it all off – from the beginning.'

'But doesn't it make any difference to you now?' the nurse asked curiously. 'Now that you're rightfully a woman?'

Conroy, busy with his bag, had not heard. Miss Henschil stared across, and her beauty, freed from the shadow of any fear, blazed up within her. 'I see what you mean,' she said. 'But it hasn't changed anything. I want Toots. *He* has never been out of his mind in his life – except over silly me.'

'It's all right,' said Conroy, stooping under the lamp, Bradshaw in hand. 'If I change at Templecombe – for Bristol (Bristol – Hereford – yes) – I can be with mother for breakfast in her room and find out.'

'Quick, then,' said Nurse Blaber. 'We've passed Gillingham quite a while. You'd better take some of our sandwiches.' She went out to get them. Conroy and Miss Henschil would have danced, but there is no room for giants in a South-Western compartment.

'Goodbye, good luck, lad. Eh, but you've changed already – like me. Send a wire to our hotel as soon as you're sure,' said Miss Henschil. 'What should I have done without you?'

'Or I?' said Conroy. 'But it's Nurse that's saving us really.'

'Then thank her,' said Miss Henschil, looking straight at him. 'Yes, I would. She'd like it.'

When Nurse Blaber came back after the parting at Templecombe her nose and her eyelids were red, but, for all that, her face reflected a great light even while she sniffed over *The Cloister and the Hearth*.

Miss Henschil, deep in a house furnisher's catalogue, did not speak for twenty minutes. Then she said, between adding totals of best, guest, and servants' sheets, 'But why should our times have been the same, Nursey?'

'Because a child is born somewhere every second of the clock,' Nurse Blaber answered. 'And besides that, you probably set each other off by talking and thinking about it. You shouldn't, you know.'

'Ay, but you've never been in Hell,' said Miss Henschil.

The telegram handed in at Hereford at 12.46 and delivered to Miss Henschil on the beach of a certain village at 2.7 ran thus:

ABSOLUTELY CONFIRMED. SHE SAYS SHE REMEMBERS HEARING NOISE OF ACCIDENT IN ENGINE-ROOM RETURNING FROM INDIA EIGHTY-FIVE.

'He means the year, not the thermometer,' said Nurse Blaber, throwing pebbles at the cold sea.

AND TWO MEN SCALDED THUS EXPLAINING MY HOOTS. ('The idea of telling me that!') SUBSEQUENTLY SILLY CLERGYMAN PASSENGER RAN UP BEHIND HER CALLING FOR JOKE, 'FRIEND, ALL IS LOST', THUS ACCOUNTING VERY WORDS.

Nurse Blaber purred audibly.

SHE SAYS ONLY REMEMBERS BEING UPSET MINUTE OR TWO. UNSPEAK-ABLE RELIEF. BEST LOVE NURSEY, WHO IS JEWEL. GET OUT OF HER WHAT SHE WOULD LIKE BEST.

'Oh, I oughtn't to have read that,' said Miss Henschil.

'It doesn't matter. I don't want anything,' said Nurse Blaber, 'and if I did I shouldn't get it.'

The Dog Hervey

My friend Attley, who would give away his own head if you told him you had lost yours, was giving away a six-months-old litter of Bettina's pups, and half-a-dozen women were in raptures at the show on Mittleham lawn.

We picked by lot. Mrs Godfrey drew first choice; her married daughter, second. I was third, but waived my right because I was already owned by Malachi, Bettina's full brother, whom I had brought over in the car to visit his nephews and nieces, and he would have slain them all if I had taken home one. Milly, Mrs Godfrey's younger daughter, pounced on my rejection with squeals of delight, and Attley turned to a dark, sallow-skinned, slack-mouthed girl, who had come over for tennis, and invited her to pick. She put on a pince-nez that made her look like a camel, knelt clumsily, for she was long from the hip to the knee, breathed hard, and considered the last couple.

'I think I'd like that sandy-pied one,' she said.

'Oh, not him, Miss Sichliffe!' Attley cried. 'He was overlaid or had sunstroke or something. They call him The Looney in the kennels. Besides, he squints.'

'I think that's rather fetching,' she answered. Neither Malachi nor I had ever seen a squinting dog before.

'That's chorea – St. Vitus's dance,' Mrs Godfrey put in. 'He ought to have been drowned.'

'But I like his cast of countenance,' the girl persisted.

'He doesn't look a good life,' I said, 'but perhaps he can be patched up.' Miss Sichliffe turned crimson; I saw Mrs Godfrey exchange a glance with her married daughter, and knew I had said something which would have to be lived down.

'Yes,' Miss Sichliffe went on, her voice shaking, 'he isn't a good life, but perhaps I can – patch him up. Come here, sir.' The mis-shapen beast lurched toward her, squinting down his own nose till he fell over his own toes. Then, luckily, Bettina ran across the lawn and reminded Malachi of their puppyhood. All that family are as queer as

Dick's hatband, and fight like man and wife. I had to separate them, and Mrs Godfrey helped me till they retired under the rhododendrons and had it out in silence.

'D'you know what that girl's father was?' Mrs Godfrey asked.

'No,' I replied. 'I loathe her for her own sake. She breathes through her mouth.'

'He was a retired doctor,' she explained. 'He used to pick up stormy young men in the repentant stage, take them home, and patch them up till they were sound enough to be insured. Then he insured them heavily, and let them out into the world again – with an appetite. Of course, no-one knew him while he was alive, but he left pots of money to his daughter.'

'Strictly legitimate – highly respectable,' I said. 'But what a life for the daughter!'

'Mustn't it have been! *Now* d'you realise what you said just now?'

'Perfectly; and now you've made me quite happy, shall we go back to the house?'

When we reached it they were all inside, sitting in committee on names.

'What shall you call yours?' I heard Milly ask Miss Sichliffe.

'Harvey,' she replied – 'Harvey's Sauce, you know. He's going to be quite saucy when I've – ' she saw Mrs Godfrey and me coming through the French window – 'when he's stronger.'

Attley, the well-meaning man, to make me feel at ease, asked what I thought of the name.

'Oh, splendid,' I said at random. 'H with an A, A with an R, R with a – '

'But that's Little Bingo,' someone said, and they all laughed.

Miss Sichliffe, her hands joined across her long knees, drawled, 'You ought always to verify your quotations.'

It was not a kindly thrust, but something in the word 'quotation' set the automatic side of my brain at work on some shadow of a word or phrase that kept itself out of memory's reach as a cat sits just beyond a dog's jump. When I was going home, Miss Sichliffe came up to me in the twilight, the pup on a leash, swinging her big shoes at the end of her tennis racket.

"Sorry,' she said in her thick schoolboy-like voice. 'I'm sorry for what I said to you about verifying quotations. I didn't know you well enough and – anyhow, I oughtn't to have.'

'But you were quite right about Little Bingo,' I answered. 'The spelling ought to have reminded me.'

'Yes, of course. It's the spelling,' she said, and slouched off with the pup sliding after her. Once again my brain began to worry after something that would have meant something if it had been properly spelled. I confided my trouble to Malachi on the way home, but Bettina had bitten him in four places, and he was busy.

Weeks later, Attley came over to see me, and before his car stopped Malachi let me know that Bettina was sitting beside the chauffeur. He greeted her by the scruff of the neck as she hopped down; and I greeted Mrs Godfrey, Attley, and a big basket.

'You've got to help me,' said Attley tiredly. We took the basket into the garden, and there staggered out the angular shadow of a sandy-pied, broken-haired terrier, with one imbecile and one delirious ear, and two most hideous squints. Bettina and Malachi, already at grips on the lawn, saw him, let go, and fled in opposite directions.

'Why have you brought that fetid hound here?' I demanded.

'Harvey? For you to take care of,' said Attley. 'He's had distemper, but *I'm* going abroad.'

'Take him with you. I won't have him. He's mentally afflicted.'

'Look here,' Attley almost shouted, 'do I strike you as a fool?'

'Always,' said I.

'Well, then, if you say so, and Ella says so, that proves I ought to go abroad.'

'Will's wrong, quite wrong,' Mrs Godfrey interrupted; 'but you must take the pup.'

'My dear boy, my dear boy, don't you ever give anything to a woman,' Attley snorted.

Bit by bit I got the story out of them in the quiet garden (never a sign from Bettina and Malachi), while Harvey stared me out of countenance, first with one cuttlefish eye and then with the other.

It appeared that, a month after Miss Sichliffe took him, the dog Harvey developed distemper. Miss Sichliffe had nursed him herself for some time; then she carried him in her arms the two miles to Mittleham, and wept – actually wept – at Attley's feet, saying that Harvey was all she had or expected to have in this world, and Attley must cure him. Attley, being by wealth, position, and temperament guardian to all lame dogs, had put everything aside for this unsavoury job, and, he asserted, Miss Sichliffe had virtually lived with him ever since.

'She went home at night, of course,' he exploded, 'but the rest of the time she simply infested the premises. Goodness knows, I'm not particular, but it was a scandal. Even the servants! . . . Three and four times a day, and notes in between, to know how the beast was. Hang it all, don't laugh! And wanting to send me flowers and goldfish. Do I look as if I wanted goldfish? Can't you two stop for a minute?' (Mrs Godfrey and I were clinging to each other for support.) 'And it isn't as if I was – was so alluring a personality, is it?'

Attley commands more trust, goodwill, and affection than most men, for he is that rare angel, an absolutely unselfish bachelor, content to be run by contending syndicates of zealous friends. His situation seemed desperate, and I told him so.

'Instant flight is your only remedy,' was my verdict. I'll take care of both your cars while you're away, and you can send me over all the greenhouse fruit.'

'But why should I be chased out of my house by a she-dromedary?' he wailed.

'Oh, stop! Stop!' Mrs Godfrey sobbed. 'You're both wrong. I admit you're right, but I *know* you're wrong.'

'Three *and* four times a day,' said Attley, with an awful countenance. 'I'm not a vain man, but – look here, Ella, I'm not sensitive, I hope, but if you persist in making a joke of it – '

'Oh, be quiet!' she almost shrieked. 'D'you imagine for one instant that your friends would ever let Mittleham pass out of their hands? I quite agree it is unseemly for a grown girl to come to Mittleham at all hours of the day and night – '

'I told you she went home o' nights,' Attley growled.

'Specially if she goes home o' nights. Oh, but think of the life she must have led, Will!'

'I'm not interfering with it; only she must leave me alone.'

'She may want to patch you up and insure you,' I suggested.

'D'you know what *you* are?' Mrs Godfrey turned on me with the smile I have feared for the last quarter of a century. 'You're the nice, kind, wise, doggy friend. You don't know how wise and nice you are supposed to be. Will has sent Harvey to you to complete the poor angel's convalescence. You know all about dogs, or Will wouldn't have done it. He's written her that. You're too far off for her to make daily calls on you. P'r'aps she'll drop in two or three times a week, and write on other days. But it doesn't matter what she does, because you don't own Mittleham, don't you see?'

I told her I saw most clearly.

'Oh, you'll get over that in a few days,' Mrs Godfrey countered. 'You're the sporting, responsible, doggy friend who – '

'He used to look at me like that at first,' said Attley, with a visible shudder, 'but he gave it up after a bit. It's only because you're new to him.'

'But, confound you! he's a ghoul – ' I began.

'And when he gets quite well, you'll send him back to her direct with your love, and she'll give you some pretty four-tailed goldfish,' said Mrs Godfrey, rising. 'That's all settled. Car, please. We're going to Brighton to lunch together.'

They ran before I could get into my stride, so I told the dog Harvey what I thought of them and his mistress. He never shifted his position, but stared at me, an intense, lopsided stare, eye after eye. Malachi came along when he had seen his sister off, and from a distance counselled me to drown the brute and consort with gentlemen again. But the dog Harvey never even cocked his cockable ear.

And so it continued as long as he was with me. Where I sat, he sat and stared; where I walked, he walked beside, head stiffly slewed over one shoulder in single-barrelled contemplation of me. He never gave tongue, never closed in for a caress, seldom let me stir a step alone. And, to my amazement, Malachi, who suffered no stranger to live within our gates, saw this gaunt, growing, green-eyed devil wipe him out of my service and company without a whimper. Indeed, one would have said the situation interested him, for he would meet us returning from grim walks together, and look alternately at Harvey and at me with the same quivering interest that he showed at the mouth of a rat-hole. Outside these inspections, Malachi withdrew himself as only a dog or a woman can.

Miss Sichliffe came over after a few days (luckily I was out) with some elaborate story of paying calls in the neighbourhood. She sent me a note of thanks next day. I was reading it when Harvey and Malachi entered and disposed themselves as usual, Harvey close up to stare at me, Malachi half under the sofa, watching us both. Out of curiosity I returned Harvey's stare, then pulled his lopsided head on to my knee, and took his eye for several minutes. Now, in Malachi's eye I can see at any hour all that there is of the normal decent dog, flecked here and there with that strained half-soul which man's love and association have added to his nature. But with Harvey the eye was perplexed, as a tortured man's. Only by looking far into its deeps could one make out the spirit of the proper animal, beclouded and cowering beneath some unfair burden.

Leggatt, my chauffeur, came in for orders.

'How d'you think Harvey's coming on?' I said, as I rubbed the brute's gulping neck. The vet had warned me of the possibilities of spinal trouble following distemper.

'He ain't *my* fancy,' was the reply. 'But *I* don't question his comings and goings so long as I 'aven't to sit alone in a room with him.'

'Why? He's as meek as Moses,' I said.

'He fair gives me the creeps. P'r'aps he'll go out in fits.'

But Harvey, as I wrote his mistress from time to time, throve, and when he grew better, would play by himself grisly games of spying, walking up, hailing, and chasing another dog. From these he would break off of a sudden and return to his normal stiff gait, with the air of one who had forgotten some matter of life and death, which could be reached only by staring at me. I left him one evening posturing with the unseen on the lawn, and went inside to finish some letters for the post. I must have been at work nearly an hour, for I was going to turn on the lights, when I felt there was somebody in the room whom, the short hairs at the back of my neck warned me, I was not in the least anxious to face. There was a mirror on the wall. As I lifted my eyes to it I saw the dog Harvey reflected near the shadow by the closed door. He had reared himself full-length on his hind legs, his head a little one side to clear a sofa between us, and he was looking at me. The face, with its knitted brows and drawn lips, was the face of a dog, but the look, for the fraction of time that I caught it, was human – wholly and horribly human. When the blood in my body went forward again he had dropped to the floor, and was merely studying me in his usual one-eyed fashion. Next day I returned him to Miss Sichliffe. I would not have kept him another day for the wealth of Asia, or even Ella Godfrey's approval.

Miss Sichliffe's house I discovered to be a mid-Victorian mansion of peculiar villainy even for its period, surrounded by gardens of conflicting colours, all dazzling with glass and fresh paint on ironwork. Striped blinds, for it was a blazing autumn morning, covered most of the windows, and a voice sang to the piano an almost forgotten song of Jean Ingelow's –

> 'Methought that the stars were blinking bright,
>   And the old brig's sails unfurled – '

Down came the loud pedal, and the unrestrained cry swelled out across a bed of tritomas consuming in their own fires –

> 'When I said I will sail to my love this night
>   On the other side of the world.'

I have no music, but the voice drew. I waited till the end:

> 'Oh, maid most dear, I am not here,
>> I have no place apart –
> No dwelling more on sea or shore,
>> But only in thy heart.'

It seemed to me a poor life that had no more than that to do at eleven o'clock of a Tuesday forenoon. Then Miss Sichliffe suddenly lumbered through a French window in clumsy haste, her brows contracted against the light.

'Well?' she said, delivering the word like a spear-thrust, with the full weight of a body behind it.

'I've brought Harvey back at last,' I replied. 'Here he is.'

But it was at me she looked, not at the dog who had cast himself at her feet – looked as though she would have fished my soul out of my breast on the instant.

'Wha – what did you think of him? What did *you* make of him?' she panted. I was too taken aback for the moment to reply. Her voice broke as she stooped to the dog at her knees. 'O Harvey, Harvey! You utterly worthless old devil!' she cried, and the dog cringed and abased himself in servility that one could scarcely bear to look upon. I made to go.

'Oh, but please, you mustn't!' She tugged at the car's side. 'Wouldn't you like some flowers or some orchids? We've really splendid orchids, and – ' she clasped her hands – 'there are Japanese goldfish – real Japanese goldfish, with four tails. If you don't care for 'em, perhaps your friends or somebody – oh, please!'

Harvey had recovered himself, and I realised that this woman beyond the decencies was fawning on me as the dog had fawned on her.

'Certainly,' I said, ashamed to meet her eye. 'I'm lunching at Mittleham, but – '

'There's plenty of time,' she entreated. 'What do *you* think of Harvey?'

'He's a queer beast,' I said, getting out. 'He does nothing but stare at me.'

'Does he stare at you all the time he's with you?'

'Always. He's doing it now. Look!'

We had halted. Harvey had sat down, and was staring from one to the other with a weaving motion of the head.

'He'll do that all day,' I said. 'What is it, Harvey?'

'Yes, what *is* it, Harvey?' she echoed. The dog's throat twitched, his body stiffened and shook as though he were going to have a fit. Then he came back with a visible wrench to his unwinking watch.

'Always so?' she whispered.

'Always,' I replied, and told her something of his life with me. She nodded once or twice, and in the end led me into the house.

There were unaging pitch-pine doors of Gothic design in it; there were inlaid marble mantelpieces and cut-steel fenders; there were stupendous wallpapers, and octagonal, medallioned Wedgwood what-nots, and black-and-gilt Austrian images holding candelabra, with every other refinement that Art had achieved or wealth had bought between 1851 and 1878. And everything reeked of varnish.

'Now!' she opened a baize door, and pointed down a long corridor flanked with more Gothic doors. 'This was where we used to – to patch 'em up. You've heard of us. Mrs Godfrey told you in the garden the day I got Harvey given me. I – ' she drew in her breath – 'I live here by myself, and I have a very large income. Come back, Harvey.'

He had tiptoed down the corridor, as rigid as ever, and was sitting outside one of the shut doors. 'Look here!' she said, and planted herself squarely in front of me. 'I tell you this because you – you've patched up Harvey, too. Now, I want you to remember that my name is Moira. Mother calls me Marjorie because it's more refined; but my real name is Moira, and I am in my thirty-fourth year.'

'Very good,' I said. 'I'll remember all that.'

'Thank you.' Then with a sudden swoop into the humility of an abashed boy – 'Sorry if I haven't said the proper things. You see – there's Harvey looking at us again. Oh, I want to say – if ever you want anything in the way of orchids or goldfish or – or anything else that would be useful to you, you've only to come to me for it. Under the will I'm perfectly independent, and we're a long-lived family, worse luck!' She looked at me, and her face worked like glass behind driven flame. 'I may reasonably expect to live another fifty years,' she said.

'Thank you, Miss Sichliffe,' I replied. 'If I want anything, you may be sure I'll come to you for it.' She nodded. 'Now I must get over to Mittleham,' I said.

'Mr Attley will ask you all about this.' For the first time she laughed aloud. 'I'm afraid I frightened him nearly out of the county. I didn't think, of course. But I dare say he knows by this time he was wrong. Say goodbye to Harvey.'

'Goodbye, old man,' I said. 'Give me a farewell stare, so we shall know each other when we meet again.'

The dog looked up, then moved slowly toward me, and stood, head bowed to the floor, shaking in every muscle as I patted him; and when I turned, I saw him crawl back to her feet.

That was not a good preparation for the rampant boy-and-girl-dominated lunch at Mittleham, which, as usual, I found in possession of everybody except the owner.

'But what did the dromedary say when you brought her beast back?' Attley demanded.

'The usual polite things,' I replied. 'I'm posing as the nice doggy friend nowadays.'

'I don't envy you. She's never darkened my doors, thank goodness, since I left Harvey at your place. I suppose she'll run about the county now swearing you cured him. That's a woman's idea of gratitude.' Attley seemed rather hurt, and Mrs Godfrey laughed.

'That proves you were right about Miss Sichliffe, Ella,' I said. 'She had no designs on anybody.'

'I'm always right in these matters. But didn't she even offer you a goldfish?'

'Not a thing,' said I. 'You know what an old maid's like where her precious dog's concerned.' And though I have tried vainly to lie to Ella Godfrey for many years, I believe that in this case I succeeded.

When I turned into our drive that evening, Leggatt observed half aloud: 'I'm glad Zvengali's back where he belongs. It's time our Mike had a look in.'

Sure enough, there was Malachi back again in spirit as well as flesh, but still with that odd air of expectation he had picked up from Harvey.

*   *   *

It was in January that Attley wrote me that Mrs Godfrey, wintering in Madeira with Milly, her unmarried daughter, had been attacked with something like enteric; that the hotel, anxious for its good name, had thrust them both out into a cottage annexe; that he was off with a nurse, and that I was not to leave England till I heard from him again. In a week he wired that Milly was down as well, and that I must bring out two more nurses, with suitable delicacies.

Within seventeen hours I had got them all aboard the Cape boat, and had seen the women safely collapsed into seasickness. The next few weeks were for me, as for the invalids, a low delirium, clouded with fantastic memories of Portuguese officials trying to tax calvesfoot jelly; voluble doctors insisting that true typhoid was unknown in the island; nurses who had to be exercised, taken out of themselves, and returned on the tick of change of guard; night slides down glassy, cobbled streets, smelling of sewage and flowers, between walls whose every stone and patch Attley and I knew; vigils in stucco verandahs, watching the curve and descent of great stars or drawing auguries from the break of dawn; insane interludes of gambling at the local Casino, where we won heaps of unconsoling silver; blasts of steamers arriving and departing in the roads; help offered by total strangers, grabbed at or thrust aside; the long nightmare crumbling back into sanity one forenoon under a vine-covered trellis, where Attley sat hugging a nurse, while the others danced a noiseless, neat-footed breakdown never learned at the Middlesex Hospital. At last, as the tension came out all over us in aches and tingles that we put down to the country wine, a vision of Mrs Godfrey, her grey hair turned to spun glass, but her eyes triumphant over the shadow of retreating death beneath them, with Milly, enormously grown, and clutching life back to her young breast, both stretched out on cane chairs, clamouring for food.

In this ungirt hour there imported himself into our life a youngish-looking middle-aged man of the name of Shend, with a blurred face and deprecating eyes. He said he had gambled with me at the Casino, which was no recommendation, and I remember that he twice gave me a basket of champagne and liqueur brandy for the invalids, which a sailor in a red-tasselled cap carried up to the cottage for me at 3 a.m. He turned out to be the son of some merchant prince in the oil and colour line, and the owner of a four-hundred-ton steam yacht, into which, at his gentle insistence, we later shifted our camp, staff, and equipage, Milly weeping with delight to escape from the horrible cottage. There we lay off Funchal for weeks, while Shend did miracles of luxury and attendance through deputies, and never once asked how his guests were enjoying themselves. Indeed, for several days at a time we would see nothing of him. He was, he said, subject to malaria. Giving as they do with both hands, I knew that Attley and Mrs Godfrey could take nobly; but I never met a man who so nobly gave and so nobly received thanks as Shend did.

'Tell us why you have been so unbelievably kind to us gypsies,' Mrs Godfrey said to him one day on deck.

He looked up from a diagram of some Thamesmouth shoals which he was explaining to me, and answered with his gentle smile: 'I will.

It's because it makes me happy – it makes me more than happy – to be with you. It makes me comfortable. You know how selfish men are? If a man feels comfortable all over with certain people, he'll bore them to death, just like a dog. You always make me feel as if pleasant things were going to happen to me.'

'Haven't any ever happened before?' Milly asked.

'This is the most pleasant thing that has happened to me in ever so many years,' he replied. 'I feel like the man in the Bible, "It's good for me to be here." Generally, I don't feel that it's good for me to be anywhere in particular.' Then, as one begging a favour. 'You'll let me come home with you – in the same boat, I mean? I'd take you back in this thing of mine, and that would save you packing your trunks, but she's too lively for spring work across the Bay.'

We booked our berths, and when the time came, he wafted us and ours aboard the Southampton mailboat with the pomp of plenipotentiaries and the precision of the Navy. Then he dismissed his yacht, and became an inconspicuous passenger in a cabin opposite to mine, on the port side.

We ran at once into early British spring weather, followed by sou'west gales. Mrs Godfrey, Milly, and the nurses disappeared. Attley stood it out, visibly yellowing, till the next meal, and followed suit, and Shend and I had the little table all to ourselves. I found him even more attractive when the women were away. The natural sweetness of the man, his voice and bearing, all fascinated me, and his knowledge of practical seamanship (he held an extra master's certificate) was a real joy. We sat long in the empty saloon and longer in the smoking-room, making dashes downstairs over slippery decks at the eleventh hour.

It was on Friday night, just as I was going to bed, that he came into my cabin, after cleaning his teeth, which he did half a dozen times a day.

'I say,' he began hurriedly, 'do you mind if I come in here for a little? I'm a bit edgy.' I must have shown surprise. 'I'm ever so much better about liquor than I used to be, but – it's the whisky in the suitcase that throws me. For God's sake, old man, don't go back on me tonight! Look at my hands!'

They were fairly jumping at the wrists. He sat down on a trunk that had slid out with the roll. We had reduced speed, and were surging in confused seas that pounded on the black port-glasses. The night promised to be a pleasant one!

'You understand, of course, don't you?' he chattered.

'Oh yes,' I said cheerily; 'but how about – '

'No, no; on no account the doctor. 'Tell a doctor, tell the whole ship. Besides, I've only got a touch of 'em. You'd never have guessed it, would you? The toothwash does the trick. I'll give you the prescription.'

I'll send a note to the doctor for a prescription, shall I?' I suggested.

'Right! I put myself unreservedly in your hands. 'Fact is, I always did. I said to myself – sure I don't bore you? – the minute I saw you, I said, "Thou art the man." ' He repeated the phrase as he picked at his knees. 'All the same, you can take it from me that the ewe-lamb business is a rotten bad one. I don't care how unfaithful the shepherd may be. Drunk or sober, 'tisn't cricket.'

A surge of the trunk threw him across the cabin as the steward answered my bell. I wrote my requisition to the doctor while Shend was struggling to his feet.

'What's wrong?' he began. 'Oh, I know. We're slowing for soundings off Ushant. It's about time, too. You'd better ship the deadlights when you come back, Matchem. It'll save you waking us later. This sea's going to get up when the tide turns. That'll show you,' he said as the man left, 'that I am to be trusted. You – you'll stop me if I say anything I shouldn't, won't you?'

'Talk away,' I replied, 'if it makes you feel better.'

'That's it; you've hit it exactly. You always make me feel better. I can rely on you. It's awkward soundings but you'll see me through it. We'll defeat him yet . . . I may be an utterly worthless devil, but I'm not a brawler . . . I told him so at breakfast. I said, "Doctor, I detest brawling, but if ever you allow that girl to be insulted again as Clements insulted her, I will break your neck with my own hands." You think I was right?'

'Absolutely,' I agreed.

'Then we needn't discuss the matter any further. That man was a murderer in intention – outside the law, you understand, as it was then. They've changed it since – but he never deceived *me*. I told him so. I said to him at the time, "I don't know what price you're going to put on my head, but if ever you allow Clements to insult her again, you'll never live to claim it." '

'And what did he do?' I asked, to carry on the conversation, for Matchem entered with the bromide.

'Oh, crumpled up at once. 'Lead still going, Matchem?'

'I 'aven't 'eard,' said that faithful servant of the Union Castle Company.

'Quite right. Never alarm the passengers. Ship the deadlight, will you?' Matchem shipped it, for we were rolling very heavily. There were tramplings and gull-like cries from on deck. Shend looked at me with a mariner's eye.

'That's nothing,' he said protectingly.

'Oh, it's all right for you,' I said, jumping at the idea. '*I* haven't an extra master's certificate. I'm only a passenger. I confess it funks me.'

Instantly his whole bearing changed to answer the appeal.

'My dear fellow, it's as simple as houses. We're hunting for sixty-five fathom water. Anything short of sixty, with a sou'west wind means – but I'll get my Channel Pilot out of my cabin and give you the general idea. I'm only too grateful to do anything to put your mind at ease.'

And so, perhaps, for another hour – he declined the drink – Channel Pilot in hand, he navigated us round Ushant, and at my request up-channel to Southampton, light by light, with explanations and reminiscences. I professed myself soothed at last, and suggested bed.

'In a second,' said he. 'Now, you wouldn't think, would you' – he glanced off the book toward my wildly swaying dressing-gown on the door – 'that I've been seeing things for the last half-hour? 'Fact is, I'm just on the edge of 'em, skating on thin ice round the corner – nor'east as near as nothing – where that dog's looking at me.'

'What's the dog like?' I asked.

'Ah, that *is* comforting of you! Most men walk through 'em to show me they aren't real. As if I didn't know! But *you're* different. Anybody could see that with half an eye.' He stiffened and pointed. 'Damn it all! The dog sees it too with half an – Why, he knows you! Knows you perfectly. D'you know *him*?'

'How can I tell if he isn't real?' I insisted.

'But you can! *You're* all right. I saw that from the first. Don't go back on me now or I shall go to pieces like the *Drummond Castle*. I beg your pardon, old man; but, you see, you *do* know the dog. I'll prove it. What's that dog doing? Come on! *You* know.' A tremor shook him, and he put his hand on my knee, and whispered with great meaning: 'I'll letter or halve it with you. There! You begin.'

'S,' said I to humour him, for a dog would most likely be standing or sitting, or may be scratching or sniffling or staring.

'Q,' he went on, and I could feel the heat of his shaking hand.

'U,' said I. There was no other letter possible; but I was shaking too.

'I.'

'N.'

'T-i-n-g,' he ran out. 'There! That proves it. I knew you knew him. You don't know what a relief that is. Between ourselves, old man, he – he's been turning up lately a – a damn sight more often than I cared for. And a squinting dog – a dog that squints! I mean that's a bit *too* much. Eh? What?' He gulped and half rose, and I thought that the full tide of delirium would be on him in another sentence.

'Not a bit of it,' I said as a last chance, with my hand over the bellpush. 'Why, you've just proved that I know him; so there are two of us in the game, anyhow.'

'By Jove! that *is* an idea! Of course there are. I knew you'd see me through. We'll defeat them yet. Hi, pup! . . . He's gone. Absolutely disappeared!' He sighed with relief, and I caught the lucky moment.

'Good business! I expect he only came to have a look at me,' I said. 'Now, get this drink down and turn in to the lower bunk.'

He obeyed, protesting that he could not inconvenience me, and in the midst of apologies sank into a dead sleep. I expected a wakeful night, having a certain amount to think over; but no sooner had I scrambled into the top bunk than sleep came on me like a wave from the other side of the world.

In the morning there were apologies, which we got over at breakfast before our party were about.

'I suppose – after this – well, I don't blame you. I'm rather a lonely chap, though.' His eyes lifted dog-like across the table.

'Shend,' I replied, 'I'm not running a Sunday school. You're coming home with me in my car as soon as we land.'

'That is kind of you – kinder than you think.'

'That's because you're a little jumpy still. Now, I don't want to mix up in your private affairs – '

'But I'd like you to,' he interrupted.

'Then, would you mind telling me the Christian name of a girl who was insulted by a man called Clements?'

'Moira,' he whispered; and just then Mrs Godfrey and Milly came to table with their shoregoing hats on.

We did not tie up till noon, but the faithful Leggatt had intrigued his way down to the dock-edge, and beside him sat Malachi, wearing his collar of gold, or Leggatt makes it look so, as eloquent as Demosthenes. Shend flinched a little when he saw him. We packed Mrs Godfrey and Milly into Attley's car – they were going with him to Mittleham, of course – and drew clear across the

railway lines to find England all lit and perfumed for spring. Shend
sighed with happiness.

'D'you know,' he said, 'if – if you'd chucked me – I should have
gone down to my cabin after breakfast and cut my throat. And now –
it's like a dream – a good dream, you know.'

We lunched with the other three at Romsey. Then I sat in front for
a little while to talk to my Malachi. When I looked back, Shend was
solidly asleep, and stayed so for the next two hours, while Leggatt
chased Attley's fat Daimler along the green-speckled hedges. He
woke up when we said goodbye at Mittleham, with promises to meet
again very soon.

'And I hope,' said Mrs Godfrey, 'that everything pleasant will
happen to you.'

'Heaps and heaps – all at once,' cried long, weak Milly, waving her
wet handkerchief.

'I've just got to look in at a house near here for a minute to enquire
about a dog,' I said, 'and then we will go home.'

'I used to know this part of the world,' he replied, and said no
more till Leggatt shot past the lodge at the Sichliffes's gate. Then I
heard him gasp.

Miss Sichliffe, in a green waterproof, an orange jersey, and a pinkish
leather hat, was working on a bulb-border. She straightened herself as
the car stopped, and breathed hard. Shend got out and walked towards
her. They shook hands, turned round together, and went into the
house. Then the dog Harvey pranced out corkily from under the lee
of a bench. Malachi, with one joyous swoop, fell on him as an enemy
and an equal. Harvey, for his part, freed from all burden whatsoever
except the obvious duty of a man-dog on his own ground, met
Malachi without reserve or remorse, and with six months' additional
growth to come and go on.

'Don't check 'em!' cried Leggatt, dancing round the flurry.
'They've both been saving up for each other all this time. It'll do
'em worlds of good.'

'Leggatt,' I said, 'will you take Mr Shend's bag and suitcase up
to the house and put them down just inside the door? Then we
will go on.'

So I enjoyed the finish alone. It was a dead heat, and they licked
each other's jaws in amity till Harvey, one imploring eye on me,
leaped into the front seat, and Malachi backed his appeal. It was
theft, but I took him, and we talked all the way home of r-rats and r-
rabbits and bones and baths and the other basic facts of life. That

evening after dinner they slept before the fire, with their warm chins across the hollows of my ankles – to each chin an ankle – till I kicked them upstairs to bed.

* * *

I was not at Mittleham when she came over to announce her engagement, but I heard of it when Mrs Godfrey and Attley came, forty miles an hour, over to me, and Mrs Godfrey called me names of the worst for suppression of information.

'As long as it wasn't me, I don't care,' said Attley.

'I believe you knew it all along,' Mrs Godfrey repeated. 'Else what made you drive that man literally into her arms?'

'To ask after the dog Harvey,' I replied.

'Then, what's the beast doing here?' Attley demanded, for Malachi and the dog Harvey were deep in a council of the family with Bettina, who was being out-argued.

'Oh, Harvey seemed to think himself *de trop* where he was,' I said. 'And she hasn't sent after him. You'd better save Bettina before they kill her.'

'There's been enough lying about that dog,' said Mrs Godfrey to me. 'If he wasn't born in lies, he was baptized in 'em. D'you know why she called him Harvey? It only occurred to me in those dreadful days when I was ill, and one can't keep from thinking, and thinks everything. D'you know your Boswell? What did Johnson say about Hervey – with an e?'

'Oh, *that's* it, is it?' I cried incautiously. 'That was why I ought to have verified my quotations. The spelling defeated me. Wait a moment, and it will come back. Johnson said: "He was a vicious man",' I began.

' "But very kind to me",' Mrs Godfrey prompted. Then, both together, ' "If you call a dog Hervey, I shall love him." '

'So you *were* mixed up in it. At any rate, you had your suspicions from the first? Tell me,' she said.

'Ella,' I said, 'I don't know anything rational or reasonable about any of it. It was all – all woman-work, and it scared me horribly.'

'Why?' she asked.

That was six years ago. I have written this tale to let her know – wherever she may be.

The House Surgeon

On an evening after Easter Day, I sat at a table in a homeward bound steamer's smoking-room, where half a dozen of us told ghost stories. As our party broke up a man, playing Patience in the next alcove, said to me: 'I didn't quite catch the end of that last story about the Curse on the family's first-born.'

'It turned out to be drains,' I explained. 'As soon as new ones were put into the house the Curse was lifted, I believe. I never knew the people myself.'

'Ah! I've had my drains up twice; I'm on gravel too.'

'You don't mean to say you've a ghost in your house? Why didn't you join our party?'

'Any more orders, gentlemen, before the bar closes?' the steward interrupted.

'Sit down again, and have one with me,' said the Patience player. 'No, it isn't a ghost. Our trouble is more depression than anything else.'

'How interesting? Then it's nothing anyone can see?'

'It's – it's nothing worse than a little depression. And the odd part is that there hasn't been a death in the house since it was built – in 1863. The lawyer said so. That decided me – my good lady, rather – and he made me pay an extra thousand for it.'

'How curious. Unusual, too!' I said.

'Yes; ain't it? It was built for three sisters – Moultrie was the name – three old maids. They all lived together; the eldest owned it. I bought it from her lawyer a few years ago, and if I've spent a pound on the place first and last, I must have spent five thousand. Electric light, new servants' wing, garden – all that sort of thing. A man and his family ought to be happy after so much expense, ain't it?' He looked at me through the bottom of his glass.

'Does it affect your family much?'

'My good lady – she's a Greek, by the way – and myself are middle-aged. We can bear up against depression; but it's hard on my little girl. I say little; but she's twenty. We send her visiting to escape it. She almost lived at hotels and hydros, last year, but that isn't pleasant for her. She used to be a canary – a perfect canary – always singing. You ought to hear her. She doesn't sing now. That sort of thing's unwholesome for the young, ain't it?'

'Can't you get rid of the place?' I suggested.

'Not except at a sacrifice, and we are fond of it. Just suits us three. We'd love it if we were allowed.'

'What do you mean by not being allowed?'

'I mean because of the depression. It spoils everything.'

'What's it like exactly?'

'I couldn't very well explain. It must be seen to be appreciated, as the auctioneers say. Now, I was much impressed by the story you were telling just now.'

'It wasn't true,' I said.

'My tale is true. If you would do me the pleasure to come down and spend a night at my little place, you'd learn more than you would if I talked till morning. Very likely 'twouldn't touch your good self at all. You might be – immune, ain't it? On the other hand, if this influenza – influence does happen to affect you, why, I think it will be an experience.'

While he talked he gave me his card, and I read his name was L. Maxwell M'Leod, Esq., of Holmescroft. A City address was tucked away in a corner.

'My business,' he added, 'used to be furs. If you are interested in furs – I've given thirty years of my life to 'em.'

'You're very kind,' I murmured.

'Far from it, I assure you. I can meet you next Saturday afternoon anywhere in London you choose to name, and I'll be only too happy to motor you down. It ought to be a delightful run – at this time of year the rhododendrons will be out. I mean it. You don't know how truly I mean it. Very probably – it won't affect you at all. And – I think I may say I have the finest collection of narwhal tusks in the world. All the best skins and horns have to go through London, and L. Maxwell M'Leod, he knows where they come from, and where they go to. That's his business.'

For the rest of the voyage up-channel Mr M'Leod talked to me of the assembling, preparation, and sale of the rarer furs; and told me things about the manufacture of fur-lined coats which quite shocked me. Somehow or other, when we landed on Wednesday, I found myself pledged to spend that weekend with him at Holmescroft.

On Saturday he met me with a well-groomed motor, and ran me out, in an hour and a half, to an exclusive residenti:l district of dustless roads and elegantly designed country villas, each standing in from three to five acres of perfectly appointed land. He told me land was selling at eight hundred pounds the acre, and the new golf links, whose Queen Anne pavilion we passed, had cost nearly twenty-four thousand pounds to create.

Holmescroft was a large, two-storeyed, low, creeper-covered resid- ence. A verandah at the south side gave on to a garden and two tennis courts, separated by a tasteful iron fence from a most park-like meadow of five or six acres, where two Jersey cows grazed. Tea was ready in the shade of a promising copper beech, and I could see groups on the lawn of young men and maidens appropriately clothed, playing lawn tennis in the sunshine.

'A pretty scene, ain't it?' said Mr M'Leod. 'My good lady's sitting under the tree, and that's my little girl in pink on the far court. But I'll take you to your room, and you can see 'em all later.'

He led me through a wide parquet-floored hall furnished in pale lemon, with huge *cloisonnée* vases, an ebonised and gold grand piano, and banks of pot flowers in Benares brass bowls, up a pale oak staircase to a spacious landing, where there was a green velvet settee trimmed with silver. The blinds were down, and the light lay in parallel lines on the floors.

He showed me my room, saying cheerfully: 'You may be a little tired. One often is without knowing it after a run through traffic. Don't come down till you feel quite restored. We shall all be in the garden.'

My room was rather warm, and smelt of perfumed soap. I threw up the window at once, but it opened so close to the floor and worked so clumsily that I came within an ace of pitching out, where I should certainly have ruined a rather lopsided laburnum below. As I set about washing off the journey's dust, I began to feel a little tired. But, I reflected, I had not come down here in this weather and among these new surroundings to be depressed; so I began to whistle.

And it was just then that I was aware of a little grey shadow, as it might have been a snowflake seen against the light, floating at an immense distance in the background of my brain. It annoyed me, and I shook my head to get rid of it. Then my brain telegraphed that it was the forerunner of a swift-striding gloom which there was yet time to escape if I would force my thoughts away from it, as a man leaping for life forces his body forward and away from the fall of a wall. But the gloom overtook me before I could take in the meaning of the message. I moved toward the bed, every nerve already aching with the foreknowledge of the pain that was to be dealt it, and sat down, while my amazed and angry soul dropped, gulf by gulf, into that horror of great darkness which is spoken of in the Bible, and which, as auctioneers say, must be experienced to be appreciated.

Despair upon despair, misery upon misery, fear after fear, each causing their distinct and separate woe, packed in upon me for an unrecorded length of time, until at last they blurred together, and I heard a click in my brain like the click in the ear when one descends in a diving bell, and I knew that the pressures were equalised within and without, and that, for the moment, the worst was at an end. But I knew also that at any moment the darkness might come down anew; and while I dwelt on this speculation precisely as a man torments a raging tooth with his tongue, it ebbed away into the little grey shadow on the brain of its first coming, and once more I heard my brain, which knew what would recur, telegraph to every quarter for help, release or diversion.

The door opened, and M'Leod reappeared. I thanked him politely, saying I was charmed with my room, anxious to meet Mrs M'Leod, much refreshed with my wash, and so on and so forth. Beyond a little stickiness at the corners of my mouth, it seemed to me that I was managing my words admirably; the while that I myself cowered at the bottom of unclimbable pits. M'Leod laid his hand on my shoulder, and said 'You've got it now already, ain't it?'

'Yes,' I answered. 'It's making me sick!'

'It will pass off when you come outside. I give you my word it will then pass off. Come!'

I shambled out behind him, and wiped my forehead in the hall.

'You mustn't mind,' he said. 'I expect the run tired you. My good lady is sitting there under the copper beech.'

She was a fat woman in an apricot-coloured gown, with a heavily powdered face, against which her black long-lashed eyes showed like currants in dough. I was introduced to many fine ladies and gentlemen of those parts. Magnificently appointed landaus and covered motors swept in and out of the drive, and the air was gay with the merry outcries of the tennis players.

As twilight drew on they all went away, and I was left alone with Mr and Mrs M'Leod, while tall menservants and maidservants took away the tennis and tea things. Miss M'Leod had walked a little down the drive with a light-haired young man, who apparently knew everything about every South American railway stock. He had told me at tea that these were the days of financial specialisation.

'I think it went off beautifully, my dear,' said Mr M'Leod to his wife; and to me: 'You feel all right now, ain't it? Of course you do.'

Mrs M'Leod surged across the gravel. Her husband skipped nimbly before her into the south verandah, turned a switch, and all Holmescroft was flooded with light.

'You can do that from your room also,' he said as they went in. 'There is something in money, ain't it?'

Miss M'Leod came up behind me in the dusk. 'We have not yet been introduced,' she said, 'but I suppose you are staying the night?'

'Your father was kind enough to ask me,' I replied.

She nodded. 'Yes, I know; and you know too, don't you? I saw your face when you came to shake hands with mamma. You felt the depression very soon. It is simply frightful in that bedroom sometimes. What do you think it is – bewitchment? In Greece, where I was a little girl, it might have been; but not in England, do you think? Or do you?'

'Cheer up, Thea. It will all come right,' he insisted.

'No, papa.' She shook her dark head. 'Nothing is right while it comes.'

'It is nothing that we ourselves have ever done in our lives – that I will swear to you,' said Mrs M'Leod suddenly. 'And we have changed our servants several times. So we know it is not them.'

'Never mind. Let us enjoy ourselves while we can,' said Mr M'Leod, opening the champagne.

But we did not enjoy ourselves. The talk failed. There were long silences.

'I beg your pardon,' I said, for I thought someone at my elbow was about to speak.

'Ah! That is the other thing!' said Miss M'Leod. Her mother groaned.

We were silent again, and, in a few seconds it must have been, a live grief beyond words – not ghostly dread or horror, but aching, helpless grief – overwhelmed us, each, I felt, according to his or her nature, and held steady like the beam of a burning glass. Behind that pain I was conscious there was a desire on somebody's part to explain something on which some tremendously important issue hung.

Meantime I rolled bread pills and remembered my sins; M'Leod considered his own reflection in a spoon; his wife seemed to be praying, and the girl fidgeted desperately with hands and feet, till the darkness passed on – as though the malignant rays of a burning-glass had been shifted from us.'

'There,' said Miss M'Leod, half rising. 'Now you see what makes a happy home. Oh, sell it – sell it, father mine, and let us go away!'

'But I've spent thousands on it. You shall go to Harrogate next week, Thea dear.'

'I'm only just back from hotels. I am so tired of packing.'

'Cheer up, Thea. It is over. You know it does not often come here twice in the same night. I think we shall dare now to be comfortable.'

He lifted a dish-cover, and helped his wife and daughter. His face was lined and fallen like an old man's after debauch, but his hand did not shake, and his voice was clear. As he worked to restore us by speech and action, he reminded me of a grey-muzzled collie herding demoralised sheep.

After dinner we sat round the dining-room fire. The drawing-room might have been under the Shadow for aught we knew, talking with the intimacy of gypsies by the wayside, or of wounded comparing notes after a skirmish. By eleven o'clock the three between them had given me every name and detail they could recall that in any way bore on the house, and what they knew of its history.

We went to bed in a fortifying blaze of electric light. My one fear was that the blasting gust of depression would return – the surest way, of course, to bring it. I lay awake till dawn, breathing quickly and sweating lightly, beneath what De Quincey inadequately describes as 'the oppression of inexpiable guilt'. Now as soon as the lovely day was broken, I fell into the most terrible of all dreams – that joyous one in which all past evil has not only been wiped out of our lives, but has never been committed; and in the very bliss of our assured innocence, before our loves shriek and change countenance, we wake to the day we have earned.

It was a coolish morning, but we preferred to breakfast in the south verandah. The forenoon we spent in the garden, pretending to play games that come out of boxes, such as croquet and clock golf. But most of the time we drew together and talked. The young man who knew all about South American railways took Miss M'Leod for a walk in the afternoon, and at five M'Leod thoughtfully whirled us all up to dine in town.

'Now, don't say you will tell the Psychological Society, and that you will come again,' said Miss M'Leod, as we parted. 'Because I know you will not.'

'You should not say that,' said her mother. 'You should say, "Good-bye, Mr Perseus. Come again." '

'Not him!' the girl cried. 'He has seen the Medusa's head!'

Looking at myself in the restaurant's mirrors, it seemed to me that I had not much benefited by my weekend. Next morning I wrote out all my Holmescroft notes at fullest length, in the hope that by so doing I could put it all behind me. But the experience worked on my mind, as they say certain imperfectly understood rays work on the body.

I am less calculated to make a Sherlock Holmes than any man I know, for I lack both method and patience, yet the idea of following up the trouble to its source fascinated me. I had no theory to go on, except a vague idea that I had come between two poles of a discharge, and had taken a shock meant for someone else. This was followed by a feeling of intense irritation. I waited cautiously on myself, expecting to be overtaken by horror of the supernatural, but my self persisted in being humanly indignant, exactly as though it had been the victim of a practical joke. It was in great pains and upheavals – that I felt in every fibre – but its dominant idea, to put it coarsely, was to get back a bit of its own. By this I knew that I might go forward if I could find the way.

After a few days it occurred to me to go to the office of Mr J.M.M. Baxter – the solicitor who had sold Holmescroft to M'Leod. I explained I had some notion of buying the place. Would he act for me in the matter ?

Mr Baxter, a large, greyish, throaty-voiced man, showed no enthusiasm. 'I sold it to Mr M'Leod,' he said. 'It 'ud scarcely do for me to start on the running-down tack now. But I can recommend – '

'I know he's asking an awful price,' I interrupted, 'and atop of it he wants an extra thousand for what he calls your clean bill of health.'

Mr Baxter sat up in his chair. I had all his attention.

'Your guarantee with the house. Don't you remember it?'

'Yes, yes. That no death had taken place in the house since it was built: I remember perfectly.'

He did not gulp as untrained men do when they lie, but his jaws moved stickily, and his eyes, turning towards the deed boxes on the wall, dulled. I counted seconds, one, two, three – one, two, three up to ten. A man, I knew, can live through ages of mental depression in that time.

'I remember perfectly.' His mouth opened a little as though it had tasted old bitterness.

'Of course that sort of thing doesn't appeal to me.' I went on. 'I don't expect to buy a house free from death.'

'Certainly not. No-one does. But it was Mr M'Leod's fancy – his wife's rather, I believe; and since we could meet it – it was my duty to my clients at whatever cost to my own feelings – to make him pay.'

'That's really why I came to you. I understood from him you knew the place well.'

'Oh, yes. Always did. It originally belonged to some connections of mine.'

'The Misses Moultrie, I suppose. How interesting! They must have loved the place before the country round about was built up.'

'They were very fond of it indeed.'

'I don't wonder. So restful and sunny. I don't see how they could have brought themselves to part with it.'

Now it is one of the most constant peculiarities of the English that in polite conversation – and I had striven to be polite – no-one ever does or sells anything for mere money's sake.

'Miss Agnes – the youngest – fell ill' (he spaced his words a little), 'and, as they were very much attached to each other, that broke up the home.'

'Naturally. I fancied it must have been something of that kind. One doesn't associate the Staffordshire Moultries' (my Demon of Irresponsibility at that instant created 'em), 'with – with being hard up.'

'I don't know whether we're related to them,' he answered importantly. 'We may be, for our branch of the family comes from the Midlands.'

I give this talk at length, because I am so proud of my first attempt at detective work. When I left him, twenty minutes later, with instructions to move against the owner of Holmescroft, with a view to purchase, I was more bewildered than any Doctor Watson at the opening of a story.

Why should a middle-aged solicitor turn plovers' egg colour and drop his jaw when reminded of so innocent and festal a matter as that no death had ever occurred in a house that he had sold? If I knew my English vocabulary at all, the tone in which he said the youngest sister 'fell ill' meant that she had gone out of her mind. That might explain his change of countenance, and it was just possible that her demented influence still hung about Holmescroft; but the rest was beyond me.

I was relieved when I reached M'Leod's City office, and could tell him what I had done – not what I thought.

M'Leod was quite willing to enter into the game of the pretended purchase, but did not see how it would help if I knew Baxter.

'He's the only living soul I can get at who was connected with Holmescroft,' I said.

'Ah! Living soul is good,' said M'Leod. 'At any rate our little girl will be pleased that you are still interested in us. Won't you come down some day this week?'

'How is it there now?' I asked.

He screwed up his face. 'Simply frightful!' he said. 'Thea is at Droitwich.'

'I should like it immensely, but I must cultivate Baxter for the present. You'll be sure and keep him busy your end, won't you?'

He looked at me with quiet contempt. 'Do not be afraid. I shall be a good Jew. I shall be my own solicitor.'

Before a fortnight was over, Baxter admitted ruefully that M'Leod was better than most firms in the business: We buyers were coy, argumentative, shocked at the price of Holmescroft, inquisitive, and cold by turns, but Mr M'Leod the seller easily met and surpassed us; and Mr Baxter entered every letter, telegram, and consultation at the proper rates in a cinematograph-film of a bill. At the end of a month he said it looked as though M'Leod, thanks to him, were really going to listen to reason. I was many pounds out of pocket, but I had learned something of Mr Baxter on the human side. I deserved it. Never in my life have I worked to conciliate, amuse, and flatter a human being as I worked over my solicitor.

It appeared that he golfed. Therefore, I was an enthusiastic beginner, anxious to learn. Twice I invaded his office with a bag (M'Leod lent it) full of the spelicans needed in this detestable game, and a vocabulary to match. The third time the ice broke, and Mr Baxter took me to his links, quite ten miles off, where in a maze of tramway lines, railroads, and nurserymaids, we skelped our divoted way round nine holes like barges plunging through head seas. He played vilely and had never expected to meet anyone worse; but as he realised my form, I think he began to like me, for he took me in hand by the two hours together. After a fortnight he could give me no more than a stroke a hole, and when, with this allowance, I once managed to beat him by one, he was honestly glad, and assured me that I should be a golfer if I stuck to it. I was sticking to it for my own ends, but now and again my conscience pricked me; for the man was a nice man. Between games he supplied me with odd pieces of evidence, such as that he had known the Moultries all his life, being their cousin, and that Miss Mary, the eldest, was an unforgiving woman who would never let bygones be. I naturally wondered what she might have against him; and somehow connected him unfavourably with mad Agnes.

'People ought to forgive and forget,' he volunteered one day between rounds. 'Specially where, in the nature of things, they can't be sure of their deductions. Don't you think so?'

'It all depends on the nature of the evidence on which one forms one's judgement,' I answered.

'Nonsense!' he cried. 'I'm lawyer enough to know that there's nothing in the world so misleading as circumstantial evidence. Never was.'

'Why? Have you ever seen men hanged on it?'

'Hanged? People have been supposed to be eternally lost on it,' his face turned grey again. 'I don't know how it is with you, but my consolation is that God must know. He must! Things that seem on the face of 'em like murder, or say suicide, may appear different to God. Heh?'

'That's what the murderer and the suicide can always hope – I suppose.'

'I have expressed myself clumsily as usual. The facts as God knows 'em – may be different – even after the most clinching evidence. I've always said that – both as a lawyer and a man, but some people won't – I don't want to judge 'em – we'll say they can't – believe it; whereas I say there's always a working chance – a certainty – that the worst hasn't happened.' He stopped and cleared his throat. 'Now, let's come on! This time next week I shall be taking my holiday.'

'What links?' I asked carelessly, while twins in a perambulator got out of our line of fire.

'A potty little nine-hole affair at a hydro in the Midlands. My cousins stay there. Always will. Not but what the fourth and the seventh holes take some doing. You could manage it, though,' he said encouragingly. 'You're doing much better. It's only your approach shots that are weak.'

'You're right. I can't approach for nuts! I shall go to pieces while you're away – with no-one to coach me,' I said mournfully.

'I haven't taught you anything,' he said, delighted with the compliment.

'I owe all I've learned to you, anyhow. When will you come back?'

'Look here,' he began. 'I don't know your engagements, but I've no-one to play with at Burry Mills. Never have. Why couldn't you take a few days off and join me there? I warn you it will be rather dull. It's a throat and gout place – baths, massage, electricity, and so forth. But the fourth and the seventh holes really take some doing.'

'I'm for the game,' I answered valiantly, Heaven well knowing that I hated every stroke and word of it.

'That's the proper spirit. As their lawyer I must ask you not to say anything to my cousins about Holmescroft. It upsets 'em. Always did. But speaking as man to man, it would be very pleasant for me if you could see your way to – '

I saw it as soon as decency permitted, and thanked him sincerely. According to my now well-developed theory he had certainly misappropriated his aged cousins' monies under power of attorney, and had probably driven poor Agnes Moultrie out of her wits, but I wished that he was not so gentle, and good-tempered, and innocent eyed.

Before I joined him at Burry Mills Hydro, I spent a night at Holmescroft. Miss M'Leod had returned from her Hydro, and first we made very merry on the open lawn in the sunshine over the manners and customs of the English resorting to such places. She knew dozens of hydros, and warned me how to behave in them, while Mr and Mrs M'Leod stood aside and adored her.

'Ah! That's the way she always comes back to us,' he said. 'Pity it wears off so soon, ain't it? You ought to hear her sing "With mirth thou pretty bird".'

We had the house to face through the evening, and there we neither laughed nor sung. The gloom fell on us as we entered, and did not shift till ten o'clock, when we crawled out, as it were, from beneath it.

'It has been bad this summer,' said Mrs M'Leod in a whisper after we realised that we were freed. 'Sometimes I think the house will get up and cry out – it is so bad.'

'How?'

'Have you forgotten what comes after the depression ?'

So then we waited about the small fire, and the dead air in the room presently filled and pressed down upon us with the sensation (but words are useless here) as though some dumb and bound power were striving against gag and bond to deliver its soul of an articulate word. It passed in a few minutes, and I fell to thinking about Mr Baxter's conscience and Agnes Moultrie, gone mad in the well-lit bedroom that awaited me. These reflections secured me a night during which I rediscovered how, from purely mental causes, a man can be physically sick; but the sickness was bliss compared to my dreams when the birds waked. On my departure, M'Leod gave me a beautiful narwhal's horn, much as a nurse gives a child sweets for being brave at a dentist's.

'There's no duplicate of it in the world,' he said, 'else it would have come to old Max M'Leod;' and he tucked it into the motor. Miss M'Leod on the far side of the car whispered, 'Have you found out anything, Mr Perseus?'

I shook my head.

'Then I shall be chained to my rock all my life,' she went on. 'Only don't tell papa.'

I supposed she was thinking of the young gentleman who special-ised in South American rails, for I noticed a ring on the third finger of her left hand.

I went straight from that house to Burry Mills Hydro, keen for the first time in my life on playing golf, which is guaranteed to occupy the mind. Baxter had taken me a room communicating with his own, and after lunch introduced me to a tall, horse-headed elderly lady of decided manners, whom a white-haired maid pushed along in a bath-chair through the park-like grounds of the Hydro. She was Miss Mary Moultrie, and she coughed and cleared her throat just like Baxter. She suffered – she told me it was a Moultrie castemark – from some obscure form of chronic bronchitis, complicated with spasm of the glottis; and, in a dead, flat voice, with a sunken eye that looked and saw not, told me what washes, gargles, pastilles, and inhalations she had proved most beneficial. From her I was passed on to her younger sister, Miss Elizabeth, a small and withered thing with twitching lips, victim, she told me, to very much the same sort of throat, but secretly devoted to another set of medicines. When she went away with Baxter and the bath-chair, I fell across a major of the Indian army with gout in his glassy eyes, and a stomach which he had taken all round the Continent. He laid everything before me; and him I escaped only to be confided in by a matron with a tendency to follicular tonsillitis and eczema. Baxter waited hand and foot on his cousins till five o'clock, trying, as I saw, to atone for his treatment of the dead sister. Miss Mary ordered him about like a dog.

'I warned you it would be dull,' he said when we met in the smoking-room.

'It's tremendously interesting,' I said. 'But how about a look round the links?'

'Unluckily damp always affects my eldest cousin. I've got to buy her a new bronchitis-kettle. Arthurs broke her old one yesterday.'

We slipped out to the chemist's shop in the town, and he bought a large glittering tin thing whose workings he explained.

'I'm used to this sort of work. I come up here pretty often,' he said. 'I've the family throat too.'

'You're a good man,' I said. 'A very good man.'

He turned towards me in the evening light among the beeches, and his face was changed to what it might have been a generation before.

'You see,' he said huskily, 'there was the youngest – Agnes. Before she fell ill, you know. But she didn't like leaving her sisters. Never would.' He hurried on with his odd-shaped load and left me among the ruins of my black theories. The man with that face had done Agnes Moultrie no wrong.

We never played our game. I was waked between two and three in the morning from my hygienic bed by Baxter in an ulster over orange and white pyjamas, which I should never have suspected from his character.

'My cousin has had some sort of a seizure,' he said. 'Will you come? I don't want to wake the doctor. Don't want to make a scandal. Quick!'

So I came quickly, and led by the white-haired Arthurs in a jacket and petticoat, entered a double-bedded room reeking with steam and Friar's Balsam. The electrics were all on. Miss Mary – I knew her by her height – was at the open window, wrestling with Miss Elizabeth, who gripped her round the knees.

Miss Mary's hand was at her own throat, which was streaked with blood.

'She's done it. She's done it too!' Miss Elizabeth panted. 'Hold her! Help me!'

'Oh, I say! Women don't cut their throats,' Baxter whispered.

'My God! Has she cut her throat?' the maid cried out, and with no warning rolled over in a faint. Baxter pushed her under the washbasins, and leaped to hold the gaunt woman who crowed and whistled as she struggled toward the window. He took her by the shoulder, and she struck out wildly: 'All right! She's only cut her hand,' he said. 'Wet towel quick!'

While I got that he pushed her backward. Her strength seemed almost as great as his. I swabbed at her throat when I could, and found no mark; then helped him to control her a little. Miss Elizabeth leaped back to bed, wailing like a child.

'Tie up her hand somehow,' said Baxter. 'Don't let it drip about the place. She – ' he stepped on broken glass in his slippers, 'she must have smashed a pane.'

Miss Mary lurched towards the open window again, dropped on her knees, her head on the sill, and lay quiet, surrendering the cut hand to me.

'What did she do?' Baxter turned towards Miss Elizabeth in the far bed.

'She was going to throw herself out of the window,' was the answer. 'I stopped her, and sent Arthurs for you. Oh, we can never hold up our heads again!'

Miss Mary writhed and fought for breath. Baxter found a shawl which he threw over her shoulders.

'Nonsense!' said he. 'That isn't like Mary;' but his face worked when he said it.

'You wouldn't believe about Aggie, John. Perhaps you will now!' said Miss Elizabeth. 'I saw her do it, and she's cut her throat too!'

'She hasn't,' I said. 'It's only her hand.'

Miss Mary suddenly broke from us with an indescribable grunt, flew, rather than ran, to her sister's bed, and there shook her as one furious schoolgirl would shake another.

'No such thing,' she croaked. 'How dare you think so, you wicked little fool?'

'Get into bed, Mary,' said Baxter. 'You'll catch a chill.'

She obeyed, but sat up with the grey shawl round her lean shoulders, glaring at her sister. 'I'm better now,' she panted. 'Arthurs let me sit out too long. Where's Arthurs? The kettle.'

'Never mind Arthurs,' said Baxter. 'You get the kettle.' I hastened to bring it from the side table. 'Now, Mary, as God sees you, tell me what you've done.'

His lips were dry, and he could not moisten. them with his tongue.

Miss Mary applied herself to the mouth of the kettle, and between indraws of steam said: 'The spasm came on just now, while I was asleep. I was nearly choking to death. So I went to the window. I've done it often before, without waking anyone. Bessie's such an old maid about draughts. I tell you I was choking to death. I couldn't manage the catch, and I nearly fell out. That window opens too low. I cut my hand trying to save myself. Who has tied it up in this filthy handkerchief? I wish you had had my throat, Bessie. I never was nearer dying!' She scowled on us all impartially, while her sister sobbed.

From the bottom of the bed we heard a quivering voice: 'Is she dead? Have they took her away? Oh, I never could bear the sight o' blood!'

'Arthurs,' said Miss Mary, 'you are an hireling. Go away!'

It is my belief that Arthurs crawled out on all fours, but I was busy picking up broken glass from the carpet.

Then Baxter, seated by the side of the bed, began to cross-examine in a voice I scarcely recognised. No-one could for an instant have doubted the genuine rage of Miss Mary against her sister, her cousin, or her maid; and that a doctor should have been called in – for she did me the honour of calling me doctor – was the last drop. She was choking with her throat; had rushed to the window for air; had near pitched out, and in catching at the window bars had cut her hand. Over and over she made this clear to the intent Baxter. Then she turned on her sister and tongue-lashed her savagely.

'You mustn't blame me,' Miss Bessie faltered at last. 'You know what we think of night and day.'

'I'm coming to that,' said Baxter. 'Listen to me. What you did, Mary, misled four people into thinking you – you meant to do away with yourself.'

'Isn't one suicide in the family enough? Oh God, help and pity us! You couldn't have believed that!' she cried.

'The evidence was complete. Now, don't you think,' Baxter's finger wagged under her nose – 'can't you think that poor Aggie did the same thing at Holmescroft when she fell out of the window?'

'She had the same throat,' said Miss Elizabeth. 'Exactly the same symptoms. Don't you remember, Mary?'

'Which was her bedroom?' I asked of Baxter in an undertone.

'Over the south verandah, looking on to the tennis lawn.'

'I nearly fell out of that very window when I was at Holmescroft – opening it to get some air. The sill doesn't come much above your knees,' I said.

'You hear that, Mary? Mary, do you hear What this gentleman says? Won't you believe that what nearly happened to you must have happened to poor Aggie that night? For God's sake – for her sake – Mary, won't you believe?'

There was a long silence while the steam kettle puffed.

'If I could have proof – if I could have proof,' said she, and broke into most horrible tears.

Baxter motioned to me, and I crept away to my room, and lay awake till morning, thinking more specially of the dumb Thing at

Holmescroft which wished to explain itself. I hated Miss Mary as perfectly as though I had known her for twenty years, but I felt that, alive or dead, I should not like her to condemn me.

Yet at midday, when I saw Miss Mary in her bath-chair, Arthurs behind and Baxter and Miss Elizabeth on either side, in the park-like grounds of the Hydro, I found it difficult to arrange my words.

'Now that you know all about it,' said Baxter aside, after the first strangeness of our meeting was over, 'it's only fair to tell you that my poor cousin did not die in Holmescroft at all. She was dead when they found her under the window in the morning. Just dead.'

'Under that laburnum outside the window?' I asked, for I suddenly remembered the crooked evil thing.

'Exactly. She broke the tree in falling. But no death has ever taken place in the house, so far as we were concerned. You can make yourself quite easy on that point. Mr M'Leod's extra thousand for what you called the "clean bill of health" was something toward my cousins' estate when we sold. It was my duty as their lawyer to get it for them – at any cost to my own feelings.'

I know better than to argue when the English talk about their duty. So I agreed with my solicitor.

'Their sister's death must have been a great blow to your cousins,' I went on. The bath-chair was behind me.

'Unspeakable,' Baxter whispered. 'They brooded on it day and night. No wonder. If their theory of poor Aggie making away with herself was correct, she was eternally lost!'

'Do you believe that she made away with herself?'

'No, thank God! Never have! And after what happened to Mary last night, I see perfectly what happened to poor Aggie. She had the family throat too. By the way, Mary thinks you are a doctor. Otherwise she wouldn't like your having been in her room.'

'Very good. Is she convinced now about her sister's death?'

'She'd give anything to be able to believe it, but she's a hard woman, and brooding along certain lines makes one groovy. I have sometimes been afraid of her reason – on the religious side, don't you know. Elizabeth doesn't matter. Brain of a hen. Always had.'

Here Arthurs summoned me to the bath-chair, and the ravaged face, beneath its knitted Shetland wool hood, of Miss Mary Moultrie.

'I need not remind you, I hope, of the seal of secrecy – absolute secrecy – in your profession,' she began. 'Thanks to my cousin's and my sister's stupidity, you have found out – ' she blew her nose.

'Please don't excite her, sir,' said Arthurs at the back.

'But, my dear Miss Moultrie, I only know what I've seen, of course, but it seems to me that what you thought was a tragedy in your sister's case, turns out, on your own evidence, so to speak, to have been an accident – a dreadfully sad one – but absolutely an accident.'

'Do you believe that too?' she cried. 'Or are you only saying it to comfort me?'

'I believe it from the bottom of my heart. Come down to Holmescroft for an hour – for half an hour and satisfy yourself.'

'Of what? You don't understand. I see the house every day – every night. I am always there in spirit – waking or sleeping. I couldn't face it in reality.'

'But you must,' I said. 'If you go there in the spirit the greater need for you to go there in the flesh. Go to your sister's room once more, and see the window – I nearly fell out of it myself. It's – it's awfully low and dangerous. That would convince you,' I pleaded.

'Yet Aggie had slept in that room for years,' she interrupted.

'You've slept in your room here for a long time, haven't you? But you nearly fell out of the window when you were choking.'

'That is true. That is one thing true,' she nodded. 'And I might have been killed as – perhaps Aggie was killed.'

'In that case your own sister and cousin and maid would have said you had committed suicide, Miss Moultrie. Come down to Holmescroft, and go over the place just once.'

'You are lying,' she said quite quietly. 'You don't want me to come down to see a window. It is something else. I warn you we are Evangelicals. We don't believe in prayers for the dead. "As the tree falls – "'

'Yes. I dare say. But you persist in thinking that your sister committed suicide.'

'No! No! I have always prayed that I might have misjudged her.'

Arthurs at the bath-chair spoke up: 'Oh, Miss Mary! you would 'ave it from the first that poor Miss Aggie 'ad made away with herself; an', of course, Miss Bessie took the notion from you: Only Master – Mister John stood out – and – and I'd 'ave taken my Bible oath you was making away with yourself last night.'

Miss Mary leaned towards me, one finger on my sleeve.

'If going to Holmescroft kills me,' she said, 'you will have the murder of a fellow-creature on your conscience for all eternity.'

'I'll risk it,' I answered. Remembering what torment the mere reflection of her torments had cast on Holmescroft, and remembering, above all, the dumb Thing that filled the house with its desire to speak, I felt that there might be worse things.

Baxter was amazed at the proposed visit, but at a nod from that terrible woman went off to make arrangements. Then I sent a telegram to M'Leod bidding him and his vacate Holmescroft for that afternoon. Miss Mary should be alone with her dead, as I had been alone.

I expected untold trouble in transporting her, but to do her justice, the promise given for the journey, she underwent it without murmur, spasm, or unnecessary word. Miss Bessie, pressed in a corner by the window, wept behind her veil, and from time to time tried to take hold of her sister's hand. Baxter wrapped himself in his newly found happiness as selfishly as a bridegroom, for he sat still and smiled.

'So long as I know that Aggie didn't make away with herself,' he explained, 'I tell you frankly I don't care what happened. She's as hard as a rock – Mary. Always was. She won't die.'

We led her out on to the platform like a blind woman, and so got her into the fly. The half-hour crawl to Holmescroft was the most racking experience of the day. M'Leod had obeyed my instructions. There was no-one visible in the house or the gardens; and the front door stood open.

Miss Mary rose from beside her sister, stepped forth first, and entered the hall.

'Come, Bessie,' she cried.

'I daren't. Oh, I daren't.'

'Come!' Her voice had altered. I felt Baxter start. 'There's nothing to be afraid of.'

'Good heavens!' said Baxter. 'She's running up the stairs. We'd better follow.'

'Let's wait below. She's going to the room.'

We heard the door of the bedroom I knew open and shut, and we waited in the lemon-coloured hall, heavy with the scent of flowers.

'I've never been into it since it was sold,' Baxter sighed. 'What a lovely, restful place it is! Poor Aggie used to arrange the flowers.'

'Restful?' I began, but stopped of a sudden, for I felt all over my bruised soul that Baxter was speaking truth. It was a light, spacious, airy house, full of the sense of wellbeing and peace – above all things, of peace. I ventured into the dining-room where the thoughtful M'Leod's had left a small fire. There was no terror there, present or lurking; and in the drawing-room, which for good reasons we had never cared to enter, the sun and the peace and the scent of the flowers worked together as is fit in an inhabited house. When I returned to the hall, Baxter was sweetly asleep on a couch, looking most unlike a middle-aged solicitor who had spent a broken night with an exacting cousin.

There was ample time for me to review it all – to felicitate myself upon my magnificent acumen (barring some errors about Baxter as a thief and possibly a murderer), before the door above opened, and Baxter, evidently a light sleeper, sprang awake.

'I've had a heavenly little nap,' he said, rubbing his eyes with the backs of his hands like a child. 'Good Lord! That's not their step!'

But it was. I had never before been privileged to see the Shadow turned backward on the dial – the years ripped bodily off poor human shoulders – old sunken eyes filled and alight – harsh lips moistened and human.

'John,' Miss Mary called, 'I know now. Aggie didn't do it!' and 'She didn't do it!' echoed Miss Bessie.

'I did not think it wrong to say a prayer,' Miss Mary continued. 'Not for her soul, but for our peace. Then I was convinced.'

'Then we got conviction,' the younger sister piped.

'We've misjudged poor Aggie, John. But I feel she knows now. Wherever she is, she knows that we know she is guiltless.'

'Yes, she knows. I felt it too,' said Miss Elizabeth.

'I never doubted,' said John Baxter, whose face was beautiful at that hour. 'Not from the first. Never have!'

'You never offered me proof, John. Now, thank God, it will not be the same any more. I can think henceforward of Aggie without sorrow.' She tripped, absolutely tripped, across the hall. 'What ideas these Jews have of arranging furniture!' She spied me behind a big *cloisonnée* vase. 'I've seen the window,' she said remotely. 'You took a great risk in advising me to undertake such a journey. However, as it turns out . . . I forgive you, and I pray you may never know what mental anguish means! Bessie! Look at this peculiar piano! Do you suppose, Doctor, these people would offer one tea? I miss mine.'

'I will go and see,' I said, and explored M'Leod's new-built servants' wing. It was in the servants' hall that I unearthed the M'Leod family, bursting with anxiety.

'Tea for three, quick,' I said. 'If you ask me any questions now, I shall have a fit!' So Mrs M'Leod got it, and I was butler, amid murmured apologies from Baxter, still smiling and self-absorbed, and the cold disapproval of Miss Mary, who thought the pattern of the china vulgar. However, she ate well, and even asked me whether I would not like a cup of tea for myself.

They went away in the twilight – the twilight that I had once feared. They were going to an hotel in London to rest after the fatigues of the day, and as their fly turned down the drive, I capered on the doorstep, with the all-darkened house behind me.

Then I heard the uncertain feet of the M'Leods and bade them not to turn on the lights, but to feel – to feel what I had done; for the Shadow was gone, with the dumb desire in the air. They drew short, but afterwards deeper, breaths, like bathers entering chill water, separated one from the other, moved about the hall, tiptoed upstairs, raced down, and then Miss M'Leod, and I believe her mother, though she denies this, embraced me. I know M'Leod did.

It was a disgraceful evening. To say we rioted through the house is to put it mildly. We played a sort of Blind Man's Buff along the darkest passages, in the unlighted drawing-room, and little dining-room, calling cheerily to each other after each exploration that here, and here, and here, the trouble – had removed itself. We came up to the bedroom – mine for the night again – and sat, the women on the bed, and we men on chairs, drinking in blessed draughts of peace and comfort and cleanliness of soul, while I told them my tale in full, and received fresh praise, thanks, and blessings.

When the servants, returned from their day's outing, gave us a supper of cold fried fish, M'Leod had sense enough to open no wine. We had been practically drunk since nightfall, and grew incoherent on water and milk.

'I like that Baxter,' said M'Leod. 'He's a sharp man. The death wasn't in the house, but he ran it pretty close, ain't it?'

'And the joke of it is that he supposes I want to buy the place from you,' I said. 'Are you selling?'

'Not for twice what I paid for it – now,' said M'Leod. 'I'll keep you in furs all your life, but not our Holmescroft.'

'No – never our Holmescroft,' said Miss M'Leod. 'We'll ask him here on Tuesday, mamma.' They squeezed each other's hands.

'Now tell me,' said Mrs M'Leod – 'that tall one, I saw out of the scullery window – did she tell you she was always here in the spirit? I hate her. She made all this trouble. It was not her house after she had sold it. What do you think?'

'I suppose,' I answered, 'she brooded over what she believed was her sister's suicide night and day – she confessed she did – and her thoughts being concentrated on this place, they felt like a – like a burning glass.'

'Burning glass is good,' said M'Leod.

'I said it was like a light of blackness turned on us,' cried the girl, twiddling her ring. 'That must have been when the tall one thought worst about her sister and the house.'

'Ah, the poor Aggie!' said Mrs M'Leod. 'The poor Aggie, trying to tell everyone it was not so! No wonder we felt Something wished to say Something. Thea, Max, do you remember that night '

'We need not remember any more,' M'Leod interrupted. 'It is not our trouble. They have told each other now.'

'Do you think, then,' said Miss M'Leod, 'that those two, the living ones, were actually told something – upstairs – in your – in the room?'

'I can't say. At any rate they were made happy, and they ate a big tea afterwards. As your father says, it is not our trouble any longer – thank God!'

'Amen!' said M'Leod. 'Now, Thea, let us have some music after all these months. "With mirth, thou pretty bird", ain't it? You ought to hear that.'

And in the half-lighted hall, Thea sang an old English song that I had never heard before.

> With mirth, thou pretty bird, rejoice
>   Thy Maker's praise enhanced;
> Lift up thy shrill and pleasant voice,
>   Thy God is high advanced!
> Thy food before He did provide,
>   And gives it in a fitting side,
> Wherewith be thou sufficed!
>   Why shouldst thou now unpleasant be,
> Thy wrath against God venting,
>   That He a little bird made thee,
> Thy silly head tormenting,
>   Because He made thee not a man?
> Oh, Peace! He hath well thought thereon,
>   Therewith be thou sufficed!

The Rabbi's Song

The Wish House

'Late came the god.'

The new Church Visitor had just left after a twenty minutes' call. During that time, Mrs Ashcroft had used such English as an elderly, experienced, and pensioned cook should, who had seen life in London. She was the readier, therefore, to slip back into easy, ancient Sussex (To softening the 'd's as one warmed) when the 'bus brought Mrs Fettley from thirty miles away for a visit, that pleasant March Saturday. The two had been friends since childhood; but, of late, destiny had separated their meetings by long intervals.

Much was to be said, and many ends, loose since last time, to be ravelled up on both sides, before Mrs Fettley, with her bag of quilt-patches, took the couch beneath the window commanding the garden, and the football-ground in the valley below.

'Most folk got out at Bush Tye for the match there,' she explained, 'so there weren't no-one for me to cushion agin, the last five mile. An' she *do* just-about bounce ye.'

'You've took no hurt,' said her hostess. 'You don't brittle by agein', Liz.'

Mrs Fettley chuckled and made to match a couple of patches to her liking. 'No, or I'd ha' broke twenty year back. You can't ever mind when I was so's to be called round, can ye?'

Mrs Ashcroft shook her head slowly – she never hurried – and went on stitching a sack-cloth lining into a list-bound rush tool-basket. Mrs Fettley laid out more patches in the spring light through the geraniums on the window-sill, and they were silent awhile.

'What like's this new Visitor o' yourn?' Mrs Fettley enquired, with a nod towards the door. Being very short-sighted, she had, on her entrance, almost bumped into the lady.

Mrs Ashcroft suspended the big packing-needle judicially on high, ere she stabbed home. 'Settin' aside she don't bring much news with her yet, I dunno as I've anythin' special agin her.'

'Ourn, at Keyneslade,' said Mrs Fettley, 'she's full o' words an' pity, but she don't stay for answers. Ye can get on with your thoughts while she clacks.'

'This 'un don't clack. She's aimin' to be one o' those High Church nuns, like.'

'Ourn's married, but, by what they say, she've made no great gains of it . . . ' Mrs Fettley threw up her sharp chin. 'Lord! How they dam' cherubim do shake the very bones o' the place!'

The tile-sided cottage trembled at the passage of two specially chartered forty-seat charabancs on their way to the Bush Tye match; a regular Saturday shopping 'bus, for the county's capital, fumed behind them; while, from one of the crowded inns, a fourth car backed out to join the procession, and held up the stream of through pleasure-traffic.

'You're as free-tongued as ever, Liz,' Mrs Ashcroft observed.

'Only when I'm with you. Otherwhiles, I'm Granny – three times over. I lay that basket's for one o' your gran'chiller – ain't it?'

' 'Tis for Arthur – my Jane's eldest.'

'But he ain't workin' nowheres, is he?'

'No. 'Tis a picnic-basket.'

'You're let off light. My Willie, he's allus at me for money for them aireated wash-poles folk puts up in their gardens to draw the music from Lunnon, like. An' I give it 'im – pore fool me!'

'An' he forgets to give you the promise-kiss after, don't he?' Mrs Ashcroft's heavy smile seemed to strike inwards.

'He do. No odds 'twixt boys now an' forty year back. Take all an' give naught – an' we to put up with it! Pore fool we! Three shillin' at a time Willie'll ask me for!'

'They don't make nothin' o' money these days,' Mrs Ashcroft said.

'An' on'y last week,' the other went on, 'me daughter, she ordered a quarter pound suet at the butchers's; an' she sent it back to 'im to be chopped. She said she couldn't bother with choppin' it.'

'I lay he charged her, then.'

'I lay he did. She told me there was a whisk-drive that afternoon at the Institute, an' she couldn't bother to do the choppin'.'

'Tck!'

Mrs Ashcroft put the last firm touches to the basket-lining. She had scarcely finished when her sixteen-year-old grandson, a maiden of the moment in attendance, hurried up the garden-path shouting to know if the thing were ready, snatched it, and made off without acknowledgment. Mrs Fettley peered at him closely.

'They're goin' picnickin' somewheres,' Mrs Ashcroft explained.

'Ah,' said the other, with narrowed eyes. 'I lay *he* won't show much mercy to any he comes across, either. Now 'oo the dooce do he remind me of, all of a sudden? '

'They must look arter theirselves – same as we did.' Mrs Ashcroft began to set out the tea.

'No denyin' *you* could, Gracie,' said Mrs Fettley.

'What's in your head now?'

'Dunno . . . But it come over me, sudden-like – about dat woman from Rye – I've slipped the name – Barnsley, wadn't it?'

'Batten – Polly Batten, you're thinkin' of.'

'That's it – Polly Batten. That day she had it in for you with a hay-fork – 'time we was all hayin' at Smalldene – for stealin' her man.'

'But you heered me tell her she had my leave to keep him?' Mrs Ashcroft's voice and smile were smoother than ever.

'I did – an' we was all looking that she'd prod the fork spang through your breastes when you said it.'

'No-oo. She'd never go beyond bounds – Polly. She shruck too much for reel doin's.'

'Allus seems to *me*,' Mrs Fettley said after a pause, 'that a man 'twixt two fightin' women is the foolishest thing on earth. Like a dog bein' called two ways.'

'Mebbe. But what set ye off on those times, Liz?'

'That boy's fashion o' carryin' his head an' arms. I haven't rightly looked at him since he's growed. Your Jane never showed it, but – *him*! Why, 'tis Jim Batten and his tricks come to life again! . . . Eh?'

'Mebbe. There's some that would ha' made it out so – bein' barren-like, themselves.'

'Oho! Ah well! Dearie, dearie me, now! . . . An' Jim Batten's been dead this – '

'Seven and twenty year,' Mrs Ashcroft answered briefly. 'Won't ye draw up, Liz?'

Mrs Fettley drew up to buttered toast, currant bread, stewed tea, bitter as leather, some home-preserved pears, and a cold boiled pig's tail to help down the muffins. She paid all the proper compliments.

'Yes. I dunno as I've ever owed me belly much,' said Mrs Ashcroft thoughtfully. 'We only go through this world once.'

'But don't it lay heavy on ye, sometimes?' her guest suggested.

'Nurse says I'm a sight liker to die o' me indigestion than me leg.' For Mrs Ashcroft had a long-standing ulcer on her shin, which needed regular care from the Village Nurse, who boasted (or others did, for her) that she had dressed it one hundred and three times already during her term of office.

'An' you that *was* so able, too! It's all come on ye before your full time, like. *I*'ve watched ye goin'.' Mrs Fettley spoke with real affection.

'Somethin's bound to find ye sometime. I've me 'eart left me still,' Mrs Ashcroft returned.

'You was always big-hearted enough for three. That's somethin' to look back on at the day's eend.'

'I reckon you've *your* back-lookin's, too,' was Mrs Ashcroft's answer.

'You know it. But I don't think much regardin' such matters excep' when I'm along with you, Gra'. Takes two sticks to make a fire.'

Mrs Fettley stared, with jaw half-dropped, at the grocer's bright calendar on the wall. The cottage shook again to the roar of the motor traffic, and the crowded football-ground below the garden roared almost as loudly; for the village was well set to its Saturday leisure.

* * *

Mrs Fettley had spoken very precisely for some time without interruption, before she wiped her eyes. 'And,' she concluded, 'they read 'is death-notice to me, out o' the paper last month. O' course it wadn't any o' *my* becomin' concerns – let be I 'adn't set eyes on him for so long. O' course *I* couldn't say nor show nothin'. Nor I've no rightful call to go to Eastbourne to see 'is grave, either. I've been schemin' to slip over there by the 'bus some day; but they'd ask questions at 'ome past endurance. So I 'aven't even *that* to stay me.'

'But you've 'ad your satisfactions?'

'Godd! Yess! Those four years 'e was workin' on the rail near us. An' the other drivers they gave him a brave funeral, too.'

'Then you've naught to cast-up about. 'Nother cup o' tea?'

* * *

The light and air had changed a little with the sun's descent, and the two elderly ladies closed the kitchen-door against chill. A couple of jays squealed and skirmished through the undraped apple trees in the garden. This time, the word was with Mrs Ashcroft, her elbows on the tea-table, and her sick leg propped on a stool . . .

'Well I never! But what did your 'usband say to that?' Mrs Fettley asked, when the deep-toned recital halted.

' 'E said I might go where I pleased for all of 'im. But seein' 'e was bed-rid, I said I'd 'tend 'im out. 'E knowed I wouldn't take no advantage of 'im in that state. 'E lasted eight or nine week. Then he was took with a seizure-like; an' laid stone-still for days. Then 'e propped 'imself up abed an' says: "You pray no man'll ever deal with you like you've dealed with some." "An' you?" I says, for *you* know, Liz, what a rover 'e was. "It cuts both ways," says 'e, "but *I*'m death-wise, an' I can see what's comin' to you." He died a-Sunday an' was buried a-Thursday . . . An' yet I'd set a heap by him – one time or – did I ever?'

'You never told me that before,' Mrs Fettley ventured.

'I'm payin' ye for what ye told me just now. Him bein' dead, I wrote up, sayin' I was free for good, to that Mrs Marshall in Lunnon – which gave me my first place as kitchen-maid – Lord, how long ago! She was well pleased, for they two was both gettin' on, an' I knowed their ways. You remember, Liz, I used to go to 'em in service between whiles, for years – when we wanted money, or – or my 'usband was away – on occasion.'

' 'E *did* get that six months at Chichester, didn't 'e?' Mrs Fettley whispered. 'We never rightly won to the bottom of it.'

' 'E'd ha' got more, but the man didn't die.'

'None o' your doin's, was it, Gra'?'

'No! 'Twas the woman's husband this time. An' so, my man bein' dead, I went back to them Marshall's, as cook, to get me legs under a gentleman's table again, and be called with a handle to me name. That was the year you shifted to Portsmouth.'

'Cosham,' Mrs Fettley corrected. 'There was a middlin' lot o' new buildin' bein' done there. My man went first, an' got the room, an' I follered.'

'Well, then, I was a year-abouts in Lunnon, all at a breath, like, four meals a day an' livin' easy. Then, 'long towards autumn, they two went travellin', like, to France; keepin' me on, for they couldn't do without me. I put the house to rights for the caretaker, an' then I slipped down 'ere to me sister Bessie – me wages in me pockets, an' all 'ands glad to be'old of me.'

'That would be when I was at Cosham,' said Mrs Fettley.

'*You* know, Liz, there wasn't no cheap-dog pride to folk, those days, no more than there was cinemas nor whisk-drives. Man or woman 'ud lay hold o' any job that promised a shillin' to the backside of it, didn't they? I was all peaked up after Lunnon, an' I thought the fresh airs 'ud serve me. So I took on at Smalldene, obligin' with a hand at the early potato-liftin', stubbin' hens, an' such-like. They'd ha' mocked me sore in my kitchen in Lunnon, to see me in men's boots, an me petticoats all shorted.'

'Did it bring ye any good?' Mrs Fettley asked.

' 'Twadn't for that I went. You know, 's well's me, that na'un happens to ye till it 'as 'appened. Your mind don't warn ye before'and of the road ye've took, till you're at the far eend of it. We've only a backwent view of our proceedin's.'

' 'Oo was it?'

' 'Arry Mockler.' Mrs Ashcroft's face puckered to the pain of her sick leg.

Mrs Fettley gasped. ' 'Arry? Bert Mockler's son! An' *I* never guessed!'

Mrs Ashcroft nodded. 'An' I told myself – *an'* I beleft it – that I wanted field-work.'

'What did ye get out of it?'

'The usuals. Everythin' at first – worse than naught after. I had signs an' warnings a-plenty, but I took no heed of 'em. For we was burnin' rubbish one day, just when we'd come to know how 'twas with – with both of us. 'Twas early in the year for burnin', an' I said so. "No!" says he. "The sooner dat old stuff's off an' done with," 'e says, "the better." 'Is face was harder'n rocks when he spoke. Then it come over me that I'd found me master, which I 'adn't ever before. I'd allus owned 'em, like.'

'Yes ! Yes ! They're yourn or you're theirn,' the other sighed. 'I like the right way best.'

'I didn't. But 'Arry did . . . 'Long then, it come time for me to go back to Lunnon. I couldn't. I clean couldn't! So, I took an' tipped a dollop o' scaldin' water out o' the copper one Monday mornin' over me left 'and and arm. Dat stayed me where I was for another fortnight.'

'Was it worth it?' said Mrs Fettley, looking at the silvery scar on the wrinkled fore-arm.

Mrs Ashcroft nodded. 'An' after that, we two made it up 'twixt us so's 'e could come to Lunnon for a job in a liv'ry stable not far from me. 'E got it. *I* 'tended to that. There wadn't no talk nowhere. His own mother never suspicioned how 'twas. He just slipped up to Lunnon, an' there we abode that winter, not 'alf a mile 'tother from each.'

'Ye paid 'is fare an' all, though'; Mrs Fettley spoke convincedly.

Again Mrs Ashcroft nodded. 'Dere wadn't much I didn't do for him.

'E was me master, an' – O God, help us! – we'd laugh over it walkin' together after dark in them paved streets, an' me corns fair wrenchin' in me boots! I'd never been like that before. Ner he! Ner he!'

Mrs Fettley clucked sympathetically.

'An' when did ye come to the eend?' she asked.

'When 'e paid it all back again, every penny. Then I knowed, but I wouldn't *suffer* meself to know. "You've been mortal kind to me," he says. "Kind!" I said. " 'Twixt *us*?" But 'e kep' all on tellin' me 'ow kind I'd been an' 'e'd never forget it all his days. I held it from off o' me for three evenin's, because I would *not* believe. Then 'e talked about not bein' satisfied with 'is job in the stables, an' the men there puttin' tricks on 'im, an' all they lies which a man tells when 'e's leavin' ye. I heard 'im out, neither 'elpin' nor 'inderin'. At the last, I took off a fiddle brooch which he'd give me an' I says: "Dat'll do. *I* ain't askin' na'un'." An' I turned me round an' walked off to me own sufferin's. 'E didn't make 'em worse. 'E didn't come nor write after that. 'E slipped off 'ere back 'ome to 'is mother again.'

'An' 'ow often did ye look for 'en to come back?' Mrs Fettley demanded mercilessly.

'More'n once – more'n once! Goin' over the streets we'd used, I thought de very pave-stones 'ud shruck out under me feet.'

'Yes,' said Mrs Fettley. 'I dunno but dat don't 'urt as much as aught else. An' dat was all ye got? '

'No. 'Twadn't. That's the curious part, if you'll believe it, Liz.'

'I do. I lay you're further off lyin' now than in all your life, Gra'.'

'I am . . . An' I suffered, like I'd not wish my most arrantest enemies to. God's Own Name! I went through the hoop that spring! One part of it was 'eddicks which I'd never known all me days before. Think o' *me* with an 'eddick! But I come to be grateful for 'em. They kep' me from thinkin' . . .'

' 'Tis like a tooth,' Mrs Fettley commented. 'It must rage an' rugg till it tortures itself quiet on ye; an' then – then there's na'un left.'

'*I* got enough lef' to last me all my days on earth. It come about through our charwoman's fiddle girl – Sophy Ellis was 'er name – all eyes an' elbers an' hunger. I used to give 'er vittles. Otherwhiles, I took no special notice of 'er, an' a sight less, o' course, when me trouble about 'Arry was on me. But – you know how fiddle maids first feel it sometimes – she come to be crazy-fond o' me, pawin' an' cuddlin' all whiles; an' I 'adn't the 'eart to beat 'er off . . . One afternoon, early in spring 'twas, 'er mother 'ad sent 'er round to scutchel up what vittles she could off of us. I was settin' by the fire, me apern over me head, half-mad with the 'eddick, when she slips in. I reckon I was middlin' short with 'er. "Lor'!" she says. "Is *that* all? I'll take it off you in two-twos! " I told her not to lay a finger on me, for I thought she'd want to stroke my forehead; an' – I ain't that make. "*I* won't tech ye," she says, an' slips out again. She 'adn't been gone ten minutes 'fore me old 'eddick took off quick as bein' kicked. So I went about my work. Prasin'ly, Sophy comes back, an' creeps into my chair quiet as a mouse. 'Er eyes was deep in 'er 'ead an' 'er face all drawed. I asked 'er what 'ad 'appened. "Nothin'," she says. "On'y *I*'ve got it now." "Got what?" I says. " Your 'eddick," she says, all hoarse an' sticky-tipped. "I've took it on me." "Nonsense," I says, "it went of itself when you was out. Lay still an' I'll make ye a cup o' tea." " 'Twon't do no good," she says, "till your time's up. 'Ow long do *your* 'eddicks last?" "Don't talk silly," I says, "or I'll send for the Doctor." It looked to me like she might be hatchin' de measles. "Oh, Mrs Ashcroft," she says, stretchin' out 'er fiddle thin arms. "I do love ye." There wasn't any holdin' agin that. I took 'er into me lap an' made much of 'er. "Is it truly gone?" she says. "Yes," I says, "an' if 'twas you took it away, I'm truly grateful." " '*Twas* me," she says, layin' 'er cheek to mine. "No-one but me knows how." An' then she said she'd changed me 'eddick for me at a Wish 'Ouse.'

'Whatt?' Mrs Fettley spoke sharply.

'A Wish House. No! *I* 'adn't 'eard o' such things, either. I couldn't get it straight at first, but, puttin' all together, I made out that a Wish 'Ouse 'ad to be a house which 'ad stood unlet an' empty long enough for Someone, like, to come an' in'abit there. She said a fiddle girl that she'd played with in the livery-stables where 'Arty worked 'ad told 'er so. She said the girl 'ad belonged in a caravan that laid up, o' winters, in Lunnon. Gypsy, I judge.'

'Ooh! There's no sayin' what Gippos know, but *I*'ve never 'eard of a Wish 'Ouse, an' I know – some things,' said Mrs Fettley.

'Sophy said there was a Wish 'Ouse in Wadloes Road just a few streets off, on the way to our greengrocer's. All you 'ad to do, she said, was to ring the bell an' wish your wish through the slit o' the letter-box. I asked 'er if the fairies give it 'er? "Don't ye know," she says, "there's no fairies in a Wish 'Ouse? There's on'y a Token." '

'Goo' Lord A'mighty! Where did she come by *that* word?' cried Mrs Fettley; for a Token is a wraith of the dead or, worse still, of the living.

'The caravan-girl 'ad told 'er, she said. Well, Liz, it troubled me to 'ear 'er, an' lyin' in me arms she must ha' felt it. "That's very kind o' you," I says, holdin' 'er tight, "to wish me 'eddick away. But why didn't ye ask somethin' nice for yourself?" "You can't do that," she says. "All you'll get at a Wish 'Ouse is leave to take someone else's trouble. I've took Ma's 'eddicks, when she's been kind to me; but this is the first time I've been able to do aught for you. Oh, Mrs Ashcroft, I *do* just – about love you." An' she goes on all like that. Liz, I tell you my 'air e'en a'most stood on end to 'ear 'er. I asked 'er what like a Token was. "I dunno," she says, "but after you've ringed the bell, you'll 'ear it run up from the basement, to the front door. Then say your wish," she says, "an' go away." "The Token don't open de door to ye, then?" I says. "Oh no," she says. "You on'y 'ear gigglin', like, be'ind the front door. Then you say you'll take the trouble off of 'oo ever 'tis you've chose for your love; an' ye'll get it," she says. I didn't ask no more – she was too 'ot an' fevered. I made much of 'er till it come time to light de gas, an' a fiddle after that, 'er 'eddick – mine, I suppose – took off, an' she got down an' played with the cat.'

'Well, I never!' said Mrs Fettley. 'Did – did ye foller it up, anyways?'

'She askt me to, but I wouldn't 'ave no such dealin's with a child.'

'What *did* ye do, then?'

'Sat in me own room 'stid o' the kitchen when me 'eddicks come on. But it lay at de back o' me mind.'

' 'Twould. Did she tell ye more, ever?'

'No. Besides what the Gippo girl 'ad told 'er, she knew naught, 'cept that the charm worked. An', next after that – in May 'twas – I suffered the summer out in Lunnon. 'Twas hot an' windy for weeks, an' the streets stinkin' o' dried 'orsedung blowin' from side to side an' lyin' level with the kerb. We don't get that nowadays. I 'ad my 'ol'day just before hoppin', an' come down 'ere to stay with Bessie again. She noticed I'd lost flesh, an' was all poochy under the eyes.'

'Did ye see 'Arry?''

Mrs Ashcroft nodded. 'The fourth – no, the fifth day. Wednesday 'twas. I knowed 'e was workin' at Smalldene again. I asked 'is mother in the street, bold as brass. She 'adn't room to say much, for Bessie – you know 'er tongue – was talkin' full-clack. But that Wednesday, I was walkin' with one o' Bessie's chillern hangin' on me skirts, at de back o' Chanter's Tot. Prasin'ly, I felt 'e was be'ind me on the footpath, an' I knowed by 'is tread 'e'd changed 'is nature. I slowed, an' I heard 'im slow. Then I fussed a piece with the child, to force him past me, like. So 'e 'ad to come past. 'E just says "Good-evenin' ", and goes on, tryin' to pull 'isself together.'

'Drunk, was he?' Mrs Fettley asked.

'Never! S'runk an' wizen; 'is clothes 'angin' on 'im like bags, an' the back of 'is neck whiter'n chalk. 'Twas all I could do not to oppen my arms an' cry after him. But I swallered me spittle till I was back 'ome again an' the chillern abed. Then I says to Bessie, after supper, "What in de world's come to 'Arry Mockler?" Bessie told me 'e'd been a-Hospital for two months, 'long o' cuttin' 'is foot wid a spade, muckin' out the old pond at Smalldene. There was poison in de dirt, an' it rooshed up 'is leg, like, an' come out all over him. 'E 'adn't been back to 'is job – carterin' at Smalldene – more'n a fortnight. She told me the Doctor said he'd go off, likely, with the November frosts; an' 'is mother 'ad told 'er that 'e didn't rightly eat nor sleep, an' sweated 'imself into pools, no odds 'ow chill 'e lay. An' spit terrible o' mornin's. "Dearie me," I says. "But, mebbe, hoppin' 'll set 'im right again," an' I licked me thread-point an' I fetched me needle's eye up to it an' I threads me needle under de lamp, steady as rocks. An' dat night (me bed was in de wash-house) I cried an' I cried. An' *you* know, Liz – for you've been with me in my throes – it takes summat to make me cry.'

'Yes; but Chile-bearin' is on'y just pain,' said Mrs Fettley.

'I come round by cock-crow, an' dabbed cold tea on me eyes to take away the signs. Long towards nex' evenin' – I was settin' out to lay some flowers on me 'usband's grave, for the look o' the thing – I met 'Arry over against where the War Memorial is now. 'E was comin' back from 'is 'orses, so 'e couldn't *not* see me. I looked 'im all over, an' " 'Arry," I says twix' me teeth, "come back an' rest-up in Lunnon." "I won't take it," he says, "for I can give ye naught." "I don't ask it," I says. "By God's Own Name, I don't ask na'un ! On'y come up an' see a Lunnon doctor." 'E lifts 'is two 'eavy eyes at me: " 'Tis past that, Gra'," 'e says. "I've but a few months left." " 'Arry!" I says. "*My* man!" I says. I couldn't say no more. 'Twas all up in me throat. "Thank ye kindly, Gra'," 'e says (but 'e never says "my woman"), an' 'e went on upstreet an' 'is mother – Oh, damn 'er! – she was watchin' for 'im, an' she shut de door be'ind 'im.'

Mrs Fettley stretched an arm across the table, and made to finger Mrs Ashcroft's sleeve at the wrist, but the other moved it out of reach.

'So I went on to the churchyard with my flowers, an' I remembered my 'usband's warnin' that night he spoke. 'E *was* death-wise, an' it *'ad* 'appened as 'e said. But as I was settin' down de jam-pot on the grave-mound, it come over me there was one thing I *could* do for 'Arry. Doctor or no Doctor, I thought I'd make a trial of it. So I did.

Nex' mornin', a bill came down from our Lunnon greengrocer. Mrs Marshall, she'd lef' me petty cash for suchlike – o' course – but I tole Bess 'twas for me to come an' open the 'ouse. So I went up, afternoon train.'

'An' – but I know you 'adn't – 'adn't you no fear?'

'What for? There was nothin' front o' me but my own shame an' God's croolty. I couldn't ever get 'Arry – 'ow *could* I? I knowed it must go on burnin' till it burned me out.'

'Aie!' said Mrs Fettley, reaching for the wrist again, and this time Mrs Ashcroft permitted it.

'Yit 'twas a comfort to know I could try *this* for 'im. So I went an' I paid the green-grocer's bill, an' put 'is receipt in me handbag, an' then I stepped round to Mrs Ellis – our char – an' got the 'ouse-keys an' opened the 'ouse. First, I made me bed to come back to (God's Own Name! Me bed to lie upon!). Nex' I made me a cup o' tea an' sat down in the kitchen thinkin', till 'long towards dusk. Terrible close, 'twas. Then I dressed me an' went out with the receipt in me 'andbag, feignin' to study it for an address, like. Fourteen, Wadloes Road, was the place – a liddle basement-kitchen 'ouse, in a row of twenty-thirty such, an' tiddy strips o' walled garden in front – the paint off the front doors, an' na'un done to na'un since ever so long. There wasn't 'ardly no-one in the streets 'cept the cats. 'Twas 'ot, too! I turned into the gate bold as brass; up de steps I went an' I ringed the front-door bell. She pealed loud, like it do in an empty house. When she'd all ceased, I 'eard a cheer, like, pushed back on de floor o' the kitchen. Then I 'eard feet on de kitchen-stairs, like it might ha' been a heavy woman in slippers. They come up to de stairhead, acrost the hall – I 'eard the bare boards creak under 'em – an' at de front door dey stopped. I stooped me to the letter-box slit, an' I says: "Let me take everythin' bad that's in store for my man, 'Arry Mockler, for love's sake." Then, whatever it was 'tother side de door let its breath out, like, as if it 'ad been holdin' it for to 'ear better.'

'Nothin' was *said* to ye?' Mrs Fettley demanded.

'Na'un. She just breathed out – a sort of *A-ah*, like. Then the steps went back an' downstairs to the kitchen – all draggy – an' I heard the cheer drawed up again.'

'An' you abode on de doorstep, throughout all, Gra'? '

Mrs Ashcroft nodded.

'Then I went away, an' a man passin' says to me: "Didn't you know that house was empty?" "No," I says. "I must ha' been give the wrong number." An' I went back to our 'ouse, an' I went to bed; for I was fair flogged out. 'Twas too 'ot to sleep more'n snatches, so I walked me about, lyin' down betweens, till crack o' dawn. Then I went to the kitchen to make me a cup o' tea, an' I hitted meself just above the ankle on an old roastin' jack o' mine that Mrs Ellis had moved out from the corner, her last cleanin'. An' so – nex' after that – I waited till the Marshalls come back o' their holiday.'

'Alone there? I'd ha' thought you'd 'ad enough of empty houses,' said Mrs Fettley, horrified.

'Oh, Mrs Ellis an' Sophy was runnin' in an' out soon's I was back, an' 'twixt us we cleaned de house again top-to-bottom. There's allus a hand's turn more to do in every house. An' that's 'ow 'twas with me that autumn an' winter, in Lunnon.'

'Then na'un hap – overtook ye for your doin's? '

Mrs Ashcroft smiled. 'No. Not then. 'Long in November I sent Bessie ten shillin's.'

'You was allus free-'anded,' Mrs Fettley interrupted.

'An' I got what I paid for, with the rest o' the news. She said the hoppin' 'ad set 'im up wonderful. 'E'd 'ad six weeks of it, and now 'e was back again carterin' at Smalldene. No odds to me 'ow it 'ad 'appened – 'slong's it 'ad. But I dunno as my ten shillin's eased me much. 'Arry bein' dead, like, 'e'd ha' been mine, till Judgment. 'Arry bein' alive, 'e'd like as not pick up with some woman middlin' quick. I raged over that. Come spring, I 'ad somethin' else to rage for. I'd growed a nasty little weepin' boil, like, on me shin, just above the boot-top, that wouldn't heal no shape. It made me sick to look at it, for I'm clean-fleshed by nature. Chop me all over with a spade, an' I'd heal like turf. Then Mrs Marshall she set 'er own doctor at me. 'E said I ought to ha' come to him at first go-off, 'stead o' drawn' all manner o' dyed stockm's over it for months. 'E said I'd stood up too much to me work, for it was settin' very close atop of a big swelled vein, like, behither the small o' me ankle. "Slow come, slow go," 'e says. "Lay your leg up on high an' rest it," he says, "an' 'twill ease off. Don't let it close up too soon. You've got a very fine leg, Mrs Ashcroft," 'e says. An' he put wet dressin's on it.'

' 'E done right.' Mrs Fettley spoke firmly. 'Wet dressin's to wet wounds. They draw de humours, same's a lamp-wick draws de oil.'

'That's true. An' Mrs Marshall was allus at me to make me set down more, an' dat nigh healed it up. An' then after a while they packed me off down to Bessie's to finish the cure; for I ain't the sort to sit down when I ought to stand up. You was back in the village then, Liz.'

'I was. I was, but – never did I guess!'

'I didn't desire ye to.' Mrs Ashcroft smiled. 'I saw 'Arry once or twice in de street, wonnerful fleshed up an' restored back. Then, one day I didn't see 'im, an' 'is mother told me one of 'is 'orses 'ad lashed out an' caught 'im on the 'ip. So 'e was abed an' middlin' painful. An' Bessie, she says to his mother, 'twas a pity 'Arry 'adn't a woman of 'is own to take the nursin' off 'er. And the old lady *was* mad! She told us that 'Arry 'ad never looked after any woman in 'is born days, an' as long as she was atop the mowlds, she'd contrive for 'im till 'er two 'ands dropped off. So I knowed she'd do watch-dog for me, 'thout askin' for bones.'

Mrs Fettley rocked with small laughter.

'That day,' Mrs Ashcroft went on, 'I'd stood on me feet nigh all the time, watchin' the doctor go in an' out; for they thought it might be 'is ribs, too. That made my boil break again, issuin' an' weepin'. But it turned out 'twadn't ribs at all, an' 'Arry 'ad a good night. When I heard that, nex' mornin', I says to meself, "I won't lay two an' two together *yit*. I'll keep me leg down a week, an' see what comes of it." It didn't hurt me that day, to speak of – 'seemed more to draw the strength out o' me like – an' 'Arry 'ad another good night. That made me persevere; but I didn't dare lay two an' two together till the weekend, an' then, 'Arry come forth e'en a'most 'imself again – na'un hurt outside ner in of him. I nigh fell on me knees in de washhouse when Bessie was up-street. "I've got ye now, my man," I says. "You'll take your good from me 'thout knowin' it till my life's end. O God, send me long to live for 'Arry's sake!" I says. An' I dunno that didn't still me ragin's.'

'For good?' Mrs Fettley asked.

'They come back, plenty times, but, let be how 'twould, I knowed I was doin' for 'im. I *knowed* it. I took an' worked me pains on an' off, like regulatin' my own range, till I learned to 'ave 'em at my commandments. An' that was funny, too. There was times, Liz, when my trouble 'ud all s'rink an' dry up, like. First, I used to try an' fetch it on again; bein' fearful to leave 'Arry alone too long for anythin' to lay 'old of. Prasin'ly I come to see that was a sign he'd do all right awhile, an' so I saved myself.'

' 'Ow long for?' Mrs Fettley asked, with deepest interest.

'I've gone de better part of a year once or twice with na'un more to show than the liddle weepin' core of it, like. *All* s'rinked up an' dried off. Then he'd inflame up – for a warnin' – an' I'd suffer it. When I couldn't no more – an' I '*ad* to keep on goin' with my Lunnon work – I'd lay me leg high on a cheer till it eased. Not too quick. I knowed by the feel of it, those times, dat 'Arry was in need. Then I'd send another five shillin's to Bess, or somethin' for the chillern, to find out if, mebbe, 'e'd took any hurt through my neglects. 'Twas *so*! Year in, year out, I worked it dat way, Liz, an' 'e got 'is good from me 'thout knowin' – for years and years.'

'But what did *you* get out of it, Gra'?' Mrs Fettley almost wailed. 'Did ye see 'im reg'lar? '

'Times – when I was 'ere on me 'ol'days. An' more, now that I'm 'ere for good. But 'e's never looked at me, ner any other woman 'cept 'is mother. '*Ow* I used to watch an' listen! So did she.'

'Years an' years!' Mrs Fettley repeated. 'An' where's 'e workin' at now?'

'Oh, 'e's give up carterin' quite a while. He's workin' for one o' them big tractorisin' firms – plowin' sometimes, an' sometimes off with lorries – fur as Wales, I've 'eard. He comes 'ome to 'is mother 'tween whiles; but I don't set eyes on him now, fer weeks on end. No odds! 'Is job keeps 'im from continuin' in one stay anywheres.'

'But just for de sake o' sayin' somethin' – s'pose 'Arry *did* get married?' said Mrs Fettley.

Mrs Ashcroft drew her breath sharply between her still even and natural teeth. 'Dat ain't been required of me,' she answered. 'I reckon my pains 'ull be counted agin that. Don't *you*, Liz?'

'It ought to be, dearie. It ought to be.'

'It *do* 'urt sometimes. You shall see it when Nurse comes. She thinks I don't know it's turned.'

Mrs Fettley understood. Human nature seldom walks up to the word 'cancer'.

'Be ye certain sure, Gra'?' she asked.

'I was sure of it when old Mr Marshall 'ad me up to 'is study an' spoke a long piece about my faithful service. I've obliged 'em on an' off for a goodish time, but not enough for a pension. But they give me a weekly 'lowance for life. I knew what *that* sinnified – as long as three years ago.'

'Dat don't *prove* it, Gra'.'

'To give fifteen bob a week to a woman 'oo'd live twenty year in the course o' nature? It *do*!'

'You're mistook! You're mistook!' Mrs Fettley insisted.

'Liz, there's *no* mistakin' when the edges are all heaped up, like –

same as a collar. You'll see it. An' I laid out Dora Wickwood, too. *She* 'ad it under the arm-pit, like.'

Mrs Fettley considered awhile, and bowed her head in finality.

' 'Ow long d'you reckon 'twill allow ye, countin' from now, dearie?'

'Slow come, slow go. But if I don't set eyes on ye 'fore next hoppin', this'll be goodbye, Liz.'

'Dunno as I'll be able to manage by then – not 'thout I have a liddle dog to lead me. For de chillern, dey won't be troubled, an' – O Gra'! I'm blindin' up – I'm blindin' up!'

'Oh, *dat* was why you didn't more'n finger with your quilt-patches all this while! I was wonderin' . . . But the pain *do* count, don't ye think, Liz? The pain *do* count to keep 'Arry where I want 'im. Say it can't be wasted, like.'

'I'm sure of it – sure of it, dearie. You'll 'ave your reward.'

'I don't want no more'n this – *if* de pain is taken into de reckonin'.'

' 'Twill be – 'twill be, Gra'.'

There was a knock on the door.

'That's Nurse. She's before 'er time,' said Mrs Ashcroft. 'Open to 'er.'

The young lady entered briskly, all the bottles in her bag clicking. 'Evenin', Mrs Ashcroft,' she began. 'I've come raound a little earlier than usual because of the Institute dance to-na-ite. You won't ma-ind, will you? ,

'Oh, no. Me dancin' days are over.' Mrs Ashcroft was the self-contained domestic at once.

'My old friend, Mrs Fettley 'ere, has been settin' talkin' with me a while.'

'I hope she 'asn't been fatiguing you?' said the Nurse a little frostily.

'Quite the contrary. It 'as been a pleasure. Only – only – just at the end I felt a bit – a bit flogged out like.'

'Yes, yes.' The Nurse was on her knees already, with the washes to hand. 'When old ladies get together they talk a deal too much, I've noticed.'

'Mebbe we do,' said Mrs Fettley, rising. 'So now I'll make myself scarce.'

'Look at it first, though,' said Mrs Ashcroft feebly. 'I'd like ye to look at it.'

Mrs Fettley looked, and shivered. Then she leaned over, and kissed Mrs Ashcroft once on the waxy yellow forehead, and again on the faded grey eyes.

'It *do* count, don't it – de pain?' The lips that still kept trace of their original moulding hardly more than breathed the words.

Mrs Fettley kissed them and moved towards the door.

A Matter of Fact

And if ye doubt the tale I tell,
Steer through the South Pacific swell;
Go where the branching coral hives
Unending strife of endless lives,
Where, leagued about the 'wildered boat,
The rainbow jellies fill and float;
And, lilting where the laver lingers,
The starfish trips on all her fingers;
Where, 'neath his myriad spines ashock,
The sea-egg ripples down the rock;
An orange wonder dimly guessed,
From darkness where the cuttles rest,
Moored o'er the darker deeps that hide
The blind white Sea-snake and his bride
Who, drowsing, nose the long-lost ships
Let down through darkness to their lips.

The Palms

Once a priest, always a priest; once a mason, always a mason; but once a journalist, always and for ever a journalist.

There were three of us, all newspaper men, the only passengers on a little tramp steamer that ran where her owners told her to go. She had once been in the Bilbao iron ore business, had been lent to the Spanish Government for service at Manilla; and was ending her days in the Cape Town coolie-trade, with occasional trips to Madagascar and even as far as England. We found her going to Southampton in ballast, and shipped in her because the fares were nominal. There was Keller, of an American paper, on his way back to the States from palace executions in Madagascar; there was a burly half-Dutchman, called Zuyland, who owned and edited a paper up country near Johannesburg; and there was myself, who had solemnly put away all journalism, vowing to forget that I had ever known the difference between an imprint and a stereo advertisement.

Ten minutes after Keller spoke to me, as the *Rathmines* cleared Cape Town, I had forgotten the aloofness I desired to feign, and was in heated discussion on the immorality of expanding telegrams beyond a certain fixed point. Then Zuyland came out of his cabin, and we were all at home instantly, because we were men of the same profession needing no introduction. We annexed the boat formally, broke open the passengers' bathroom door – on the Manilla lines the Dons do not wash – cleaned out the orange-peel and cigar-ends at the bottom of the bath, hired a Lascar to shave us throughout the voyage, and then asked each other's names.

Three ordinary men would have quarrelled through sheer boredom before they reached Southampton. We, by virtue of our craft, were anything but ordinary men. A large percentage of the tales of the world, the thirty-nine that cannot be told to ladies and the one that can, are common property coming of a common stock. We told them all, as a matter of form, with all their local and specific variants which are surprising. Then came, in the intervals of steady card-play, more personal histories of adventure and things seen and suffered: panics among white folk, when the blind terror ran from man to man on the Brooklyn Bridge, and the people crushed each other to death they knew not why; fires, and faces that opened and shut their mouths horribly at red-hot window frames; wrecks in frost and snow, reported from the sleet-sheathed rescue-tug at the risk of frostbite; long rides after diamond thieves; skirmishes on the veldt and in municipal committees with the Boers; glimpses of lazy tangled Cape politics and the mule-rule in the Transvaal; card-tales, horse-tales, woman-tales, by the score and the half hundred; till the first mate, who had seen more than us all put together, but lacked words to clothe his tales with, sat open-mouthed far into the dawn.

When the tales were done we picked up cards till a curious hand or a chance remark made one or other of us say, 'That reminds me of a man who – or a business which – ' and the anecdotes would continue while the *Rathmines* kicked her way northward through the warm water.

In the morning of one specially warm night we three were sitting immediately in front of the wheel-house, where an old Swedish boatswain whom we called 'Frithiof the Dane' was at the wheel, pretending that he could not hear our stories. Once or twice Frithiof spun the spokes curiously, and Keller lifted his head from a long chair to ask, 'What is it? Can't you get any steerage-way on her?'

'There is a feel in the water,' said Frithiof, 'that I cannot understand. I think that we run downhills or somethings. She steers bad this morning.'

Nobody seems to know the laws that govern the pulse of the big waters. Sometimes even a landsman can tell that the solid ocean is atilt, and that the ship is working herself up a long unseen slope; and sometimes the captain says, when neither full steam nor fair wind justifies the length of a day's run, that the ship is sagging downhill; but how these ups and downs come about has not yet been settled authoritatively.

'No, it is a following sea,' said Frithiof; 'and with a following sea you shall not get good steerage-way.'

The sea was as smooth as a duck-pond, except for a regular oily swell. As I looked over the side to see where it might be following us from, the sun rose in a perfectly clear sky and struck the water with its light so sharply that it seemed as though the sea should clang like a burnished gong. The wake of the screw and the little white streak cut by the log-line hanging over the stern were the only marks on the water as far as eye could reach.

Keller rolled out of his chair and went aft to get a pineapple from the ripening stock that was hung inside the after awning.

'Frithiof, the log-line has got tired of swimming. It's coming home,' he drawled.

'What?' said Frithiof, his voice jumping several octaves.

'Coming home,' Keller repeated, leaning over the stern. I ran to his side and saw the log-line, which till then had been drawn tense over the stern railing, slacken, loop, and come up off the port quarter. Frithiof called up the speaking-tube to the bridge, and the bridge answered, 'Yes, nine knots.' Then Frithiof spoke again, and the answer was, 'What do you want of the skipper?' and Frithiof bellowed, 'Call him up.'

By this time Zuyland, Keller, and myself had caught something of Frithiof's excitement, for any emotion on shipboard is most contagious. The captain ran out of his cabin, spoke to Frithiof, looked at the log-line, jumped on the bridge, and in a minute we felt the steamer swing round as Frithiof turned her.

'Going back to Cape Town?' said Keller.

Frithiof did not answer, but tore away at the wheel. Then he beckoned us three to help, and we held the wheel down till the

Rathmines answered it, and we found ourselves looking into the white of our own wake, with the still oily sea tearing past our bows, though we were not going more than half steam ahead.

The captain stretched out his arm from the bridge and shouted. A minute later I would have given a great deal to have shouted too, for one-half of the sea seemed to shoulder itself above the other half, and came on in the shape of a hill. There was neither crest, comb, nor curl-over to it; nothing but black water with little waves chasing each other about the flanks. I saw it stream past and on a level with the *Rathmines*' bow-plates before the steamer hove up her bulk to rise, and I argued that this would be the last of all earthly voyages for me. Then we lifted for ever and ever and ever, till I heard Keller saying in my ear, 'The bowels of the deep, good Lord!' and the *Rathmines* stood poised, her screw racing and drumming on the slope of a hollow that stretched downwards for a good half-mile.

We went down that hollow, nose under for the most part, and the air smelt wet and muddy, like that of an emptied aquarium. There was a second hill to climb; I saw that much: but the water came aboard and carried me aft till it jammed me against the wheel-house door, and before I could catch breath or clear my eyes again we were rolling to and fro in torn water, with the scuppers pouring like eaves in a thunderstorm.

'There were three waves,' said Keller; 'and the stokehold's flooded.'

The firemen were on deck waiting, apparently, to be drowned. The engineer came and dragged them below, and the crew, gasping, began to work the clumsy Board of Trade pump. That showed nothing serious, and when I understood that the *Rathmines* was really on the water, and not beneath it, I asked what had happened.

'The captain says it was a blow-up under the sea – a volcano,' said Keller.

'It hasn't warmed anything,' I said. I was feeling bitterly cold, and cold was almost unknown in those waters. I went below to change my clothes, and when I came up everything was wiped out in clinging white fog.

'Are there going to be any more surprises?' said Keller to the captain.

'I don't know. Be thankful you're alive, gentlemen. That's a tidal wave thrown up by a volcano. Probably the bottom of the sea has been lifted a few feet somewhere or other. I can't quite understand this cold spell. Our sea-thermometer says the surface water is 44°, and it should be 68° at least.'

'It's abominable,' said Keller, shivering. 'But hadn't you better attend to the fog-horn? It seems to me that I heard something.'

'Heard! Good heavens!' said the captain from the bridge, 'I should think you did.' He pulled the string of our fog-horn, which was a weak one. It sputtered and choked, because the stokehold was full of water and the fires were half-drowned, and at last gave out a moan. It was answered from the fog by one of the most appalling steam-sirens I have ever heard. Keller turned as white as I did, for the fog, the cold fog, was upon us, and any man may be forgiven for fearing a death he cannot see.

'Give her steam there!' said the captain to the engine-room. 'Steam for the whistle, if we have to go dead slow.'

We bellowed again, and the damp dripped off the awnings on to the deck as we listened for the reply. It seemed to be astern this time, but much nearer than before.

'The *Pembroke Castle* on us!' said Keller; and then, viciously, 'Well, thank God, we shall sink her too.'

'It's a side-wheel steamer,' I whispered. 'Can't you hear the paddles?'

This time we whistled and roared till the steam gave out, and the answer nearly deafened us. There was a sound of frantic threshing in the water, apparently about fifty yards away, and something shot past in the whiteness that looked as though it were grey and red.

'The *Pembroke Castle* bottom up,' said Keller, who, being a journalist, always sought for explanations. 'That's the colours of a Castle liner. We're in for a big thing.'

'The sea is bewitched,' said Frithiof from the wheel-house. 'There are *two* steamers!'

Another siren sounded on our bow, and the little steamer rolled in the wash of something that had passed unseen.

'We're evidently in the middle of a fleet,' said Keller quietly. 'If one doesn't run us down, the other will. Phew! What in creation is that?'

I sniffed, for there was a poisonous rank smell in the cold air – a smell that I had smelt before.

'If I was on land I should say that it was an alligator. It smells like musk,' I answered.

'Not ten thousand alligators could make that smell,' said Zuyland; 'I have smelt them.'

'Bewitched! Bewitched!' said Frithiof. 'The sea she is turned upside down, and we are walking along the bottom.'

Again the *Rathmines* rolled in the wash of some unseen ship, and a silver-grey wave broke over the bow, leaving on the deck a sheet of sediment – the grey broth that has its place in the fathomless deeps of the sea. A sprinkling of the wave fell on my face, and it was so cold that it stung as boiling water stings. The dead and most untouched deep water of the sea had been heaved to the top by the submarine volcano – the chill still water that kills all life and smells of desolation and emptiness. We did not need either the blinding fog or that indescribable smell of musk to make us unhappy – we were shivering with cold and wretchedness where we stood.

'The hot air on the cold water makes this fog,' said the captain; 'it ought to clear in a little time.'

'Whistle, oh! whistle, and let's get out of it,' said Keller.

The captain whistled again, and far and far astern the invisible twin steam-sirens answered us. Their blasting shriek grew louder, till at last it seemed to tear out of the fog just above our quarter, and I cowered while the *Rathmines* plunged bows under on a double swell that crossed.

'No more,' said Frithiof, 'it is not good any more. Let us get away, in the name of God.'

'Now if a torpedo-boat with a *City of Paris* siren went mad and broke her moorings and hired a friend to help her, it's just conceivable that we might be carried as we are now. Otherwise this thing is – '

The last words died on Keller's lips, his eyes began to start from his head, and his jaw fell. Some six or seven feet above the port bulwarks, framed in fog, and as utterly unsupported as the full moon, hung a Face. It was not human, and it certainly was not animal, for it did not belong to this earth as known to man. The mouth was open, revealing a ridiculously tiny tongue – as absurd as the tongue of an elephant; there were tense wrinkles of white skin at the angles of the drawn lips, white feelers like those of a barbel sprung from the lower jaw, and there was no sign of teeth within the mouth. But the horror of the face lay in the eyes, for those were sightless – white, in sockets as white as scraped bone, and blind. Yet for all this the face, wrinkled as the mask of a lion is drawn in Assyrian sculpture, was alive with rage and terror. One long white feeler touched our bulwarks. Then the face disappeared with the swiftness of a blindworm popping into its burrow, and the next thing that I remember is my own voice in my own ears, saying gravely to the mainmast, 'But the air-bladder ought to have been forced out of its mouth, you know.'

Keller came up to me, ashy white. He put his hand into his pocket, took a cigar, bit it, dropped it, thrust his shaking thumb into his mouth and mumbled, 'The giant gooseberry and the raining frogs! Gimme a light – gimme a light! Say, gimme a light.' A little bead of blood dropped from his thumb joint.

I respected the motive, though the manifestation was absurd. 'Stop, you'll bite your thumb off,' I said, and Keller laughed brokenly as he picked up his cigar. Only Zuyland, leaning over the port bulwarks, seemed self-possessed. He declared later that he was very sick.

'We've seen it,' he said, turning round. 'That is it.'

'What?' said Keller, chewing the unlighted cigar.

As he spoke the fog was blown into shreds, and we saw the sea, grey with mud, rolling on every side of us and empty of all life. Then in one spot it bubbled and became like the pot of ointment that the Bible speaks of. From that wide-ringed trouble a Thing came up – a grey and red Thing with a neck – a Thing that bellowed and writhed in pain. Frithiof drew in his breath and held it till the red letters of the ship's name, woven across his jersey, straggled and opened out as though they had been type badly set. Then he said with a little cluck in his throat, 'Ah me! It is blind. *Hur illa*! That thing is blind,' and a murmur of pity went through us all, for we could see that the thing on the water was blind and in pain. Something had gashed and cut the great sides cruelly and the blood was spurting out. The grey ooze of the undermost sea lay in the monstrous wrinkles of the back, and poured away in sluices. The blind white head flung back and battered the wounds, and the body in its torment rose clear of the red and grey waves till we saw a pair of quivering shoulders streaked with weed and rough with shells, but as white in the clear spaces as the hairless, maneless, blind, toothless head. Afterwards, came a dot on the horizon and the sound of a shrill scream, and it was as though a shuttle shot all across the sea in one breath, and a second head and neck tore through the levels, driving a whispering wall of water to right and left. The two Things met – the one untouched and the other in its death-throe – male and female, we said, the female coming to the male. She circled round him bellowing, and laid her neck across the curve of his great turtle-back, and he disappeared under water for an instant, but flung up again, grunting in agony while the blood ran. Once the entire head and neck shot clear of the water and stiffened, and I heard Keller saying, as though he was watching a street accident, 'Give him air. For God's sake, give him air.' Then the death-struggle began, with crampings and twistings and jerkings of the white bulk to and fro, till our little steamer rolled again, and each grey wave coated her plates with the grey slime. The sun was clear, there was no wind, and we watched, the whole crew, stokers and all, in wonder and pity, but chiefly pity. The Thing was so helpless, and, save for his mate, so alone. No human eye should have beheld him; it was monstrous and indecent to exhibit him there in trade waters between atlas degrees of latitude. He had been spewed up, mangled and dying, from his rest on the sea-floor, where he might have lived till the Judgment Day, and we saw the tides of his life go from him as an angry tide goes out across rocks in the teeth of a landward gale. His mate lay rocking on the water a little distance off, bellowing continually, and the smell of musk came down upon the ship making us cough.

At last the battle for life ended in a batter of coloured seas. We saw the writhing neck fall like a flail, the carcase turn sideways, showing the glint of a white belly and the inset of a gigantic hind leg or flipper. Then all sank, and sea boiled over it, while the mate swam round and round, darting her head in every direction. Though we might have feared that she would attack the steamer, no power on earth could have drawn any one of us from our places that hour. We watched, holding our breaths. The mate paused in her search; we could hear the wash beating along her sides; reared her neck as high as she could reach, blind and lonely in all that loneliness of the sea, and sent one desperate bellow booming across the swells as an oyster-shell skips across a pond. Then she made off to the westward, the sun shining on the white head and the wake behind it, till nothing was left to see but a little pinpoint of silver on the horizon. We stood on our course again; and the *Rathmines*, coated with the sea-sediment from bow to stern, looked like a ship made grey with terror.

* * *

'We must pool our notes,' was the first coherent remark from Keller. 'we're three trained journalists – we hold absolutely the biggest scoop on record. Start fair.'

I objected to this. Nothing is gained by collaboration in journalism when all deal with the same facts, so we went to work each according to his own lights. Keller triple-headed his account, talked about our 'gallant captain', and wound up with an allusion to American enterprise in that it was a citizen of Dayton, Ohio, that had seen the sea-serpent. This sort of thing would have discredited the Creation, much more a mere sea tale, but as a specimen of the picture-writing of a half-civilised people it was very interesting. Zuyland took a heavy column and a half, giving approximate lengths and breadths, and the whole list of the crew whom he had sworn on oath to testify to his facts. There was nothing fantastic or flamboyant in Zuyland. I wrote three-quarters of a leaded bourgeois column, roughly speaking, and refrained from putting any journalese into it for reasons that had begun to appear to me.

Keller was insolent with joy. He was going to cable from South-ampton to the New York *World*, mail his account to America on the same day, paralyse London with his three columns of loosely knitted headlines, and generally efface the earth. 'You'll see how I work a big scoop when I get it,' he said.

'Is this your first visit to England?' I asked.

'Yes,' said he. 'You don't seem to appreciate the beauty of our scoop. It's pyramidal – the death of the sea-serpent! Good heavens alive, man, it's the biggest thing ever vouchsafed to a paper!'

'Curious to think that it will never appear in any paper, isn't it?' I said.

Zuyland was near me, and he nodded quickly.

'What do you mean?' said Keller. 'If you're enough of a Britisher to throw this thing away, I shan't. I thought you were a news-paperman.'

'I am. That's why I know. Don't be an ass, Keller. Remember, I'm seven hundred years your senior, and what your grandchildren may learn five hundred years hence, I learned from my grand-fathers about five hundred years ago. You won't do it, because you can't.'

This conversation was held in open sea, where everything seems possible, some hundred miles from Southampton. We passed the Needles Light at dawn, and the lifting day showed the stucco villas on the green and the awful orderliness of England – line upon line, wall upon wall, solid stone dock and monolithic pier. We waited an hour in the Customs shed, and there was ample time for the effect to soak in.

'Now, Keller, you face the music. The *Havel* goes out today. Mail by her, and I'll take you to the telegraph-office,' I said.

I heard Keller gasp as the influence of the land closed about him, cowing him as they say Newmarket Heath cows a young horse unused to open courses.

'I want to retouch my stuff. Suppose we wait till we get to London?' he said.

Zuyland, by the way, had torn up his account and thrown it over-board that morning early. His reasons were my reasons.

In the train Keller began to revise his copy, and every time that he looked at the trim little fields, the red villas, and the embankments of the line, the blue pencil plunged remorselessly through the slips. He appeared to have dredged the dictionary for adjectives. I could think of none that he had not used. Yet he was a perfectly sound poker-player and never showed more cards than were sufficient to take the pool.

'Aren't you going to leave him a single bellow?' I asked sympath-etically. 'Remember, everything goes in the States, from a trouser-button to a double-eagle.'

'That's just the curse of it,' said Keller below his breath. 'We've played 'em for suckers so often that when it comes to the golden truth – I'd like to try this on a London paper. You have first call there, though.'

'Not in the least. I'm not touching the thing in our papers. I shall be happy to leave 'em all to you; but surely you'll cable it home?'

'No. Not if I can make the scoop here and see the Britishers sit up.'

'You won't do it with three columns of slushy headline, believe me. They don't sit up as quickly as some people.'

'I'm beginning to think that too. Does *nothing* make any difference in this country?' he said, looking out of the window. 'How old is that farmhouse?'

'New. It can't be more than two hundred years at the most.'

'Um. Fields, too?'

'That hedge there must have been clipped for about eighty years.'

'Labour cheap – eh?'

'Pretty much. Well, I suppose you'd like to try the *Times*, wouldn't you?'

'No,' said Keller, looking at Winchester Cathedral. 'Might as well try to electrify a haystack. And to think that the *World* would take three columns and ask for more – with illustrations too! It's sickening.'

'But the *Times* might,' I began.

Keller flung his paper across the carriage, and it opened in its austere majesty of solid type – opened with the crackle of an en-cyclopedia.

'Might! You *might* work your way through the bow-plates of a cruiser. Look at that first page!'

'It strikes you that way, does it?' I said. 'Then I'd recommend you to try a light and frivolous journal.'

'With a thing like this of mine – of ours? It's sacred history!'

I showed him a paper which I conceived would be after his own heart, in that it was modelled on American lines.

'That's homey,' he said, 'but it's not the real thing. Now, I should like one of these fat old *Times* columns. Probably there'd be a bishop in the office, though.'

When we reached London Keller disappeared in the direction of the Strand. What his experiences may have been I cannot tell, but it seems that he invaded the office of an evening paper. at 11.45 a.m. (I told him English editors were most idle at that hour), and mentioned my name as that of a witness to the truth of his story.

'I was nearly fired out,' he said furiously at lunch. 'As soon as I mentioned you, the old man said that I was to tell you that they didn't want any more of your practical jokes, and that you knew the hours to call if you had anything to sell, and that they'd see you condemned before they helped to puff one of your infernal yarns in advance. Say, what record do you hold for truth in this country, anyway?'

'A beauty. You ran up against it, that's all. Why don't you leave the English papers alone and cable to New York? Everything goes over there.'

'Can't you see that's just why?' he repeated.

'I saw it a long time ago. You don't intend to cable, then?'

'Yes, I do,' he answered, in the over-emphatic voice of one who does not know his own mind.

That afternoon I walked him abroad and about, over the streets that run between the pavements like channels of grooved and tongued lava, over the bridges that are made of enduring stone, through subways floored and sided with yard-thick concrete, between houses that are never rebuilt, and by river-steps hewn, to the eye, from the living rock. A black fog chased us into Westminster Abbey, and, standing there in the darkness, I could hear the wings of the dead centuries circling round the head of Litchfield A. Keller, journalist, of Dayton, Ohio, U.S.A., whose mission it was to make the Britishers sit up.

He stumbled gasping into the thick gloom, and the roar of the traffic came to his bewildered ears.

'Let's go to the telegraph-office and cable,' I said. 'Can't you hear the New York *World* crying for news of the great sea-serpent, blind, white, and smelling of musk, stricken to death by a submarine volcano, and assisted by his loving wife to die in mid-ocean, as visualised by an American citizen, the breezy, newsy, brainy news-paper man of Dayton, Ohio? 'Rah for the Buckeye State. Step lively! Both gates! Szz! Boom! Aah!' Keller was a Princeton man, and he seemed to need encouragement.

'You've got me on your own ground,' said he, tugging at his overcoat pocket. He pulled out his copy, with the cable forms – for he had written out his telegram – and put them all into my hand, groaning, 'I pass. If I hadn't come to your cursed country – if I'd sent it off at Southampton – if I ever get you west of the Alleghannies, if – '

'Never mind, Keller. It isn't your fault. It's the fault of your country. If you had been seven hundred years older you'd have done what I am going to do.'

'What are you going to do?'

'Tell it as a lie.'

'Fiction?' This with the full-blooded disgust of a journalist for the illegitimate branch of the profession.

'You can call it that if you like. I shall call it a lie.'

And a lie it has become; for Truth is a naked lady, and if by accident she is drawn up from the bottom of the sea, it behoves a gentleman either to give her a print petticoat or to turn his face to the wall and vow that he did not see.

'Swept and Garnished'

When the first waves of feverish cold stole over Frau Ebermann she very wisely telephoned for the doctor and went to bed. He diagnosed the attack as mild influenza, prescribed the appropriate remedies, and left her to the care of her one servant in her comfortable Berlin flat. Frau Ebermann, beneath the thick coverlet, curled up with what patience she could until the aspirin should begin to act, and Anna should come back from the chemist with the formamint, the ammoniated quinine, the eucalyptus, and the little tin steam-inhaler. Meantime, every bone in her body ached; her head throbbed; her hot, dry hands would not stay the same size for a minute together; and her body, tucked into the smallest possible compass, shrank from the chill of the well-warmed sheets.

Of a sudden she noticed that an imitation-lace cover which should have lain mathematically square with the imitation-marble top of the radiator behind the green plush sofa had slipped away so that one corner hung over the bronze-painted steam pipes. She recalled that she must have rested her poor head against the radiator-top while she was taking off her boots. She tried to get up and set the thing straight, but the radiator at once receded toward the horizon, which, unlike true horizons, slanted diagonally, exactly parallel with the dropped lace edge of the cover. Frau Ebermann groaned through sticky lips and lay still.

'Certainly, I have a temperature,' she said. 'Certainly, I have a grave temperature. I should have been warned by that chill after dinner.'

She resolved to shut her hot-lidded eyes, but opened them in a little while to torture herself with the knowledge of that ungeometrical thing against the far wall. Then she saw a child – an untidy, thin-faced little girl of about ten, who must have strayed in from the adjoining flat. This proved – Frau Ebermann groaned again at the way the world falls to bits when one is sick – proved that Anna had forgotten to shut the outer door of the flat when she went to the chemist. Frau Ebermann had had children of her own, but they were all grown-up now, and she had never been a child-lover in any sense. Yet the intruder might be made to serve her scheme of things.

'Make – put,' she muttered thickly, 'that white thing straight on the top of that yellow thing.'

The child paid no attention, but moved about the room, investigating everything that came in her way – the yellow cut-glass handles of the chest of drawers, the stamped bronze hook to hold back the heavy puce curtains, and the mauve enamel, New Art finger-plates on the door. Frau Ebermann watched indignantly.

'Aie! That is bad and rude. Go away!' she cried, though it hurt her to raise her voice. 'Go away by the road you came!' The child passed behind the bed-foot, where she could not see her. 'Shut the door as you go. I will speak to Anna, but – first, put that white thing straight.'

She closed her eyes in misery of body and soul. The outer door clicked, and Anna entered, very penitent that she had stayed so long at the chemist's. But it had been difficult to find the proper type of inhaler, and –

'Where did the child go?' moaned Frau Ebermann – 'the child that was here?'

'There was no child,' said startled Anna. 'How should any child come in when I shut the door behind me after I go out? All the keys of the flats are different.'

'No, no! You forgot this time. But my back is aching, and up my legs also. Besides, who knows what it may have fingered and upset? Look and see.'

'Nothing is fingered, nothing is upset,' Anna replied, as she took the inhaler from its paper box.

'Yes, there is. Now I remember all about it. Put – put that white thing, with the open edge – the lace, I mean – quite straight on that – ' she pointed. Anna, accustomed to her ways, understood and went to it.

'Now, is it quite straight?' Frau Ebermann demanded.

'Perfectly,' said Anna. 'In fact, in the very centre of the radiator.' Anna measured the equal margins with her knuckle, as she had been told to do when she first took service.

'And my tortoiseshell hairbrushes?' Frau Ebermann could not command her dressing-table from where she lay.

'Perfectly straight, side by side in the big tray, and the comb laid across them. Your watch also in the coralline watch-holder.

Everything' – she moved round the room to make sure – 'everything is as you have it when you are well.'

Frau Ebermann sighed with relief. It seemed to her that the room and her head had suddenly grown cooler. 'Good!' said she. 'Now warm my nightgown in the kitchen, so it will be ready when I have perspired. And the towels also. Make the inhaler steam, and put in the eucalyptus; that is good for the larynx. Then sit you in the kitchen, and come when I ring. But, first, my hot-water bottle.'

It was brought and scientifically tucked in.

'What news?' said Frau Ebermann drowsily. She had not been out that day.

'Another victory,' said Anna. 'Many more prisoners and guns.'

Frau Ebermann purred, one might almost say grunted, contentedly. 'That is good too,' she said; and Anna, after lighting the inhaler-lamp, went out.

Frau Ebermann reflected that in an hour or so the aspirin would begin to work, and all would be well. Tomorrow – no, the day after – she would take up life with something to talk over with her friends at coffee. It was rare – everyone knew it – that she should be overcome by any ailment. Yet in all her distresses she had not allowed the minutest deviation from daily routine and ritual. She would tell her friends – she ran over their names one by one – exactly what measures she had taken against the lace cover on the radiator-top and in regard to her two tortoiseshell hairbrushes and the comb at right angles. How she had set everything in order – everything in order. She roved further afield as she wriggled her toes luxuriously on the hot-water bottle. If it pleased our dear God to take her to Himself, and she was not so young as she had been – there was that plate of the four lower ones in the blue tooth-glass, for instance – He should find all her belongings fit to meet His eye. 'Swept and garnished' were the words that shaped themselves in her intent brain. 'Swept and garnished for – '

No, it was certainly not for the dear Lord that she had swept; she would have her room swept out tomorrow or the day after, and garnished. Her hands began to swell again into huge pillows of nothingness. Then they shrank, and so did her head, to minute dots. It occurred to her that she was waiting for some event, some tremendously important event, to come to pass. She lay with shut eyes for a long time till her head and hands should return to their proper size.

She opened her eyes with a jerk.

'How stupid of me,' she said aloud, 'to set the room in order for a parcel of dirty little children!'

They were there – five of them, two little boys and three girls – headed by the anxious-eyed ten-year-old whom she had seen before. They must have entered by the outer door, which Anna had neglected to shut behind her when she returned with the inhaler. She counted them backward and forward as one counts scales – one, two, three, four, five.

They took no notice of her, but hung about, first on one foot then on the other, like strayed chickens, the smaller ones holding by the larger. They had the air of utterly wearied passengers in a railway waiting-room, and their clothes were disgracefully dirty.

'Go away!' cried Frau Ebermann at last, after she had struggled, it seemed to her, for years to shape the words.

'You called?' said Anna at the living-room door.

'No,' said her mistress. 'Did you shut the flat door when you came in?'

'Assuredly,' said Anna. 'Besides, it is made to catch shut of itself.'

'Then go away,' said she, very little above a whisper. If Anna pretended not to see the children, she would speak to Anna later on.

'And now,' she said, turning toward them as soon as the door closed. The smallest of the crowd smiled at her, and shook his head before he buried it in his sister's skirts.

'Why – don't – you – go – away?' she whispered earnestly.

Again they took no notice, but, guided by the elder girl, set themselves to climb, boots and all, on to the green plush sofa in front of the radiator. The little boys had to be pushed, as they could not compass the stretch unaided. They settled themselves in a row, with small gasps of relief, and pawed the plush approvingly.

'I ask you – I ask you why do you not go away – why do you not go away?' Frau Ebermann found herself repeating the question twenty times. It seemed to her that everything in the world hung on the answer. 'You know you should not come into houses and rooms unless you are invited. Not houses and bedrooms, you know.'

'No,' a solemn little six-year-old repeated, 'not houses nor bed-rooms, nor dining-rooms, nor churches, nor all those places. Shouldn't come in. It's rude.'

'Yes, he said so,' the younger girl put in proudly. 'He said it. He told them only pigs would do that.' The line nodded and dimpled one to another with little explosive giggles, such as children use when they tell deeds of great daring against their elders.

'If you know it is wrong, that makes it much worse,' said Frau Ebermann.

'Oh yes; much worse,' they assented cheerfully, till the smallest boy changed his smile to a baby wail of weariness.

'When will they come for us?' he asked, and the girl at the head of the row hauled him bodily into her square little capable lap.

'He's tired,' she explained. 'He is only four. He only had his first breeches this spring.' They came almost under his armpits, and were held up by broad linen braces, which, his sorrow diverted for the moment, he patted proudly.

'Yes, beautiful, dear,' said both girls.

'Go away!' said Frau Ebermann. 'Go home to your father and mother!'

Their faces grew grave at once.

'H'sh! We *can't*,' whispered the eldest. 'There isn't anything left.'

'All gone,' a boy echoed, and he puffed through pursed lips. 'Like *that*, uncle told me. Both cows too.'

'And my own three ducks,' the boy on the girl's lap said sleepily.

'So, you see, we came here.' The elder girl leaned forward a little, caressing the child she rocked.

'I – I don't understand,' said Frau Ebermann 'Are you lost, then? You must tell our police.'

'Oh no; we are only waiting.'

'But what are you waiting *for*?'

'We are waiting for our people to come for us. They told us to come here and wait for them. So we are waiting till they come,' the eldest girl replied.

'Yes. We are waiting till our people come for us,' said all the others in chorus.

'But,' said Frau Ebermann very patiently – 'but now tell me, for I tell you that I am not in the least angry, where do you come from? Where do you come from?'

The five gave the names of two villages of which she had read in the papers,

'That is silly,' said Frau Ebermann. 'The people fired on us, and they were punished. Those places are wiped out, stamped flat.'

'Yes, yes, wiped out, stamped flat. That is why and – I have lost the ribbon off my pigtail,' said the younger girl. She looked behind her over the sofa-back.

'It is not here,' said the elder. 'It was lost before. Don't you remember?'

'Now, if you are lost, you must go and tell our police. They will take care of you and give you food,' said Frau Ebermann. 'Anna will show you the way there.'

'No,' – this was the six-year-old with the smile – 'we must wait here till our people come for us. Mustn't we, sister?'

'Of course. We wait here till our people come for us. All the world knows that,' said the eldest girl.

'Yes.' The boy in her lap had waked again. 'Little children, too – as little as Henri, and *he* doesn't wear trousers yet. As little as all that.'

'I don't understand,' said Frau Ebermann, shivering. In spite of the heat of the room and the damp breath of the steam-inhaler, the aspirin was not doing its duty.

The girl raised her blue eyes and looked at the woman for an instant.

'You see,' she said, emphasising her statements with her fingers, '*they* told *us* to wait *here* till *our* people came for us. So we came. We wait till our people come for us.'

'That is silly again,' said Frau Ebermann. 'It is no good for you to wait here. Do you know what this place is? You have been to school? It is Berlin, the capital of Germany.'

'Yes, yes,' they all cried; 'Berlin, capital of Germany. We know that. That is why we came.'

'So, you see, it is no good,' she said triumphantly, 'because your people can never come for you here.'

'They told us to come here and wait till our people came for us.' They delivered this as if it were a lesson in school. Then they sat still, their hands orderly folded on their laps, smiling as sweetly as ever.

'Go away! Go away!' Frau Ebermann shrieked.

'You called?' said Anna, entering.

'No. Go away! Go away!'

'Very good, old cat,' said the maid under her breath. 'Next time you *may* call,' and she returned to her friend in the kitchen.

'I ask you – ask you, *please* to go away,' Frau Ebermann pleaded. 'Go to my Anna through that door, and she will give you cakes and sweeties. It is not kind of you to come into my room and behave so badly.'

'Where else shall we go now?' the elder girl demanded, turning to her little company. They fell into discussion. One preferred the broad street with trees, another the railway station; but when she suggested an Emperor's palace, they agreed with her.

'We will go then,' she said, and added half apologetically to Frau Ebermann, 'You see, they are so little they like to meet all the others.'

'What others?' said Frau Ebermann.

'The others – hundreds and hundreds and thousands and thousands of the others.'

'That is a lie. There cannot be a hundred even, much less a thousand,' cried Frau Ebermann.

'So?' said the girl politely.

'Yes. *I* tell you; and I have very good information. I know how it happened. You should have been more careful. You should not have run out to see the horses and guns passing. That is how it is done when our troops pass through. My son has written me so.'

They had clambered down from the sofa, and gathered round the bed with eager, interested eyes.

'Horses and guns going by – how fine!' someone whispered.

'Yes, yes; believe me, *that* is how the accidents to the children happen. You must know yourself that it is true. One runs out to look – '

'But I never saw any at all,' a boy cried sorrowfully. 'Only one noise I heard. That was when Aunt Emmeline's house fell down.'

'But listen to me. *I* am telling you! One runs out to look, because one is little and cannot see well. So one peeps between the man's legs, and then – you know how close those big horses and guns turn the corners – then one's foot slips and one gets run over. That's how it happens. Several times it had happened, but not many times; certainly not a hundred, perhaps not twenty. So, you see, you *must* be all. Tell me now that you are all that there are, and Anna shall give you the cakes.'

'Thousands,' a boy repeated monotonously. 'Then we all come here to wait till our people come for us.'

'But now we will go away from here. The poor lady is tired,' said the elder girl, plucking his sleeve.

'Oh, you hurt, you hurt!' he cried, and burst into tears.

'What is that for?' said Frau Ebermann. 'To cry in a room where a poor lady is sick is very inconsiderate.'

'Oh, but look, lady!' said the elder girl.

Frau Ebermann looked and saw.

'*Au revoir*, lady.' They made their little smiling bows and curtseys undisturbed by her loud cries. '*Au revoir*, lady. We will wait till our people come for us.'

When Anna at last ran in, she found her mistress on her knees, busily cleaning the floor with the lace cover from the radiator, because, she explained, it was all spotted with the blood of five children – she was perfectly certain there could not be more than five in the whole world – who had gone away for the moment, but were now waiting round the corner, and Anna was to find them and give them cakes to stop the bleeding, while her mistress swept and garnished that Our dear Lord when He came might find everything as it should be.

Mary Postgate

Of Miss Mary Postgate, Lady McCausland wrote that she was 'thoroughly conscientious, tidy, companionable, and ladylike. I am very sorry to part with her, and shall always be interested in her welfare.'

Miss Fowler engaged her on this recommendation, and to her surprise, for she had had experience of companions, found that it was true. Miss Fowler was nearer sixty than fifty at the time, but though she needed care she did not exhaust her attendant's vitality. On the contrary, she gave out, stimulatingly and with reminiscences. Her father had been a minor Court official in the days when the Great Exhibition of 1851 had just set its seal on Civilisation made perfect. Some of Miss Fowler's tales, none the less, were not always for the young. Mary was not young, and though her speech was as colourless as her eyes or her hair, she was never shocked. She listened unflinchingly to everyone; said at the end, 'How interesting!' or 'How shocking!' as the case might be, and never again referred to it, for she prided herself on a trained mind, which 'did not dwell on these things'. She was, too, a treasure at domestic accounts, for which the village tradesmen, with their weekly books, loved her not. Otherwise she had no enemies; provoked no jealousy even among the plainest; neither gossip nor slander had ever been traced to her; she supplied the odd place at the Rector's or the Doctor's table at half an hour's notice; she was a sort of public aunt to very many small children of the village street, whose parents, while accepting everything, would have been swift to resent what they called 'patronage'; she served on the Village Nursing Committee as Miss Fowler's nominee when Miss Fowler was crippled by rheumatoid arthritis, and came out of six months' fortnightly meetings equally respected by all the cliques.

And when Fate threw Miss Fowler's nephew, an unlovely orphan of eleven, on Miss Fowler's hands, Mary Postgate stood to her share of the business of education as practised in private and public schools. She checked printed clothes-lists, and unitemised bills of extras; wrote to Head and House masters, matrons, nurses and doctors, and grieved or rejoiced over half-term reports. Young Wyndham Fowler repaid her in his holidays by calling her 'Gatepost', 'Postey', or 'Packthread', by thumping her between her narrow shoulders, or by chasing her bleating, round the garden, her large mouth open, her large nose high in air, at a stiff-necked shamble very like a camel's. Later on he filled the house with clamour, argument, and harangues as to his personal needs, likes and dislikes, and the limitations of 'you women', reducing Mary to tears of physical fatigue, or, when he chose to be humorous, of helpless laughter. At crises, which multiplied as he grew older, she was his ambassadress and his interpretress to Miss Fowler, who had no large sympathy with the young; a vote in his interest at the councils on his future; his sewing-woman, strictly accountable for mislaid boots and garments; always his butt and his slave.

And when he decided to become a solicitor, and had entered an office in London; when his greeting had changed from 'Hullo, Postey, you old beast', to 'Mornin', Packthread', there came a war which, unlike all wars that Mary could remember, did not stay decently outside England and in the newspapers, but intruded on the lives of people whom she knew. As she said to Miss Fowler, it was 'most vexatious'. It took the Rector's son who was going into business with his elder brother; it took the Colonel's nephew on the eve of fruit-farming in Canada; it took Mrs Grant's son who, his mother said, was devoted to the ministry; and, very early indeed, it took Wynn Fowler, who announced on a postcard that he had joined the Flying Corps and wanted a cardigan waistcoat.

'He must go, and he must have the waistcoat,' said Miss Fowler. So Mary got the proper-sized needles and wool, while Miss Fowler told the men of her establishment – two gardeners and an odd man, aged sixty – that those who could join the Army had better do so. The gardeners left. Cheape, the odd man, stayed on, and was promoted to the gardener's cottage. The cook, scorning to be limited in luxuries, also left, after a spirited scene with Miss Fowler, and took the housemaid with her. Miss Fowler gazetted Nellie, Cheape's seventeen-year-old daughter, to the vacant post; Mrs Cheape to the rank of cook, with occasional cleaning bouts; and the reduced establishment moved forward smoothly.

Wynn demanded an increase in his allowance. Miss Fowler, who always looked facts in the face, said, 'He must have it. The chances are he won't live long to draw it, and if three hundred makes him happy – '

Wynn was grateful, and came over, in his tight-buttoned uniform, to say so. His training centre was not thirty miles away, and his talk was so technical that it had to be explained by charts of the various types of machines. He gave Mary such a chart.

'And you'd better study it, Postey,' he said. 'You'll be seeing a lot of 'em soon.' So Mary studied the chart, but when Wynn next arrived to swell and exalt himself before his womenfolk, she failed badly in cross-examination, and he rated her as in the old days.

'You *look* more or less like a human being,' he said in his new Service voice. 'You *must* have had a brain at some time in your past. What have you done with it? Where d'you keep it? A sheep would know more than you do, Postey. You're lamentable. You are less use than an empty tin can, you dowey old cassowary.'

'I suppose that's how your superior officer talks to *you*?' said Miss Fowler from her chair.

'But Postey doesn't mind,' Wynn replied. 'Do you, Packthread?'

'Why? Was Wynn saying anything? I shall get this right next time you come,' she muttered, and knitted her pale brows again over the diagrams of Taubes, Farmans, and Zeppelins.

In a few weeks the mere land and sea battles which she read to Miss Fowler after breakfast passed her like idle breath. Her heart and her interest were high in the air with Wynn, who had finished 'rolling' (whatever that might be) and had gone on from a 'taxi' to a machine more or less his own. One morning it circled over their very chimneys, alighted on Vegg's Heath, almost outside the garden gate, and Wynn came in, blue with cold, shouting for food. He and she drew Miss Fowler's bath-chair, as they had often done, along the Heath footpath to look at the bi-plane. Mary observed that 'it smelt very badly'.

'Postey, I believe you think with your nose,' said Wynn. 'I know you don't with your mind. Now, what type's that?'

'I'll go and get the chart,' said Mary.

'You're hopeless! You haven't the mental capacity of a white mouse,' he cried, and explained the dials and the sockets for bomb-dropping till it was time to mount and ride the wet clouds once more.

'Ah!' said Mary, as the stinking thing flared upward. 'Wait till our Flying Corps gets to work! Wynn says it's much safer than in the trenches.'

'I wonder,' said Miss Fowler. 'Tell Cheape to come and tow me home again.'

'It's all downhill. I can do it,' said Mary, 'if you put the brake on.' She laid her lean self against the pushing-bar and home they trundled.

'Now, be careful you aren't heated and catch a chill,' said over-dressed Miss Fowler.

'Nothing makes me perspire,' said Mary. As she bumped the chair under the porch she straightened her long back. The exertion had given her a colour, and the wind had loosened a wisp of hair across her forehead. Miss Fowler glanced at her.

'What do you ever think of, Mary?' she demanded suddenly.

'Oh, Wynn says he wants another three pairs of stockings – as thick as we can make them.'

'Yes. But I mean the things that women think about. Here you are, more than forty – '

'Forty-four,' said truthful Mary.

'Well?'

'Well?' Mary offered Miss Fowler her shoulder as usual.

'And you've been with me ten years now.'

'Let's see,' said Mary. 'Wynn was eleven when he came. He's twenty now, and I came two years before that. It must be eleven.'

'Eleven! And you've never told me anything that matters in all that while. Looking back, it seems to me that I've done all the talking.'

'I'm afraid I'm not much of a conversationalist. As Wynn says, I haven't the mind. Let me take your hat.'

Miss Fowler, moving stiffly from the hip, stamped her rubber-tipped stick on the tiled hall floor. 'Mary, aren't you *anything* except a companion? Would you *ever* have been anything except a companion?'

Mary hung up the garden hat on its proper peg. 'No,' she said after consideration. 'I don't imagine I ever should. But I've no imagination, I'm afraid.'

She fetched Miss Fowler her eleven-o'clock glass of Contrexéville.

That was the wet December when it rained six inches to the month, and the women went abroad as little as might be. Wynn's flying chariot visited them several times, and for two mornings (he had warned her by postcard) Mary heard the thresh of his propellers at dawn. The second time she ran to the window, and stared at the whitening sky. A little blur passed overhead. She lifted her lean arms towards it.

That evening at six o'clock there came an announcement in an official envelope that Second Lieutenant W. Fowler had been killed during a trial flight. Death was instantaneous. She read it and carried it to Miss Fowler.

'I never expected anything else,' said Miss Fowler; 'but I'm sorry it happened before he had done anything.'

The room was whirling round Mary Postgate, but she found herself quite steady in the midst of it.

'Yes,' she said. 'It's a great pity he didn't die in action after he had killed somebody.'

'He was killed instantly. That's one comfort,' Miss Fowler went on.

'But Wynn says the shock of a fall kills a man at once – whatever happens to the tanks,' quoted Mary.

The room was coming to rest now. She heard Miss Fowler say impatiently, 'But why can't we cry, Mary?' and herself replying, 'There's nothing to cry for. He has done his duty as much as Mrs Grant's son did.'

'And when he died, *she* came and cried all the morning,' said Miss Fowler. 'This only makes me feel tired – terribly tired. Will you help me to bed, please, Mary? – And I think I'd like the hot-water bottle.'

So Mary helped her and sat beside, talking of Wynn in his riotous youth.

'I believe,' said Miss Fowler suddenly, 'that old people and young people slip from under a stroke like this. The middle-aged feel it most.'

'I expect that's true,' said Mary, rising. 'I'm going to put away the things in his room now. Shall we wear mourning?'

'Certainly not,' said Miss Fowler. 'Except, of course, at the funeral. I can't go. You will. I want you to arrange about his being buried here. What a blessing it didn't happen at Salisbury!'

Everyone, from the Authorities of the Flying Corps to the Rector, was most kind and sympathetic. Mary found herself for the moment in a world where bodies were in the habit of being despatched by all sorts of conveyances to all sorts of places. And at the funeral two young men in buttoned-up uniforms stood beside the grave and spoke to her afterwards.

'You're Miss Postgate, aren't you?' said one. 'Fowler told me about you. He was a good chap – a first-class fellow – a great loss.'

'Great loss!' growled his companion. 'We're all awfully sorry.'

'How high did he fall from?' Mary whispered.

'Pretty nearly four thousand feet, I should think, didn't he? You were up that day, Monkey?'

'All of that,' the other child replied. 'My bar made three thousand, and I wasn't as high as him by a lot.'

'Then *that*'s all right,' said Mary. 'Thank you very much.'

They moved away as Mrs Grant flung herself weeping on Mary's flat chest, under the lych-gate, and cried, '*I* know how it feels! *I* know how it feels!'

'But both his parents are dead,' Mary returned, as she fended her off. 'Perhaps they've all met by now,' she added vaguely as she escaped towards the coach.

'I've thought of that too,' wailed Mrs Grant; 'but then he'll be practically a stranger to them. Quite embarrassing!'

Mary faithfully reported every detail of the ceremony to Miss Fowler, who, when she described Mrs Grant's outburst, laughed aloud.

'Oh, how Wynn would have enjoyed it! He was always utterly unreliable at funerals. D'you remember – ' And they talked of him again, each piecing out the other's gaps. 'And now,' said Miss Fowler, 'we'll pull up the blinds and we'll have a general tidy. That always does us good. Have you seen to Wynn's things?'

'Everything – since he first came,' said Mary. 'He was never destructive – even with his toys.'

They faced that neat room.

'It can't be natural not to cry,' Mary said at last. 'I'm *so* afraid you'll have a reaction.'

'As I told you, we old people slip from under the stroke. It's you I'm afraid for. Have you cried yet?'

'I can't. It only makes me angry with the Germans.'

'That's sheer waste of vitality,' said Miss Fowler. 'We must live till the war's finished.' She opened a full wardrobe. 'Now, I've been thinking things over. This is my plan. All his civilian clothes can be given away – Belgian refugees, and so on.'

Mary nodded. 'Boots, collars, and gloves?'

'Yes. We don't need to keep anything except his cap and belt.'

'They came back yesterday with his Flying Corps clothes' – Mary pointed to a roll on the little iron bed.

'Ah, but keep his Service things. Someone may be glad of them later. Do you remember his sizes?'

'Five feet eight and a half; thirty-six inches round the chest. But he told me he's just put on an inch and a half. I'll mark it on a label and tie it on his sleeping-bag.'

'So that disposes of *that*,' said Miss Fowler, tapping the palm of one hand with the ringed third finger of the other. 'What waste it all is! We'll get his old school trunk tomorrow and pack his civilian clothes.'

'And the rest?' said Mary. 'His books and pictures and the games and the toys – and – and the rest?'

'My plan is to burn every single thing,' said Miss Fowler. 'Then we shall know where they are and no-one can handle them afterwards. What do you think?'

'I think that would be much the best,' said Mary. 'But there's such a lot of them.'

'We'll burn them in the destructor,' said Miss Fowler.

This was an open-air furnace for the consumption of refuse; a little circular four-foot tower of pierced brick over an iron grating. Miss Fowler had noticed the design in a gardening journal years ago, and had had it built at the bottom of the garden. It suited her tidy soul, for it saved unsightly rubbish-heaps, and the ashes lightened the stiff clay soil.

Mary considered for a moment, saw her way clear, and nodded again. They spent the evening putting away well-remembered civilian suits, underclothes that Mary had marked, and the regiments of very gaudy socks and ties. A second trunk was needed, and, after that, a little packing-case, and it was late next day when Cheape and the local carrier lifted them to the cart. The Rector luckily knew of a friend's son, about five feet eight and a half inches high, to whom a complete Flying Corps outfit would be most acceptable, and sent his gardener's son down with a barrow to take delivery of it. The cap was hung up in Miss Fowler's bedroom, the belt in Miss Postgate's; for, as Miss Fowler said, they had no desire to make tea-party talk of them.

'That disposes of *that*,' said Miss Fowler. 'I'll leave the rest to you, Mary. I can't run up and down the garden. You'd better take the big clothes-basket and get Nellie to help you.'

'I shall take the wheelbarrow and do it myself,' said Mary, and for once in her life closed her mouth.

Miss Fowler, in moments of irritation, had called Mary deadly methodical. She put on her oldest waterproof and gardening-hat and her ever-slipping galoshes, for the weather was on the edge of more rain. She gathered fire-lighters from the kitchen, a half-scuttle of coals, and a faggot of brushwood. These she wheeled in the barrow down the mossed paths to the dank little laurel shrubbery where the destructor stood under the drip of three oaks. She climbed the wire fence into the Rector's glebe just behind, and from his tenant's rick pulled two large armfuls of good hay, which she spread neatly on the fire-bars. Next, journey by journey, passing Miss Fowler's white face at the morning-room window each time, she brought down in the towel-covered clothes-basket, on the wheelbarrow, thumbed and used Hentys, Marryats, Levers, Stevensons, Baroness Orczys, Garvices, schoolbooks and atlases, unrelated piles of the *Motor Cyclist*, the *Light Car*, and catalogues of Olympia Exhibitions; the remnants of a fleet of sailing-ships from ninepenny cutters to a three-guinea yacht; a prep-school dressing-gown; bats from three-and-sixpence to twenty-four shillings; cricket and tennis balls; disintegrated steam and clockwork locomotives with their twisted rails; a grey and red tin model of a submarine; a dumb gramophone and cracked records; golf clubs that had to be broken across the knee, like his walking-sticks, and an assegai; photographs of private and public school cricket and football elevens, and his O.T.C. on the line of march; kodaks and film-rolls; some pewters, and one real silver cup, for boxing competitions and Junior Hurdles; sheaves of school photographs; Miss Fowler's photograph; her own which he had borne off in fun and (good care she took not to ask!) had never returned; a playbox with a secret drawer; a load of flannels, belts and jerseys, and a pair of spiked shoes unearthed in the attic; a packet of all the letters that Miss Fowler and she had ever written to him, kept for some absurd reason through all these years; a five-day attempt at a diary; framed pictures of racing motors in full Brooklands career, and load upon load of undistinguishable wreckage of tool-boxes, rabbit-hutches, electric batteries, tin soldiers, fretsaw outfits, and jigsaw puzzles.

Miss Fowler at the window watched her come and go, and said to herself, 'Mary's an old woman. I never realised it before.'

After lunch she recommended her to rest.

'I'm not in the least tired,' said Mary. 'I've got it all arranged. I'm going to the village at two o'clock for some paraffin. Nellie hasn't enough, and the walk will do me good.'

She made one last quest round the house before she started, and found that she had overlooked nothing. It began to mist as soon as she had skirted Vegg's Heath, where Wynn used to descend – it seemed to her that she could almost hear the beat of his propellers overhead, but there was nothing to see. She hoisted her umbrella and lunged into the blind wet till she had reached the shelter of the empty village. As she came out of Mr Kidd's shop with a bottle full of paraffin in her string shopping-bag, she met Nurse Eden, the village nurse, and fell into talk with her, as usual, about the village children. They were just parting opposite the 'Royal Oak', when a gun, they fancied, was fired immediately behind the house. It was followed by a child's shriek dying into a wail.

'Accident!' said Nurse Eden promptly, and dashed through the empty bar, followed by Mary. They found Mrs Gerritt, the publican's wife, who could only gasp and point to the yard, where a little cart-lodge was sliding sideways amid a clatter of tiles. Nurse Eden snatched up a sheet drying before the fire, ran out, lifted something from the ground, and flung the sheet round it. The sheet turned scarlet and half her uniform too, as she bore the load into the kitchen. It was little Edna Gerritt, aged nine, whom Mary had known since her perambulator days.

'Am I hurted bad?' Edna asked, and died between Nurse Eden's dripping hands. The sheet fell aside and for an instant, before she could shut her eyes, Mary saw the ripped and shredded body.

'It's a wonder she spoke at all,' said Nurse Eden. 'What in God's name was it?'

'A bomb,' said Mary.

'One o' the Zeppelins?'

'No. An aeroplane. I thought I heard it on the Heath, but I fancied it was one of ours. It must have shut off its engines as it came down. That's why we didn't notice it.'

'The filthy pigs!' said Nurse Eden, all white and shaken. 'See the pickle I'm in! Go and tell Dr Hennis, Miss Postgate.' Nurse looked at the mother, who had dropped face down on the floor. 'She's only in a fit. Turn her over.'

Mary heaved Mrs Gerritt right side up, and hurried off for the doctor. When she told her tale, he asked her to sit down in the surgery till he got her something.

'But I don't need it, I assure you,' said she. 'I don't think it would be wise to tell Miss Fowler about it, do you? Her heart is so irritable in this weather.'

Dr Hennis looked at her admiringly as he packed up his bag.

'No. Don't tell anybody till we're sure,' he said, and hastened to the 'Royal Oak', while Mary went on with the paraffin. The village behind her was as quiet as usual, for the news had not yet spread. She frowned a little to herself, her large nostrils expanded uglily, and from time to time she muttered a phrase which Wynn, who never restrained himself before his womenfolk, had applied to the enemy. 'Bloody pagans! They *are* bloody pagans. But,' she continued, falling back on the teaching that had made her what she was, 'one mustn't let one's mind dwell on these things.'

Before she reached the house Dr Hennis, who was also a special constable, overtook her in his car.

'Oh, Miss Postgate,' he said, 'I wanted to tell you that that accident at the "Royal Oak" was due to Gerritt's stable tumbling down. It's been dangerous for a long time. It ought to have been condemned.'

'I thought I heard an explosion too,' said Mary.

'You might have been misled by the beams snapping. I've been looking at 'em. They were dry-rotted through and through. Of course, as they broke, they would make a noise just like a gun.'

'Yes?' said Mary politely.

'Poor little Edna was playing underneath it,' he went on, still holding her with his eyes, 'and that and the tiles cut her to pieces, you see?'

'I saw it,' said Mary, shaking her head. 'I heard it too.'

'Well, we cannot be sure.' Dr Hennis changed his tone completely. 'I know both you and Nurse Eden (I've been speaking to her) are perfectly trustworthy, and I can rely on you not to say anything – yet at least. It is no good to stir up people unless – '

'Oh, I never do – anyhow,' said Mary, and Dr Hennis went on to the county town.

After all, she told herself, it might, just possibly, have been the collapse of the old stable that had done all those things to poor little Edna. She was sorry she had even hinted at other things, but Nurse Eden was discretion itself. By the time she reached home the affair seemed increasingly remote by its very monstrosity. As she came in, Miss Fowler told her that a couple of aeroplanes had passed half an hour ago.

'I thought I heard them,' she replied, 'I'm going down to the garden now. I've got the paraffin.'

'Yes, but – what *have* you got on your boots? They're soaking wet. Change them at once.'

Not only did Mary obey but she wrapped the boots in a newspaper, and put them into the string bag with the bottle. So, armed with the longest kitchen poker, she left.

'It's raining again,' was Miss Fowler's last word, 'but – I know you won't be happy till that's disposed of.'

'It won't take long. I've got everything down there, and I've put the lid on the destructor to keep the wet out.'

The shrubbery was filling with twilight by the time she had completed her arrangements and sprinkled the sacrificial oil. As she lit the match that would burn her heart to ashes, she heard a groan or a grunt behind the dense Portugal laurels.

'Cheape?' she called impatiently, but Cheape, with his ancient lumbago, in his comfortable cottage, would be the last man to profane the sanctuary. 'Sheep,' she concluded, and threw in the fusee. The pyre went up in a roar, and the immediate flame hastened night around her.

'How Wynn would have loved this!' she thought, stepping back from the blaze.

By its light she saw, half hidden behind a laurel not five paces away, a bareheaded man sitting very stiffly at the foot of one of the oaks. A broken branch lay across his lap – one booted leg protruding from beneath it. His head moved ceaselessly from side to side, but his body was as still as the tree's trunk. He was dressed – she moved sideways to look more closely – in a uniform something like Wynn's, with a flap buttoned across the chest. For an instant, she had some idea that it might be one of the young flying men she had met at the funeral. But their heads were dark and glossy. This man's was as pale as a baby's, and so closely cropped that she could see the disgusting pinky skin beneath. His lips moved.

'What do you say?' Mary moved towards him and stooped.

'Laty! Laty! Laty!' he muttered, while his hands picked at the dead wet leaves. There was no doubt as to his nationality. It made her so angry that she strode back to the destructor, though it was still too hot to use the poker there. Wynn's books seemed to be catching well. She looked up at the oak behind the man; several of the light upper and two or three rotten lower branches had broken and scattered their rubbish on the shrubbery path. On the lowest fork a helmet with dependent strings, showed like a bird's-nest in the light of a long-tongued flame. Evidently this person had fallen through the tree. Wynn had told her that it was quite possible for people to fall out of aeroplanes. Wynn told her too, that trees were useful things to break an aviator's fall, but in this case the aviator must have been broken or he would have moved from his queer position. He seemed helpless except for his horrible rolling head. On the other hand, she could see a pistol case at his belt – and Mary loathed pistols. Months ago, after reading certain Belgian reports together, she and Miss Fowler had had dealings with one – a huge revolver with flat-nosed bullets, which latter, Wynn said, were forbidden by the rules of war to be used against civilised enemies. 'They're good enough for us,' Miss Fowler had replied. 'Show Mary how it works.' And Wynn, laughing at the mere possibility of any such need, had led the craven winking Mary into the Rector's disused quarry, and had shown her how to fire the terrible machine. It lay now in the top left-hand drawer of her toilet-table – a memento not included in the burning. Wynn would be pleased to see how she was not afraid.

She slipped up to the house to get it. When she came through the rain, the eyes in the head were alive with expectation. The mouth even tried to smile. But at sight of the revolver its corners went down just like Edna Gerritt's. A tear trickled from one eye, and the head rolled from shoulder to shoulder as though trying to point out something.

'*Cassée. Tout cassée,*' it whimpered.

'What do you say?' said Mary disgustedly, keeping well to one side, though only the head moved.

'*Cassée,*' it repeated. '*Che me rends. Le médicin! Toctor!*'

'*Nein!*' said she, bringing all her small German to bear with the big pistol. '*Ich haben der todt Kinder gesehn.*'

The head was still. Mary's hand dropped. She had been careful to keep her finger off the trigger for fear of accidents. After a few moments' waiting, she returned to the destructor, where the flames were falling, and churned up Wynn's charring books with the poker. Again the head groaned for the doctor.

'Stop that!' said Mary, and stamped her foot. 'Stop that, you bloody pagan!'

The words came quite smoothly and naturally. They were Wynn's own words, and Wynn was a gentleman who for no consideration on earth would have torn little Edna into those vividly coloured strips and strings. But this thing hunched under the oak tree had done that thing. It was no question of reading horrors out of newspapers to Miss Fowler. Mary had seen it with her own eyes on the 'Royal Oak' kitchen table. She must not allow her mind to dwell upon it. Now Wynn was dead, and everything connected with him was lumping and rustling and tinkling under her busy poker into red black dust and grey leaves of ash. The thing beneath the oak would die too. Mary had seen death more than once. She came of a family that had a knack of dying under, as she told Miss Fowler, 'most distressing circumstances'. She would stay where she was till she was entirely satisfied that It was dead – dead as dear papa in the late 'eighties; aunt Mary in 'eighty-nine; mamma in 'ninety-one; cousin

Dick in 'ninety-five; Lady McCausland's housemaid in 'ninety-nine; Lady McCausland's sister in nineteen hundred and one; Wynn buried five days ago; and Edna Gerritt still waiting for decent earth to hide her. As she thought – her underlip caught up by one faded canine, brows knit and nostrils wide – she wielded the poker with lunges that jarred the grating at the bottom, and careful scrapes round the brickwork above. She looked at her wrist-watch. It was getting on to half-past four, and the rain was coming down in earnest. Tea would be at five. If It did not die before that time, she would be soaked and would have to change. Meantime, and this occupied her, Wynn's things were burning well in spite of the hissing wet, though now and again a book-back with a quite distinguishable title would be heaved up out of the mass. The exercise of stoking had given her a glow which seemed to reach to the marrow of her bones. She hummed – Mary never had a voice – to herself. She had never believed in all those advanced views – though Miss Fowler herself leaned a little that way – of woman's work in the world; but now she saw there was much to be said for them. This, for instance, was *her* work – work which no man, least of all Dr Hennis, would ever have done. A man, at such a crisis, would be what Wynn called a 'sportsman'; would leave everything to fetch help, and would certainly bring It into the house. Now a woman's business was to make a happy home for – for a husband and children. Failing these – it was not a thing one should allow one's mind to dwell upon – but – 'Stop it!' Mary cried once more across the shadows. '*Nein*, I tell you! *Ich haben der todt Kinder gesehn.*'

But it was a fact. A woman who had missed these things could still be useful – more useful than a man in certain respects. She thumped like a pavior through the settling ashes at the secret thrill of it. The rain was damping the fire, but she could feel – it was too dark to see – that her work was done. There was a dull red glow at the bottom of the destructor, not enough to char the wooden lid if she slipped it half over against the driving wet. This arranged, she leaned on the poker and waited, while an increasing rapture laid hold on her. She ceased to think. She gave herself up to feel. Her long pleasure was broken by a sound that she had waited for in agony several times in her life. She leaned forward and listened, smiling. There could be no mistake. She closed her eyes and drank it in. Once it ceased abruptly.

'Go on,' she murmured, half aloud. 'That isn't the end.'

Then the end came very distinctly in a lull between two rain-gusts. Mary Postgate drew her breath short between her teeth and shivered from head to foot. '*That*'s all right,' said she contentedly, and went up to the house, where she scandalised the whole routine by taking a luxurious hot bath before tea, and came down looking, as Miss Fowler said when she saw her lying all relaxed on the other sofa, 'quite handsome!'

A Madonna of the Trenches

Gipsy Vans

Whatever a man of the sons of men
Shall say to his heart of the lords above,
They have shown man, verily, once and again,
Marvellous mercies and infinite love.

*   *   *

O sweet one love, O my life's delight,
Dear, though the days have divided us,
Lost beyond hope, taken far out of sight,
Not twice in the world shall the Gods do thus.

Swinburne, *Les Noyades*

Seeing how many unstable ex-soldiers came to the Lodge of Instruction (attached to Faith and Works E.C. 5837) in the years after the war, the wonder is there was not more trouble from Brethren whom sudden meetings with old comrades jerked back into their still raw past. But our round, torpedo-bearded local Doctor – Brother Keede, Senior Warden – always stood ready to deal with hysteria before it got out of hand; and when I examined Brethren unknown or imperfectly vouched for on the Masonic side, I passed on to him anything that seemed doubtful. He had had his experience as medical officer of a South London Battalion, during the last two years of the war; and, naturally, often found friends and acquaintants among the visitors.

Brother C. Strangwick, a young, tallish, new-made Brother, hailed from some South London Lodge. His papers and his answers were above suspicion, but his red-rimmed eyes had a puzzled glare that might mean nerves. So I introduced him particularly to Keede, who discovered in him a Headquarters Orderly of his old Battalion, congratulated him on his return to fitness – he had been discharged for some infirmity or other – and plunged at once into Somme memories.

'I hope I did right, Keede,' I said when we were robing before Lodge.

'Oh, quite. He reminded me that I had him under my hands at Sampoux in 'Eighteen, when he went to bits. He was a Runner.'

'Was it shock?' I asked.

'Of sorts – but not what he wanted me to think it was. No, he wasn't shamming. He had jumps to the limit – but he played up to mislead me about the reason of 'em . . . . Well, if we could stop patients from lying, medicine would be too easy, I suppose.'

I noticed that, after Lodge-working, Keede gave him a seat a couple of rows in front of us, that he might enjoy a lecture on the Orientation of King Solomon's Temple, which an earnest Brother thought would be a nice interlude between Labour and the high tea that we called our 'Banquet'. Even helped by tobacco it was a dreary performance. About halfway through, Strangwick, who had been fidgeting and twitching for some minutes, rose, drove back his chair grinding across the tessellated floor, and yelped 'Oh, My Aunt! I can't stand this any longer.' Under cover of a general laugh of assent he brushed past us and stumbled towards the door.

'I thought so!' Keede whispered to me. 'Come along!' We overtook him in the passage, crowing hysterically and wringing his hands. Keede led him into the Tyler's Room, a small office where we stored odds and ends of regalia and furniture, and locked the door.

'I'm – I'm all right,' the boy began, piteously.

''Course you are.' Keede opened a small cupboard which I had seen called upon before, mixed sal volatile and water in a graduated glass, and, as Strangwick drank, pushed him gently on to an old sofa. 'There,' he went on. 'It's nothing to write home about. I've seen you ten times worse. I expect our talk has brought things back.'

He hooked up a chair behind him with one foot, held the patient's hands in his own, and sat down. The chair creaked.

'Don't!' Strangwick squealed. 'I can't stand it! There's nothing on earth creaks like they do! And – and when it thaws we – we've got to slap 'em back with a spa-ade! Remember those Frenchmen's little boots under the duckboards? . . . What'll I do? What'll I do about it?'

Someone knocked at the door, to know if all were well.

'Oh, quite, thanks!' said Keede over his shoulder. 'But I shall need this room awhile. Draw the curtains, please.'

We heard the rings of the hangings that drape the passage from Lodge to Banquet Room click along their poles, and what sound there had been, of feet and voices, was shut off.

Strangwick, retching impotently, complained of the frozen dead who creak in the frost.

'He's playing up still,' Keede whispered. '*That's* not his real trouble – any more than 'twas last time.'

'But surely,' I replied, 'men get those things on the brain pretty badly. 'Remember in October – '

'This chap hasn't, though. I wonder what's really helling him. What are you thinking of?' said Keede peremptorily.

'French End an' Butcher's Row,' Strangwick muttered.

'Yes, there were a few there. But suppose we face Bogey instead of giving him best every time.' Keede turned towards me with a hint in his eye that I was to play up to his leads.

'What was the trouble with French End?' I opened at a venture.

'It was a bit by Sampoux, that we had taken over from the French. They're tough, but you wouldn't call 'em tidy as a nation. They had faced both sides of it with dead to keep the mud back. All those trenches were like gruel in a thaw. Our people had to do the same sort of thing – elsewhere; but Butcher's Row in French End was the – er – showpiece. Luckily, we pinched a salient from Jerry just then, an' straightened things out – so we didn't need to use the Row after November. You remember, Strangwick?'

'My God, yes! When the buckboard-slats were missin' you'd tread on 'em, an' they'd creak.'

'They're bound to. Like leather,' said Keede. 'It gets on one's nerves a bit, but – '

'Nerves? It's real! It's real!' Strangwick gulped.

'But at your time of life, it'll all fall behind you in a year or so. I'll give you another sip of – paregoric, an' we'll face it quietly. Shall we?'

Keede opened his cupboard again and administered a carefully dropped dark dose of something that was not sal volatile. 'This'll settle you in a few minutes,' he explained. 'Lie still, an' don't talk unless you feel like it.'

He faced me, fingering his beard.

'Ye-es. Butcher's Row wasn't pretty,' he volunteered. 'Seeing Strangwick here, has brought it all back to me again. 'Funny thing! We had a Platoon Sergeant of Number Two – what the deuce was his name? – an elderly bird who must have lied like a patriot to get out to the front at his age; but he was a first-class Non-Com., and the last person, you'd think, to make mistakes. Well, he was due for a fortnight's home leave in January, 'Eighteen. You were at B.H.Q. then, Strangwick, weren't you?'

'Yes. I was Orderly. It was January twenty-first'; Strangwick spoke with a thickish tongue, and his eyes burned. Whatever drug it was, had taken hold.

'About then,' Keede said. 'Well, this Sergeant, instead of coming down from the trenches the regular way an' joinin' Battalion Details after dark, an' takin' that funny little train for Arras, thinks he'll warm himself first. So he gets into a dug-out, in Butcher's Row, that used to be an old French dressing-station, and fugs up between a couple of braziers of pure charcoal! As luck 'ud have it, that was the only dug-out with an inside door opening inwards – some French anti-gas fitting, I expect – and, by what we could make out, the door must have swung to while he was warming. Anyhow, he didn't turn up at the train. There was a search at once. We couldn't afford to waste Platoon Sergeants. We found him in the morning. He'd got his gas all right. A machine-gunner reported him, didn't he, Strangwick?'

'No, Sir. Corporal Grant – o' the Trench Mortars.'

'So it was. Yes, Grant – the man with that little wen on his neck. Nothing wrong with your memory, at any rate. What was the Sergeant's name?'

'Godsoe – John Godsoe,' Strangwick answered.

'Yes, that was it. I had to see him next mornin' – frozen stiff between the two braziers – and not a scrap of private papers on him. *That* was the only thing that made me think it mightn't have been – quite an accident.'

Strangwick's relaxing face set, and he threw back at once to the Orderly Room manner.

'I give my evidence – at the time – to you, sir. He passed – overtook me, I should say – comin' down from supports, after I'd warned him for leaf. I thought he was goin' through Parrot Trench as usual; but 'e must 'ave turned off into French End where the old bombed barricade was.'

'Yes. I remember now. You were the last man to see him alive. That was on the twenty-first of January, you say? Now, *when* was it that Dearlove and Billings brought you to me – clean out of your head?' . . . Keede dropped his hand, in the style of magazine detectives, on Strangwick's shoulder. The boy looked at him with

cloudy wonder, and muttered: 'I was took to you on the evenin'
of the twenty-fourth of January. But you don't think I did him
in, do you?'

I could not help smiling at Keede's discomfiture; but he recovered
himself. 'Then what the dickens *was* on your mind that evening –
before I gave you the hypodermic?'

'The – the things in Butcher's Row. They kept on comin' over me.
You've seen me like this before, sir.'

'But I knew that it was a lie. You'd no more got stiffs on the brain
then than you have now. You've got something, but you're hiding it.'

' 'Ow do *you* know, Doctor?' Strangwick whimpered.

'D'you remember what you said to me, when Dearlove and Billings
were holding you down that evening?'

'About the things in Butcher's Row?'

'Oh, no! You spun me a lot of stuff about corpses creaking; but you
let yourself go in the middle of it – when you pushed that telegram at
me. What did you mean, f'rinstance, by asking what advantage it was
for you to fight beasts of officers if the dead didn't rise?'

'Did I say "Beasts of Officers"?'

'You did. It's out of the Burial Service.'

'I suppose, then, I must have heard it. As a matter of fact, I 'ave.'
Strangwick shuddered extravagantly.

'Probably. And there's another thing – that hymn you were shouting till I put you under. It was something about Mercy and Love.
Remember it?'

'I'll try,' said the boy obediently, and began to paraphrase, as
nearly as possible thus: ' "Whatever a man may say in his heart unto
the Lord, yea, verily I say unto you – Gawd hath shown man, again
and again, marvellous mercy an' – an' somethin' or other love." '
He screwed up his eyes and shook.

'Now where did you get *that* from?' Keede insisted.

'From Godsoe – on the twenty-first Jan . . . 'Ow could I tell what 'e
meant to do?' he burst out in a high, unnatural key – 'Any more than
I knew *she* was dead.'

'Who was dead?' said Keede.

'Me Auntie Armine.'

'The one the telegram came to you about, at Sampoux, that you
wanted me to explain – the one that you were talking of in the
passage out here just now when you began: "O Auntie", and changed
it to "O Gawd", when I collared you?'

'That's her! I haven't a chance with you, Doctor. *I* didn't know there was anything wrong with those braziers. How could I? We're always usin' 'em. Honest to God, I thought at first go-off he might wish to warm himself before the leaf-train. I – I didn't know Uncle John meant to start – 'ouse-keepin'.' He laughed horribly, and then the dry tears came.

Keede waited for them to pass in sobs and hiccoughs before he continued: 'Why? Was Godsoe your Uncle?'

'No,' said Strangwick, his head between his hands. 'Only we'd known him ever since we were born. Dad 'ad known him before that. He lived almost next street to us. Him an' Dad an' Ma an' – an' the rest had always been friends. So we called him Uncle – like children do.'

'What sort of man was he?'

'One o' *the* best, sir. Pensioned Sergeant with a little money left him – quite independent – and very superior. They had a sittin'-room full o' Indian curios that him and his wife used to let sister an' me see when we'd been good.'

'Wasn't he rather old to join up?'

'That made no odds to him. He joined up as Sergeant Instructor at the first go-off, an' when the Battalion was ready he got 'imself sent along. He wangled me into 'is Platoon when I went out – early in 'Seventeen. Because Ma wanted it, I suppose.'

'I'd no notion you knew him that well,' was Keede's comment.

'Oh, it made no odds to him. He 'ad no pets in the Platoon, but 'e'd write 'ome to Ma about me an' all the doin's. You see – ' Strangwick stirred uneasily on the sofa – 'we'd known him all our lives – lived in the next street an' all . . . An' him well over fifty. Oh dear me! *Oh* dear me! What a bloody mix-up things are, when one's as young as me!' he wailed of a sudden.

But Keede held him to the point. 'He wrote to your Mother about you?'

'Yes. Ma's eyes had gone bad followin' on air-raids. Blood-vessels broke behind 'em from sittin' in cellars an' bein' sick. She had to 'ave 'er letters read to her by Auntie. Now I think of it, that was the only thing that you might have called anything at all – '

'Was that the Aunt that died, and that you got the wire about?' Keede drove on.

'Yes – Auntie Armine – Ma's younger sister, an' she nearer fifty than forty. What a mix-up! An' if I'd been asked any time about it, I'd 'ave sworn there wasn't a single sol'tary item concernin' her that everybody didn't know an' hadn't known all along. No more conceal to her doin's than – than so much shop-front. She'd looked after sister an' me, when needful – whoopin' cough an' measles just the same as Ma. We was in an' out of her house like rabbits. You see, Uncle Armine is a cabinet-maker, an' second-'and furniture, an' we liked playin' with the things. She 'ad no children, and when the war came, she said she was glad of it. But she never talked much of her feelin's. She kept herself to herself, you understand.' He stared most earnestly at us to help out our understandings.

'What was she like?' Keede enquired.

'A biggish woman, an' had been 'andsome, I believe, but, bein' used to her, we two didn't notice much – except, per'aps, for one thing. Ma called her 'er proper name, which was Bella; but Sis an' me always called 'er Auntie Armine. See?'

'What for?'

'We thought it sounded more like her – like somethin' movin' slow, in armour.'

'Oh! And she read your letters to your mother, did she?'

'Every time the post came in she'd slip across the road from opposite an' read 'em. An' – an' I'll go bail for it that that was all there was to it for as far back as I remember. Was I to swing tomorrow, I'd go bail for *that*! 'Tisn't fair of 'em to 'ave unloaded it all on me, because – because – if the dead *do* rise, why, what in 'ell becomes of me an' all I've believed all me life? I want to know *that*! I – I –'

But Keede would not be put off. 'Did the Sergeant give you away at all in his letters?' he demanded, very quietly.

'There was nothin' to give away – we was too busy – but his letters about me were a great comfort to Ma. I'm no good at writin'. I saved it all up for my leafs. I got me fourteen days every six months an' one over . . . I was luckier than most, that way.'

'And when you came home, used you to bring 'em news about the Sergeant?' said Keede.

'I expect I must have; but I didn't think much of it at the time. I was took up with me own affairs – naturally. Uncle John always wrote to me once each leaf, tellin' me what was doin' an' what I was li'ble to expect on return, an' Ma 'ud 'ave that read to her. Then o' course I had to slip over to his wife an' pass her the news. An' then there was the young lady that I'd thought of marryin' if I came through. We'd got as far as pricin' things in the windows together.'

'And you didn't marry her – after all?'

Another tremor shook the boy. '*No*!' he cried. ' 'Fore it ended, I knew what reel things reelly mean! I – I never dreamed such things could be! . . . An' she nearer fifty than forty an' me own Aunt! . . . But there wasn't a sign nor a hint from first to last, so 'ow *could* I tell? Don't you *see* it? All she said to me after me Christmas leaf in' '18, when I come to say goodbye – all Auntie Armine said to me was: "You'll be seein' Mister Godsoe soon?" "Too soon for my likings," I says. " Well then, tell 'im from me," she says, "that I expect to be through with my little trouble by the twenty-first of next month, an' I'm dyin' to see him as soon as possible after that date." '

'What sort of trouble was it?' Keede turned professional at once.

'She'd 'ad a bit of a gatherin' in 'er breast, I believe. But she never talked of 'er body much to anyone.'

'I see,' said Keede. 'And she said to you?'

Strangwick repeated: ' "Tell Uncle John I hope to be finished of my drawback by the twenty-first, an' I'm dying to see 'im as soon as 'e can after that date." An' then she says, laughin': "But you've a head like a sieve. I'll write it down, an' you can give it him when you see 'im." So she wrote it on a bit o' paper an' I kissed 'er goodbye – I was always her favourite, you see – an' I went back to Sampoux. The thing hardly stayed in my mind at all, d'you see. But the next time I was up in the front line – I was a Runner, d'ye see – our platoon was in North Bay Trench an' I was up with a message to the Trench Mortar there that Corporal Grant was in charge of. Followin' on receipt of it, he borrowed a couple of men off the platoon, to slew 'er round or somethin'. I give Uncle John Auntie Armine's paper, an' I give Grant a fag, an' we warmed up a bit over a brazier. Then Grant says to me: "I don't like it"; an' he jerks 'is thumb at Uncle John in the bay studyin' Auntie's message. Well, *you* know, sir, you had to speak to Grant about 'is way of prophesyin' things – after Rankine shot himself with the Very light.'

'I did,' said Keede, and he explained to me 'Grant had the Second Sight – confound him! It upset the men. I was glad when he got pipped. What happened after that, Strangwick?'

'Grant whispers to me: "Look, you damned Englishman. 'E's for it." Uncle John was leanin' up against the bay, an' hummin' that hymn I was tryin' to tell you just now. He looked different all of a sudden – as if 'e'd got shaved. *I* don't know anything of these things, but I cautioned Grant as to his style of speakin', if an officer 'ad 'eard him, an' I went on. Passin' Uncle John in the bay, 'e nods an' smiles, which he didn't often, an' he says, pocketin' the paper "This suits *me*. I'm for leaf on the twenty-first, too." '

'He said that to you, did he?' said Keede.

'*Pre*cisely the same as passin' the time o' day. O' course I returned the agreeable about hopin' he'd get it, an' in due course I returned to 'Eadquarters. The thing 'ardly stayed in my mind a minute. That was the eleventh January – three days after I'd come back from leaf. You remember, sir, there wasn't anythin' doin' either side round Sampoux the first part o' the month. Jerry was gettin' ready for his March Push, an' as long as he kept quiet, we didn't want to poke 'im up.'

'I remember that,' said Keede. 'But what about the Sergeant?'

'I must have met him, on an' off, I expect, goin' up an' down, through the ensuin' days, but it didn't stay in me mind. Why needed it? And on the twenty-first Jan., his name was on the leaf-paper when I went up to warn the leaf-men. I noticed *that*, o' course. Now that very afternoon Jerry 'ad been tryin' a new trench-mortar, an' before our 'Eavies could out it, he'd got a stinker into a bay an' mopped up 'alf a dozen. They were bringin' 'em down when I went up to the supports, an' that blocked Little Parrot, same as it always did. *You* remember, sir?'

'Rather! And there was that big machine-gun behind the Half-House waiting for you if you got out,' said Keede.

'I remembered that too. But it was just on dark an' the fog was comin' off the Canal, so I hopped out of Little Parrot an' cut across the open to where those four dead Warwicks are heaped up. But the fog turned me round, an' the next thing I knew I was knee-over in that old 'alf-trench that runs west o' Little Parrot into French End. I dropped into it – almost atop o' the machine-gun platform by the side o' the old sugar boiler an' the two Zoo-ave skel'tons. That gave me my bearin's, an' so I went through French End, all up those missin' buckboards, into Butcher's Row where the *poy-looz* was laid in six deep each side, an' stuffed under the buckboards. It had froze tight, an' the drippin's had stopped, an' the creakin's had begun.'

'Did that really worry you at the time?' Keede asked.

'No,' said the boy with professional scorn. 'If a Runner starts noticin' such things he'd better chuck. In the middle of the Row, just before the old dressin'-station you referred to, sir, it come over me that somethin' ahead on the buckboards was just like Auntie Armine, waitin' beside the door; an' I thought to meself 'ow truly comic it would be if she could be dumped where I was then. In 'alf a second I saw it was only the dark an' some rags o' gas-screen, 'angin' on a bit of board, 'ad played me the trick. So I went on up to the supports an' warned the leaf-men there, includin' Uncle John. Then I went up

Rake Alley to warn 'em in the front line. I didn't hurry because I didn't want to get there till Jerry 'ad quieted down a bit. Well, then a Company Relief dropped in – an' the officer got the wind up over some lights on the flank, an' tied 'em into knots, an' I 'ad to hunt up me leaf-men all over the blinkin' shop. What with one thing an' another, it must 'ave been 'alf-past eight before I got back to the supports. There I run across Uncle John, scrapin' mud off himself, havin' shaved – quite the dandy. He asked about the Arras train, an' I said, if Jerry was quiet, it might be ten o'clock. "Good!" says 'e. "I'll come with you." So we started back down the old trench that used to run across Halnaker, back of the support dug-outs. *You* know, sir.'

Keede nodded.

'Then Uncle John says something to me about seein' Ma an' the rest of 'em in a few days, an' had I any messages for 'em? Gawd knows what made me do it, but I told 'im to tell Auntie Armine I never expected to see anything like *her* up in our part of the world. And while I told him I laughed. That's the last time I *'ave* laughed." Oh – you've seen 'er, 'ave you? says he, quite natural-like. Then I told 'im about the sand-bags an' rags in the dark, playin' the trick. "Very likely," says he, brushin' the mud off his putties. By this time, we'd got to the corner where the old barricade into French End was – before they bombed it down, sir. He turns right an' climbs across it. "No, thanks," says I. "I've been there once this evenin'." But he wasn't attendin' to me. He felt behind the rubbish an' bones just inside the barricade, an' when he straightened up, he had a full brazier in each hand.

'"Come on, Clem," he says, an' he very rarely give me me own name. "You aren't afraid, are you?" he says. "It's just as short, an' if Jerry starts up again he won't waste stuff here. He knows it's abandoned." "Who's afraid now?" I says. "Me for one," says he. "I don't want *my* leaf spoiled at the last minute." Then 'e wheels round an' speaks that bit you said come out o' the Burial Service.'

For some reason Keede repeated it in full, slowly: 'If after the manner of men I have fought with beasts at Ephesus, what advantageth it me, if the dead rise not?'

'That's it,' said Strangwick. 'So we went down French End together – everything froze up an' quiet, except for their creakin's. I remember thinkin' – ' his eyes began to flicker.

'Don't think. Tell what happened,' Keede ordered.

'Oh! Beg y' pardon! He went on with his braziers, hummin' his hymn, down Butcher's Row. Just before we got to the old dressin' station he stops and sets 'em down an' says "Where did you say she was, Clem? Me eyes ain't as good as they used to be."

' "In 'er bed at 'ome," I says. "Come on down. It's perishin' cold, an' *I'm* not due for leaf."

' "Well, I am," 'e says. "*I* am . . . " An' then – give you me word I didn't recognise the voice – he stretches out 'is neck a bit, in a way 'e 'ad, an' he says: "Why, Bella!" 'e says. "Oh, Bella!" 'e says. "Thank Gawd!" 'e says. Just like that! An' then I saw – I tell you I saw – Auntie Armine herself standin' by the old dressin' station door where first I'd thought I'd seen her. He was lookin' at 'er an' she was lookin' at him. I saw it, an' me soul turned over inside me because – because it knocked out everything I'd believed in. I 'ad nothin' to lay 'old of, d'ye see? An' 'e was lookin' at 'er as though he could 'ave et 'er, an' she was lookin' at 'im the same way, out of 'er eyes. Then he says: "Why, Bella," 'e says, "this must be only the second time we've been alone together in all these years." An' I saw 'er half hold out her arms to 'im in that perishin' cold. An' she nearer fifty than forty an' me own Aunt! You can shop me for a lunatic tomorrow, but I saw it – I *saw* 'er answerin' to his spoken word . . . Then 'e made a snatch to unsling 'is rifle. Then 'e cuts 'is hand away saying: "No! Don't tempt me, Bella. We've all Eternity ahead of us. An hour or two won't make any odds." Then he picks up the braziers an' goes on to the dug-out door. He'd finished with me. He pours petrol on 'em, an' lights it with a match, an' carries 'em inside, flarin'. All that time Auntie Armine stood with 'er arms out – an' a look in 'er face! *I* didn't know such things was or could be! Then he comes out an' says: "Come in, my dear"; an' she stoops an' goes into the dug-out with that look on her face – that look on her face! An' then 'e shuts the door from inside an' starts wedgin' it up. So 'elp me Gawd, I saw an' 'eard all these things with my own eyes an' ears!'

He repeated his oath several times. After a long pause Keede asked him if he recalled what happened next.

'It was a bit of a mix-up, for me, from then on. I must have carried on – they told me I did, but – but I was – I felt a – a long way inside of meself, like – if you've ever had that feelin'. I wasn't rightly on the spot at all. They woke me up some time next morning, because 'e 'adn't showed up at the train; an' someone had seen him with me. I wasn't 'alf cross-examined by all an' sundry till dinner-time.

'Then, I think, I volunteered for Dearlove, who 'ad a sore toe, for a front-line message. I had to keep movin', you see, because I hadn't anything to hold *on* to. Whilst up there, Grant informed me how he'd found Uncle John with the door wedged an' sandbags stuffed in the cracks. I hadn't waited for that. The knockin' when 'e wedged up was enough for me. Like Dad's coffin.'

'No-one told *me* the door had been wedged.' Keede spoke severely.

'No need to black a dead man's name, sir.'

'What made Grant go to Butcher's Row?'

'Because he'd noticed Uncle John had been pinchin' charcoal for a week past an' layin' it up behind the old barricade there. So when the 'unt began, he went that way straight as a string, an' when he saw the door shut, he knew. He told me he picked the sandbags out of the cracks an' shoved 'is hand through and shifted the wedges before anyone come along. It looked all right. You said yourself, sir, the door must 'ave blown to.'

'Grant knew what Godsoe meant, then?' Keede snapped.

'Grant knew Godsoe was for it; an' nothin' earthly could 'elp or 'inder. He told me so.'

'And then what did you do?'

'I expect I must 'ave kept on carryin' on, till Headquarters give me that wire from Ma – about Auntie Armine dyin'.'

'When had your Aunt died?'

'On the mornin' of the twenty-first. The mornin' of the 21st! That tore it, d'ye see? As long as I could think, I had kep' tellin' myself it was like those things you lectured about at Arras when we was billeted in the cellars – the Angels of Mons, and so on. But that wire tore it.'

'Oh! Hallucinations! I remember. And that wire tore it?' said Keede.

'Yes! You see' – he half lifted himself off the sofa – 'there wasn't a single gor-dam thing left abidin' for me to take hold of, here or hereafter. If the dead *do* rise – and I saw 'em – why – why, *anything* can 'appen. Don't you understand?'

He was on his feet now, gesticulating stiffly.

'For I saw 'er,' he repeated. 'I saw 'im an' 'er – she dead since mornin' time, an' he killin' 'imself before my livin' eyes so's to carry on with 'er for all Eternity – an' she 'oldin' out 'er arms for it! I want to know where I'm *at*! Look 'ere, you two – why stand *we* in jeopardy every hour?'

'God knows,' said Keede to himself.

'Hadn't we better ring for someone?' I suggested. 'He'll go off the handle in a second.'

'No, he won't. It's the last kick-up before it takes hold. I know how the stuff works. Hul-lo!'

Strangwick, his hands behind his back and his eyes set, gave tongue in the strained, cracked voice of a boy reciting. 'Not twice in the world shall the Gods do thus,' he cried again and again.

'And I'm damned if it's goin' to be even once for me!' he went on with sudden insane fury. '*I* don't care whether we *'ave* been pricin' things in the windows.... *Let* 'er sue if she likes! She don't know what reel things mean. *I* do – I've 'ad occasion to notice 'em . . . *No*, I tell you! I'll 'ave 'em when I want 'em, an' be done with 'em; but not till I see that look on a face . . . that look . . . I'm not takin' any. The reel thing's life an' death. It *begins* at death, d'ye see. *She* can't understand . . . Oh, go on an' push off to Hell, you an' your lawyers. I'm fed up with it – fed up!'

He stopped as abruptly as he had started, and the drawn face broke back to its natural irresolute lines. Keede, holding both his hands, led him back to the sofa, where he dropped like a wet towel, took out some flamboyant robe from a press, and drew it neatly over him.

'Ye-es. *That's* the real thing at last,' said Keede. 'Now he's got it off his mind he'll sleep. By the way, who introduced him?'

'Shall I go and find out?' I suggested.

'Yes; and you might ask him to come here. There's no need for us to stand to all night.'

So I went to the Banquet, which was in full swing, and was seized by an elderly, precise Brother from a South London Lodge, who followed me, concerned and apologetic. Keede soon put him at his ease.

'The boy's had trouble,' our visitor explained. 'I'm most mortified he should have performed his bad turn here. I thought he'd put it be'ind him.'

'I expect talking about old days with me brought it all back,' said Keede. 'It does sometimes.'

'Maybe! Maybe! But over and above that, Clem's had post-war trouble, too.'

'Can't he get a job? He oughtn't to let that weigh on him, at his time of life,' said Keede cheerily.

' 'Tisn't that – he's provided for – but – ' he coughed confidentially behind his dry hand – 'as a matter of fact, Worshipful Sir, he's – he's implicated for the present in a little breach of promise action.'

'Ah! That's a different thing,' said Keede.

'Yes. That's his reel trouble. No reason given, you understand.

The young lady in every way suitable, an' she'd make him a good little wife too, if I'm any judge. But he says she ain't his ideel or something. No getting at what's in young people's minds these days, is there?'

'I'm afraid there isn't,' said Keede. 'But he's all right now. He'll sleep. You sit by him, and when he wakes, take him home quietly . . . Oh, we're used to men getting a little upset here. You've nothing to thank us for, Brother – Brother – '

'Armine,' said the old gentleman. 'He's my nephew by marriage.'

'That's all that's wanted!' said Keede.

Brother Armine looked a little puzzled. Keede hastened to explain. 'As I was saying, all he wants now is to be kept quiet till he wakes.'

'At the End of the Passage'

The sky is lead and our faces are red,
And the gates of Hell are opened and riven,
And the winds of Hell are loosened and driven,
And the dust flies up in the face of Heaven,
And the clouds come down in a fiery sheet,
Heavy to raise and hard to be borne.
And the soul of man is turned from his meat,
Turned from the trifles for which he has striven
Sick in his body, and heavy-hearted,
And his soul flies up like the dust in the sheet
Breaks from his flesh and is gone and departed,
As the blasts they blow on the cholera-horn.

Himalayan

Four men, each entitled to 'life, liberty, and the pursuit of happiness', sat at a table playing whist. The thermometer marked – for them – one hundred and one degrees of heat. The room was darkened till it was only just possible to distinguish the pips of the cards and the very white faces of the players. A tattered, rotten punkah of whitewashed calico was puddling the hot air and whining dolefully at each stroke. Outside lay gloom of a November day in London. There was neither sky, sun, nor horizon – nothing but a brown purple haze of heat. It was as though the earth were dying of apoplexy.

From time to time clouds of tawny dust rose from the ground without wind or warning, flung themselves tablecloth-wise among the tops of the parched trees, and came down again. Then a whirling dust-devil would scutter across the plain for a couple of miles, break, and fall outward, though there was nothing to check its flight save a long low line of piled railway-sleepers white with the dust, a cluster of huts made of mud, condemned rails, and canvas, and the one squat four-roomed bungalow that belonged to the assistant engineer in charge of a section of the Gaudhari State line then under construction.

The four, stripped to the thinnest of sleeping-suits, played whist crossly, with wranglings as to leads and returns. It was not the best kind of whist, but they had taken some trouble to arrive at it. Mottram of the Indian Survey had ridden thirty and railed one hundred miles from his lonely post in the desert since the night before; Lowndes of the Civil Service, on special duty in the political department, had come as far to escape for an instant the miserable intrigues of an impoverished native State whose king alternately fawned and blustered for more money from the pitiful revenues contributed by hard-wrung peasants and despairing camel-breeders; Spurstow, the doctor of the line, had left a cholera-stricken camp of coolies to look after itself for forty-eight hours while he associated with white men once more. Hummil, the assistant engineer, was the host. He stood fast and received his friends thus every Sunday if they could come in. When one of them failed to appear, he would send a telegram to his last address, in order that he might know whether the defaulter were dead or alive. There are very many places in the East where it is not good or kind to let your acquaintances drop out of sight even for one short week.

The players were not conscious of any special regard for each other. They squabbled whenever they met; but they ardently desired to meet, as men without water desire to drink. They were lonely folk who understood the dread meaning of loneliness. They were all under thirty years of age – which is too soon for any man to possess that knowledge.

'Pilsener?' said Spurstow, after the second rubber, mopping his forehead.

'Beer's out, I'm sorry to say, and there's hardly enough soda-water for tonight,' said Hummil.

'What filthy bad management!' Spurstow snarled.

'Can't help it. I've written and wired; but the trains don't come through regularly yet. Last week the ice ran out – as Lowndes knows.'

'Glad I didn't come. I could ha' sent you some if I had known, though. Phew! it's too hot to go on playing bumblepuppy.' This with a savage scowl at Lowndes, who only laughed. He was a hardened offender.

Mottram rose from the table and looked out of a chink in the shutters.

'What a sweet day!' said he.

The company yawned all together and betook themselves to an aimless investigation of all Hummil's possessions – guns, tattered novels, saddlery, spurs, and the like. They had fingered them a score of times before, but there was really nothing else to do.

'Got anything fresh?' said Lowndes.

'Last week's *Gazette of India*, and a cutting from a home paper. My father sent it out. It's rather amusing.'

'One of those vestrymen that call 'emselves MPs again, is it?' said Spurstow, who read his newspapers when he could get them.

'Yes. Listen to this. It's to your address, Lowndes. The man was making a speech to his constituents, and he piled it on. Here's a sample: "And I assert unhesitatingly that the Civil Service in India is the preserve – the pet preserve – of the aristocracy of England. What does the democracy – what do the masses – get from that country, which we have step by step fraudulently annexed? I answer, nothing whatever. It is farmed with a single eye to their own interests by the scions of the aristocracy. They take good care to maintain their lavish scale of incomes, to avoid or stifle any enquiries into the nature and conduct of their administration, while they themselves force the unhappy peasant to pay with the sweat of his brow for all the luxuries in which they are lapped." ' Hummil waved the cutting above his head. ' 'Ear! 'ear!' said his audience.

Then Lowndes, meditatively: 'I'd give – I'd give three months' pay to have that gentleman spend one month with me and see how the free and independent native prince works things. Old Timbersides' – this was his flippant title for an honoured and decorated feudatory prince – 'has been wearing my life out this week past for money. By Jove, his latest performance was to send me one of his women as a bribe!'

'Good for you! Did you accept it?' said Mottram.

'No. I rather wish I had, now. She was a pretty little person, and she yarned away to me about the horrible destitution among the king's womenfolk. The darlings haven't had any new clothes for nearly a month, and the old man wants to buy a new drag from Calcutta – solid silver railings and silver lamps, and trifles of that kind. I've tried to make him understand that he has played the deuce with the revenues for the last twenty years and must go slow. He can't see it.'

'But he has the ancestral treasure-vaults to draw on. There must be three millions at least in jewels and coin under his palace,' said Hummil.

'Catch a native king disturbing the family treasure! The priests forbid it except as the last resort. Old Timbersides has added something like a quarter of a million to the deposit in his reign.'

'Where the mischief does it all come from?' said Mottram.

'The country. The state of the people is enough to make you sick. I've known the taxmen wait by a milch-camel till the foal was born and then hurry off the mother for arrears. And what can I do? I can't get the court clerks to give me any accounts; I can't raise anything more than a fat smile from the commander-in-chief when I find out the troops are three months in arrears; and old Timbersides begins to weep when I speak to him. He has taken to the King's Peg heavily – liqueur brandy for whisky, and Heidsieck for soda-water.'

'That's what the Rao of Jubela took to. Even a native can't last long at that,' said Spurstow. 'He'll go out.'

'And a good thing, too. Then I suppose we'll have a council of regency, and a tutor for the young prince, and hand him back his kingdom with ten years' accumulations.'

'Whereupon that young prince, having been taught all the vices of the English, will play ducks and drakes with the money and undo ten years' work in eighteen months. I've seen that business before,' said Spurstow. 'I should tackle the king with a light hand, if I were you, Lowndes. They'll hate you quite enough under any circumstances.'

'That's all very well. The man who looks on can talk about the light hand; but you can't clean a pigsty with a pen dipped in rose-water. I know my risks; but nothing has happened yet. My servant's an old Pathan, and he cooks for me. They are hardly likely to bribe him, and I don't accept food from my true friends, as they call themselves. Oh, but it's weary work! I'd sooner be with you, Spurstow. There's shooting near your camp.'

'Would you? I don't think it. About fifteen deaths a day don't incite a man to shoot anything but himself. And the worst of it is that the poor devils look at you as though you ought to save them. Lord knows, I've tried everything. My last attempt was empirical, but it pulled an old man through. He was brought to me apparently past hope, and I gave him gin and Worcester sauce with cayenne. It cured him; but I don't recommend it.'

'How do the cases run generally?' said Hummil.

'Very simply indeed. Chlorodyne, opium pill, chlorodyne, collapse, nitre, bricks to the feet, and then – the burning-ghât. The last seems to be the only thing that stops the trouble. It's black cholera, you know. Poor devils! But, I will say, little Bunsee Lal, my apothecary, works like a demon. I've recommended him for promotion if he comes through it all alive.'

'And what are your chances, old man?' said Mottram.

'Don't know; don't care much; but I've sent the letter in. What are you doing with yourself generally?'

'Sitting under a table in the tent and spitting on the sextant to keep it cool,' said the man of the survey. 'Washing my eyes to avoid ophthalmia, which I shall certainly get, and trying to make a sub-surveyor understand that an error of five degrees in an angle isn't quite so small as it looks. I'm altogether alone, y' know, and shall be till the end of the hot weather.'

'Hummil's the lucky man,' said Lowndes, flinging himself into a long chair. 'He has an actual roof – torn as to the ceiling-cloth, but still a roof – over his head. He sees one train daily. He can get beer and soda-water and ice 'em when God is good. He has books, pictures' (they were torn from the *Graphic*) 'and the society of the excellent subcontractor Jevins, besides the pleasure of receiving us weekly.'

Hummil smiled grimly. 'Yes, I'm the lucky man, I suppose. Jevins is luckier.'

'How? Not –'

'Yes. Went out. Last Monday.'

'By his own hand?' said Spurstow quickly, hinting the suspicion that was in everybody's mind. There was no cholera near Hummil's section. Even fever gives a man at least a week's grace, and sudden death generally implied self-slaughter.

'I judge no man this weather,' said Hummil. 'He had a touch of the sun, I fancy; for last week, after you fellows had left, he came into the verandah and told me that he was going home to see his wife, in Market Street, Liverpool, that evening.

'I got the apothecary in to look at him, and we tried to make him lie down. After an hour or two he rubbed his eyes and said he believed he had had a fit – hoped he hadn't said anything rude. Jevins had a great idea of bettering himself socially. He was very like Chucks in his language.'

'Well?'

'Then he went to his own bungalow and began cleaning a rifle. He told the servant that he was going to shoot buck in the morning. Naturally he fumbled with the trigger, and shot himself through the head – accidentally. The apothecary sent in a report to my chief, and Jevins is buried somewhere out there. I'd have wired to you, Spurstow, if you could have done anything.'

'You're a queer chap,' said Mottram. 'If you'd killed the man yourself you couldn't have been more quiet about the business.'

'Good Lord! what does it matter?' said Hummil calmly. 'I've got to do a lot of his overseeing work in addition to my own. I'm the only person that suffers. Jevins is out of it – by pure accident, of course, but out of it. The apothecary was going to write a long screed on suicide. Trust a *babu* to drivel when he gets the chance.'

'Why didn't you let it go in as suicide?' said Lowndes.

'No direct proof. A man hasn't many privileges in this country, but he might at least be allowed to mishandle his own rifle. Besides, some day I may need a man to smother up an accident to myself. Live and let live. Die and let die.'

'You take a pill,' said Spurstow, who had been watching Hummil's white face narrowly. 'Take a pill, and don't be an ass. That sort of talk is skittles. Anyhow, suicide is shirking your work. If I were Job ten times over, I should be so interested in what was going to happen next that I'd stay on and watch.'

'Ah! I've lost that curiosity,' said Hummil.

'Liver out of order?' said Lowndes feelingly.

'No. Can't sleep. That's worse.'

'By Jove, it is!' said Mottram. 'I'm that way every now and then, and the fit has to wear itself out. What do you take for it?'

'Nothing. What's the use? I haven't had ten minutes' sleep since Friday morning.'

'Poor chap! Spurstow, you ought to attend to this,' said Mottram. 'Now you mention it, your eyes are rather gummy and swollen.'

Spurstow, still watching Hummil, laughed lightly. 'I'll patch him up, later on. Is it too hot, do you think, to go for a ride?'

'Where to?' said Lowndes wearily. 'We shall have to go away at eight, and there'll be riding enough for us then. I hate a horse, when I have to use him as a necessity. Oh, heavens! what is there to do?'

'Begin whist again, at chick points ['a chick' is supposed to be eight shillings] and a gold mohur on the rub,' said Spurstow promptly.

'Poker. A month's pay all round for the pool – no limit – and fifty-rupee raises. Somebody would be broken before we got up,' said Lowndes.

'Can't say that it would give me any pleasure to break any man in this company,' said Mottram. 'There isn't enough excitement in it, and it's foolish.' He crossed over to the worn and battered little camp-piano – wreckage of a married household that had once held the bungalow – and opened the case.

'It's used up long ago,' said Hummil. 'The servants have picked it to pieces.'

The piano was indeed hopelessly out of order, but Mottram managed to bring the rebellious notes into a sort of agreement, and there rose from the ragged keyboard something that might once have been the ghost of a popular music-hall song. The men in the long chairs turned with evident interest as Mottram banged the more lustily.

'That's good!' said Lowndes. 'By Jove! the last time I heard that song was in '79, or thereabouts, just before I came out.'

'Ah!' said Spurstow with pride,' I was home in '80.' And he mentioned a song of the streets popular at that date.

Mottram executed it roughly. Lowndes criticised and volunteered emendations. Mottram dashed into another ditty, not of the music-hall character, and made as if to rise.

'Sit down,' said Hummil. 'I didn't know that you had any music in your composition. Go on playing until you can't think of anything more. I'll have that piano tuned up before you come again. Play something festive.'

Very simple indeed were the tunes to which Mottram's art and the limitations of the piano could give effect, but the men listened with pleasure, and in the pauses talked all together of what they had seen or heard when they were last at home. A dense dust-storm sprung up outside, and swept roaring over the house, enveloping it in the choking darkness of midnight, but Mottram continued unheeding, and the crazy tinkle reached the ears of the listeners above the flapping of the tattered ceiling-cloth.

In the silence after the storm he glided from the more directly personal songs of Scotland, half humming them as he played, into the Evening Hymn.

'Sunday,' said he, nodding his head.

'Go on. Don't apologise for it,' said Spurstow.

Hummil laughed long and riotously. 'Play it, by all means. You're full of surprises today. I didn't know you had such a gift of finished sarcasm. How does that thing go?'

Mottram took up the tune.

'Too slow by half. You miss the note of gratitude,' said Hummil. 'It ought to go to the "Grasshopper's Polka" – this way.' And he chanted, *prestissimo* –

'Glory to thee, my God, this night,
For all the blessings of the light.

'That shows we really feel our blessings. How does it go on? –

> 'If in the night I sleepless lie,
> My soul with sacred thoughts supply;
> May no ill dreams disturb my rest, – Quicker, Mottram! –
> Or powers of darkness me molest!

'Bah! what an old hypocrite you are!'

'Don't be an ass,' said Lowndes. 'You are at full liberty to make fun of anything else you like, but leave that hymn alone. It's associated in my mind with the most sacred recollections – '

'Summer evenings in the country – stained-glass window – light going out, and you and she jamming your heads together over one hymn-book,' said Mottram.

'Yes, and a fat old cockchafer hitting you in the eye when you walked home. Smell of hay, and a moon as big as a bandbox sitting on the top of a haycock; bats – roses – milk and midges,' said Lowndes.

'Also mothers. I can just recollect my mother singing me to sleep with that when I was a little chap,' said Spurstow.

The darkness had fallen on the room. They could hear Hummil squirming in his chair.

'Consequently,' said he testily, 'you sing it when you are seven fathom deep in Hell! It's an insult to the intelligence of the Deity to pretend we're anything but tortured rebels.'

'Take *two* pills,' said Spurstow; 'that's tortured liver.'

'The usually placid Hummil is in a vile bad temper. I'm sorry for his coolies tomorrow,' said Lowndes, as the servants brought in the lights and prepared the table for dinner.

As they were settling into their places about the miserable goat-chops, and the smoked tapioca pudding, Spurstow took occasion to whisper to Mottram, 'Well done, David!'

'Look after Saul, then,' was the reply.

'What are you two whispering about?' said Hummil suspiciously.

'Only saying that you are a damned poor host. This fowl can't be cut,' returned Spurstow with a sweet smile. 'Call this a dinner?'

'I can't help it. You don't expect a banquet, do you?'

Throughout that meal Hummil contrived laboriously to insult directly and pointedly all his guests in succession, and at each insult Spurstow kicked the aggrieved persons under the table; but he dared not exchange a glance of intelligence with either of them. Hummil's face was white and pinched, while his eyes were unnaturally large. No man dreamed for a moment of resenting his savage personalities, but as soon as the meal was over they made haste to get away. 'Don't go. You're just getting amusing, you fellows. I hope I haven't said anything that annoyed you. You're such touchy devils.' Then, changing the note into one of almost abject entreaty, Hummil added, 'I say, you surely aren't going?'

'In the language of the blessed Jorrocks, where I dines I sleeps,' said Spurstow. 'I want to have a look at your coolies tomorrow, if you don't mind. You can give me a place to lie down in, I suppose?'

The others pleaded the urgency of their several duties next day, and, saddling up, departed together, Hummil begging them to come next Sunday. As they jogged off, Lowndes unbosomed himself to Mottram – ' . . . And I never felt so like kicking a man at his own table in my life. He said I cheated at whist, and reminded me I was in debt! Told you you were as good as a liar to your face! You aren't half indignant enough over it.'

'Not I,' said Mottram. 'Poor devil! Did you ever know old Hummy behave like that before or within a hundred miles of it?'

'That's no excuse. Spurstow was hacking my shin all the time, so I kept a hand on myself. Else I should have – '

'No, you wouldn't. You'd have done as Hummy did about Jevins; judge no man this weather. By Jove! the buckle of my bridle is hot in my hand! Trot out a bit, and 'ware rat-holes.'

Ten minutes' trotting jerked out of Lowndes one very sage remark when he pulled up, sweating from every pore – 'Good thing Spurstow's with him tonight.'

'Ye-es. Good man, Spurstow. Our roads turn here. See you again next Sunday, if the sun doesn't bowl me over.'

'S'pose so, unless old Timbersides' finance minister manages to dress some of my food. Good-night, and – God bless you!'

'What's wrong now?'

'Oh, nothing.' Lowndes gathered up his whip, and, as he flicked Mottram's mare on the flank, added, 'You're not a bad little chap – that's all.' And the mare bolted half a mile across the sand, on the word.

In the assistant engineer's bungalow Spurstow and Hummil smoked the pipe of silence together, each narrowly watching the other. The capacity of a bachelor's establishment is as elastic as its arrangements are simple. A servant cleared away the dining-room table, brought in a couple of rude native bedsteads made of tape strung on a light wood frame, flung a square of cool Calcutta matting over each, set them side by side, pinned two towels to the punkah so that their fringes should just sweep clear of the sleepers' nose and mouth, and announced that the couches were ready.

The men flung themselves down, ordering the punkah-coolies by all the powers of Hell to pull. Every door and window was shut, for the outside air was that of an oven. The atmosphere within was only 104 degrees, as the thermometer bore witness, and heavy with the foul smell of badly-trimmed kerosene lamps; and this stench, combined with that of native tobacco, baked brick, and dried earth, sends the heart of many a strong man down to his boots, for it is the smell of the Great Indian Empire when she turns herself for six months into a house of torment. Spurstow packed his pillows craftily so that he reclined rather than lay, his head at a safe elevation above his feet. It is not good to sleep on a low pillow in the hot weather if you happen to be of thick-necked build, for you may pass with lively snores and gugglings from natural sleep into the deep slumber of heat-apoplexy.

'Pack your pillows,' said the doctor sharply, as he saw Hummil preparing to lie down at full length.

The night-light was trimmed; the shadow of the punkah wavered across the room, and the 'flick' of the punkah-towel and the soft whine of the rope through the wall-hole followed it. Then the punkah flagged, almost ceased. The sweat poured from Spurstow's brow. Should he go out and harangue the coolie? It started forward again with a savage jerk, and a pin came out of the towels. When this was replaced, a tomtom in the coolie-lines began to beat with the steady throb of a swollen artery inside some brain-fevered skull. Spurstow turned on his side and swore gently. There was no movement on Hummil's part. The man had composed himself as rigidly as a corpse, his hands clinched at his sides. The respiration was too hurried for any suspicion of sleep. Spurstow looked at the set face. The jaws were clinched, and there was a pucker round the quivering eyelids.

'He's holding himself as tightly as ever he can,' thought Spurstow. 'What in the world is the matter with him?' – 'Hummil!'

'Yes,' in a thick constrained voice.

'Can't you get to sleep?'

'No.'

'Head hot? 'Throat feeling bulgy? or how?'

'Neither, thanks. I don't sleep much, you know.'

'Feel pretty bad?'

'Pretty bad, thanks. There is a tomtom outside, isn't there? I thought it was my head at first . . . Oh, Spurstow, for pity's sake give me something that will put me asleep – sound asleep – if it's only for six hours!' He sprang up, trembling from head to foot. 'I haven't been able to sleep naturally for days, and I can't stand it! – I can't stand it!'

'Poor old chap!'

'That's no use. Give me something to make me sleep. I tell you I'm nearly mad. I don't know what I say half my time. For three weeks I've had to think and spell out every word that has come through my lips before I dared say it. Isn't that enough to drive a man mad? I can't see things correctly now, and I've lost my sense of touch. My skin aches – my skin aches! Make me sleep. Oh, Spurstow, for the love of God make me sleep sound. It isn't enough merely to let me dream. Let me sleep!'

'All right, old man, all right. Go slow; you aren't half as bad as you think.' The floodgates of reserve once broken, Hummil was clinging to him like a frightened child. 'You're pinching my arm to pieces.'

'I'll break your neck if you don't do something for me. No, I didn't mean that. Don't be angry, old fellow.' He wiped the sweat off himself as he fought to regain composure. 'I'm a bit restless and off my oats, and perhaps you could recommend some sort of sleeping mixture – bromide of potassium.'

'Bromide of skittles! Why didn't you tell me this before? Let go of my arm, and I'll see if there's anything in my cigarette-case to suit your complaint.' Spurstow hunted among his day-clothes, turned up the lamp, opened a little silver cigarette-case, and advanced on the expectant Hummil with the daintiest of fairy squirts.

'The last appeal of civilisation,' said he, 'and a thing I hate to use. Hold out your arm. Well, your sleeplessness hasn't ruined your muscle; and what a thick hide it is! Might as well inject a buffalo subcutaneously. Now in a few minutes the morphia will begin working. Lie down and wait.'

A smile of unalloyed and idiotic delight began to creep over Hummil's face. 'I think,' he whispered – 'I think I'm going off now. Gad! it's positively heavenly! Spurstow, you must give me that case to keep; you – ' The voice ceased as the head fell back.

'Not for a good deal,' said Spurstow to the unconscious form. 'And now, my friend, sleeplessness of your kind being very apt to relax the moral fibre in little matters of life and death, I'll just take the liberty of spiking your guns.'

He paddled into Hummil's saddle-room in his bare feet and uncased a twelve-bore rifle, an express, and a revolver. Of the first he unscrewed the nipples and hid them in the bottom of a saddlery-case; of the second he abstracted the lever, kicking it behind a big wardrobe. The third he merely opened, and knocked the doll-head bolt of the grip up with the heel of a riding-boot.

'That's settled,' he said, as he shook the sweat off his hands. 'These little precautions will at least give you time to turn. You have too much sympathy with gun-room accidents.'

And as he rose from his knees, the thick muffled voice of Hummil cried in the doorway, 'You fool!'

Such tones they use who speak in the lucid intervals of delirium to their friends a little before they die.

Spurstow started, dropping the pistol. Hummil stood in the door-way, rocking with helpless laughter.

'That was awf'ly good of you, I'm sure,' he said, very slowly, feeling for his words. 'I don't intend to go out by my own hand at present. I say, Spurstow, that stuff won't work. What shall I do? What shall I do?' And panic terror stood in his eyes.

'Lie down and give it a chance. Lie down at once.'

'I daren't. It will only take me halfway again, and I shan't be able to get away this time. Do you know it was all I could do to come out just now? Generally I am as quick as lightning; but you had clogged my feet. I was nearly caught.'

'Oh yes, I understand. Go and lie down.'

'No, it isn't delirium; but it was an awfully mean trick to play on me. Do you know I might have died?'

As a sponge rubs a slate clean, so some power unknown to Spurstow had wiped out of Hummil's face all that stamped it for the face of a man, and he stood at the doorway in the expression of his lost innocence. He had slipped back into terrified childhood.

'Is he going to die on the spot?' thought Spurstow. Then, aloud, 'All right, my son. Come back to bed, and tell me all about it. You couldn't sleep; but what was all the rest of the nonsense?'

'A place – a place down there,' said Hummil, with simple sincerity. The drug was acting on him by waves, and he was flung from the fear of a strong man to the fright of a child as his nerves gathered sense or were dulled.

'Good God! I've been afraid of it for months past, Spurstow. It has made every night hell to me; and yet I'm not conscious of having done anything wrong.'

'Be still, and I'll give you another dose. We'll stop your night-mares, you unutterable idiot!'

'Yes, but you must give me so much that I can't get away. You must make me quite sleepy – not just a little sleepy. It's so hard to run then.'

'I know it; I know it. I've felt it myself. The symptoms are exactly as you describe.'

'Oh, don't laugh at me, confound you! Before this awful sleep-lessness came to me I've tried to rest on my elbow and put a spur in the bed to sting me when I fell back. Look!'

'By Jove! the man has been rowelled like a horse! Ridden by the nightmare with a vengeance! And we all thought him sensible enough. Heaven send us understanding! You like to talk, don't you?'

'Yes, sometimes. Not when I'm frightened. *Then* I want to run. Don't you?'

'Always. Before I give you your second dose try to tell me exactly what your trouble is.'

Hummil spoke in broken whispers for nearly ten minutes, whilst Spurstow looked into the pupils of his eyes and passed his hand before them once or twice.

At the end of the narrative the silver cigarette-case was produced, and the last words that Hummil said as he fell back for the second time were, 'Put me quite to sleep; for if I'm caught I die – I die!'

'Yes, yes; we all do that sooner or later – thank Heaven who has set a term to our miseries,' said Spurstow, settling the cushions under the head. 'It occurs to me that unless I drink something I shall go out before my time. I've stopped sweating, and – I wear a seventeen-inch collar.' He brewed himself scalding hot tea, which is an excellent remedy against heat-apoplexy if you take three or four cups of it in time. Then he watched the sleeper.

'A blind face that cries and can't wipe its eyes, a blind face that chases him down corridors! H'm! Decidedly, Hummil ought to go on leave as soon as possible; and, sane or otherwise, he undoubtedly did rowel himself most cruelly. Well, Heaven send us understanding!'

At midday Hummil rose, with an evil taste in his mouth, but an unclouded eye and a joyful heart.

'I was pretty bad last night, wasn't I?' said he.

'I have seen healthier men. You must have had a touch of the sun. Look here: if I write you a swingeing medical certificate, will you apply for leave on the spot?'

'No.'

'Why not? You want it.'

'Yes, but I can hold on till the weather's a little cooler.'

'Why should you, if you can get relieved on the spot?'

'Burkett is the only man who could be sent; and he's a born fool.'

'Oh, never mind about the line. You aren't so important as all that. Wire for leave, if necessary.'

Hummil looked very uncomfortable.

'I can hold on till the Rains,' he said evasively.

'You can't. Wire to headquarters for Burkett.'

'I won't. If you want to know why, particularly, Burkett is married, and his wife's just had a kid, and she's up at Simla, in the cool, and Burkett has a very nice billet that takes him into Simla from Saturday to Monday. That little woman isn't at all well. If Burkett was transferred she'd try to follow him. If she left the baby behind she'd fret herself to death. If she came – and Burkett's one of those selfish little beasts who are always talking about a wife's place being with her husband – she'd die. It's murder to bring a woman here just now. Burkett hasn't the physique of a rat. If he came here he'd go out; and I know she hasn't any money, and I'm pretty sure she'd go out too. I'm salted in a sort of way, and I'm not married. Wait till the Rains, and then Burkett can get thin down here. It'll do him heaps of good.'

'Do you mean to say that you intend to face – what you have faced, till the Rains break?'

'Oh, it won't be so bad, now you've shown me a way out of it. I can always wire to you. Besides, now I've once got into the way of sleeping, it'll be all right. Anyhow, I shan't put in for leave. That's the long and the short of it.'

'My great Scott! I thought all that sort of thing was dead and done with.'

'Bosh! You'd do the same yourself. I feel a new man, thanks to that cigarette-case. You're going over to camp now, aren't you?'

'Yes; but I'll try to look you up every other day, if I can.'

'I'm not bad enough for that. I don't want you to bother. Give the coolies gin and ketchup.'

'Then you feel all right?'

'Fit to fight for my life, but not to stand out in the sun talking to you. Go along, old man, and bless you!'

Hummil turned on his heel to face the echoing desolation of his bungalow, and the first thing he saw standing in the verandah was the figure of himself. He had met a similar apparition once before, when he was suffering from overwork and the strain of the hot weather.

'This is bad – already,' he said, rubbing his eyes. 'If the thing slides away from me all in one piece, like a ghost, I shall know it is only my eyes and stomach that are out of order. If it walks – my head is going.'

He approached the figure, which naturally kept at an unvarying distance from him, as is the use of all spectres that are born of overwork. It slid through the house and dissolved into swimming specks within the eyeball as soon as it reached the burning light of the garden. Hummil went about his business till even. When he came in to dinner he found himself sitting at the table. The vision rose and walked out hastily. Except that it cast no shadow it was in all respects real.

No living man knows what that week held for Hummil. An increase of the epidemic kept Spurstow in camp among the coolies, and all he could do was to telegraph to Mottram, bidding him go to the bungalow and sleep there. But Mottram was forty miles away from the nearest telegraph, and knew nothing of anything save the needs of the survey till he met, early on Sunday morning, Lowndes and Spurstow heading towards Hummil's for the weekly gathering.

'Hope the poor chap's in a better temper,' said the former, swinging himself off his horse at the door. 'I suppose he isn't up yet.'

'I'll just have a look at him,' said the doctor. 'If he's asleep there's no need to wake him.'

And an instant later, by the tone of Spurstow's voice calling upon them to enter, the men knew what had happened. There was no need to wake him.

The punkah was still being pulled over the bed, but Hummil had departed this life at least three hours.

The body lay on its back, hands clinched by the side, as Spurstow had seen it lying seven nights previously. In the staring eyes was written terror beyond the expression of any pen.

Mottram, who had entered behind Lowndes, bent over the dead and touched the forehead lightly with his lips. 'Oh, you lucky, lucky devil!' he whispered.

But Lowndes had seen the eyes, and withdrew shuddering to the other side of the room.

'Poor chap! poor old chap! And the last time I met him I was angry. Spurstow, we should have watched him. Has he – ?'

Deftly Spurstow continued his investigations, ending by a search round the room.

'No, he hasn't,' he snapped. 'There's no trace of anything. Call the servants.'

They came, eight or ten of them, whispering and peering over each other's shoulders.

'When did your Sahib go to bed?' said Spurstow.

'At eleven or ten, we think,' said Hummil's personal servant.

'He was well then? But how should you know?'

'He was not ill, as far as our comprehension extended. But he had slept very little for three nights. This I know, because I saw him walking much, and specially in the heart of the night.'

As Spurstow was arranging the sheet, a big straight-necked hunting-spur tumbled on the ground. The doctor groaned. The personal servant peeped at the body.

'What do you think, Chuma?' said Spurstow, catching the look on the dark face.

'Heaven-born, in my poor opinion, this that was my master has descended into the Dark Places, and there has been caught because he was not able to escape with sufficient speed. We have the spur for evidence that he fought with Fear. Thus have I seen men of my race do with thorns when a spell was laid upon them to overtake them in their sleeping hours and they dared not sleep.'

'Chuma, you're a mud-head. Go out and prepare seals to be set on the Sahib's property.'

'God has made the Heaven-born. God has made me. Who are we, to enquire into the dispensations of God? I will bid the other servants hold aloof while you are reckoning the tale of the Sahib's property. They are all thieves, and would steal.'

'As far as I can make out, he died from – oh, anything; stoppage of the heart's action, heat-apoplexy, or some other visitation,' said Spurstow to his companions. 'We must make an inventory of his effects, and so on.'

'He was scared to death,' insisted Lowndes. 'Look at those eyes! For pity's sake don't let him be buried with them open!'

'Whatever it was, he's clear of all the trouble now,' said Mottram softly.

Spurstow was peering into the open eyes.

'Come here,' said he. 'Can you see anything there?'

'I can't face it!' whimpered Lowndes. 'Cover up the face! Is there any fear on earth that can turn a man into that likeness? It's ghastly. Oh, Spurstow, cover it up!'

'No fear – on earth,' said Spurstow. Mottram leaned over his shoulder and looked intently.

'I see nothing except some grey blurs in the pupil. There can be nothing there, you know.'

'Even so. Well, let's think. It'll take half a day to knock up any sort of coffin; and he must have died at midnight. Lowndes, old man, go out and tell the coolies to break ground next to Jevins's grave. Mottram, go round the house with Chuma and see that the seals are put on things. Send a couple of men to me here, and I'll arrange.'

The strong-armed servants when they returned to their own kind told a strange story of the doctor Sahib vainly trying to call their master back to life by magic arts – to wit, the holding of a little green box that clicked to each of the dead man's eyes, and of a bewildered muttering on the part of the doctor Sahib, who took the little green box away with him.

The resonant hammering of a coffin-lid is no pleasant thing to hear, but those who have experience maintain that much more terrible is the soft swish of the bed-linen, the reeving and unreeving of the bed-tapes, when he who has fallen by the roadside is apparelled for burial, sinking gradually as the tapes are tied over, till the swaddled shape touches the floor and there is no protest against the indignity of hasty disposal.

At the last moment Lowndes was seized with scruples of conscience. 'Ought you to read the service – from beginning to end?' said he to Spurstow.

'I intend to. You're my senior as a civilian. You can take it if you like.'

'I didn't mean that for a moment. I only thought if we could get a chaplain from somewhere – I'm willing to ride anywhere – and give poor Hummil a better chance. That's all.'

'Bosh!' said Spurstow, as he framed his lips to the tremendous words that stand at the head of the burial service.

After breakfast they smoked a pipe in silence to the memory of the dead. Then Spurstow said absently – ' 'Tisn't in medical science.'

'What?'

'Things in a dead man's eye.'

'For goodness' sake leave that horror alone!' said Lowndes. 'I've seen a native die of pure fright when a tiger chivvied him. I know what killed Hummil.'

'The deuce you do! I'm going to try to see.' And the doctor retreated into the bathroom with a Kodak camera. After a few minutes there was the sound of something being hammered to pieces, and he emerged, very white indeed.

'Have you got a picture?' said Mottram. 'What does the thing look like?'

'It was impossible, of course. You needn't look, Mottram. I've torn up the films. There was nothing there. It was impossible.'

'That,' said Lowndes, very distinctly, watching the shaking hand striving to relight the pipe, 'is a damned lie.'

Mottram laughed uneasily. 'Spurstow's right,' he said. 'We're all in such a state now that we'd believe anything. For pity's sake let's try to be rational.'

There was no further speech for a long time. The hot wind whistled without, and the dry trees sobbed. Presently the daily train, winking brass, burnished steel, and spouting steam, pulled up panting in the intense glare. 'We'd better go on on that,' said Spurstow. 'Go back to work. I've written my certificate. We can't do any more good here, and work'll keep our wits together. Come on.'

No-one moved. It is not pleasant to face railway journeys at midday in June. Spurstow gathered up his hat and whip, and, turning in the doorway, said – 'There may be Heaven – there must be Hell. Meantime, there is our life here. We-ell?'

Neither Mottram nor Lowndes had any answer to the question.

The Bisara of Pooree

Little Blind Fish, thou art marvellous wise,
Little Blind Fish, who put out thy eyes?
Open thine ears while I whisper my wish –
Bring me a lover, thou little Blind Fish.

The Charm of the Bisara

Some natives say that it came from the other side of Kulu, where the eleven-inch Temple Sapphire is. Others that it was made at the Devil-Shrine of Ao-Chung in Thibet, was stolen by a Kafir, from him by a Gurkha, from him again by a Lahouli, from him by a *khitmatgar*, and by this latter sold to an Englishman, so all its virtue was lost: because, to work properly, the Bisara of Pooree must be stolen – with bloodshed if possible, but, at any rate, stolen.

These stories of the coming into India are all false. It was made at Pooree ages since – the manner of its making would fill a small book – was stolen by one of the Temple dancing-girls there, for her own purposes, and then passed on from hand to hand, steadily northward, till it reached Hanla: always bearing the same name – the Bisara of Pooree. In shape it is a tiny, square box of silver, studded outside with eight small balas-rubies. Inside the box, which opens with a spring, is a little eyeless fish, carved from some sort of dark, shiny nut and wrapped in a shred of faded gold-cloth. That is the Bisara of Pooree, and it were better for a man to take a king cobra in his hand than to touch the Bisara of Pooree.

All kinds of magic are out of date and done away with except in India where nothing changes in spite of the shiny, toy-scum stuff that people call 'civilisation'. Any man who knows about the Bisara of Pooree will tell you what its powers are – always supposing that it has been honestly stolen. It is the only regularly working, trustworthy love-charm in the country, with one exception.

[The other charm is in the hands of a trooper of the Nizam's Horse, at a place called Tuprani, due north of Hyderabad.]

This can be depended upon for a fact. Someone else may explain it. If the Bisara be not stolen, but given or bought or found, it turns against its owner in three years, and leads to ruin or death. This is another fact which you may explain when you have time. Meanwhile, you can laugh at it. At present, the Bisara is safe on an ekka-pony's neck, inside the blue bead-necklace that keeps off the Evil Eye. If the ekka-driver ever finds it, and wears it, or gives it to his wife, I am sorry for him.

A very dirty hill-cooly woman, with goitre, owned it at Theog in 1884. It came into Simla from the north before Churton's *khitmatgar* bought it, and sold it, for three times its silver-value, to Churton, who collected curiosities. The servant knew no more what he had bought than the master; but a man looking over Churton's collection of curiosities – Churton was an Assistant Commissioner by the way – saw and held his tongue. He was an Englishman; but knew how to believe. Which shows that he was different from most Englishmen. He knew that it was dangerous to have any share in the little box when working or dormant; for unsought Love is a terrible gift.

Pack – 'Grubby' Pack, as we used to call him – was, in every way, a nasty little man who must have crawled into the Army by mistake. He was three inches taller than his sword, but not half so strong. And the sword was a fifty-shilling, tailor-made one. Nobody liked him, and, I suppose, it was his wizenedness and worthlessness that made him fall so hopelessly in love with Miss Hollis, who was good and sweet, and five foot seven in her tennis shoes. He was not content with falling in love quietly, but brought all the strength of his miserable little nature into the business. If he had not been so objectionable, one might have pitied him. He vapoured, and fretted, and fumed, and trotted up and down, and tried to make himself pleasing in Miss Hollis's big, quiet, grey eyes, and failed. It was one of the cases that you sometimes meet, even in this country where we marry by Code, of a really blind attachment all on one side, without the faintest possibility of return. Miss Hollis looked on Pack as some sort of vermin running about the road. He had no prospects beyond Captain's pay, and no wits to help that out by one anna. In a large-sized man, love like his would have been touching. In a good man it would have been grand. He being what he was, it was only a nuisance.

You will believe this much. What you will not believe, is what follows: Churton, and The Man who Knew what the Bisara was, were lunching at the Simla Club together. Churton was complaining of life in general. His best mare had rolled out of stable down the hill and had broken her back; his decisions were being reversed by the upper Courts, more than an Assistant Commissioner of eight years' standing has a right to expect; he knew liver and fever, and, for weeks past, had felt out of sorts. Altogether, he was disgusted and disheartened.

Simla Club dining-room is built, as all the world knows, in two sections, with an arch-arrangement dividing them. Come in, turn to your own left, take the table under the window, and you cannot see anyone who has come in, turning to the right, and taken a table on the right side of the arch. Curiously enough, every word that you say can be heard, not only by the other diner, but by the servants beyond the screen through which they bring dinner. This is worth knowing: an echoing room is a trap to be forewarned against.

Half in fun, and half hoping to be believed, The Man who Knew told Churton the story of the Bisara of Pooree at rather greater length than I have told it to you in this place; winding up with the suggestion that Churton might as well throw the little box down the hill and see whether all his troubles would go with it. In ordinary ears, English ears, the tale was only an interesting bit of folklore. Churton laughed, said that he felt better for his tiffin, and went out. Pack had been tiffining by himself to the right of the arch, and had heard everything. He was nearly mad with his absurd infatuation for Miss Hollis that all Simla had been laughing about.

It is a curious thing that, when a man hates or loves beyond reason, he is ready to go beyond reason to gratify his feelings. Which he would not do for money or power merely. Depend upon it, Solomon would never have built altars to Ashtaroth and all those ladies with queer names, if there had not been trouble of some kind in his *zenana*, and nowhere else. But this is beside the story. The facts of the case are these: Pack called on Churton next day when Churton was out, left his card, and *stole* the Bisara of Pooree from its place under the clock on the mantelpiece! Stole it like the thief he was by nature. Three days later, all Simla was electrified by the news that Miss Hollis had accepted Pack – the shrivelled rat, Pack! Do you desire clearer evidence than this? The Bisara of Pooree had been stolen, and it worked as it had always done when won by foul means.

There are three or four times in a man's life when he is justified in meddling with other people's affairs to play Providence.

The Man who Knew felt that he *was* justified; but believing and acting on a belief are quite different things. The insolent satisfaction of Pack as he ambled by the side of Miss Hollis, and Churton's striking release from liver, as soon as the Bisara of Pooree had gone, decided the Man. He explained to Churton and Churton laughed, because he was not brought up to believe that men on the Government House List steal – at least little things. But the miraculous acceptance by Miss Hollis of that tailor, Pack, decided him to take steps on suspicion. He vowed that he only wanted to find out where his ruby-studded silver box had vanished to. You cannot accuse a man on the Government House List of stealing. And if you rifle his room you are a thief yourself. Churton, prompted by The Man who Knew, decided on burglary. If he found nothing in Pack's room . . . but it is not nice to think of what would have happened in that case.

Pack went to a dance at Benmore – Benmore *was* Benmore in those days, and not an office – and danced fifteen waltzes out of twenty-two with Miss Hollis. Churton and The Man took all the keys that they could lay hands on, and went to Pack's room in the hotel, certain that his servants would be away. Pack was a cheap soul. He had not purchased a decent cashbox to keep his papers in, but one of those native imitations that you buy for ten rupees. It opened to any sort of key, and there at the bottom, under Pack's Insurance Policy, lay the Bisara of Pooree!

Churton called Pack names, put the Bisara of Pooree in his pocket, and went to the dance with The Man. At least, he came in time for supper, and saw the beginning of the end in Miss Hollis's eyes. She was hysterical after supper, and was taken away by her Mamma.

At the dance, with the abominable Bisara in his pocket, Churton twisted his foot on one of the steps leading down to the old Rink, and had to be sent home in a rickshaw, grumbling. He did not believe in the Bisara of Pooree any the more for this manifestation, but he sought out Pack and called him some ugly names; and 'thief' was the mildest of them. Pack took the names with the nervous smile of a little man who wants both soul and body to resent an insult, and went his way. There was no public scandal.

A week later, Pack got his definite dismissal from Miss Hollis. There had been a mistake in the placing of her affections, she said. So he went away to Madras, where he can do no great harm even if he lives to be a Colonel.

Churton insisted upon The Man who Knew taking the Bisara of Pooree as a gift. The Man took it, went down to the Cart Road at once, found an ekka pony with a blue head-necklace, fastened the Bisara of Pooree inside the necklace with a piece of shoestring and thanked Heaven that he was rid of a danger. Remember, in case you ever find it, that you must not destroy the Bisara of Pooree. I have not time to explain why just now, but the power lies in the little wooden fish. Mister Gubernatis or Max Muller could tell you more about it than I.

You will say that all this story is made up. Very well. If ever you come across a little silver, ruby-studded box, seven-eighths of an inch long by three-quarters wide, with a dark-brown wooden fish, wrapped in gold cloth, inside it, keep it. Keep it for three years, and then you will discover for yourself whether my story is true or false.

Better still, steal it as Pack did, and you will be sorry that you had not killed yourself in the beginning.

The Lost Legion

When the Indian Mutiny broke out, and a little time before the siege of Delhi, a regiment of Native Irregular Horse was stationed at Peshawar on the frontier of India. That regiment caught what John Lawrence called at the time 'the prevalent mania', and would have thrown in its lot with the mutineers had it been allowed to do so. The chance never came, for, as the regiment swept off down south, it was headed up by a remnant of an English corps into the hills of Afghanistan, and there the newly-conquered tribesmen turned against it as wolves turn against buck. It was hunted for the sake of its arms and accoutrements from hill to hill, from ravine to ravine, up and down the dried beds of rivers and round the shoulders of bluffs, till it disappeared as water sinks in the sand – this officerless, rebel regiment. The only trace left of its existence today is a nominal roll drawn up in neat round hand and countersigned by an officer who called himself 'Adjutant, late – Irregular Cavalry.' The paper is yellow with years and dirt, but on the back of it you can still read a pencil note by John Lawrence, to this effect: 'See that the two native officers who remained loyal are not deprived of their estates. – J. L.' Of six hundred and fifty sabres only two stood strain, and John Lawrence in the midst of all the agony of the first months of the Mutiny found time to think about their merits.

That was more that thirty years ago, and the tribesmen across the Afghan border who helped to annihilate the regiment are now old men. Sometimes a greybeard speaks of his share in the massacre. 'They came,' he will say, 'across the border, very proud, calling upon us to rise and kill the English, and go down to the sack of Delhi. But we who had just been conquered by the same English knew that they were over bold, and that the Government could account easily for those down-country dogs. This Hindustani regiment, therefore, we treated with fair words, and kept standing in one place till the redcoats came after them very hot and angry. Then this regiment ran forward a little more into our hills to avoid the wrath of the English,

and we lay upon their flanks watching from the sides of the hills till
we were well assured that their path was lost behind them. Then we
came down, for we desired their clothes, and their bridles, and their
rifles, and their boots – more especially their boots. That was a great
killing – done slowly.' Here the old man will rub his nose, and shake
his long snaky locks, and lick his bearded lips, and grin till the yellow
tooth-stumps show. 'Yes, we killed them because we needed their
gear, and we knew that their lives had been forfeited to God on
account of their sin – the sin of treachery to the salt which they had
eaten. They rode up and down the valleys, stumbling and rocking in
their saddles, and howling for mercy. We drove them slowly like
cattle till they were all assembled in one place, the flat wide valley of
Sheor Kôt. Many had died from want of water, but there still were
many left, and they could not make any stand. We went among
them, pulling them down with our hands two at a time, and our boys
killed them who were new to the sword. My share of the plunder was
such and such – so many guns, and so many saddles. The guns were
good in those days. Now we steal the Government rifles, and despise
smooth barrels. Yes, beyond doubt we wiped that regiment from off
the face of the earth, and even the memory of the deed is now dying.
But men say – '

At this point the tale would stop abruptly, and it was impossible to
find out what men said across the border. The Afghans were always
a secretive race, and vastly preferred doing something wicked to
saying anything at all. They would be quiet and well-behaved for
months, till one night, without word or warning, they would rush a
police-post, cut the throats of a constable or two, dash through a
village, carry away three or four women, and withdraw, in the red
glare of burning thatch, driving the cattle and goats before them to
their own desolate hills. The Indian Government would become
almost tearful on these occasions. First it would say, 'Please be good
and we'll forgive you.' The tribe concerned in the latest depredation
would collectively put its thumb to its nose and answer rudely. Then
the Government would say: 'Hadn't you better pay up a little money
for those few corpses you left behind you the other night?' Here the
tribe would temporise, and lie and bully, and some of the younger
men, merely to show contempt of authority, would raid another
police-post and fire into some frontier mud fort, and, if lucky, kill a
real English officer. Then the Government would say: 'Observe; if
you really persist in this line of conduct you will be hurt.' If the tribe
knew exactly what was going on in India, it would apologise or be

rude, according as it learned whether the Government was busy with other things, or able to devote its full attention to their perform- ances. Some of the tribes knew to one corpse how far to go. Others became excited, lost their heads, and told the Government to come on. With sorrow and tears, and one eye on the British taxpayer at home, who insisted on regarding these exercises as brutal wars of annexation, the Government would prepare an expensive little field- brigade and some guns, and send all up into the hills to chase the wicked tribe out of the valleys, where the corn grew, into the hill- tops where there was nothing to eat. The tribe would turn out in full strength and enjoy the campaign, for they knew that their women would never be touched, that their wounded would be nursed, not mutilated, and that as soon as each man's bag of corn was spent they could surrender and palaver with the English General as though they had been a real enemy. Afterwards, years afterwards, they would pay the blood-money, driblet by driblet, to the Government and tell their children how they had slain the redcoats by thousands. The only drawback to this kind of picnic-war was the weakness of the redcoats for solemnly blowing up with powder their fortified towers and keeps. This the tribes always considered mean.

Chief among the leaders of the smaller tribes – the little clans who knew to a penny the expense of moving white troops against them – was a priest-bandit-chief whom we will call the Gulla Kutta Mullah. His enthusiasm for border murder as an art was almost dignified. He would cut down a mail-runner from pure wantonness, or bombard a mud fort with rifle fire when he knew that our men needed to sleep. In his leisure moments he would go on circuit among his neighbours, and try to incite other tribes to devilry. Also, he kept a kind of hotel for fellow-outlaws in his own village, which lay in a valley called Bersund. Any respectable murderer on that section of the frontier was sure to lie up at Bersund, for it was reckoned an exceedingly safe place. The sole entry to it ran through a narrow gorge which could be converted into a death-trap in five minutes. It was surrounded by high hills, reckoned inaccessible to all save born mountaineers, and here the Gulla Kutta Mullah lived in great state, the head of a colony of mud and stone huts, and in each mud but hung some portion of a red uniform and the plunder of dead men. The Government particularly wished for his capture, and once invited him formally to come out and be hanged on account of a few of the murders in which he had taken a direct part. He replied: 'I am only twenty miles, as the crow flies, from your border. Come and fetch me.'

'Some day we will come,' said the Government, 'and hanged you will be.'

The Gulla Kutta Mullah let the matter from his mind. He knew that the patience of the Government was as long as a summer day; but he did not realise that its arm was as long as a winter night. Months afterwards, when there was peace on the border, and all India was quiet, the Indian Government turned in its sleep and remembered the Gulla Kutta Mullah at Bersund with his thirteen outlaws. The movement against him of one single regiment – which the telegrams would have translated as war – would have been highly impolitic. This was a time for silence and speed, and, above all, absence of bloodshed.

You must know that all along the north-west frontier of India there is spread a force of some thirty thousand foot and horse, whose duty it is quietly and unostentatiously to shepherd the tribes in front of them. They move up and down, and down and up, from one desolate little post to another; they are ready to take the field at ten minutes' notice; they are always half in and half out of a difficulty somewhere along the monotonous line; their lives are as hard as their own muscles, and the papers never say anything about them. It was from this force that the Government picked its men.

One night at a station where the mounted Night Patrol fire as they challenge, and the wheat rolls in great blue-green waves under our cold northern moon, the officers were playing billiards in the mud-walled club-house, when orders came to them that they were to go on parade at once for a night-drill. They grumbled, and went to turn out their men – a hundred English troops, let us say, two hundred Goorkhas, and about a hundred cavalry of the finest native cavalry in the world.

When they were on the parade-ground, it was explained to them in whispers that they must set off at once across the hills to Bersund. The English troops were to post themselves round the hills at the side of the valley; the Goorkhas would command the gorge and the death-trap, and the cavalry would fetch a long march round and get to the back of the circle of hills, whence, if there were any difficulty, they could charge down on the Mullah's men. But orders were very strict that there should be no fighting and no noise. They were to return in the morning with every round of ammunition intact, and the Mullah and the thirteen outlaws bound in their midst. If they were successful, no-one would know or care anything about their work; but failure meant probably a small border war, in which the

Gulla Kutta Mullah would pose as a popular leader against a big bullying power, instead of a common border murderer.

Then there was silence, broken only by the clicking of the compass needles and snapping of watch-cases, as the heads of columns compared bearings and made appointments for the rendezvous. Five minutes later the parade-ground was empty; the green coats of the Goorkhas and the overcoats of the English troops had faded into the darkness, and the cavalry were cantering away in the face of a blinding drizzle.

What the Goorkhas and the English did will be seen later on. The heavy work lay with the horses, for they had to go far and pick their way clear of habitations. Many of the troopers were natives of that part of the world, ready and anxious to fight against their kin, and some of the officers had made private and unofficial excursions into those hills before. They crossed the border, found a dried river bed, cantered up that, walked through a stony gorge, risked crossing a low hill under cover of the darkness, skirted another hill, leaving their hoof-marks deep in some ploughed ground, felt their way along another watercourse, ran over the neck of a spur, praying that no-one would hear their horses grunting, and so worked on in the rain and the darkness, till they had left Bersund and its crater of hills a little behind them, and to the left, and it was time to swing round. The ascent commanding the back of Bersund was steep, and they halted to draw breath in a broad level valley below the height. That is to say, the men reined up, but the horses, blown as they were, refused to halt. There was unchristian language, the worse for being delivered in a whisper, and you heard the saddles squeaking in the darkness as the horses plunged.

The subaltern at the rear of one troop turned in his saddle and said very softly: 'Carter, what the blessed heavens are you doing at the rear? Bring your men up, man.'

There was no answer, till a trooper replied: 'Carter Sahib is forward – not there. There is nothing behind us.'

'There is,' said the subaltern. 'The squadron's walking on its own tail.'

Then the Major in command moved down to the rear swearing softly and asking for the blood of Lieutenant Halley – the subaltern who had just spoken.

'Look after your rearguard,' said the Major. 'Some of your infernal thieves have got lost. They're at the head of the squadron, and you're several kinds of idiot.'

'Shall I tell off my men, sir?' said the subaltern sulkily, for he was feeling wet and cold.

'Tell 'em off!' said the Major. '*Whip* 'em off, by Gad! You're squandering them all over the place. There's a troop behind you *now*!'

'So I was thinking,' said the subaltern calmly. 'I have all my men here, sir. Better speak to Carter.'

'Carter Sahib sends salaam and wants to know why the regiment is stopping,' said a trooper to Lieutenant Halley.

'Where under heaven *is* Carter?' said the Major.

'Forward with his troop,' was the answer.

'Are we walking in a ring, then, or are we the centre of a blessed brigade?' said the Major.

By this time there was silence all along the column. The horses were still; but, through the drive of the fine rain, men could hear the feet of many horses moving over stony ground.

'We're being stalked,' said Lieutenant Halley.

'They've no horses here. Besides they'd have fired before this,' said the Major. 'It's – it's villagers' ponies.'

'Then our horses would have neighed and spoilt the attack long ago. They must have been near us for half an hour,' said the subaltern.

'Queer that we can't smell the horses,' said the Major, damping his finger and rubbing it on his nose as he sniffed up wind.

'Well, it's a bad start,' said the subaltern, shaking the wet from his overcoat. 'What shall we do, sir?'

'Get on,' said the Major. 'We shall catch it tonight.'

The column moved forward very gingerly for a few paces. Then there was an oath, a shower of blue sparks as shod hooves crashed on small stones, and a man rolled over with a jangle of accoutrements that would have waked the dead.

'Now we've gone and done it,' said Lieutenant Halley. 'All the hillside awake, and all the hillside to climb in the face of musketry-fire. This comes of trying to do night-hawk work.'

The trembling trooper picked himself up, and tried to explain that his horse had fallen over one of the little cairns that are built of loose stones on the spot where a man has been murdered. There was no need for reasons. The Major's big Australian charger blundered next, and the column came to a halt in what seemed to be a very graveyard of little cairns all about two feet high. The manoeuvres of the squadron are not reported. Men said that it felt like mounted quadrilles without training and without the music; but at last the horses, breaking rank and choosing their own way, walked clear of the cairns, till every man of the squadron re-formed and drew rein a few yards up the slope of the hill. Then, according to Lieutenant Halley, there was another scene very like the one which has been described. The Major and Carter insisted that all the men had not joined ranks, and that there were more of them in the rear clicking and blundering among the dead men's cairns. Lieutenant Halley told off his own troopers again and resigned himself to wait. Later on he told me: 'I didn't much know, and I didn't much care what was going on. The row of that trooper falling ought to have scared half the country, and I would take my oath that we were being stalked by a full regiment in the rear, and *they* were making row enough to rouse all Afghanistan. I sat tight, but nothing happened.'

The mysterious part of the night's work was the silence on the hillside. Everybody knew that the Gulla Kutta Mullah had his out-post huts on the reverse side of the hill, and everybody expected by the time that the Major had sworn himself into a state of quiet that the watchmen there would open fire. When nothing occurred, they said that the gusts of the rain had deadened the sound of the horses, and thanked Providence. At last the Major satisfied himself (*a*) that he had left no-one behind among the cairns, and (*b*) that he was not being taken in the rear by a large and powerful body of cavalry. The men's tempers were thoroughly spoiled, the horses were lathered and unquiet, and one and all prayed for the daylight.

They set themselves to climb up the hill, each man leading his mount carefully. Before they had covered the lower slopes or the breastplates had begun to tighten, a thunderstorm came up behind, rolling across the low hills and drowning any noise less than that of cannon. The first flash of the lightning showed the bare ribs of the ascent, the hill-crest standing steely blue against the black sky, the little falling lines of the rain, and, a few yards to their left flank, an Afghan watch-tower, two-storeyed, built of stone, and entered by a ladder from the upper storey. The ladder was up, and a man with a rifle was leaning from the window. The darkness and the thunder rolled down in an instant, and, when the lull followed, a voice from the watch-tower cried, 'Who goes there?'

The cavalry were very quiet, but each man gripped his carbine and stood beside his horse. Again the voice called, 'Who goes there?' and in a louder key, 'O, brothers, give the alarm!' Now, every man in the cavalry would have died in his long boots sooner than have asked for quarter; but it is a fact that the answer to the second call was a long wail of '*Marf karo*! *Marf karo*!' which means, 'Have mercy! Have mercy!' It came from the climbing regiment.

The cavalry stood dumbfounded, till the big troopers had time to whisper one to another 'Mir Khan, was that thy voice? Abdullah, didst *thou* call?' Lieutenant Halley stood beside his charger and waited. So long as no firing was going on he was content. Another flash of lightning showed the horses with heaving flanks and nodding heads, the men, white-eyeballed, glaring beside them, and the stone watch-tower to the left. This time there was no head at the window, and the rude iron-clamped shutter that could turn a rifle bullet was closed.

'Go on, men,' said the Major. 'Get up to the top at any rate.' The squadron toiled forward, the horses wagging their tails and the men pulling at the bridles, the stones rolling down the hillside and the sparks flying. Lieutenant Halley declares that he never heard a squadron make so much noise in his life. They scrambled up, he said, as though each horse had eight legs and a spare horse to follow him. Even then there was no sound from the watch-tower, and the men stopped exhausted on the ridge that overlooked the pit of darkness in which the village of Bersund lay. Girths were loosed, curb-chains shifted, and saddles adjusted, and the men dropped down among the stones. Whatever might happen now, they had the upper ground of any attack.

The thunder ceased, and with it the rain, and the soft thick darkness of a winter night before the dawn covered them all. Except for the sound of falling water among the ravines below, everything was still. They heard the shutter of the watch-tower below them thrown back with a clang, and the voice of the watcher calling: 'Oh, Hafiz Ullah!'

The echoes took up the call, 'La-la-la!' And an answer came from the watch-tower hidden round the curve of the hill, 'What is it, Shahbaz Khan?'

Shahbaz Khan replied in the high-pitched voice of the mountaineer: 'Hast thou seen?'

The answer came back: 'Yes. God deliver us from all evil spirits!'

There was a pause, and then: 'Hafiz Ullah, I am alone! Come to me!'

'Shahbaz Khan, I am alone also; but I dare not leave my post!'

'That is a lie; thou art afraid.'

A longer pause followed, and then: 'I am afraid. Be silent! They are below us still. Pray to God and sleep.'

The troopers listened and wondered, for they could not understand what save earth and stone could lie below the watch-towers.

Shahbaz Khan began to call again: 'They are below us. I can see
them. For the pity of God come over to me, Hafiz Ullah ! My father
slew ten of them. Come over!'

Hafiz Ullah answered in a very loud voice, 'Mine was guiltless.
Hear, ye Men of the Night, neither my father nor my blood had any
part in that sin. Bear thou thy own punishment, Shahbaz Khan.'

'Oh, someone ought to stop those two chaps crowing away like
cocks there,' said Lieutenant Halley, shivering under his rock.

He had hardly turned round to expose a new side of him to the rain
before a bearded, long-locked, evil-smelling Afghan rushed up the
hill, and tumbled into his arms. Halley sat upon him, and thrust as
much of a sword-hilt as could be spared down the man's gullet. 'If
you cry out, I kill you,' he said cheerfully.

The man was beyond any expression of terror. He lay and quaked,
grunting. When Halley took the sword-hilt from between his teeth,
he was still inarticulate, but clung to Halley's arm, feeling it from
elbow to wrist.

'The Rissala! The dead Rissala!' he gasped. 'It is down there!'

'No; the Rissala, the very much alive Rissala. It is up here,' said
Halley, unshipping his watering-bridle, and fastening the man's
hands. 'Why were you in the towers so foolish as to let us pass?'

'The valley is full of the dead,' said the Afghan. 'It is better to fall
into the hands of the English than the hands of the dead. They
march to and fro below there. I saw them in the lightning.'

He recovered his composure after a little, and whispering, because
Halley's pistol was at his stomach, said: 'What is this? There is
no war between us now, and the Mullah will kill me for not seeing
you pass!'

'Rest easy,' said Halley; 'we are coming to kill the Mullah, if God
please. His teeth have grown too long. No harm will come to thee
unless the daylight shows thee as a face which is desired by the
gallows for crime done. But what of the dead regiment?'

'I only kill within my own border,' said the man, immensely
relieved. 'The Dead Regiment is below. The men must have passed
through it on their journey – four hundred dead on horses, stumbling among their own graves, among the little heaps – dead men
all, whom we slew.'

'Whew!' said Halley. 'That accounts for my cursing Carter and the
Major cursing me. Four hundred sabres, eh? No wonder we thought

there were a few extra men in the troop. Kurruk Shah,' he whispered to a grizzled native officer that lay within a few feet of him, 'hast thou heard anything of a dead Rissala in these hills?'

'Assuredly,' said Kurruk Shah with a grim chuckle. 'Otherwise, why did I, who have served the Queen for seven-and-twenty years, and killed many hill-dogs, shout aloud for quarter when the lightning revealed us to the watch-towers? When I was a young man I saw the killing in the valley of Sheor-Kot there at our feet, and I know the tale that grew up therefrom. But how can the ghosts of unbelievers prevail against us who are of the Faith? Strap that dog's hands a little tighter, Sahib. An Afghan is like an eel.'

'But a dead Rissala,' said Halley, jerking his captive's wrist. 'That is foolish talk, Kurruk Shah. The dead are dead. Hold still, *sag*.' The Afghan wriggled.

'The dead are dead, and for that reason they walk at night. What need to talk? We be men; we have our eyes and ears. Thou canst both see and hear them, down the hillside,' said Kurruk Shah composedly.

Halley stared and listened long and intently. The valley was full of stifled noises, as every valley must be at night; but whether he saw or heard more than was natural Halley alone knows, and he does not choose to speak on the subject.

At last, and just before the dawn, a green rocket shot up from the far side of the valley of Bersund, at the head of the gorge, to show that the Goorkhas were in position. A red light from the infantry at left and right answered it, and the cavalry burnt a white flare. Afghans in winter are late sleepers, and it was not till full day that the Gulla Kutta Mullah's men began to straggle from their huts, rubbing their eyes. They saw men in green, and red, and brown uniforms, leaning on their arms, neatly arranged all round the crater of the village of Bersund, in a cordon that not even a wolf could have broken. They rubbed their eyes the more when a pink-faced young man, who was not even in the Army, but represented the Political Department, tripped down the hillside with two orderlies, rapped at the door of the Gulla Kutta Mullah's house, and told him quietly to step out and be tied up for safe transport. That same young man passed on through the huts, tapping here one cateran and there another lightly with his cane; and as each was pointed out, so he was tied up, staring hopelessly at the crowned heights around where the English soldiers looked down with incurious eyes. Only the Mullah tried to carry it off with curses and high words, till a soldier who was tying his hands said: 'None o' your lip!' Why didn't you come out when you was ordered, instead o' keepin' us awake all night? You're no better than my own barrack-sweeper, you white-'eaded old polyanthus! Kim up!'

Half an hour later the troops had gone away with the Mullah and his thirteen friends. The dazed villagers were looking ruefully at a pile of broken muskets and snapped swords, and wondering how in the world they had come so to miscalculate the forbearance of the Indian Government.

It was a very neat little affair, neatly carried out, and the men concerned were unofficially thanked for their services.

Yet it seems to me that much credit is also due to another regiment whose name did not appear in the brigade orders, and whose very existence is in danger of being forgotten.

The Dream of Duncan Parrenness

Like Mr Bunyan of old, I, Duncan Parrenness, Writer to the Most Honourable the East India Company, in this God-forgotten city of Calcutta, have dreamed a dream, and never since that Kitty my mare fell lame have I been so troubled. Therefore, lest I should forget my dream, I have made shift to set it down here. Though Heaven knows how unhandy the pen is to me who was always readier with sword than ink-horn when I left London two long years since.

When the Governor-General's great dance (that he gives yearly at the latter end of November) was finisht, I had gone to mine own room which looks over that sullen, un-English stream, the Hoogly, scarce so sober as I might have been. Now, roaring drunk in the West is but fuddled in the East, and I was drunk Nor'-Nor' Easterly as Mr Shakespeare might have said. Yet, in spite of my liquor, the cool night winds (though I have heard that they breed chills and fluxes innumerable) sobered me somewhat; and I remembered that I had been but a little wrung and wasted by all the sicknesses of the past four months, whereas those young bloods that came eastward with me in the same ship had been all, a month back, planted to Eternity in the foul soil north of Writers' Buildings. So then, I thanked God mistily (though, to my shame, I never kneeled down to do so) for licence to live, at least till March should be upon us again.

Indeed, we that were alive (and our number was less by far than those who had gone to their last account in the hot weather late past) had made very merry that evening, by the ramparts of the Fort, over this kindness of Providence; though our jests were neither witty nor such as I should have liked my Mother to hear.

When I had lain down (or rather thrown me on my bed) and the fumes of my drink had a little cleared away, I found that I could get no sleep for thinking of a thousand things that were better left alone. First, and it was a long time since I had thought of her, the sweet face of Kitty Somerset, drifted, as it might have been drawn in a picture, across the foot of my bed, so plainly, that I almost thought she had been present in the body. Then I remembered how she drove me to this accursed country to get rich, that I might the more quickly marry her, our parents on both sides giving their consent; and then how she thought better (or worse maybe) of her troth, and wed Tom Sanderson but a short three months after I had sailed. From Kitty I fell a-musing on Mrs Vansuythen, a tall pale woman with violet eyes that had come to Calcutta from the Dutch Factory at Chinsura, and had set all our young men, and not a few of the factors, by the ears. Some of our ladies, it is true, said that she had never a husband or marriage-lines at all; but women, and specially those who have led only indifferent good lives themselves, are cruel hard one on another. Besides, Mrs Vansuythen was far prettier than them all. She had been most gracious to me at the Governor-General's rout, and indeed I was looked upon by all as her *preux chevalier* – which is French for a much worse word. Now, whether I cared so much as the scratch of a pin for this same Mrs Vansuythen (albeit I had vowed eternal love three days after we met) I knew not then nor did till later on; but mine own pride, and a skill in the smallsword that no man in Calcutta could equal, kept me in her affections. So that I believed I worship her.

When I had dismist her violet eyes from my thoughts, my reason reproacht me for ever having followed her at all; and I saw how the one year that I had lived in this land had so burnt and seared my mind with the flames of a thousand bad passions and desires, that I had aged ten months for each one in the Devil's school. Whereat I thought of my Mother for a while, and was very penitent: making in my sinful tipsy mood a thousand vows of reformation – all since broken, I fear me, again and again. Tomorrow, says I to myself, I will live cleanly for ever. And I smiled dizzily (the liquor being still strong in me) to think of the dangers I had escaped; and built all manner of fine Castles in Spain, whereof a shadowy Kitty Somerset that had the violet eyes and the sweet slow speech of Mrs Vansuythen, was always Queen.

Lastly, a very fine and magnificent courage (that doubtless had its birth in Mr Hastings' Madeira) grew upon me, till it seemed that I could become Governor-General, Nawab, Prince, ay, even the Great Mogul himself, by the mere wishing of it. Wherefore, taking my first steps, random and unstable enough, towards my new kingdom, I kickt my servants sleeping without till they howled and ran from me, and called Heaven and Earth to witness that I, Duncan Parrenness, was a Writer in the service of the Company and afraid of no man. Then, seeing that neither the Moon nor the Great Bear were minded to accept my challenge, I lay down again and must have fallen asleep.

I was waked presently by my last words repeated two or three times, and I saw that there had come into the room a drunken man, as I thought, from Mr Hastings' rout. He sate down at the foot of my bed in all the world as it belonged to him, and I took note, as well as I could, that his face was somewhat like mine own grown older, save when it changed to the face of the Governor-General or my father, dead these six months. But this seemed to me only natural, and the due result of too much wine; and I was so angered at his entry all unannounced, that I told him, not over civilly, to go. To all my words he made no answer whatever, only saying slowly, as though it were some sweet morsel: 'Writer in the Company's service and afraid of no man'. Then he stops short, and turning round sharp upon me, says that one of my kidney need fear neither man nor devil; that I was a brave young man, and like enough, should I live so long, to be Governor-General. But for all these things (and I suppose that he meant thereby the changes and chances of our shifty life in these parts) I must pay my price. By this time I had sobered somewhat, and being well waked out of my first sleep, was disposed to look upon the matter as a tipsy man's jest. So, says I merrily: 'And what price shall I pay for this palace of mine, which is but twelve feet square, and my five poor pagodas a month? The Devil take you and your jesting: I have paid my price twice over in sickness.' At that moment my man turns full towards me: so that by the moonlight I could see every line and wrinkle of his face. Then my drunken mirth died out of me, as I have seen the waters of our great rivers die away in one night; and I, Duncan Parrenness, who was afraid of no man, was taken with a more deadly terror than I hold it has ever been the lot of mortal man to know. For I saw that his face was my very own, but marked and lined and scarred with the furrows of disease and much evil living – as I once, when I was (Lord help me) very drunk indeed, have seen mine own face, all white and drawn and grown old, in a mirror. I take it that any man would have been even more greatly feared than I. For I am in no way wanting in courage.

After I had lain still for a little, sweating in my agony and waiting until I should awake from this terrible dream (for dream I knew it to be) he says again, that I must pay my price, and a little after, as though it were to be given in pagodas and sicca rupees: 'What price will you pay?' Says I, very softly: 'For God's sake let me be, whoever you are, and I will mend my ways from tonight.' Says he, laughing a little at my words, but otherwise making no motion of having heard them: 'Nay, I would only rid so brave a young ruffler as yourself of much that will be a great hindrance to you on your way through life in the Indies; for believe me,' and here he looks full on me once more, 'there is no return.' At all this rigmarole, which I could not then understand, I was a good deal put aback and waited for what should come next. Says he very calmly, 'Give me your trust in man.' At that I saw how heavy would be my price, for I never doubted but that he could take from me all that he asked, and my head was, through terror and wakefulness, altogether cleared of the wine I had drunk. So I takes him up very short, crying that I was not so wholly bad as he would make believe, and that I trusted my fellows to the full as much as they were worthy of it. 'It was none of my fault,' says I, 'if one half of them were liars and the other half deserved to be burnt in the hand, and I would once more ask him to have done with his questions.' Then I stopped, a little afraid, it is true, to have let my tongue so run away with me, but he took no notice of this, and only laid his hand lightly on my left breast and I felt very cold there for a while. Then he says, laughing more: 'Give me your faith in women.' At that I started in my bed as though I had been stung, for I thought of my sweet mother in England, and for a while fancied that my faith in God's best creatures could neither be shaken nor stolen from me. But later, Myself's hard eyes being upon me, I fell to thinking, for the second time that night, of Kitty (she that jilted me and married Tom Sanderson) and of Mistress Vansuythen, whom only my devilish pride made me follow, and how she was even worse than Kitty, and I worst of them all – seeing that with my life's work to be done, I must needs go dancing down the Devil's swept and garnished causeway, because, forsooth, there was a light woman's smile at the end of it. And I thought that all women in the world were either like Kitty or Mistress Vansuythen (as indeed they have ever since been to me) and this put me to such an extremity of rage and sorrow, that I was beyond word glad when Myself's hand fell again on my left breast, and I was no more troubled by these follies.

After this he was silent for a little, and I made sure that he must go or I awake ere long: but presently he speaks again (and very softly) that I was a fool to care for such follies as those he had taken from me, and that ere he went he would only ask me for a few other trifles such as no man, or for matter of that boy either, would keep about him in this country. And so it happened that he took from out of my very heart as it were, looking all the time into my face with my own eyes, as much as remained to me of my boy's soul and conscience. This was to me a far more terrible loss than the two that I had suffered before. For though, Lord help me, I had travelled far enough from all paths of decent or godly living, yet there was in me, though I myself write it, a certain goodness of heart which, when I was sober (or sick) made me very sorry of all that I had done before the fit came on me. And this I lost wholly: having in place thereof another deadly coldness at the heart. I am not, as I have before said, ready with my pen, so I fear that what I have just written may not be readily understood. Yet there be certain times in a young man's life, when, through great sorrow or sin, all the boy in him is burnt and seared away so that he passes at one step to the more sorrowful state of manhood: as our staring Indian day changes into night with never so much as the grey of twilight to temper the two extremes. This shall perhaps make my state more clear, if it be remembered that my torment was ten times as great as comes in the natural course of nature to any man. At that time I dared not think of the change that had come over me, and all in one night: though I have often thought of it since. 'I have paid the price,' says I, my teeth chattering, for I was deadly cold, 'and what is my return?' At this time it was nearly dawn, and Myself had begun to grow pale and thin against the white light in the east, as my mother used to tell me is the custom of ghosts and devils and the like. He made as if he would go, but my words stopt him and he laughed – as I remember that I laughed when I ran Angus Macalister through the sword-arm last August, because he said that Mrs Vansuythen was no better than she should be. 'What return?' – says he, catching up my last words – 'Why, strength to live as long as God or the Devil pleases, and so long as you live my young master, my gift.' With that he puts something into my hand, though it was still too dark to see what it was, and when next I lookt up he was gone.

When the light came I made shift to behold his gift, and saw that it was a little piece of dry bread.

L'Envoi

My new-cut ashlar takes the light
Where crimson-blank the windows flare;
By my own work, before the night,
Great Overseer, I make my prayer.

If there be good in that I wrought,
Thy hand compelled it, Master, Thine;
Where I have failed to meet Thy thought
I know, through Thee, the blame is mine.

One instant's toil to Thee denied
Stands all Eternity's offence,
Of that I did with Thee to guide
To Thee, through Thee, be excellence.

Who, lest all thought of Eden fade,
Bring'st Eden to the craftsman's brain,
Godlike to muse o'er his own trade
And Manlike stand with God again.

The depth and dream of my desire,
The bitter paths wherein I stray,
Thou knowest Who has made the Fire,
Thou knowest Who has made the Clay.

One stone the more swings to her place
In that dread Temple of Thy Worth –
It is enough that through Thy grace
I saw naught common on Thy earth.

Take not that vision from my ken;
Oh whatsoe'er may spoil or speed,
Help me to need no aid from men
That I may help such men as need.

The Tomb of his Ancestors

Some people will tell you that if there were but a single loaf of bread in all India it would be divided equally between the Plowdens, the Trevors, the Beadons, and the Rivett-Carnacs. That is only one way of saying that certain families serve India generation after generation, as dolphins follow in line across the open sea.

Let us take a small and obscure case. There has been at least one representative of the Devonshire Chinns in or near Central India since the days of Lieutenant-Fireworker Humphrey Chinn, of the Bombay European Regiment, who assisted at the capture of Seringapatam in 1799. Alfred Ellis Chinn, Humphrey's younger brother, commanded a regiment of Bombay grenadiers from 1804 to 1813, when he saw some mixed fighting; and in 1834 John Chinn of the same family – we will call him John Chinn the First – came to light as a level-headed administrator in time of trouble at a place called Mundesur. He died young, but left his mark on the new country, and the Honourable the Board of Directors of the Honourable the East India Company embodied his virtues in a stately resolution, and paid for the expenses of his tomb among the Satpura hills.

He was succeeded by his son, Lionel Chinn, who left the little old Devonshire home just in time to be severely wounded in the Mutiny. He spent his working life within a hundred and fifty miles of John Chinn's grave, and rose to the command of a regiment of small, wild hill-men, most of whom had known his father. His son John was born in the small thatched-roofed, mud-walled cantonment, which is even today eighty miles from the nearest railway, in the heart of a scrubby, tigerish country. Colonel Lionel Chinn served thirty years and retired. In the Canal his steamer passed the outward-bound troopship carrying his son eastward to the family duty.

The Chinns are luckier than most folk, because they know exactly what they must do. A clever Chinn passes for the Bombay Civil Service, and gets away to Central India, where everybody is glad to see him. A dull Chinn enters the Police Department or the Woods and Forest, and sooner or later he, too, appears in Central India, and that is what gave rise to the saying, 'Central India is inhabited by Bhils, Mairs, and Chinns, all very much alike.' The breed is small-boned, dark, and silent, and the stupidest of them are good shots. John Chinn the Second was rather clever, but as the eldest son he entered the army, according to Chinn tradition. His duty was to abide in his father's regiment for the term of his natural life, though the corps was one which most men would have paid heavily to avoid. They were irregulars, small, dark, and blackish, clothed in rifle-green with black-leather trimmings; and friends called them the 'Wuddars', which means a race of low-caste people who dig up rats to eat. But the Wuddars did not resent it. They were the only Wuddars, and their points of pride were these:

Firstly, they had fewer English officers than any native regiment. Secondly, their subalterns were not mounted on parade, as is the general rule, but walked at the head of their men. A man who can hold his own with the Wuddars at their quickstep must be sound in wind and limb. Thirdly, they were the most *pukka shikarries* (out-and-out hunters) in all India. Fourthly – up to one-hundredthly – they were the Wuddars – Chinn's Irregular Bhil Levies of the old days, but now, henceforward and for ever, the Wuddars.

No Englishman entered their mess except for love or through family usage. The officers talked to their soldiers in a tongue not two hundred white folk in India understood; and the men were their children, all drawn from the Bhils, who are, perhaps, the strangest of the many strange races in India. They were, and at heart are, wild men, furtive, shy, full of untold superstitions. The races whom we call natives of the country found the Bhil in possession of the land when they first broke into that part of the world thousands of years ago. The books call them Pre-Aryan, Aboriginal, Dravidian, and so forth; and, in other words, that is what the Bhils call themselves. When a Rajput chief whose bards can sing his pedigree backwards for twelve hundred years is set on the throne, his investiture is not complete till he has been marked on the forehead with blood from the veins of a Bhil. The Rajputs say the ceremony has no meaning, but the Bhil knows that it is the last, last shadow of his old rights as the long-ago owner of the soil.

Centuries of oppression and massacre made the Bhil a cruel and half-crazy thief and cattle-stealer, and when the English came he seemed to be almost as open to civilisation as the tigers of his own jungles. But John Chinn the First, father of Lionel, grandfather of our John, went into his country, lived with him, learned his language, shot the deer that stole his poor crops, and won his confidence, so that some Bhils learned to plough and sow, while others were coaxed into the Company's service to police their friends.

When they understood that standing in line did not mean instant execution, they accepted soldiering as a cumbrous but amusing kind of sport, and were zealous to keep the wild Bhils under control. That was the thin edge of the wedge. John Chinn the First gave them written promises that, if they were good from a certain date, the Government would overlook previous offences; and since John Chinn was never known to break his word – he promised once to hang a Bhil locally esteemed invulnerable, and hanged him in front of his tribe for seven proved murders – the Bhils settled down as steadily as they knew how. It was slow, unseen work, of the sort that is being done all over India today; and though John Chinn's only reward came, as I have said, in the shape of a grave at Government expense, the little people of the hills never forgot him.

Colonel Lionel Chinn knew and loved them, too, and they were very fairly civilised, for Bhils, before his service ended. Many of them could hardly be distinguished from low-caste Hindoo farmers; but in the south, where John Chinn the First was buried, the wildest still clung to the Satpura ranges, cherishing a legend that some day Jan Chinn, as they called him, would return to his own. In the meantime they mistrusted the white man and his ways. The least excitement would stampede them, plundering at random, and now and then killing; but if they were handled discreetly they grieved like children, and promised never to do it again.

The Bhils of the regiment – the uniformed men – were virtuous in many ways, but they needed humouring. They felt bored and homesick unless taken after tiger as beaters; and their cold-blooded daring – all Wuddars shoot tigers on foot: it is their caste-mark – made even the officers wonder. They would follow up a wounded tiger as unconcernedly as though it were a sparrow with a broken wing; and this through a country full of caves and rifts and pits, where a wild beast could hold a dozen men at his mercy. Now and then some little man was brought to barracks with his head smashed in or his ribs torn away; but his companions never learned caution; they contented themselves with settling the tiger.

Young John Chinn was decanted at the verandah of the Wuddars' lonely mess-house from the back seat of a two-wheeled cart, his gun-cases cascading all round him. The slender little hookey-nosed boy looked forlorn as a strayed goat when he slapped the white dust off his knees, and the cart jolted down the glaring road. But in his heart he was contented. After all, this was the place where he had been born, and things were not much changed since he had been sent to England, a child, fifteen years ago.

There were a few new buildings, but the air and the smell and the sunshine were the same; and the little green men who crossed the parade-ground looked very familiar. Three weeks ago John Chinn would have said he did not remember a word of the Bhil tongue, but at the mess door he found his lips moving in sentences that he did not understand – bits of old nursery rhymes, and tail-ends of such orders as his father used to give the men.

The Colonel watched him come up the steps, and laughed.

'Look!' he said to the Major. 'No need to ask the young un's breed. He's a *pukka* Chinn. Might be his father in the Fifties over again.'

'Hope he'll shoot as straight,' said the Major. 'He's brought enough ironmongery with him.'

'Wouldn't be a Chinn if he didn't. Watch him blowin' his nose. Regular Chinn beak. Flourishes his handkerchief like his father. It's the second edition – line for line.'

'Fairy tale, by Jove!' said the Major, peering through the slats of the jalousies. 'If he's the lawful heir, he'll . . . Now old Chinn could no more pass that chick without fiddling with it than . . .'

'His son!' said the Colonel, jumping up.

'Well, I be blowed!' said the Major. The boy's eye had been caught by a split-reed screen that hung on a slew between the veranda pillars, and, mechanically, he had tweaked the edge to set it level. Old Chinn had sworn three times a day at that screen for many years; he could never get it to his satisfaction.

His son entered the anteroom in the middle of a fivefold silence. They made him welcome for his father's sake and, as they took stock of him, for his own. He was ridiculously like the portrait of the Colonel on the wall, and when he had washed a little of the dust from his throat he went to his quarters with the old man's short, noiseless jungle-step.

'So much for heredity,' said the Major. 'That comes of four generations among the Bhils.'

'And the men know it,' said a Wing officer. 'They've been waiting for this youth with their tongues hanging out. I am persuaded that, unless he absolutely beats 'em over the head, they'll lie down by companies and worship him.'

'Nothin' like havin' a father before you,' said the Major. 'I'm a *parvenu* with my chaps. I've only been twenty years in the regiment, and my revered parent he was a simple squire. There's no getting at the bottom of a Bhil's mind. Now, why is the superior bearer that young Chinn brought with him fleeing across country with his bundle?' He stepped into the verandah, and shouted after the man – a typical new-joined subaltern's servant who speaks English and cheats in proportion.

What is it?' he called.

Plenty bad man here. I going, sar,' was the reply. 'Have taken Sahib's keys, and say will shoot.'

Doocid lucid – doocid convincin'. How those up-country thieves can leg it! He has been badly frightened by someone.' The Major strolled to his quarters to dress for mess.

Young Chinn, walking like a man in a dream, had fetched a compass round the entire cantonment before going to his own tiny cottage. The captain's quarters, in which he had been born, delayed him for a little; then he looked at the well on the parade-ground, where he had sat of evenings with his nurse, and at the ten-by-fourteen church, where the officers went to service if a chaplain of any official creed happened to come along. It seemed very small as compared with the gigantic buildings he used to stare up at, but it was the same place.

From time to time he passed a knot of silent soldiers, who saluted. They might have been the very men who had carried him on their backs when he was in his first knickerbockers. A faint light burned in his room, and, as he entered, hands clasped his feet, and a voice murmured from the floor.

'Who is it?' said young Chinn, not knowing he spoke in the Bhil tongue.

'I bore you in my arms, Sahib, when I was a strong man and you were a small one – crying, crying, crying! I am your servant, as I was your father's before you. We are all your servants.'

Young Chinn could not trust himself to reply, and the voice went on: 'I have taken your keys from that fat foreigner, and sent him away; and the studs are in the shirt for mess. Who should know, if I do not know? And so the baby has become a man, and forgets his nurse; but my nephew shall make a good servant, or I will beat him twice a day.'

Then there rose up, with a rattle, as straight as a Bhil arrow, a little white-haired wizened ape of a man, with medals and orders on his tunic, stammering, saluting, and trembling. Behind him a young and wiry Bhil, in uniform, was taking the trees out of Chinn's mess-boots.

Chinn's eyes were full of tears. The old man held out his keys.

'Foreigners are bad people. He will never come back again. We are all servants of your father's son. Has the Sahib forgotten who took him to see the trapped tiger in the village across the river, when his mother was so frightened and he was so brave?'

The scene came back to Chinn in great magic-lantern flashes. 'Bukta!' he cried; and all in a breath: 'You promised nothing should hurt me. *Is* it Bukta?'

The man was at his feet a second time. 'He has not forgotten. He remembers his own people as his father remembered. Now can I die. But first I will live and show the Sahib how to kill tigers. That yonder is my nephew. If he is not a good servant, beat him and send him to me, and I will surely kill him, for now the Sahib is with his own people. Ai, *Jan baba – Jan baba*! My *Jan baba*! I will stay here and see that this does his work well. Take off his boots, fool. Sit down upon the bed, Sahib, and let me look. It is *Jan baba*.'

He pushed forward the hilt of his sword as a sign of service, which is an honour paid only to viceroys, governors, generals, or to little children whom one loves dearly. Chinn touched the hilt mechanically with three fingers, muttering he knew not what. It happened to be the old answer of his childhood, when Bukta in jest called him the little General Sahib.

The Major's quarters were opposite Chinn's, and when he heard his servant gasp with surprise he looked across the room. Then the Major sat on the bed and whistled; for the spectacle of the senior native commissioned officer of the regiment, an 'unmixed' Bhil, a Companion of the Order of British India, with thirty-five years' spotless service in the army, and a rank among his own people superior to that of many Bengal princelings, valeting the last-joined subaltern, was a little too much for his nerves.

The throaty bugles blew the Mess-call that has a long legend behind it. First a few piercing notes like the shrieks of beaters in a far-away cover, and next, large, full, and smooth, the refrain of the wild song: 'And oh, and oh, the green pulse of Mundore – Mundore!'

'All little children were in bed when the Sahib heard that call last,' said Bukta, passing Chinn a clean handkerchief. The call brought back memories of his cot under the mosquito-netting, his mother's kiss, and the sound of footsteps growing fainter as he dropped asleep among his men. So he hooked the dark collar of his new mess-jacket, and went to dinner like a prince who has newly inherited his father's crown.

Old Bukta swaggered forth curling his whiskers. He knew his own value, and no money and no rank within the gift of the Government would have induced him to put studs in young officers' shirts, or to hand them clean ties. Yet, when he took off his uniform that night, and squatted among his fellows for a quiet smoke, he told them what he had done, and they said that he was entirely right. Thereat Bukta propounded a theory which to a white mind would have seemed raving insanity; but the whispering, level-headed little men of war considered it from every point of view, and thought that there might be a great deal in it.

At mess under the oil-lamps the talk turned as usual to the unfailing subject of *shikar* – big game shooting of every kind and under all sorts of conditions. Young Chinn opened his eyes when he understood that each one of his companions had shot several tigers in the Wuddar style – on foot, that is – making no more of the business than if the brute had been a dog.

'In nine cases out of ten,' said the Major, 'a tiger is almost as dangerous as a porcupine. But the tenth time you come home feet first.'

That set all talking, and long before midnight Chinn's brain was in a whirl with stories of tigers – man-eaters and cattle-killers each pursuing his own business as methodically as clerks in an office; new tigers that had lately come into such-and-such a district; and old, friendly beasts of great cunning, known by nicknames in the mess – such as 'Puggy', who was lazy, with huge paws, and 'Mrs Malaprop', who turned up when you never expected her, and made female noises. Then they spoke of Bhil superstitions, a wide and picturesque field, till young Chinn hinted that they must be pulling his leg.

' 'Deed, we aren't,' said a man on his left. 'We know all about you. You're a Chinn and all that, and you've a sort of vested right here; but if you don't believe what we're telling you, what will you do when old Bukta begins his stories? He knows about ghost-tigers, and tigers that go to a hell of their own; and tigers that walk on their hind feet; and your grandpapa's riding-tiger, as well. Odd he hasn't spoken of that yet.'

'You know you've an ancestor buried down Satpura way, don't you?' said the Major, as Chinn smiled irresolutely.

'Of course I do,' said Chinn, who had the chronicle of the Book of Chinn by heart. It lies in a worn old ledger on the Chinese lacquer table behind the piano in the Devonshire home, and the children are allowed to look at it on Sundays.

'Well, I wasn't sure. Your revered ancestor, my boy, according to the Bhils, has a tiger of his own – a saddle-tiger that he rides round the country whenever he feels inclined. *I* don't call it decent in an ex-Collector's ghost; but that is what the Southern Bhils believe. Even our men, who might be called moderately cool, don't care to beat that country if they hear that Jan Chinn is running about on his tiger. It is supposed to be a clouded animal – not stripy, but blotchy, like a tortoiseshell tomcat. No end of a brute, it is, and a sure sign of war or pestilence or – or something. There's a nice family legend for you.'

'What's the origin of it, d' you suppose?' said Chinn.

'Ask the Satpura Bhils. Old Jan Chinn was a mighty hunter before the Lord. Perhaps it was the tiger's revenge, or perhaps he's huntin' 'em still. You must go to his tomb one of these days and enquire. Bukta will probably attend to that. He was asking me before you came whether by any ill-luck you had already bagged your tiger. If not, he is going to enter you under his own wing. Of course, for you of all men it's imperative. You'll have a first-class time with Bukta.'

The Major was not wrong. Bukta kept an anxious eye on young Chinn at drill, and it was noticeable that the first time the new officer lifted up his voice in an order the whole line quivered. Even the Colonel was taken aback, for it might have been Lionel Chinn returned from Devonshire with a new lease of life. Bukta had continued to develop his peculiar theory among his intimates, and it was accepted as a matter of faith in the lines, since every word and gesture on young Chinn's part so confirmed it.

The old man arranged early that his darling should wipe out the reproach of not having shot a tiger; but he was not content to take the first or any beast that happened to arrive. In his own villages he dispensed the high, low, and middle justice, and when his people – naked and fluttered – came to him with word of a beast marked down, he bade them send spies to the kills and the watering-places, that he might be sure the quarry was such an one as suited the dignity of such a man.

Three or four times the reckless trackers returned, most truthfully saying that the beast was mangy, undersized – a tigress worn with nursing, or a broken-toothed old male – and Bukta would curb young Chinn's impatience.

At last, a noble animal was marked down – a ten-foot cattle-killer with a huge roll of loose skin along the belly, glossy-hided, full-frilled about the neck, whiskered, frisky, and young. He had slain a man in pure sport, they said.

'Let him be fed,' quoth Bukta, and the villagers dutifully drove out a cow to amuse him, that he might lie up near by.

Princes and potentates have taken ship to India and spent great moneys for the mere glimpse of beasts one-half as fine as this of Bukta's.

'It is not good,' said he to the Colonel, when he asked for shooting-leave, 'that my Colonel's son who may be – that my Colonel's son should lose his maidenhead on any small jungle beast. That may come after. I have waited long for this which is a tiger. He has come in from the Mair country. In seven days we will return with the skin.'

The mess gnashed their teeth enviously. Bukta, had he chosen, might have invited them all. But he went out alone with Chinn, two days in a shooting-cart and a day on foot, till they came to a rocky, glary valley with a pool of good water in it. It was a parching day, and the boy very naturally stripped and went in for a bathe, leaving Bukta by the clothes. A white skin shows far against brown jungle, and what Bukta beheld on Chinn's back and right shoulder dragged him forward step by step with staring eyeballs.

'I'd forgotten it isn't decent to strip before a man of his position,' said Chinn, flouncing in the water. 'How the little devil stares! What is it, Bukta?' 'The Mark!' was the whispered answer.

'It is nothing. You know how it is with my people!' Chinn was annoyed. The dull-red birthmark on his shoulder, something like a conventionalised Tartar cloud, had slipped his memory or he would not have bathed. It occurred, so they said at home, in alternate generations, appearing, curiously enough, eight or nine years after birth, and, save that it was part of the Chinn inheritance, would not be considered pretty. He hurried ashore, dressed again, and went on till they met two or three Bhils, who promptly fell on their faces. 'My people,' grunted Bukta, not condescending to notice them. 'And so your people, Sahib. When I was a young man we were fewer, but not so weak. Now we are many, but poor stock. As may be remembered. How will you shoot him, Sahib? From a tree? From a shelter which my people shall build? By day or by night?'

'On foot and in the daytime,' said young Chinn.

'That was your custom, as I have heard,' said Bukta to himself. 'I will get news of him. Then you and I will go to him. I will carry one gun. You have yours. There is no need of more. What tiger shall stand against *thee*?'

He was marked down by a little waterhole at the head of a ravine, full-gorged and half asleep in the May sunlight. He was walked up like a partridge, and he turned to do battle for his life. Bukta made no motion to raise his rifle, but kept his eyes on Chinn, who met the shattering roar of the charge with a single shot – it seemed to him hours as he sighted – which tore through the throat, smashing the backbone below the neck and between the shoulders. The brute couched, choked, and fell, and before Chinn knew well what had happened Bukta bade him stay still while he paced the distance between his feet and the ringing jaws.

'Fifteen,' said Bukta. 'Short paces. No need for a second shot, Sahib. He bleeds cleanly where he lies, and we need not spoil the skin. I said there would be no need of these, but they came – in case.'

Suddenly the sides of the ravine were crowned with the heads of Bukta's people – a force that could have blown the ribs out of the beast had Chinn's shot failed; but their guns were hidden, and they appeared as interested beaters, some five or six waiting the word to skin. Bukta watched the life fade from the wild eyes, lifted one hand, and turned on his heel.

'No need to show that we care,' said he. 'Now, after this, we can kill what we choose. Put out your hand, Sahib.'

Chinn obeyed. It was entirely steady, and Bukta nodded. 'That also was your custom. My men skin quickly. They will carry the skin to cantonments. Will the Sahib come to my poor village for the night and, perhaps, forget that I am his officer?'

'But those men, the beaters. They have worked hard, and perhaps – '

'Oh, if they skin clumsily, we will skin them. They are my people. In the lines I am one thing. Here I am another.'

This was very true. When Bukta doffed uniform and reverted to the fragmentary dress of his own people, he left his civilisation of drill in the next world. That night, after a little talk with his subjects, he devoted to an orgie; and a Bhil orgie is a thing not to be safely written about. Chinn, flushed with triumph, was in the thick of it, but the meaning of the mysteries was hidden. Wild folk came and pressed about his knees with offerings. He gave his flask to the elders of the village. They grew eloquent, and wreathed him about with flowers. Gifts and loans, not all seemly, were thrust upon him, and infernal music rolled and maddened round red fires, while singers sang songs of the ancient times, and danced peculiar dances. The aboriginal liquors are very potent, and Chinn was compelled to taste them often, but, unless the stuff had been drugged, how came he to fall asleep suddenly, and to waken late the next day – half a march from the village?

'The Sahib was very tired. A little before dawn he went to sleep,' Bukta explained. 'My people carried him here, and now it is time we should go back to cantonments.'

The voice, smooth and deferential, the step, steady and silent, made it hard to believe that only a few hours before Bukta was yelling and capering with naked fellow-devils of the scrub.

'My people were very pleased to see the Sahib. They will never forget. When next the Sahib goes out recruiting, he will go to my people, and they will give him as many men as we need.'

Chinn kept his own counsel, except as to the shooting of the tiger, and Bukta embroidered that tale with a shameless tongue. The skin was certainly one of the finest ever hung up in the mess, and the first of many. When Bukta could not accompany his boy on shooting-trips, he took care to put him in good hands, and Chinn learned more of the mind and desire of the wild Bhil in his marches and campings, by talks at twilight or at wayside pools, than an uninstruc-ted man could have come at in a lifetime.

Presently his men in the regiment grew bold to speak of their relatives – mostly in trouble – and to lay cases of tribal custom before him. They would say, squatting in his verandah at twi-light, after the easy, confidential style of the Wuddars, that such-and-such a bachelor had run away with such-and-such a wife at a far-off village. Now, how many cows would Chinn Sahib consider a just fine? Or, again, if written order came from the Government that a Bhil was to repair to a walled city of the plains to give evidence in a law-court, would it be wise to disregard that order? On the other hand, if it were obeyed, would the rash voyager return alive?

'But what have I to do with these things?' Chinn demanded of Bukta, impatiently. 'I am a soldier. I do not know the law.'

'Hoo! Law is for fools and white men. Give them a large and loud order, and they will abide by it. Thou art their law.'

'But wherefore?'

Every trace of expression left Bukta's countenance. The idea might have smitten him for the first time. 'How can I say?' he replied. 'Perhaps it is on account of the name. A Bhil does not love strange things. Give them orders, Sahib – two, three, four words at a time such as they can carry away in their heads. That is enough.'

Chinn gave orders then, valiantly, not realising that a word spoken in haste before mess became the dread unappealable law of villages beyond the smoky hills – was, in truth, no less than the Law of Jan Chinn the First, who, so the whispered legend ran, had come back to earth, to oversee the third generation, in the body and bones of his grandson.

There could be no sort of doubt in this matter. All the Bhils knew that Jan Chinn reincarnated had honoured Bukta's village with his presence after slaying his first-in-this-life tiger; that he had eaten and drunk with the people, as he was used; and – Bukta must have drugged Chinn's liquor very deeply – upon his back and right shoulder all men had seen the same angry red Flying Cloud that the high Gods had set on the flesh of Jan Chinn the First when first he came to the Bhil. As concerned the foolish white world which has no eyes, he was a slim and young officer in the Wuddars; but his own people knew he was Jan Chinn, who had made the Bhil a man; and, believing, they hastened to carry his words, careful never to alter them on the way.

Because the savage and the child who plays lonely games have one horror of being laughed at or questioned, the little folk kept their convictions to themselves; and the Colonel, who thought he knew his regiment, never guessed that each one of the six hundred quick-footed, beady-eyed rank-and-file, to attention beside their rifles, believed serenely and unshakenly that the subaltern on the left flank of the line was a demigod twice born – tutelary deity of their land and people. The Earth-gods themselves had stamped the incarnation, and who would dare to doubt the handiwork of the Earth-gods?

Chinn, being practical above all things, saw that his family name served him well in the lines and in camp. His men gave no trouble – one does not commit regimental offences with a god in the chair of justice – and he was sure of the best beaters in the district when he needed them. They believed that the protection of Jan Chinn the First cloaked them, and were bold in that belief beyond the utmost daring of excited Bhils.

His quarters began to look like an amateur natural history museum, in spite of duplicate heads and horns and skulls that he sent home to Devonshire. The people, very humanly, learned the weak side of their god. It is true he was unbribable, but bird-skins, butterflies, beetles, and, above all, news of big game pleased him. In other respects, too, he lived up to the Chinn tradition. He was fever-proof. A night's sitting out over a tethered goat in a damp valley, that would have filled the Major with a month's malaria, had no effect on him. He was, as they said, 'salted before he was born'.

Now in the autumn of his second year's service an uneasy rumour crept out of the earth and ran about among the Bhils. Chinn heard nothing of it till a brother-officer said across the mess-table: 'Your revered ancestor's on the rampage in the Satpura country. You'd better look him up.'

'I don't want to be disrespectful, but I'm a little sick of my revered ancestor. Bukta talks of nothing else. What's the old boy supposed to be doing now?'

'Riding cross-country by moonlight on his processional tiger. That's the story. He's been seen by about two thousand Bhils, skipping along the tops of the Satpuras, and scaring people to death. They believe it devoutly, and all the Satpura chaps are worshipping away at his shrine-tomb, I mean like good uns. You really ought to go down there. Must be a queer thing to see your grandfather treated as a god.'

'What makes you think there's any truth in the tale?' said Chinn.

'Because all our men deny it. They say they've never heard of Chinn's tiger. Now that's a manifest lie, because every Bhil *has*.'

'There's only one thing you've overlooked,' said the Colonel, thoughtfully. 'When a local god reappears on earth, it's always an excuse for trouble of some kind; and those Satpura Bhils are about as wild as your grandfather left them, young un. It means something.'

'Meanin' they may go on the warpath?' said Chinn.

'Can't say – as yet. Shouldn't be surprised a little bit.'

'I haven't been told a syllable.'

'Proves it all the more. They are keeping something back.'

'Bukta tells me everything, too, as a rule. Now, why didn't he tell me that?'

Chinn put the question directly to the old man that night, and the answer surprised him.

'Why should I tell what is well known? Yes, the Clouded Tiger is out in the Satpura country.'

'What do the wild Bhils think that it means?'

'They do not know. They wait. Sahib, what is coming? Say only one little word, and we will be content.'

'We? What have tales from the south, where the jungly Bhils live, to do with drilled men?'

'When Jan Chinn wakes is no time for any Bhil to be quiet.'

'But he has not waked, Bukta.'

'Sahib – ' the old man's eyes were full of tender reproof – 'if he does not wish to be seen, why does he go abroad in the moonlight? We know he is awake, but we do not know what he desires. Is it a sign for all the Bhils, or one that concerns the Satpura folk alone? Say one little word, Sahib, that I may carry it to the lines, and send on to our villages. Why does Jan Chinn ride out? Who has done wrong? Is it pestilence? Is it murrain? Will our children die? Is it a sword? Remember, Sahib, we are thy people and thy servants, and in this life I bore thee in my arms – not knowing.'

'Bukta has evidently looked on the cup this evening,' Chinn thought; 'but if I can do anything to soothe the old chap I must. It's like the Mutiny rumours on a small scale.'

He dropped into a deep wicker chair, over which was thrown his first tiger-skin, and his weight on the cushion flapped the clawed paws over his shoulders. He laid hold of them mechanically as he spoke, drawing the painted hide, cloak-fashion, about him.

'Now will I tell the truth, Bukta,' he said, leaning forward, the dried muzzle on his shoulder, to invent a specious lie.

'I see that it is the truth,' was the answer, in a shaking voice.

'Jan Chinn goes abroad among the Satpuras, riding on the Clouded Tiger, ye say? Be it so. Therefore the sign of the wonder is for the Satpura Bhils only, and does not touch the Bhils who plough in the north and east, the Bhils of the Khandesh, or any others, except the Satpura Bhils, who, as we know, are wild and foolish.'

'It is, then, a sign for *them*. Good or bad?'

'Beyond doubt, good. For why should Jan Chinn make evil to those whom he has made men? The nights over yonder are hot; it is ill to lie in one bed over-long without turning, and Jan Chinn would look again upon his people. So he rises, whistles his Clouded Tiger, and goes abroad a little to breathe the cool air. If the Satpura Bhils kept to their villages, and did not wander after dark, they would not see him. Indeed, Bukta, it is no more than that he would see the light again in his own country. Send this news south, and say that it is my word.'

Bukta bowed to the floor. 'Good Heavens!' thought Chinn, 'and this blinking pagan is a first-class officer, and as straight as a die! I may as well round it off neatly.' He went on: 'If the Satpura Bhils ask the meaning of the sign, tell them that Jan Chinn would see how they kept their old promises of good living. Perhaps they have plundered; perhaps they mean to disobey the orders of the Government; perhaps there is a dead man in the jungle; and so Jan Chinn has come to see.'

'Is he, then, angry?'

'Bah! Am *I* ever angry with my Bhils? I say angry words, and threaten many things. *Thou* knowest, Bukta. I have seen thee smile behind the hand. I know, and thou knowest. The Bhils are my children. I have said it many times.'

'Ay. We be thy children,' said Bukta.

'And no otherwise is it with Jan Chinn, my father's father. He would see the land he loved and the people once again. It is a good ghost, Bukta. I say it. Go and tell them. And I do hope devoutly,' he added, 'that it will calm 'em down.' Flinging back the tiger-skin, he rose with a long, unguarded yawn that showed his well-kept teeth.

Bukta fled, to be received in the lines by a knot of panting enquirers.

'It is true,' said Bukta. 'He wrapped himself in the skin, and spoke from it. He would see his own country again. The sign is not for us; and, indeed, he is a young man. How should he lie idle of nights? He says his bed is too hot and the air is bad. He goes to and fro for the love of night-running. He has said it.'

The grey-whiskered assembly shuddered.

'He says the Bhils are his children. Ye know he does not lie. He has said it to me.'

'But what of the Satpura Bhils? What means the sign for them?'

'Nothing. It is only night-running, as I have said. He rides to see if they obey the Government, as he taught them to do in his first life.'

'And what if they do not?'

'He did not say.'

The light went out in Chinn's quarters.

'Look,' said Bukta. 'Now he goes away. None the less it is a good ghost, as he has said. How shall we fear Jan Chinn, who made the Bhil a man? His protection is on us; and ye know Jan Chinn never broke a protection spoken or written on paper. When he is older and has found him a wife he will lie in his bed till morning.'

A commanding officer is generally aware of the regimental state of mind a little before the men; and this is why the Colonel said, a few days later, that someone had been putting the Fear of God into the Wuddars. As he was the only person officially entitled to do this, it distressed him to see such unanimous virtue. 'It's too good to last,' he said. 'I only wish I could find out what the little chaps mean.'

The explanation, as it seemed to him, came at the change of the moon, when he received orders to hold himself in readiness to 'allay any possible excitement' among the Satpura Bhils, who were, to put it mildly, uneasy because a paternal Government had sent up against them a Mahratta State-educated vaccinator, with lancets, lymph, and an officially registered calf. In the language of State, they had 'manifested a strong objection to all prophylactic measures', had 'forcibly detained the vaccinator', and 'were on the point of neglecting or evading their tribal obligations'.

'That means they are in a blue funk – same as they were at census-time,' said the Colonel; 'and if we stampede them into the hills we'll never catch 'em, in the first place, and, in the second, they'll whoop off plundering till further orders. Wonder who the God-forsaken idiot is who is trying to vaccinate a Bhil. I knew trouble was coming. One good thing is that they'll only use local corps, and we can knock up something we'll call a campaign, and let them down easy. Fancy us potting our best beaters because they don't want to be vaccinated! They're only crazy with fear.'

'Don't you think, sir,' said Chinn, the next day, 'that perhaps you could give me a fortnight's shooting-leave?'

'Desertion in the face of the enemy, by Jove!' The Colonel laughed. 'I might, but I'd have to antedate it a little, because we're warned for service, as you might say. However, we'll assume that you applied for leave three days ago, and are now well on your way south.'

'I'd like to take Bukta with me.'

'Of course, yes. I think that will be the best plan. You've some kind of hereditary influence with the little chaps, and they may listen to you when a glimpse of our uniforms would drive them wild. You've never been in that part of the world before, have you? Take care they don't send you to your family vault in your youth and innocence. I believe you'll be all right if you can get 'em to listen to you.'

'I think so, sir; but if – if they should accidentally put an – make asses of 'emselves – they might, you know – I hope you'll represent that they were only frightened. There isn't an ounce of real vice in 'em, and I should never forgive myself if anyone of – of my name got them into trouble.'

The Colonel nodded, but said nothing.

Chinn and Bukta departed at once. Bukta did not say that, ever since the official vaccinator had been dragged into the hills by indignant Bhils, runner after runner had skulked up to the lines, entreating, with forehead in the dust, that Jan Chinn should come and explain this unknown horror that hung over his people.

The portent of the Clouded Tiger was now too clear. Let Jan Chinn comfort his own, for vain was the help of mortal man. Bukta toned down these beseechings to a simple request for Chinn's presence. Nothing would have pleased the old man better than a rough-and-tumble campaign against the Satpuras, whom he, as an 'unmixed' Bhil, despised; but he had a duty to all his nation as Jan Chinn's interpreter; and he devoutly believed that forty plagues would fall on his village if he tampered with that obligation. Besides, Jan Chinn knew all things, and he rode the Clouded Tiger.

They covered thirty miles a day on foot and pony, raising the blue wall-like line of the Satpuras as swiftly as might be. Bukta was very silent.

They began the steep climb a little after noon, but it was near sunset ere they reached the stone platform clinging to the side of a rifted, jungle-covered hill, where Jan Chinn the First was laid, as he had desired, that he might overlook his people. All India is full of neglected graves that date from the beginning of the eighteenth century – tombs of forgotten colonels of corps long since disbanded; mates of East India men who went on shooting expeditions and never came back; factors, agents, writers, and ensigns of the Honourable the East India Company by hundreds and thousands and tens of thousands. English folk forget quickly, but natives have long memories, and if a man has done good in his life it is remembered after his death. The weathered marble four-square tomb of Jan Chinn was hung about with wild flowers and nuts, packets of wax and honey, bottles of native spirits, and infamous cigars, with buffalo horns and plumes of dried grass. At one end was a rude clay image of a white man, in the old-fashioned top hat, riding on a bloated tiger.

Bukta salaamed reverently as they approached. Chinn bared his head and began to pick out the blurred inscription. So far as he could read it ran thus – word for word, and letter for letter:

To the Memory of JOHN CHINN, Esq.
Late Collector of . . . .
. . . . . ithout Bloodshed or . . error of Authority
Employ . . only . . cans of Conciliat . . . and Confiden .

accomplished the . . . tire Subjection . . .
a Lawless and Predatory Peop . . .
. . . taching them to . . . ish Government
by a Conquest . . over . . . . Minds
The most perma . . . and rational Mode of Domini . .
. . Governor General and Counc . . . engal
have ordered thi . . . . . erected
. . . arted this Life Aug. 19, 184 . . Ag . . .

On the other side of the grave were ancient verses, also very worn.
As much as Chinn could decipher said:

. . . . the savage band.
Forsook their Haunts and b . . . . . is Command
. . . . mended . . rals check a . . . . st for spoil.
And . . s . . ing Hamlets prove his gene . . . . toil.
Humanit . . . survey . . . . . . ights restor . .
A Nation . . ield . . subdued without a Sword.

For some little time he leaned on the tomb thinking of this
dead man of his own blood, and of the house in Devonshire;
then, nodding to the plains: 'Yes; it's a big work, all of it, even my
little share. He must have been worth knowing . . . Bukta, where
are my people?'

'Not here, Sahib. No man comes here except in full sun. They wait
above. Let us climb and see.'

But Chinn, remembering the first law of Oriental diplomacy, in an
even voice answered: 'I have come this far only because the Satpura
folk are foolish, and dared not visit our lines. Now bid them wait on
me *here*. I am not a servant, but the master of Bhils.'

'I go – I go,' clucked the old man. Night was falling, and at any
moment Jan Chinn might whistle up his dreaded steed from the
darkening scrub.

Now for the first time in a long life Bukta disobeyed a lawful
command and deserted his leader; for he did not come back, but
pressed to the flat table-top of the hill, and called softly. Men stirred

all about him – little trembling men with bows and arrows who had watched the two since noon.

'Where is he?' whispered one.

'At his own place. He bids you come,' said Bukta.

'Now?'

'Now.'

'Rather let him loose the Clouded Tiger upon us. We do not go.'

'Nor I, though I bore him in my arms when he was a child in this his life. Wait here till the day.'

'But surely he will be angry.'

'He will be very angry, for he has nothing to eat. But he has said to me many times that the Bhils are his children. By sunlight I believe this, but – by moonlight I am not so sure. What folly have ye Satpura pigs compassed that ye should need him at all?'

'One came to us in the name of the Government with little ghost-knives and a magic calf, meaning to turn us into cattle by the cutting off of our arms. We were greatly afraid, but we did not kill the man. He is here, bound – a black man; and we think he comes from the west. He said it was an order to cut us all with knives – especially the women and the children. We did not hear that it was an order, so we were afraid, and kept to our hills. Some of our men have taken ponies and bullocks from the plains, and others pots and cloths and earrings.'

'Are any slain?'

'By our men? Not yet. But the young men are blown to and fro by many rumours like flames upon a hill. I sent runners asking for Jan Chinn lest worse should come to us. It was this fear that he foretold by the sign of the Clouded Tiger.

He says it is otherwise,' said Bukta; and he repeated, with amplifications, all that young Chinn had told him at the conference of the wicker chair.

'Think you,' said the questioner, at last, 'that the Government will lay hands on us?'

'Not I,' Bukta rejoined. 'Jan Chinn will give an order, and ye will obey. The rest is between the Government and Jan Chinn. I myself know something of the ghost-knives and the scratching. It is a charm against the Smallpox. But how it is done I cannot tell. Nor need that concern you.'

'If he stands by us and before the anger of the Government we will most strictly obey Jan Chinn, except – except we do not go down to that place tonight.'

They could hear young Chinn below them shouting for Bukta; but they cowered and sat still, expecting the Clouded Tiger. The tomb had been holy ground for nearly half a century. If Jan Chinn chose to sleep there, who had better right? But they would not come within eyeshot of the place till broad day.

At first Chinn was exceedingly angry, till it occurred to him that Bukta most probably had a reason (which, indeed, he had), and his own dignity might suffer if he yelled without answer. He propped himself against the foot of the grave, and, alternately dozing and smoking, came through the warm night proud that he was a lawful, legitimate, fever-proof Chinn.

He prepared his plan of action much as his grandfather would have done; and when Bukta appeared in the morning with a most liberal supply of food, said nothing of the overnight desertion. Bukta would have been relieved by an outburst of human anger; but Chinn finished his victual leisurely, and a cheroot, ere he made any sign.

'They are very much afraid,' said Bukta, who was not too bold himself. 'It remains only to give orders. They said they will obey if thou wilt only stand between them and the Government.'

'That I know,' said Chinn, strolling slowly to the table-land. A few of the elder men stood in an irregular semicircle in an open glade; but the ruck of people – women and children – were hidden in the thicket. They had no desire to face the first anger of Jan Chinn the First.

Seating himself on a fragment of split rock, he smoked his cheroot to the butt, hearing men breathe hard all about him. Then he cried, so suddenly that they jumped: 'Bring the man that was bound!'

A scuffle and a cry were followed by the appearance of a Hindoo vaccinator, quaking with fear, bound hand and foot, as the Bhils of old were accustomed to bind their human sacrifices. He was pushed cautiously before the presence; but young Chinn did not look at him.

'I said – the man that *was* bound. Is it a jest to bring me one tied like a buffalo? Since when could the Bhil bind folk at his pleasure? Cut!'

Half a dozen hasty knives cut away the thongs, and the man crawled to Chinn, who pocketed his case of lancets and tubes of lymph. Then, sweeping the semicircle with one comprehensive forefinger, and in the voice of compliment, he said, clearly and distinctly: 'Pigs!'

'Ai!' whispered Bukta. 'Now he speaks. Woe to foolish people!'

'I have come on foot from my house' (the assembly shuddered) 'to make clear a matter which any other Satpura Bhil would have seen with both eyes from a distance. Ye know the Smallpox who pits and scars your children so that [they look] like wasp-combs. It is an order of the Government that whoso is scratched on the arm with these little knives which I hold up is charmed against her. All Sahibs are thus charmed, and very many Hindoos. This is the mark of the charm. Look!'

He rolled back his sleeve to the armpit and showed the white scars of the vaccination-mark on his white skin. 'Come, all, and look.'

A few daring spirits came up, and nodded their heads wisely. There was certainly a mark, and they knew well what other dread marks were hidden by the shirt. Merciful was Jan Chinn, that then and there proclaimed his godhead!

'Now all these things the man whom ye bound told you.'

'I did – a hundred times; but they answered with blows,' groaned the operator, chafing his wrists and ankles.

'But, being pigs, ye did not believe; and so came I here to save you, first from Smallpox, next from a great folly of fear, and lastly, it may be, from the rope and the jail. It is no gain to me; it is no pleasure to me: but for the sake of that one who is yonder, who made the Bhil a man' – he pointed down the hill – 'I, who am of his blood, the son of his son, come to turn your people. And I speak the truth, as did Jan Chinn.'

The crowd murmured reverently, and men stole out of the thicket by twos and threes to join it. There was no anger in their god's face.

'These are my orders. (Heaven send they'll take 'em, but I seem to have impressed 'em so far!) I myself will stay among you while this man scratches your arms with the knives, after the order of the Government. In three, or it may be five or seven, days, your arms will swell and itch and burn. That is the power of Smallpox fighting in your base blood against the orders of the Government. I will therefore stay among you till I see that Smallpox is conquered, and I will not go away till the men and the women and the little children show me upon their arms such marks as I have even now showed you. I bring with me two very good guns, and a man whose name is known among beasts and men. We will hunt together, I and he and your young men, and the others shall eat and lie still. This is my order.'

There was a long pause while victory hung in the balance. A white-haired old sinner, standing on one uneasy leg, piped up: 'There are ponies and some few bullocks and other things for which we need a *kowl* [protection]. They were *not* taken in the way of trade.'

The battle was won, and John Chinn drew a breath of relief. The young Bhils had been raiding, but if taken swiftly all could be put straight.

'I will write a *kowl* so soon as the ponies, the bullocks, and the other things are counted before me and sent back whence they came. But first we will put the Government mark on such as have not been visited by Smallpox.' In an undertone, to the vaccinator: 'If you show you are afraid you'll never see Poona again, my friend.'

'There is not sufficient ample supply of vaccination for all this population,' said the man. 'They destroyed the offeecial calf.'

'They won't know the difference. Scrape 'em and give me a couple of lancets; I'll attend to the elders.'

The aged diplomat who had demanded protection was the first victim. He fell to Chinn's hand and dared not cry out. As soon as he was freed he dragged up a companion, and held him fast, and the crisis became, as it were, a child's sport; for the vaccinated chased the unvaccinated to treatment, vowing that all the tribe must suffer equally. The women shrieked, and the children ran howling; but Chinn laughed, and waved the pink-tipped lancet.

'It is an honour,' he cried. 'Tell them, Bukta, how great an honour it is that I myself mark them. Nay, I cannot mark every one – the Hindoo must also do his work – but I will touch all marks that he makes, so there will be an equal virtue in them. Thus do the Rajputs stick pigs. Ho, brother with one eye! Catch that girl and bring her to me. She need not run away yet, for she is not married, and I do not seek her in marriage. She will not come? Then she shall be shamed by her little brother, a fat boy, a bold boy. He puts out his arm like a soldier. Look! *He* does not flinch at the blood. Some day he shall be in my regiment. And now, mother of many, we will lightly touch thee, for Smallpox has been before us here. It is a true thing, indeed, that this charm breaks the power of Mata. There will be no more pitted faces among the Satpuras, and so ye can ask many cows for each maid to be wed.'

And so on and so on – quick-poured showman's patter, sauced in the Bhil hunting-proverbs and tales of their own brand of coarse humour till the lancets were blunted and both operators worn out.

But, nature being the same the world over, the unvaccinated grew jealous of their marked comrades, and came near to blows about it. Then Chinn declared himself a court of justice, no longer a medical board, and made formal enquiry into the late robberies.

'We are the thieves of Mahadeo,' said the Bhils, simply. 'It is our fate, and we were frightened. When we are frightened we always steal.'

Simply and directly as children, they gave in the tale of the plunder, all but two bullocks and some spirits that had gone amissing (these Chinn promised to make good out of his own pocket), and ten ring-leaders were despatched to the lowlands with a wonderful document, written on the leaf of a note-book, and addressed to an Assistant District Superintendent of Police. There was warm calamity in that note, as Jan Chinn warned them, but anything was better than loss of liberty.

Armed with this protection, the repentant raiders went downhill. They had no desire whatever to meet Mr Dundas Fawne of the Police, aged twenty-two, and of a cheerful countenance, nor did they wish to revisit the scene of their robberies. Steering a middle course, they ran into the camp of the one Government chaplain allowed to the various irregular corps through a district of some fifteen thousand square miles, and stood before him in a cloud of dust. He was by way of being a priest, they knew, and, what was more to the point, a good sportsman who paid his beaters generously.

When he read Chinn's note he laughed, which they deemed a lucky omen, till he called up policemen, who tethered the ponies and the bullocks by the piled house-gear, and laid stern hands upon three of that smiling band of the thieves of Mahadeo. The chaplain himself addressed them magisterially with a riding-whip. That was painful, but Jan Chinn had prophesied it. They submitted, but would not give up the written protection, fearing the jail. On their way back they met Mr D. Fawne, who had heard about the robberies, and was not pleased.

'Certainly,' said the eldest of the gang, when the second interview was at an end, 'certainly Jan Chinn's protection has saved us our liberty, but it is as though there were many beatings in one small piece of paper. Put it away.'

One climbed into a tree, and stuck the letter into a cleft forty feet from the ground, where it could do no harm. Warmed, sore, but happy, the ten returned to Jan Chinn next day, where he sat among uneasy Bhils, all looking at their right arms, and all bound under terror of their god's disfavour not to scratch.

'It was a good *kowl*,' said the leader. 'First the chaplain, who laughed, took away our plunder, and beat three of us, as was pro-mised. Next, we meet Fawne Sahib, who frowned, and asked for the plunder. We spoke the truth, and so he beat us all, one after another, and called us chosen names. He then gave us these two bundles' – they set down a bottle of whisky and a box of cheroots – 'and we came away. The *kowl* is left in a tree, because its virtue is that so soon as we show it to a Sahib we are beaten.'

'But for that *kowl*' said Jan Chinn, sternly, 'ye would all have been marching to jail with a policeman on either side. Ye come now to serve as beaters for me. These people are unhappy, and we will go hunting till they are well. Tonight we will make a feast.'

It is written in the chronicles of the Satpura Bhils, together with many other matters not fit for print, that through five days, after the day that he had put his mark upon them, Jan Chinn the First hunted for his people; and on the five nights of those days the tribe was gloriously and entirely drunk. Jan Chinn bought country spirits of an awful strength, and slew wild pig and deer beyond counting, so that if any fell sick they might have two good reasons.

Between head- and stomach-aches they found no time to think of their arms, but followed Jan Chinn obediently through the jungles, and with each day's returning confidence men, women, and children stole away to their villages as the little army passed by. They carried news that it was good and right to be scratched with ghost-knives; that Jan Chinn was indeed reincarnated as a god of free food and drink, and that of all nations the Satpura Bhils stood first in his favour, if they would only refrain from scratching. Henceforward that kindly demigod would be connected in their minds with great gorgings and the vaccine and lancets of a paternal Government.

'And tomorrow I go back to my home,' said Jan Chinn to his faithful few, whom neither spirits, overeating, nor swollen glands could conquer. It is hard for children and savages to behave reverently at all times to the idols of their make-belief; and they had frolicked excessively with Jan Chinn. But the reference to his home cast a gloom on the people.

'And the Sahib will not come again?' said he who had been vaccinated first.

'That is to be seen,' answered Chinn, warily.

'Nay, but come as a white man – come as a young man whom we know and love; for, as thou alone knowest, we are a weak people. If we again saw thy – thy horse – ' They were picking up their courage.

'I have no horse. I came on foot with Bukta, yonder. What is this?'

'Thou knowest – the thing that thou hast chosen for a night-horse.' The little men squirmed in fear and awe.

'Night-horses? Bukta, what is this last tale of children?'

Bukta had been a silent leader in Chinn's presence since the night of his desertion, and was grateful for a chance-flung question.

'They know, Sahib,' he whispered. 'It is the Clouded Tiger. That – that comes from the place where thou didst once sleep. It is thy horse – as it has been these three generations.'

'My horse! That was a dream of the Bhils.'

'It is no dream. Do dreams leave the tracks of broad pugs on earth? Why make two faces before thy people? They know of the night-ridings, and they – and they – '

'Are afraid, and would have them cease.'

Bukta nodded. 'If thou hast no further need of him. He is thy horse.'

'The thing leaves a trail, then?' said Chinn.

'We have seen it. It is like a village road under the tomb.'

'Can ye find and follow it for me?'

'By daylight – if one comes with us, and, above all, stands nearby.'

'I will stand close, and we will see to it that Jan Chinn does not ride any more.'

The Bhils shouted the last words again and again.

From Chinn's point of view the stalk was nothing more than an ordinary one – downhill, through split and crannied rocks, unsafe, perhaps, if a man did not keep his wits by him, but no worse than twenty others he had undertaken. Yet his men – they refused absolutely to beat, and would only trail – dripped sweat at every move. They showed the marks of enormous pugs that ran, always downhill, to a few hundred feet below Jan Chinn's tomb, and disappeared in a narrow-mouthed cave. It was an insolently open road, a domestic highway, beaten without thought of concealment.

'The beggar might be paying rent and taxes,' Chinn muttered ere he asked whether his friend's taste ran to cattle or man.

'Cattle,' was the answer. 'Two heifers a week. We drive them for him at the foot of the hill. It is his custom. If we did not, he might seek us.'

'Blackmail and piracy,' said Chinn. 'I can't say I fancy going into the cave after him. What's to be done?'

The Bhils fell back as Chinn lodged himself behind a rock with his rifle ready. Tigers, he knew, were shy beasts, but one who had been long cattle-fed in this sumptuous style might prove overbold.

'He speaks!' someone whispered from the rear. 'He knows, too.'

'Well, of *all* the infernal cheek!' said Chinn. There was an angry growl from the cave – a direct challenge.

'Come out, then,' Chinn shouted. 'Come out of that. Let's have a look at you.'

The brute knew well enough that there was some connection between brown nude Bhils and his weekly allowance; but the white helmet in the sunlight annoyed him, and he did not approve of the voice that broke his rest. Lazily as a gorged snake, he dragged himself out of the cave, and stood yawning and blinking at the entrance. The sunlight fell upon his flat right side, and Chinn wondered. Never had he seen a tiger marked after this fashion. Except for his head, which was staringly barred, he was dappled – not striped, but dappled like a child's rocking-horse in rich shades of smoky black on red gold. That portion of his belly and throat which should have been white was orange, and his tail and paws were black.

He looked leisurely for some ten seconds, and then deliberately lowered his head, his chin dropped and drawn in, staring intently at the man. The effect of this was to throw forward the round arch of his skull, with two broad bands across it, while below the bands glared the unwinking eyes; so that, head on, as he stood, he showed something like a diabolically scowling pantomime-mask. It was a piece of natural mesmerism that he had practised many times on his quarry, and though Chinn was by no means a terrified heifer, he stood for a while, held by the extraordinary oddity of the attack. The head – the body seemed to have been packed away behind it – the ferocious, skull-like head, crept nearer to the switching of an angry tail-tip in the grass. Left and right the Bhils had scattered to let John Chinn subdue his own horse.

'My word!' he thought. 'He's trying to frighten me!' and fired between the saucer-like eyes, leaping aside upon the shot.

A big coughing mass, reeking of carrion, bounded past him up the hill, and he followed discreetly. The tiger made no attempt to turn into the jungle; he was hunting for sight and breath – nose up, mouth open, the tremendous fore-legs scattering the gravel in spurts.

Scuppered!' said John Chinn, watching the flight. 'Now if he was a partridge he'd tower. Lungs must be full of blood.'

The brute had jerked himself over a boulder and fallen out of sight the other side. John Chinn looked over with a ready barrel. But the red trail led straight as an arrow even to his grandfather's tomb, and there, among the smashed spirit-bottles and the fragments of the mud image, the life left, with a flurry and a grunt.

'If my worthy ancestor could see that,' said John Chinn, 'he'd have been proud of me. Eyes, lower jaw, and lungs. A very nice shot.' He whistled for Bukta as he drew the tape over the stiffening bulk.

'Ten – six – eight – by Jove! It's nearly eleven – call it eleven. Fore-arm, twenty-four-five – seven and a half. A short tail, too: three feet one. But what a skin! Oh, Bukta! Bukta! The men with the knives swiftly.'

'Is he beyond question dead?' said an awe-stricken voice behind a rock.

'That was not the way I killed my first tiger,' said Chinn. 'I did not think that Bukta would run. I had no second gun.'

'It – it is the Clouded Tiger,' said Bukta, un-heeding the taunt. 'He is dead.'

Whether all the Bhils, vaccinated and unvaccinated, of the Satpuras had lain by to see the kill, Chinn could not say; but the whole hill's flank rustled with little men, shouting, singing, and stamping. And yet, till he had made the first cut in the splendid skin, not a man would take a knife; and, when the shadows fell, they ran from the red-stained tomb, and no persuasion would bring them back till dawn. So Chinn spent a second night in the open, guarding the carcass from jackals, and thinking about his ancestor.

He returned to the lowlands to the triumphal chant of an escorting army three hundred strong, the Mahratta vaccinator close at his elbow, and the rudely dried skin a trophy before him. When that army suddenly and noiselessly disappeared, as quail in high corn, he argued he was near civilisation, and a turn in the road brought him upon the camp of a wing of his own corps. He left the skin on a cart-tail for the world to see, and sought the Colonel.

'They're perfectly right,' he explained earnestly. 'There isn't an ounce of vice in 'em. They were only frightened. I've vaccinated the whole boiling, and they like it awfully. What are – what are we doing here, sir?'

'That's what I'm trying to find out,' said the Colonel. 'I don't know yet whether we're a piece of a brigade or a police force. However, I think we'll call ourselves a police force. How did you manage to get a Bhil vaccinated?'

'Well, sir,' said Chinn, ' I've been thinking it over, and, as far as I can make out, I've got a sort of hereditary influence over 'em.'

'So I know, or I wouldn't have sent you; but *what*, exactly?'

'It's rather rummy. It seems, from what I can make out, that I'm my own grandfather reincarnated, and I've been disturbing the peace of the country by riding a pad-tiger of nights. If I hadn't done that, I don't think they'd have objected to the vaccination; but the two together were more than they could stand. And so, sir, I've vaccinated 'em, and shot my tiger-horse as a sort o' proof of good faith. You never saw such a skin in your life.'

The Colonel tugged his moustache thoughtfully. 'Now, how the deuce,' said he, 'am I to include that in my report?'

Indeed, the official version of the Bhils' anti-vaccination stampede said nothing about Lieutenant John Chinn, his godship. But Bukta knew, and the corps knew, and every Bhil in the Satpura hills knew.

And now Bukta is zealous that John Chinn shall swiftly be wedded and impart his powers to a son; for if the Chinn succession fails, and the little Bhils are left to their own imaginings, there will be fresh trouble in the Satpuras.

By Word of Mouth

Not though you die tonight, O Sweet, and wail,
  A spectre at my door,
Shall mortal Fear make Love immortal fail –
  I shall but love you more,
Who from Death's house returning, give me still
One moment's comfort in my matchless ill.

Shadow Houses

This tale may be explained by those who know how souls are made, and where the bounds of the Possible are put down. I have lived long enough in this country to know that it is best to know nothing, and can only write the story as it happened.

Dumoise was our Civil Surgeon at Meridki, and we called him 'Dormouse', because he was a round little, sleepy little man. He was a good Doctor and never quarrelled with anyone, not even with our Deputy Commissioner, who had the manners of a bargee and the tact of a horse. He married a girl as round and as sleepy-looking as himself. She was a Miss Hillardyce, daughter of 'Squash' Hillardyce of the Berars, who married his Chief's daughter by mistake. But that is another story.

A honeymoon in India is seldom more than a week long; but there is nothing to hinder a couple from extending it over two or three years. This is a delightful country for married folk who are wrapped up in one another. They can live absolutely alone and without interruption – just as the Dormice did. These two little people retired from the world after their marriage, and were very happy. They were forced, of course, to give occasional dinners, but they made no friends hereby, and the Station went its own way and forgot them; only saying, occasionally, that Dormouse was the best of good fellows, though dull. A Civil Surgeon who never quarrels is a rarity, appreciated as such.

Few people can afford to play Robinson Crusoe anywhere – least of all in India, where we are few in the land, and very much dependent on each other's kind offices. Dumoise was wrong in shutting himself from the world for a year, and he discovered his mistake when an epidemic of typhoid broke out in the Station in the heart of the cold weather, and his wife went down. He was a shy little man, and five days were wasted before he realised that Mrs Dumoise was burning with something worse than simple fever, and three days more passed before he ventured to call on Mrs Shute, the Engineer's wife, and timidly speak about his trouble. Nearly every household in India knows that Doctors are very helpless in typhoid. The battle must be fought out between Death and the Nurses, minute by minute and degree by degree. Mrs Shute almost boxed Dumoise's ears for what she called his 'criminal delay', and went off at once to look after the poor girl. We had seven cases of typhoid in the Station that winter and, as the average of death is about one in every five cases, we felt certain that we should have to lose somebody. But all did their best. The women sat up nursing the women, and the men turned to and tended the bachelors who were down, and we wrestled with those typhoid cases for fifty-six days, and brought them through the Valley of the Shadow in triumph. But, just when we thought all was over, and were going to give a dance to celebrate the victory, little Mrs Dumoise got a relapse and died in a week and the Station went to the funeral. Dumoise broke down utterly at the brink of the grave, and had to be taken away.

After the death, Dumoise crept into his own house and refused to be comforted. He did his duties perfectly, but we all felt that he should go on leave, and the other men of his own Service told him so. Dumoise was very thankful for the suggestion – he was thankful for anything in those days – and went to Chini on a walking-tour. Chini is some twenty marches from Simla, in the heart of the Hills, and the scenery is good if you are in trouble. You pass through big, still deodar-forests, and under big, still cliffs, and over big, still grass-downs swelling like a woman's breasts; and the wind across the grass, and the rain among the deodars, say: 'Hush – hush – hush.' So little Dumoise was packed off to Chini, to wear down his grief with a full-plate camera, and a rifle. He took also a useless bearer, because the man had been his wife's favourite servant. He was idle and a thief, but Dumoise trusted everything to him.

On his way back from Chini, Dumoise turned aside to Bagi, through the Forest Reserve which is on the spur of Mount Huttoo.

Some men who have travelled more than a little say that the march from Kotegarh to Bagi is one of the finest in creation. It runs through dark wet forest, and ends suddenly in bleak, nipped hillside and black rocks. Bagi *dâk*-bungalow is open to all the winds and is bitterly cold. Few people go to Bagi. Perhaps that was the reason why Dumoise went there. He halted at seven in the evening, and his bearer went down the hillside to the village to engage coolies for the next day's march. The sun had set, and the night-winds were beginning to croon among the rocks. Dumoise leaned on the railing of the verandah, waiting for his bearer to return. The man came back almost immediately after he had disappeared, and at such a rate that Dumoise fancied he must have crossed a bear. He was running as hard as he could up the face of the hill.

But there was no bear to account for his terror. He raced to the verandah and fell down, the blood spurting from his nose and his face iron-grey. Then he gurgled: 'I have seen the *Memsahib*! I have seen the *Memsahib*!'

'Where?' said Dumoise.

'Down there, walking on the road to the village. She was in a blue dress, and she lifted the veil of her bonnet and said: "Ram Dass, give my *salaams* to the *Sahib*, and tell him that I shall meet him next month at Nuddea." Then I ran away, because I was afraid.'

What Dumoise said or did I do not know. Ram Dass declares that he said nothing, but walked up and down the verandah all the cold night, waiting for the *Memsahib* to come up the hill and stretching out his arms into the dark like a madman. But no *Memsahib* came, and, next day, he went on to Simla cross-questioning the bearer every hour.

Ram Dass could only say that he had met Mrs Dumoise and that she had lifted up her veil and given him the message which he had faithfully repeated to Dumoise. To this statement Ram Dass adhered. He did not know where Nuddea was, had no friends at Nuddea, and would most certainly never go to Nuddea, even though his pay were doubled.

Nuddea is in Bengal, and has nothing whatever to do with a doctor serving in the Punjab. It must be more than twelve hundred miles from Meridki.

Dumoise went through Simla without halting, and returned to Meridki, there to take over charge from the man who had been officiating for him during his tour. There were some Dispensary accounts to be explained, and some recent orders of the Surgeon-

General to be noted, and, altogether, the taking-over was a full day's work. In the evening, Dumoise told his *locum tenens*, who was an old friend of his bachelor days, what had happened at Bagi; and the man said that Ram Dass might as well have chosen Tuticorin while he was about it.

At that moment a telegraph-peon came in with a telegram from Simla, ordering Dumoise not to take over charge at Meridki, but to go at once to Nuddea on special duty. There was a nasty outbreak of cholera at Nuddea, and the Bengal Government, being shorthanded, as usual, had borrowed a Surgeon from the Punjab.

Dumoise threw the telegram across the table and said: 'Well?'

The other Doctor said nothing. It was all that he could say.

Then he remembered that Dumoise had passed through Simla on his way from Bagi; and thus might, possibly, have heard the first news of the impending transfer.

He tried to put the question, and the implied suspicion into words, but Dumoise stopped him with: 'If I had desired *that*, I should never have come back from Chini. I was shooting there. I wish to live, for I have things to do . . . but I shall not be sorry.'

The other man bowed his head, and helped, in the twilight, to pack up Dumoise's just opened trunks. Ram Dass entered with the lamps.

'Where is the *Sahib* going?' he asked.

'To Nuddea,' said Dumoise, softly.

Ram Dass clawed Dumoise's knees and boots and begged him not to go. Ram Dass wept and howled till he was turned out of the room. Then he wrapped up all his belongings and came back to ask for a character. He was not going to Nuddea to see his *Sahib* die, and, perhaps to die himself.

So Dumoise gave the man his wages and went down to Nuddea alone, the other Doctor bidding him goodbye as one under sentence of death.

Eleven days later, he had joined his *Memsahib*; and the Bengal Government had to borrow a fresh Doctor to cope with that epidemic at Nuddea. The first importation lay dead in Chooadanga *dâk*-bungalow.

My Own True Ghost Story

As I came through the Desert thus it was –
As I came through the Desert.

The City of Dreadful Night

Somewhere in the Other World, where there are books and pictures and plays and shop windows to look at, and thousands of men who spend their lives in building up all four, lives a gentleman who writes real stories about the real insides of people; and his name is Mr Walter Besant. But he will insist upon treating his ghosts – he has published half a workshopful of them – with levity. He makes his ghost-seers talk familiarly, and, in some cases, flirt outrageously, with the phantoms. You may treat anything, from a Viceroy to a Vernacular Paper, with levity; but you must behave reverently toward a ghost, and particularly an Indian one.

There are, in this land, ghosts who take the form of fat, cold, pobby corpses, and hide in trees near the roadside till a traveller passes. Then they drop upon his neck and remain. There are also terrible ghosts of women who have died in childbed. These wander along the pathways at dusk, or hide in the crops near a village, and call seductively. But to answer their call is death in this world and the next. Their feet are turned backward that all sober men may recognise them. There are ghosts of little children who have been thrown into wells. These haunt well-curbs and the fringes of jungles, and wail under the stars, or catch women by the wrist and beg to be taken up and carried. These and the corpse ghosts, however, are only vernacular articles and do not attack Sahibs. No native ghost has yet been authentically reported to have frightened an Englishman; but many English ghosts have scared the life out of both white and black.

Nearly every other Station owns a ghost. There are said to be two at Simla, not counting the woman who blows the bellows at Syree *dâk*-bungalow on the Old Road; Mussoorie has a house haunted of a very lively Thing; a White Lady is supposed to do nightwatchman round a house in Lahore; Dalhousie says that one of her houses 'repeats' on autumn evenings all the incidents of a horrible horse-and-precipice accident; Murree has a merry ghost, and, now that she has been swept by cholera, will have room for a sorrowful one; there are Officers' Quarters in Mian Mir whose doors open without reason, and whose furniture is guaranteed to creak, not with the heat of June but with the weight of Invisibles who come to lounge in the chairs; Peshawar possesses houses that none will willingly rent; and there is something – not fever – wrong with a big bungalow in Allahabad. The older Provinces simply bristle with haunted houses, and march phantom armies along their main thoroughfares.

Some of the *dâk*-bungalows on the Grand Trunk Road have handy little cemeteries in their compound – witnesses to the 'changes and chances of this mortal life' in the days when men drove from Calcutta to the Northwest. These bungalows are objectionable places to put up in. They are generally very old, always dirty, while the *khansamah* is as ancient as the bungalow. He either chatters senilely, or falls into the long trances of age. In both moods he is useless. If you get angry with him, he refers to some Sahib dead and buried these thirty years, and says that when he was in that Sahib's service not a *khansamah* in the Province could touch him. Then he jabbers and mows and trembles and fidgets among the dishes, and you repent of your irritation.

In these *dâk*-bungalows, ghosts are most likely to be found, and when found, they should be made a note of. Not long ago it was my business to live in *dâk*-bungalows. I never inhabited the same house for three nights running, and grew to be learned in the breed. I lived in Government-built ones with red brick walls and rail ceilings, an inventory of the furniture posted in every room, and an excited snake at the threshold to give welcome. I lived in 'converted' ones – old houses officiating as *dâk*-bungalows – where nothing was in its proper place and there wasn't even a fowl for dinner. I lived in second-hand palaces where the wind blew through openwork marble tracery just as uncomfortably as through a broken pane. I lived in *dâk*-bungalows where the last entry in the visitors' book was fifteen months old, and where they slashed off the curry-kid's head with a sword. It was my good luck to meet all sorts of men, from sober travelling missionaries and deserters flying from British Regiments, to drunken loafers who threw whisky bottles at all who passed; and my still greater good fortune just to escape a maternity case. Seeing that a fair proportion of the tragedy of our lives out here acted itself in *dâk*-bungalows, I wondered that I had met no ghosts. A ghost that would voluntarily hang about a *dâk*-bungalow would be mad of course; but so many men have died mad in *dâk*-bungalows that there must be a fair percentage of lunatic ghosts.

In due time I found my ghost, or ghosts rather, for there were two of them. Up till that hour I had sympathised with Mr Besant's method of handling them, as shown in 'The Strange Case of Mr Lucraft and Other Stories'. I am now in the Opposition.

We will call the bungalow Katmal *dâk*-bungalow. But *that* was the smallest part of the horror. A man with a sensitive hide has no right to sleep in *dâk*-bungalows. He should marry. Katmal *dâk*-bungalow was old and rotten and unrepaired. The floor was of worn brick, the walls were filthy, and the windows were nearly black with grime. It stood on a bypath largely used by native Sub-Deputy Assistants of all kinds, from Finance to Forests; but real Sahibs were rare. The *khansamah*, who was nearly bent double with old age, said so.

When I arrived, there was a fitful, undecided rain on the face of the land, accompanied by a restless wind, and every gust made a noise like the rattling of dry bones in the stiff toddy palms outside. The *khan-samah* completely lost his head on my arrival. He had served a Sahib once. Did I know that Sahib? He gave me the name of a well-known man who has been buried for more than a quarter of a century, and showed me an ancient daguerreotype of that man in his prehistoric youth. I had seen a steel engraving of him at the head of a double volume of Memoirs a month before, and I felt ancient beyond telling.

The day shut in and the *khansamah* went to get me food. He did not go through the pretence of calling it '*khana*' – man's victuals. He said '*ratub*', and that means, among other things, 'grub' – dog's rations. There was no insult in his choice of the term. He had forgotten the other word, I suppose.

While he was cutting up the dead bodies of animals, I settled myself down, after exploring the *dâk*-bungalow. There were three rooms, beside my own, which was a corner kennel, each giving into the other through dingy white doors fastened with long iron bars. The bungalow was a very solid one, but the partition walls of the rooms were almost jerry-built in their flimsiness. Every step or bang of a trunk echoed from my room down the other three, and every footfall came back tremulously from the far walls. For this reason I shut the door. There were no lamps – only candles in long glass shades. An oil wick was set in the bathroom.

For bleak, unadulterated misery that *dâk*-bungalow was the worst of the many that I had ever set foot in. There was no fireplace, and the windows would not open; so a brazier of charcoal would have been useless. The rain and the wind splashed and gurgled and moaned round the house, and the toddy palms rattled and roared. Half a dozen jackals went through the compound singing, and a hyena stood afar off and mocked them. A hyena would convince a Sadducee of the Resurrection of the Dead – the worst sort of Dead. Then came the *ratub* – a curious meal, half native and half English in composition – with the old *khansamah* babbling behind my chair about dead and gone English people, and the wind-blown candles playing shadow-bo-peep with the bed and the mosquito-curtains. It was just the sort of dinner and evening to make a man think of every single one of his past sins, and of all the others that he intended to commit if he lived.

Sleep, for several hundred reasons, was not easy. The lamp in the bathroom threw the most absurd shadows into the room, and the wind was beginning to talk nonsense.

Just when the reasons were drowsy with blood-sucking I heard the regular – 'Let-us-take-and-heave-him-over' grunt of doolie-bearers in the compound. First one doolie came in, then a second, and then a third. I heard the doolies dumped on the ground, and the shutter in front of my door shook. 'That's someone trying to come in,' I said. But no-one spoke, and I persuaded myself that it was the gusty wind. The shutter of the room next to mine was attacked, flung back, and the inner door opened. 'That's some Sub-Deputy Assistant,' I said, 'and he has brought his friends with him. Now they'll talk and spit and smoke for an hour.'

But there were no voices and no footsteps. No-one was putting his luggage into the next room. The door shut, and I thanked Providence that I was to be left in peace. But I was curious to know where the doolies had gone. I got out of bed and looked into the darkness. There was never a sign of a doolie. Just as I was getting into bed again, I heard, in the next room, the sound that no man in his senses can possibly mistake – the whir of a billiard ball down the length of the slates when the striker is stringing for break. No other sound is like it. A minute afterwards there was another whir, and I got into bed. I was not frightened – indeed I was not. I was very curious to know what had become of the doolies. I jumped into bed for that reason.

Next minute I heard the double click of a cannon and my hair sat up. It is a mistake to say that hair stands up. The skin of the head tightens and you can feel a faint, prickly bristling all over the scalp. That is the hair sitting up.

There was a whir and a click, and both sounds could only have been made by one thing – a billiard ball. I argued the matter out at great length with myself; and the more I argued the less probable it seemed that one bed, one table, and two chairs – all the furniture of the room next to mine – could so exactly duplicate the sounds of a game of billiards. After another cannon, a three-cushion one to judge by the whir, I argued no more. I had found my ghost and would have given worlds to have escaped from that *dâk*-bungalow. I listened, and with each listen the game grew clearer. There was whir on whir and click on click. Sometimes there was a double click and a whir and another click. Beyond any sort of doubt, people were playing billiards in the next room. And the next room was not big enough to hold a billiard table!

Between the pauses of the wind I heard the game go forward – stroke after stroke. I tried to believe that I could not hear voices; but that attempt was a failure.

Do you know what fear is? Not ordinary fear of insult, injury or death, but abject, quivering dread of something that you cannot see – fear that dries the inside of the mouth and half of the throat – fear that makes you sweat on the palms of the hands, and gulp in order to keep the uvula at work? This is a fine Fear – a great cowardice, and must be felt to be appreciated. The very improbability of billiards in a *dâk*-bungalow proved the reality of the thing. No man – drunk or sober – could imagine a game at billiards, or invent the spitting crack of a 'screw-cannon'.

A severe course of *dâk*-bungalows has this disadvantage – it breeds infinite credulity. If a man said to a confirmed *dâk*-bungalow-haunter: 'There is a corpse in the next room, and there's a mad girl in the next but one, and the woman and man on that camel have just eloped from a place sixty miles away,' the hearer would not disbelieve because he would know that nothing is too wild, grotesque, or horrible to happen in a *dâk*-bungalow.

This credulity, unfortunately, extends to ghosts. A rational person fresh from his own house would have turned on his side and slept. I did not. So surely as I was given up as a bad carcass by the scores of things in the bed because the bulk of my blood was in my heart, so surely did I hear every stroke of a long game at billiards played in the echoing room behind the iron-barred door. My dominant fear was that the players might want a marker. It was an absurd fear, because creatures who could play in the dark would be above such super-fluities. I only know that that was my terror; and it was real.

After a long, long while the game stopped, and the door banged. I slept because I was dead tired. Otherwise I should have preferred to have kept awake. Not for everything in Asia would I have dropped the door-bar and peered into the dark of the next room.

When the morning came, I considered that I had done well and wisely, and enquired for the means of departure.

'By the way, *khansamah*,' I said, 'what were those three doolies doing in my compound in the night?'

'There were no doolies,' said the *khansamah*.

I went into the next room and the daylight streamed through the open door. I was immensely brave. I would, at that hour, have played Black Pool with the owner of the big Black Pool down below.

'Has this place always been a *dâk*-bungalow?' I asked.

'No,' said the *khansamah*. 'Ten or twenty years ago, I have for-gotten how long, it was a billiard room.'

'A how much?'

'A billiard room for the Sahibs who built the Railway. I was *khan-samah* then in the big house where all the Railway-Sahibs lived, and I used to come across with brandy-*shrab*. These three rooms were all one, and they held a big table on which the Sahibs played every evening. But the Sahibs are all dead now, and the Railway runs, you say, nearly to Kabul.'

'Do you remember anything about the Sahibs?'

'It is long ago, but I remember that one Sahib, a fat man and always angry, was playing here one night, and he said to me: "Mangal Khan, brandy-*pani do*," and I filled the glass, and he bent over the table to strike, and his head fell lower and lower till it hit the table, and his spectacles came off, and when we – the Sahibs and I myself – ran to lift him, he was dead. I helped to carry him out. Aha, he was a strong Sahib! But he is dead and I, old Mangal Khan, am still living, by your favour.'

That was more than enough! I had my ghost – a first-hand, authenticated article. I would write to the Society for Psychical Research – I would paralyse the Empire with the news! But I would, first of all, put eighty miles of assessed crop land between myself and that *dâk*-bungalow before nightfall. The Society might send their regular agent to investigate later on.

I went into my own room and prepared to pack after noting down the facts of the case. As I smoked I heard the game begin again – with a miss in baulk this time, for the whir was a short one.

The door was open and I could see into the room. *Click – click*! That was a cannon. I entered the room without fear, for there was sunlight within and a fresh breeze without. The unseen game was going on at a tremendous rate. And well it might, when a restless little rat was running to and fro inside the dingy ceiling-cloth, and a piece of loose window-sash was making fifty breaks off the window-bolt as it shook in the breeze!

Impossible to mistake the sound of billiard balls! Impossible to mistake the whir of a ball over the slate! But I was to be excused. Even when I shut my enlightened eyes the sound was marvellously like that of a fast game.

Entered angrily the faithful partner of my sorrows, Kadir Baksh.

'This bungalow is very bad and low-caste! No wonder the Presence was disturbed and is speckled. Three sets of doolie-bearers came to the bungalow late last night when I was sleeping outside, and said that it was their custom to rest in the rooms set apart for the English people! What honour has the *khansamah*? They tried to enter, but I told them to go. No wonder, if these *Oorias* have been here, that the Presence is sorely spotted. It is shame, and the work of a dirty man!'

Kadir Baksh did not say that he had taken from each gang two annas for rent in advance, and then, beyond my earshot, had beaten them with the big green umbrella whose use I could never before divine. But Kadir Baksh has no notions of morality.

There was an interview with the *khansamah*, but as he promptly lost his head, wrath gave place to pity, and pity led to a long conversation, in the course of which he put the fat Engineer-Sahib's tragic death in three separate stations – two of them fifty miles away. The third shift was to Calcutta, and there the Sahib died while driving a dogcart.

If I had encouraged him the *khansamah* would have wandered all through Bengal with his corpse.

I did not go away as soon as I intended. I stayed for the night, while the wind and the rat and the sash and the window-bolt played a ding-dong 'hundred and fifty up'. Then the wind ran out and the billiards stopped, and I felt that I had ruined my one genuine, hall-marked ghost story.

Had I only stopped at the proper time, I could have made *anything* out of it.

That was the bitterest thought of all!